CW01066490

Brittany Lifeline

by
Val Gascoyne

SURVIVAL BOOKS • LONDON • ENGLAND

First published 2005

All rights reserved. No part of this publication
may be reproduced, stored in a retrieval system or
recorded by any means, without prior written
permission from the author.

Copyright © Survival Books 2005
Cover photograph: Roger Moss (🖳 www.picturefrance.com)

Survival Books Limited
26 York Street, London W1U 6PZ, United Kingdom
☎ +44 (0)20-7788 7644, 🖺 +44 (0)870-762 3212
✉ info@survivalbooks.net
🖳 www.survivalbooks.net
To order books, please refer to page 379.

British Library Cataloguing in Publication Data.
A CIP record for this book is available
from the British Library.
ISBN 1 901130 34 7

Printed and bound in Italy by Legoprint spa.

ACKNOWLEDGEMENTS

I would like to thank all the hoteliers in Brittany who made my many nights away from home so much more bearable, Peter Elias for his specialist advice, and Robert Lérat for his translations and IT support. Another thank-you to my editor, Joe Laredo, and to his wife and colleague, Kerry, for designing and laying out the pages, producing the index and checking the proofs. A final thank-you to Jo Taylor for her superb illustrations and maps and to Jim Watson for designing the excellent cover and colour pages.

What Readers & Reviewers Have Said

If you need to find out how France works, this book is indispensable. Native French people probably have a less thorough understanding of how their country functions.

LIVING FRANCE

This book is a Godsend – a practical guide to all things French and the famous French administration – a book I am sure I will used time and time again during my stay in France.

READER

I would recommend this book to anyone considering the purchase of a French property – get it early so you do it right!

READER

Let's say it at once: David Hampshire's *Living and Working in France* is the best handbook ever produced for visitors and foreign residents in this country. It is Hampshire's meticulous detail which lifts his work way beyond the range of other books with similar titles. *Living and Working in France* is absolutely indispensable.

RIVIERA REPORTER

I found this a wonderful book crammed with facts and figures, with a straightforward approach to the problems and pitfalls you are likely to encounter. It is laced with humour and a thorough understanding of what's involved. Gets my vote!

READER

I was born in France and spent countless years there. I bought this book when I had to go back after a few years away, and this is far and away the best book on the subject. The amount of information covered is nothing short of incredible. I thought I knew enough about my native country. This book has proved me wrong. Don't go to France without it. Big mistake if you do. Absolutely priceless!

READER

If you're thinking about buying a property in France, Hampshire is totally on target. I read this book before going through the buying process and couldn't believe how perfectly his advice dovetailed with my actual experience.

READER

About Other Survival Books on France

In answer to the desert island question about the one how-to book on France, this book would be it.

THE RECORDER

It's just what I needed! Everything I wanted to know and even things I didn't know I wanted to know but was glad I discovered!

READER

There are now several books on this subject, but I've found that this book is definitely the best one. It's crammed with up-to-date information and seems to cover absolutely everything.

READER

Covers every conceivable question concerning everyday life – I know of no other book that could take the place of this one.

FRANCE IN PRINT

An excellent reference book for anyone thinking of taking the first steps towards buying a new or old property in France.

READER

Thankfully, with several very helpful pieces of information from this book, I am now the proud owner of a beautiful house in France. Thank God for David Hampshire!

READER

I saw this book advertised and thought I had better read it. It was definitely money well spent.

READER

We bought an apartment in Paris using this book as a daily reference. It helped us immensely, giving us confidence in many procedures from looking for a place initially to the closing, including great information on insurance and utilities. Definitely a great source!

READER

A comprehensive guide to all things French, written in a highly readable and amusing style, for anyone planning to live, work or retire in France.

THE TIMES

THE AUTHOR

Originally from Hertfordshire, Val Gascoyne worked as a retail manager before returning to college to qualify as an administrator and going on to run her own secretarial business for five years. Having spent most of her earnings on travelling, she eventually moved to France for fresh challenges, a calmer life and French neighbours. There she set up Purple Pages (see below). This book and its companions, *Poitou-Charentes Lifeline, Dordogne/Lot Lifeline* and *Normandy Lifeline*, are a development of that activity in collaboration with Survival Books.

Purple Pages
Grosbout, 16240 La Forêt de Tessé, France
☎ 05 45 29 59 74, UK ☎ 0871-900 8305
🖳 www.purplepages.info

This company produces tailored directories, unique to each family, which are the result of exhaustive research and contain everything you could possibly need to know about an area – from when the dustmen call and where the nearest English-speaking doctor is to be found, to facilities and services for specific medical needs or sporting passions.

CONTENTS

5 Ille-et-Vilaine 243

6 Morbihan 317

Index 371

Order Forms 379

Notes 383

IMPORTANT NOTE

Every effort has been made to ensure that the information contained in this book is accurate and up to date. Note, however, that businesses and organisations can be quite transient, particularly those operated by expatriates (French businesses tend to go on 'for ever'), and therefore information can quickly change or become outdated.

It's advisable to check with an official and reliable source before making major decisions or undertaking an irreversible course of action. If you're planning to travel long-distance to visit somewhere, always phone beforehand to check the opening times, availability of goods, prices and other relevant information.

Unless specifically stated, a reference to any company, organisation or product doesn't constitute an endorsement or recommendation.

Author's Notes

- Times are shown using the 12-hour clock, e.g. ten o'clock in the morning is written as 10am and ten in the evening as 10pm.

- Costs and prices are shown in euros (€) where appropriate. They should be taken as a guide only, although they were accurate at the time of publication.

- Unless otherwise stated, all telephone numbers have been shown as if dialling from France. To dial from abroad, use your local international access code (e.g. 00 from the UK) followed by 33 for France and omit the initial 0 of the French number.

- His/he/him/man/men (etc.) also mean her/she/her/woman/ women (no offence ladies!). This is done simply to make life easier for both the reader and, in particular, the author, and isn't intended to be sexist.

- Warnings and important points are shown in **bold** type.

- The following symbols are used in this book: ☎ (telephone), ▤ (fax), ▣ (internet) and ✉ (email).

- British English is used throughout. French words and phrases are given in italics in brackets where appropriate and are used in preference to English where no exact equivalents exist.

- If there isn't a listing for a particular town under a given heading, this facility or service wasn't available in or near that town at the time of publication. **Chapters 1 & 2** provide information about facilities and services that are available in most towns or are provided on a regional basis, and are therefore not listed in the department chapters.

Carnaret

JoTaylor

INTRODUCTION

If you're thinking of living, working, buying a home or spending an extended holiday in Brittany, this is **the book** for you. *Brittany Lifeline* has been written to answer all those important questions about life in this region that aren't answered in other books. Whether you're planning to spend a few months or a lifetime there, to work, retire or buy a holiday home, this book is essential reading.

Brittany is a popular holiday destination that has long been a magnet for discerning holiday homeowners, and its relaxed lifestyle and quality of life attract an increasing number of foreign residents. The region is one of the most attractive in France, with more coastline than any other, beautiful beaches, picturesque villages and, particularly on the south coast, an exceptionally sunny climate. Brittany is steeped in history, being world famous for its megalithic standing stones, and shares many aspects of Celtic culture with Cornwall, Wales, Ireland and Scotland.

An abundance of tourist guides and information about Brittany is available, but until now it has been difficult to find comprehensive details of local costs, facilities and services, particularly in one book. *Brittany Lifeline* fills this gap and contains accurate, up-to-date, practical information about the most important aspects of daily life in Brittany. If you've ever sought a restaurant that's open after 10pm, a 24-hour petrol station or something to do with your children on a wet day, this book will become your 'bible'.

Information is derived from a variety of sources, both official and unofficial, not least the hard-won experiences of the author, her friends, family and colleagues. *Brittany Lifeline* is a comprehensive handbook and is designed to make your stay in the region – however long or short – easier and less stressful. **It will also help you save valuable time, trouble and money, and will repay your investment many times over!** (For comprehensive information about living and working in France in general and buying a home in France, this book's sister publications, *Living and Working in France* and *Buying a Home in France*, written by David Hampshire, are highly recommended reading.)

I trust this book will help make your life easier and more enjoyable, and smooth the way to a happy and rewarding time in Brittany.

Bienvenue en Bretagne!   **Val Gascoyne**
                                                          July 2005

Vitré

JoTaylor

1

Introducing Brittany

This chapter is divided into two sections: Section 1, below, provides a general introduction to the area covered by this book and a brief description of each of its four departments and their main towns; Section 2, beginning on page 24, contains information about getting to (and from) the area and getting around by public transport once you're there.

OVERVIEW

The location of Brittany in relation to France is shown below. Relevant airports outside the region are shown here; those within it are shown on the map opposite.

The map opposite shows the region as a whole; detailed maps of each department are included in **Chapters 3, 4, 5** and **6**.

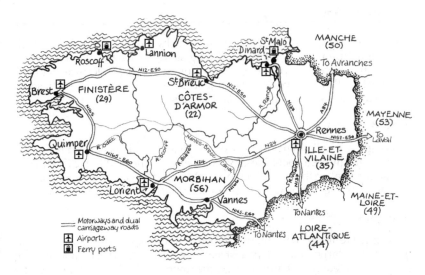

In each department, a selection of main towns has been made and facilities and services in these towns are given, although others are included where appropriate. The selected towns are geographically spread, so at least one of them should be reasonably close wherever you choose to stay or live, although not necessarily in your department. The selected towns are as follows:

Côtes-d'Armor (22)

- **Bröons**
- **Guingamp**
- **Lannion**
- **Loudéac**
- **St Brieuc**

Finistère (29)

- **Brest**
- **Carhaix-Plouguer**
- **Châteaulin**
- **Morlaix**
- **Quimper**

Ille-et-Vilaine (35)

- **Bain-de-Bretagne**
- **Combourg**
- **Fougères**
- **Redon**
- **Rennes**
- **St Malo**

Morbihan (56)

- **Le Faouët**
- **Lorient**
- **Ploërmel**
- **Vannes**

Côtes-d'Armor

The coastline of Cotes-d'Armor is dominated by the Bay of St Brieuc, which boasts a nature reserve, marina and long sandy beaches. Inland there are lakes with beaches, so you're never far from water-based leisure facilities. Architecture throughout the department is varied, and there are still some houses and bread ovens made of earth and stone.

Bröons

Although a small town, Bröons offers many facilities, including social groups and children's activities. Every other year (the next is in 2006) there's a large carnival on the second Sunday in March. The lake and park at Jugon-les-Lacs is to the north-west offering watersports, bathing and walking.

Guingamp

An attractive town, with many timbered buildings preserved in the old quarter and large areas of pedestrian streets, narrow roads and unique shops. Founded in the tenth century, the town was built up around a castle overlooking the Valley of Trieux. Guingamp has a well known football team, *En Avant de Guingamp*, which is in the first division. During the summer there's free street entertainment on Thursdays and for those that like to eat out, there seem to be restaurants at every turn.

Lannion

Lannion is set deep in the estuary and has town and woodland walks alongside the river Léguer, which runs through the centre. At its best in the summer, when it hosts a succession of festivals, the town is in flower all year long, and, although it has a wide selection of boutiques and unusual shops open daily, Thursday is the best day to shop, as there's a large open air market.

Loudéac

Loudéac is at the heart of an area referred to as Centre Bretagne, centrally placed between the north and south coasts, with a forest to the north-east and rivers on both sides. The town was once famous for a little blue flower, the flax, and the linen produced from it. Today there's an exhibition in neighbouring St Thélo, *l'Age d'Or du Lin* (The Golden Age of Linen), showing how important flax was in the 18th and 19th centuries.

St Brieuc

The bay of St Brieuc is a nature reserve and has the world's fifth biggest tides, sometimes receding 7km (4.5mi) to reveal a vast marine landscape.

The town itself has many parks and gardens, with footpaths, exercise courses (*parcours santé*) and playgrounds. There's a proposed route around the historic centre, to help you discover the history, museums, churches and ancient architecture of the town.

Finistère

This department, covering the most western point of the country, has more coastline in proportion to its size than any other in mainland France. There are several islands off the coast that can be visited by boat from various towns. There are markets throughout the year, but their number doubles in the summer months, when smaller towns and villages hold markets of local crafts and produce.

Brest

The most westerly major town in France, Brest is shielded from the Atlantic by several small islands just off the coast; a variety of boat services operate between them and the mainland. The Château du Brest overlooks the sea and is home to a collection of model ships, paintings and sculptures. Despite its extreme location, Brest is easily accessible via motorways, an airport and fast trains to Paris.

Carhaix-Plouguer

Carhaix-Plouguer is believed to be the site of the Roman city of Vorgium – one of the principal cities of Roman Brittany. Although the town lost its importance during the middle ages, it was revitalised during the first half of the 20th century and, following an ambitious programme of investment over the past 15 years, is once again one of the main towns of central Brittany. Approached from the west, it appears to be a small town; the tourist office is located at the end of a small cobbled street, the *mairie* is tucked away in the secluded *place de la Mairie* and other small streets lead off the town's main street. Carhaix-Plouguer is known for its annual pop festival, *Les Vieilles Charrues*, which has grown to be one of the biggest events of its kind in France, attracting tens of thousands of young people every year, from all over the country.

Châteaulin

In the centre of the department, Châteaulin straddles a loop of the Nantes-Brest canal. Below the railway viaduct, built in 1906, the canal is popular for salmon fishing and walking along the tow paths. Overlooking the town are the remains of a tenth century chateau and tucked away in the centre is a red, British telephone box.

Morlaix

There's a steep descent into the centre of Morlaix, which is dominated by the viaduct that crosses it. It's a bustling town, with a good selection of shops, restaurants and hotels. Although well inland, Morlaix has a marina almost at the end of the main street, one of the town's restaurants being aboard a boat moored at the quayside.

Quimper

Quimper was built on the confluence of the rivers Odet and Steir and takes its name from the Breton word for confluence: *kemper*. During the Middle Ages the town became a major strategic and administrative centre and was fortified with walls and ramparts. The city that developed within the walls comprised narrow streets and wooden houses, but in the mid-1800s it underwent redevelopment, the old walls and narrow streets being demolished to create a more open aspect.

Quimper remains the administrative centre of Finistère, the river Odet flowing straight through the middle. The town has a large pedestrian centre of cobbled streets and timbered buildings, and there's an abundance of restaurants, with one on almost every street corner and several overlooking the covered market.

Ille-et-Vilaine

The easternmost department of the region, bordering Lower Normandy, Ille-et-Vilaine is the gateway to Brittany. Rennes, the regional capital, is located in the very centre and the department's small coastline is to the north. Inland, the countryside is one of rivers, forests and stone houses in small villages.

Bain-de-Bretagne

Bain-de-Bretagne is small but picturesque town, the two spires of its church visible on the skyline from all around. The lake has a turreted chateau one side and a watersports centre and swimming pool on the other.

Combourg

This town is dominated by the Château de Combourg, which looks out across the lake. The chateau was immortalised by the famous romantic writer Francois-René de Chateaubriand and is still owned and occupied by the Chateaubriand family. The town itself is full of character and has a bustling centre.

Fougères

Fougères is home to the oldest belfry in Brittany, built in 1397, and the flamboyant gothic church of St Sulpice, one of the region's richest churches. Part of the town has preserved its 14th- and 15th-century timbered buildings. In strong contrast, there's a contemporary sculpture, made of glass, in the gardens alongside the river.

Redon

Bisected by a raised railway line and with sloping ground in every direction, Redon lies at the confluence of the Nantes-Brest canal and river Vilaine and is bounded on three sides by water. Needless to say, aquatic pursuits come high on the list of activities available, with a marina to the south of the town centre.

Rennes

The capital of the department and the region, Rennes has a bustling centre and an array of architectural styles. A historic cathedral, basilica and eight churches contrast with the curved structure of the modern school of architecture with its wooden facade. Like many towns in the region, Rennes has water running straight through its centre – in this case the river Vilaine and the Canal d'Ile-et-Rance. Rennes is unique among Breton towns in boasting an underground railway system (*métro*), to add to its already comprehensive transport network.

Morbihan

Brittany's most popular department boasts its best climate and most attractive scenery. The two main towns, Vannes and Lorient, are on the coast. Both have a variety of inlets, rivers and islands and so, unusually, they have boat taxis as an alternative to the conventional taxis. Lorient even has a boat bus service. Water is also a major feature inland, as three major rivers cross the department as well as the Nantes-Brest canal, built at the instigation of Napoleon to link the river Loire with the harbour at Brest. The canal is 360km (223mi) long and took 38 years to construct.

Le Faouët

Le Faouët is a small town dominated by a 16th century timber-covered market in the town square, whose clock chimes on the hour. The three chapels in the town have been the inspiration for a number of artists and the old convent now houses a permanent collection of art by painters who stayed in Le Faouët between 1850 and the Second World War. Surrounded by deep wooded valleys with streams and rivers, Le Faouët is an ideal location for walkers and anglers.

Lorient

A town surrounded by water, Lorient is situated on the south-west coast of Brittany, at the mouth of the river Scorff, with many sheltered waters ideal for sailing, canoeing and other watersports. The seaside town of Larmor-Plage is to the south and a large retail park at Lanester to the north. As befits a town where water plays such an important role, there's a boat transport system (*Batobus*) taking passengers up and down the estuary and across to Port Louis and Larmor-Plage. The Island of Ile-de-Groix is just off the coast, with regular boat crossings.

Ploërmel

The town of Ploërmel, on the edge of the forest of Broceliande, was founded in the sixth century. The town itself has many narrow streets within its walls, which converge in front of the Eglise St Armel, a magnificent 16th century gothic and Renaissance church. North-west of the town is a 250ha (615-acre) lake, which is the focal point for activities including golf, canoeing, sailing and waterskiing.

Vannes

Parks and gardens are dotted across this town, and the Etang au Duc reaches right into the town centre. The cathedral of St Pierre is in the centre of the old walled city, many of whose towers and ramparts can still be seen. There are half-timbered houses in the narrow streets, and the port that was frequently used by the Dukes of Brittany is now a bustling marina.

GETTING THERE & GETTING AROUND

Getting There by Air

There are several direct flights to Brittany from a variety of UK airports and numerous flights to Paris, from where you can complete your journey by air, by hired car (or helicopter, if money is no object) or by rail. Details of all three options are given in this section.

Although budget airlines can offer low fares, the major airlines also offer some good prices and are sometimes cheaper. In spring 2005, many of the flights listed below were under £100 return, plus airport taxes, but note that some airlines are planning to introduce baggage charges (see note below following table).

Airline	Website	UK/Eire	French
Aer Arann	💻 *www.aerarann.com*	☎ 0800-587 2324	
	Ireland	☎ 0818-210210	
	Ireland from abroad	☎ +353 61 70 44 28	
Air France	💻 *www.airfrance.com*	☎ 0845-084 511	☎ 08 20 82 08 20
Aurigny.com	💻 *www.aurigny.com*	☎ 0871-871 0717	
BMI	💻 *www.flybmi.com*	☎ 0870-60 70 555	
	From abroad	☎ +44 1332-854854	
Brit Air	💻 *www.britair.com*	☎ 0845-084 511	☎ 08 20 82 08 20
British Airways	💻 *www.britishairways. com*	☎ 0870-850 9850	☎ 08 25 82 54 00
Easyjet*	💻 *www.easyjet.com*	☎ 0877-750 0100	☎ 08 25 08 25 08
Flybe	💻 *www.flybe.com*	☎ 0871-700 0535	
	From abroad	☎ +44 1392-268529	
Flywest	💻 *www.flywest.fr*	-	☎ 08 92 25 93 59
KLM	💻 *www.klm.com*	☎ 0870-507 4074	☎ 08 90 71 07 10
Rockhopper	💻 *www.rockhopper.aero*	☎ 01481-824 567	☎ 0810 000 023
Ryanair*	💻 *www.ryanair.com*	☎ 0871-246 0000	☎ 08 92 55 56 66
	Ireland	☎ 0818-303030	
Thomson Fly	💻 *www.thomsonfly.com*	☎ 0870-190 0737	☎ 01 70 70 81 36

*   Ryanair are planning to charge up to £50 for all checked-in luggage, although the limit for hand luggage has been increased to 10kg from 7kg. Easyjet allows hand luggage of any weight provided it doesn't exceed certain dimensions and you can lift it into overhead lockers unaided.

First Luggage (☎ 0845-270 0670, 💻 *www.firstluggage.com*) is a new company offering a luggage transfer service from your home or office. Your belongings are transported to your destination in conjunction with FedEx, and you're kept up-to-date with their progress. Prices start at around £25 one way and include items such as prams, suitcases and sports equipment, e.g. golf clubs and skis.

The following websites may help you to find low-cost flights with scheduled airlines:

- 💻 *www.cheapflights.co.uk*
- 💻 *www.ebookers.com*
- 💻 *www.expedia.co.uk*
- 💻 *www.flightline.co.uk*
- 💻 *www.travelocity.co.uk*

International Airports

There are currently five international airports in Brittany plus Nantes just to the south. These are listed below (department numbers are given in brackets).

Brest (29)	Aéroport de Brest Guipavas 💻 *www.brest.aeroport.fr*	☎ 02 98 32 01 00
Dinard (35)	Aéroport de Dinard 💻 *www.saint-malo.cci.fr*	☎ 08 25 08 35 09
Lorient (56)	Aéroport Lann-Bihouë, Plœmeur 💻 *www.lorient.aeroport.fr*	☎ 02 97 87 21 50
Nantes (44)	Aéroport Nantes Atlantique 💻 *www.nantes.aeroport.fr*	☎ 02 40 84 80 00
Rennes (35)	Aéroport de Rennes St Jacques 💻 *www.rennes.aeroport.fr*	☎ 02 99 29 60 00
St Brieuc (22)	Aéroport St Brieuc Armor, Trémuson 💻 *www.st-brieuc.aeroport.fr*	☎ 02 96 94 95 00

The following tables list direct routes from the Channel Islands, England, Scotland and Ireland to Brittany and Paris that were in service in the spring of 2005. These are intended only as a guide, as airline services are constantly changing, and you should check with the relevant airports or airlines (see page 25) for the latest information.

Channel Islands

From	To	Airline
Guernsey	Dinard	Aurigny Air Services
	St Brieuc	Rockhopper

Jersey	Dinard	Rockhopper
	St Brieuc	Rockhopper

England

From	**To**	**Airline**
Birmingham	Brest	Flybe
	Paris CDG	Air France, British Airways, KLM
Bournemouth	Paris CDG	Thomson Fly
Bristol	Paris CDG	British Airways, KLM
Coventry	Paris CDG	Thomson Fly
Doncaster/ Sheffield	Paris CDG	Thomson Fly
Durham Tees Valley	Paris CDG	BMI
Exeter	Brest	Flybe
	Paris CDG	Flybe
Leeds	Paris CDG	BMI
Liverpool	Paris CDG	Easyjet
London City	Paris CDG	Air France
	Paris Orly	Air France
Lon. Gatwick	Nantes	Air France
Lon. Heathrow	Paris CDG	Air France, BMI, British Airways
Lon. Stansted	Dinard	Ryanair
Luton	Dinard	Ryanair
	Paris CDG	Easyjet
Manchester	Paris CDG	Air France, BMI, British Airways
Newcastle	Paris CDG	Air France, Easyjet
Southampton	Brest	Flybe
	Rennes	Flybe

Ireland

From	To	Airline
Belfast	Paris CDG	BMI
Cork	Brest	Flywest
	Paris CDG	BMI
Dublin	Paris CDG	Air France, BMI
Galway	Lorient	Aer Arann
Waterford	Lorient	Aer Arann

Scotland

From	To	Airline
Aberdeen	Paris CDG	Air France, BMI
Edinburgh	Paris CDG	Air France, BMI, British Airways
Glasgow	Paris CDG	Air France, BMI, British Airways

Domestic Airports

From the following airports you can fly to Paris or Nantes and from there connect to the UK and other countries. Some of these airports have direct flights to other continental European destinations. See the relevant website for current information.

Brest	Aéroport Brest Bretagne	☎ 02 98 32 01 00
	🖥 *www.airport.cci-brest.fr*	
	Flights to Nantes and Paris Charles de Gaulle and Orly.	
Lannion (22)	Aéroport Lannion	☎ 02 96 05 82 22
	🖥 *www.lannion.aeroport.fr*	
	Flights to Paris Orly.	
Lorient	Aéroport Lorient Bretagne Sud	☎ 02 97 87 21 50
	🖥 *www.lorient.aeroport.fr*	
	Flights to Paris Charles de Gaulle and Lyon.	
Nantes	Aéroport Nantes Atlantique	☎ 02 40 84 80 00
	🖥 *www.nantes.aeroport.fr*	
	Flights to Brest and Paris Charles de Gaulle.	
Quimper (29)	Aéroport de Quimper Cornouaille	☎ 02 98 94 30 30

🖳 *www.quimper.cci.fr*
Flights to Paris Charles de Gaulle.

Rennes (35)	Rennes Aéroport	☎ 02 99 29 60 00

🖳 *www.rennes.aeroport.fr*
Flights to Paris Charles de Gaulle and Orly.

Domestic Flights

From	To	Airline
Nantes	Brest	Air France
Paris CDG	Brest	Air France, Flywest
	Lorient	Brit Air
	Nantes	Air France
	Quimper	Air France
	Rennes	Air France
Paris Orly	Brest	Air France
	Lannion	Air France
	Rennes	Air France

Plane & Helicopter Hire

Guiscriff	Aérodrome Bretagne Atlantique	
	Pont Person	☎ 02 97 34 08 55

🖳 *www.aerodrome-bretagne.com*
(west of Le Faouët)
Helicopters and planes for charter and aeroplane-taxis.

Atlantique Air Assistance	Rezé	☎ 02 40 84 37 37

🖳 *www.atlantiqueairassistance.com*
Air taxi.

Blugeon Hélicoptères	Le Rocher, Morzine	☎ 04 50 75 99 15

🖳 *www.blugeon-helicopteres.com*
Helicopter-taxis across France.

Phénix Aviation	Le Havre	☎ 02 32 85 00 81

🖳 *www.phenix-aviation.biz*
Flights on request and air taxi.

Car Hire

Listed below are the main car hire companies in each principal town. The websites of the 'big five' companies are as follows:

Avis	🖥 *www.avis.fr*
Budget	🖥 *www.budget.fr*
Car'Go	🖥 *www.cargo.fr*
Europcar	🖥 *www.europcar-bretagne.com*
Hertz	🖥 *www.hertz.com*

Airport-based

Brest	Ada	☎ 02 98 84 63 36
	Sixt Grand West Location	☎ 08 20 88 11 81
Dinard	Ada	☎ 02 99 56 06 15
	National Citer	☎ 02 23 18 00 00
Lorient	Hertz	☎ 02 97 21 20 31
Nantes	Avis	☎ 02 51 83 01 02
	Budget	☎ 02 40 20 25 70
Paris CDG	Avis	☎ 01 48 62 34 34
	Budget	☎ 01 48 62 70 21
	Euro Rent	☎ 01 48 62 40 77
	Europcar	☎ 01 48 62 33 33
	Hertz	☎ 01 48 62 29 00
Paris Orly	Avis	☎ 08 20 61 16 19
	Budget	☎ 01 49 75 56 05
Rennes	ADA Location	☎ 02 99 27 22 22
	National Citer	☎ 02 99 29 60 22
St Brieuc	Europcar	☎ 02 96 94 45 45
	Hertz	☎ 02 96 94 25 89

Côtes-d'Armor

Guingamp	ADA, 22 boulevard de la Marne	☎ 02 96 44 32 53
Lannion	Avis, route de Perros-Guirec	☎ 02 96 48 10 98
Loudéac	Garage Loudéac Auto, 4 boulevard Peupliers	☎ 02 96 28 00 07

| St Brieuc | Ada, 57 rue de la Gare | ☎ 02 96 78 19 99 |

Finistère

Brest	ABL, 53 rue de Loscoat	☎ 02 98 47 47 00
Carhaix-Plouguer	Clovis Location, ZA Villeneuve	☎ 08 25 80 01 15
Châteaulin	Garage de Cornouaille, route de Pleyben	☎ 02 98 86 04 40
Morlaix	Avis, Gare SNCF	☎ 02 98 15 20 05
Quimper	Rent-a-Car, 6 route de Brest	☎ 02 98 64 22 34

Ille-et-Vilaine

Bain-de-Bretagne	Actuel Location, ZA Château Gaillard	☎ 02 99 43 38 39
Fougères	Car Go, 16 rue de Sévigné	☎ 02 99 99 06 88
Redon	Rent-a-Car, route de Rennes	☎ 02 99 72 14 00
Rennes	Avis, Gare SNCF	☎ 02 23 42 14 14
St Malo	National/Citer, 46 boulevard de la République 🖥 *www.citer.fr*	☎ 02 23 18 00 00

Morbihan

Lorient	ADA, 16 cours de Chazelles	☎ 02 97 21 75 06
Ploërmel	Europcar, 24 boulevard Laennec	☎ 02 97 74 39 22
Vannes	Avis, place de la Gare	☎ 02 97 47 54 54

Taxis

Côtes-d'Armor

Bröons	Taxi du Bröon, rue du Belloir	☎ 02 96 80 01 80
Guingamp	Corveller Taxi, 6 rue Maréchal Foch	☎ 02 96 21 33 05
	Grimault Taxi	☎ 02 96 44 17 17

	Taxi Guingamp Grâces, 1 rue Madeleine Prolongée	☎ 02 96 44 38 00
	Taxi Menguy, 6 rue François Ménez	☎ 02 96 44 36 39
Lannion	Allo Armor Taxi, 41 rue Hersart de la Villemarqué	☎ 06 07 06 84 27
	Anne Taxi, Nivern Bihan, route Perros-Guirec	☎ 02 96 48 75 40
	Taxi Bourdonnec, Station Gare, 34 rue Keravel	☎ 06 07 96 75 02
	Taxi Evano, Bel-Air-Loquivy	☎ 02 96 37 25 04
	Taxi Ménez, 49 rue Tréguier	☎ 02 96 46 79 79
Loudéac	Taxi Coulmé, 32 boulevard Penthièvre	☎ 02 96 28 05 71
	Taxi Hémonic, rue Glais Bizoin	☎ 02 96 28 06 33
	Taxi Marylène	☎ 06 07 35 46 80
St Brieuc	Allo les Taxis Ploufraganais, Ploufragan	☎ 02 96 78 28 28
	Armor Griffon Taxis	☎ 02 96 94 70 70
	La Maison du Taxi, Plérin	☎ 02 96 74 74 74
	Taxi Danzé, 27 avenue Tertre Notre Dame	☎ 06 82 74 43 88
	Taxi Guy Ollivro, Langueux	☎ 02 96 61 29 70
	Taxi Houée, 16 rue Béranger	☎ 02 96 78 39 24

Finistère

Brest	Allo Taxi, 245 rue Jean Jaurès	☎ 02 98 42 11 11
	Radio Taxi Brestois, 220 rue Jean Jaurès	☎ 02 98 80 43 43
	Taxi Geffroy, 6 rue de Touraine	☎ 02 98 47 29 70
Carhaix-Plouguer	Croissant, Moulin à Vent, route Rostrenen	☎ 02 98 93 04 19

	Dénès Taxi, 7 rue Docteur Menguy	☎ 02 98 93 79 90
	Taxi Rémi, 1 rue Soleil	☎ 02 98 93 24 25
	TaxiCom', 9 place de la Gare	☎ 02 98 99 38 61

This taxi service operates around the town on Tuesday
mornings, Wednesday afternoons and all day Saturdays. €2
for each journey.

Châteaulin	l'Angélus, 37 route de la Gare	☎ 02 98 86 08 62
	Atlantic, 51 rue de Kerlobret	☎ 02 98 86 03 71
	Clabon, 18 avenue de Quimper	☎ 02 98 86 00 15
	JL Louët, 1 résidence la Plaine	☎ 02 98 86 02 00
Morlaix	Poulichot	☎ 02 98 88 31 32
	Trans' Armor, 81 bis rue de Brest	☎ 02 98 63 40 40
	Taxi Huon, 43 rue Kermadiou	☎ 02 98 63 22 62
	Taxis Morlaisiens, place Otages	☎ 02 98 88 08 32
Quimper Armand	Radios Taxis Quimpérois, place Louis	☎ 02 98 90 21 21
	Abbassides Taxi Radio, 20 rue Auguste Perret	☎ 02 98 53 42 42

Ille-et-Vilaine

Bain-de-Bretagne	Taxis Bainais, La Croix Blanche	☎ 02 99 43 74 49
	Taxi Guermont, avenue Général Wood	☎ 02 99 43 83 60
	JP Geffray, route de Pierric, Grand-Fougeray	☎ 02 99 08 45 29
Combourg	Sylvie Lebreton, Le Village, La Chapelle-aux-Filzméens	☎ 06 24 37 66 05
Fougères	Allo Taxi Fougerais, 3 place des Urbanistes	☎ 02 99 99 31 84
	Christian Galeine, 77 boulevard Edmond Roussin	☎ 02 99 94 20 05

	Taxi de Beaucé, 63 route d'Ernée	☎ 02 99 94 40 30
	Taxi Gohin, 6 rue de la Forêt	☎ 02 99 99 89 80
	Taxis des Landes, ZA du Bois Menu	☎ 02 99 98 36 20
Redon	Allo Hurtel Taxi, 15 rue Thiers	☎ 02 99 71 24 64
	Bothamy Taxi, 4 place Charles de Gaulle	☎ 06 80 90 81 23
	Cheval Taxi, 5 rue Houssaye	☎ 02 99 71 10 24
	Radio Taxi Violin, 6 impasse Poiriers	☎ 02 99 71 35 05
	Taxi Saudrais, 40 rue Bahurel	☎ 02 99 71 36 36
Rennes	Radio Taxis Rennais, 2 rue Capitaine Dreyfus, St Jacques de la Lande This is a central number for all taxis in the city.	☎ 02 99 30 79 79
St Malo	Allo Taxis Malouins, 33 rue Noguette 🖳 www.allo-taxis-malouins.com	☎ 02 99 81 30 30
	Allo Taxi Minihicois, 10 rue Lambety	☎ 02 99 81 67 69
	Taxi Daniel St Malo, 24 avenue Louis Aubert	☎ 06 60 21 59 95

Morbihan

Le Faouët	Taxi Le Meur-Le Gal, 13 rue de Quimper	☎ 02 97 23 09 29
	Taxi Carcreff-Le Gac, 7 rue Croix Blanche	☎ 02 97 23 20 30
Lorient	Radio Taxi Lorientais, 27 boulevard de Normandie 🖳 www.taxilorient.com This is a central number for all taxis in the town.	☎ 02 97 21 29 29
Ploërmel	Conoir, 8 rue de l'Ancienne Caserne	☎ 02 97 63 62 93
	Davalo Taxi, 10 avenue Maréchal de Lattre de Tassigny	☎ 02 97 74 03 64

Vannes	Radio Taxis Vannetais, place de la Gare ☎ 02 97 54 34 34

A large taxi company with 19 cars.

Philippe Jégu, 10 allée de Lorraine   ☎ 06 09 70 48 87

Trains

There are trains direct from Paris Charles de Gaulle airport to Rennes and Quimper. From Rennes you can connect to Brest, Morlaix, Lannion, Guingamp, St Brieuc, Vannes and Redon. There are some trains direct to these stations from the airport but only one or two a day and it may more convenient to use these connecting services or take the underground, bus or a taxi to Montparnasse station in Paris for more frequent services (see **Getting There by Rail** on page 42). For further details, contact the SNCF:

SNCF   ☎ 3635
💻 *www.voyages-sncf.com*
The website has an English option and enables you to look up and book train travel both to and within France.

Getting There by Road

Channel Crossings

Within Brittany are the ferry ports of Roscoff and St Malo. North-east of the region are the ports of Boulogne, Caen, Calais, Cherbourg, Dieppe and Le Havre. Information on routes to these ports has been included only where there's no direct route to Roscoff or St Malo from the corresponding UK port.

Route	Vessel	Crossing Time	Company
Dover/Calais	Tunnel	35 minutes	Eurotunnel
	Seacat	1hour	Hoverspeed
	Ferry	1 hour 15 minutes	P & O, Sea France
Dover/ Boulogne	Fast ferry	50 minutes	Speed Ferries
Newhaven/ Dieppe	Ferry	4 hours	Transmanche
Plymouth/ Roscoff	Ferry	6 hours	Brittany Ferries
Poole/St Malo*	Seacat	4 hours 35 minutes	Condor Ferries

Portsmouth/ Cherbourg	Fast Ferry	3 hours	Brittany Ferries
	Ferry	4 hours 45 minutes	Brittany Ferries
Portsmouth/ St Malo	Ferry	8 hours 45 minutes	Brittany Ferries
Rosslare/ Cherbourg	Cruiser	18 hours 30 minutes	Irish Ferries
Weymouth/ St Malo	Fast ferry	5 hours 15 minutes	Condor Ferries

*   Seasonal route

Brittany Ferries   🖳 *www.brittany-ferries.co.uk*   *UK*   ☎ 0870-366 5333
  France ☎ 08 25 82 88 28
Ferries from Portsmouth to St Malo and Cherbourg, Plymouth to Roscoff.

Property Owners' Travel Club   *UK*   ☎ 0870-514 3555
Brittany Ferries' Property Owners' Travel Club offers savings of up to 33 per cent on passenger and vehicle fares and discount for three friends, providing up to 15 per cent savings on standard fares. There's a one-off registration fee of £35 and a £45 annual membership fee.

Condor Ferries   🖳 *www.condorferries.com*   *UK*   ☎ 0845-345 2000
  France ☎ 08 25 13 51 35
Seacats (fast ferries) operate from February to the end of December from Poole or Weymouth to St Malo via the Channel Islands. In the summer there are additional crossings direct from Poole to St Malo.

Frequent Traveller Membership entitles you to a 20 per cent discount on all Channel crossings and a 10 per cent discount between the Channel Islands and France. Annual membership costs £68 for an individual plus £21 for a spouse.

Eurotunnel   🖳 *www.eurotunnel.co.uk*   *UK*   ☎ 0870-535 3535
  France ☎ 08 10 63 03 04
UK lines are open Mondays to Fridays 8am to 7pm, Saturdays and bank holidays 8am to 5.30pm, Sundays 9am to 5.30pm. French lines open Mondays to Saturdays 9am to 5.30pm. There are two or three crossings per hour during the day and less frequent crossings during the night.

The Frequent Traveller loyalty scheme involves purchasing a minimum of ten, off-peak, single journeys, for which you pay

£39 each. If you want to travel at peak time there's a supplement of £20 or £30 per crossing.

Note: Eurotunnel doesn't allow vehicles that use LPG or are dual-powered. Campervans and caravans that have bottled gas for fridges and cookers, etc. are accepted provided bottles are switched off and disconnected.

Hoverspeed   🖳 *www.hoverspeed.com*   *UK*   ☎ 0870-240 8070
    France ☎ 03 21 46 14 00
The Seacat (fast ferry) operates up to eight crossings a day in high season.

There's a Frequent User loyalty scheme which offers a 20 per cent discount with free membership, but you need three booking references of crossings taken within the last six months to qualify.

Irish Ferries   🖳 *www.irishferries.com*   *Eire*   ☎ 0818-300 400
    UK   ☎ 08705-171717
    France ☎ 01 43 94 46 94
Ferries from Rosslare to Cherbourg. There's a Business Travellers' Scheme that credits you 10 per cent of your total expenditure to use against future travel if you cross six times or more in any 12-month period.

P&O Ferries   🖳 *www.poferries.com*   *UK*   ☎ 0870-598 0333
    France ☎ 08 25 12 01 56
The Dover/Calais route has crossings every day except Christmas day.

Season Ticket   *UK*   ☎ 0870-600 0613
If you travel to France five times or more per year you can save money by block booking five return crossings, which are fully flexible up to 24 hours before travel. P&O has stopped all other loyalty programmes.

Sea France   🖳 *www.seafrance.co.uk*   *UK*   ☎ 08705-711 711
    France ☎ 03 21 34 55 00
Ferry crossings all year, up to 15 each day in high season; crossing times vary between 70 and 90 minutes according to the vessel.

Speed Ferries   🖳 *www.speedferries.com*   *UK*   ☎ 0870-220 0570
    France ☎ 03 21 10 50 00
This is a 50-minute fast ferry service that operates between Dover and Boulogne. One-way fares for a car and passengers (no foot passengers are allowed) start at £25. Suitable for cars, motorbikes, small camper vans and small trailers. There are three crossings a day throughout the year with five from mid-

March to September. UK lines are open Mondays to Fridays from 9am to 7pm, Saturdays and Sundays 10am to 5pm. There's a £10 charge for bookings made through the call centre.

Transmanche Ferries   🖳 *www.transmancheferries.com*   *UK*   ☎ 0800-917 1201
  France ☎ 08 00 65 01 00

A conventional ferry service from Newhaven to Dieppe. Three crossings daily from Mondays to Fridays, two on Saturdays and Sundays.

As an alternative to booking direct with a ferry company, you can use one of several companies that will help you to obtain the cheapest fare. These include:

Cheap 4 Ferries   🖳 *www.cheap4ferries.co.uk*   *UK*   ☎ 0870-700 0138

Ferry Crossings Online   🖳 *www.ferry-crossings-online.co.uk*

Ferry Crossings UK   🖳 *www.ferrycrossings-uk.co.uk*   *UK*   ☎ 0871-222 8642

Suggested Routes

Suggested routes are given below to the main town in each department from each port. These are based on an average driving speed of 120kph (75mph) on motorways and 80kph (50mph) on other roads. Costs are based on fuel at €1.15 per litre and fuel consumption of 30mpg in towns and 40mpg on the motorway.

From Calais

● Calais ➔ St Brieuc

Suggested Route
A16 to Abbeville
A28 to junction 10
A29 to the A13
A13 to Caen
A84 to junction 34
N175, N176 & N12 to St Brieuc

Summary
Distance: 575km (356mi)
Time: 5 hours, 20 minutes
Cost: €40 plus tolls (€21.50)

● Calais ➔ Châteaulin

Suggested Route
A16 to Abbeville

Summary
Distance: 688km (426mi)

A28 to junction 10
A29 to the A13
A13 to Caen, A84 to junction 34
N175 & N176 towards St Brieuc
N12 to Guingamp
D787 to Carhaix-Plouguer
N164 to Châteaulin

Time: 5 hours, 20 minutes
Cost: €47 plus tolls (€21.50)

● Calais ➔ Rennes

Suggested Route
A16 to Abbeville
A28 to junction 10
A29 to the A13
A13 to Caen
A84 to Rennes

Summary
Distance: 520km (325mi)
Time: 4 hours, 45 minutes
Cost: €36 plus tolls (€21.50)

● Calais ➔ Lorient

Suggested Route
A16 to Abbeville
A28 to junction 10
A29 to the A13
A13 to Caen
A84 to Rennes
N24 to Lorient

Summary
Distance: 667km (417mi)
Time: 6 hours, 15 minutes
Cost: €47 plus tolls (€21.50)

From Cherbourg

● Cherbourg ➔ St Brieuc

Suggested Route
N13 south to Carentan
N174 past St Lô to join A84
A84 to junction 34
N175 & N176 towards St Brieuc
N12 to St Brieuc

Summary
Distance: 264km (163mi)
Time: 3 hours, 5 minutes
Cost: €18 (no tolls)

● Cherbourg ➔ Châteaulin

Suggested Route
N13 south to Carentan
N174 past St Lô to join A84
A84 to junction 34
N175 & N176 towards St Brieuc
N12 to Guingamp

Summary
Distance: 379km (235mi)
Time: 4 hours, 35 minutes
Cost: €26 (no tolls)

D787 to Carhaix-Plouguer
N164 to Châteaulin

- Cherbourg ➔ Rennes

  Suggested Route
  N13 south to Carentan
  N174 past St Lô to join A84
  A84 to Rennes

  Summary
  Distance: 221km (137mi)
  Time: 2 hours, 35 minutes
  Cost: €15 (no tolls)

- Cherbourg ➔ Lorient

  Suggested Route
  N13 south to Carentan
  N174 past St Lô to join A84
  A84 Rennes
  N24 to Lorient

  Summary
  Distance: 368km (228mi)
  Time: 4 hours, 5 minutes
  Cost: €25 (no tolls)

From Roscoff

- Roscoff ➔ St Brieuc

  Suggested Route
  D58 to Morlaix
  N12 past Guingamp
  Just before the airport
  D712 into St Brieuc

  Summary
  Distance: 109km (68mi)
  Time: 1 hour, 50 minutes
  Cost: €14 (no tolls)

- Roscoff ➔ Châteaulin

  Suggested Route
  D58 to D69 south of St Pol
  D69 to Landivisiau
  D30 & D18 to Le Faou
  N165 to Châteaulin

  Summary
  Distance: 75km (47mi)
  Time: 1 hour, 20 minutes
  Cost: €10 (no tolls)

- Roscoff ➔ Rennes

  Suggested Route
  D58 to Morlaix
  N12 past St Brieuc to Rennes

  Summary
  Distance: 208km (130mi)
  Time: 3 hours, 20 minutes
  Cost: €27 (no tolls)

- Roscoff ➔ Lorient

  Suggested Route
  D58 to D69 south of St Pol

  Summary
  Distance: 163km (102mi)

D69 to Landivisiau
D30 & D18 to Le Faou
N165 past Quimper and on to Lorient

Time: 2 hours, 15 minutes
Cost: €19 (no tolls)

From St Malo

● St Malo ➔ St Brieuc

Suggested Route
Leave St Malo towards Dinard
D168 past the airport
D768 to Lamballe
N12 to St Brieuc

Summary
Distance: 72km (45mi)
Time: 1 hour, 20 minutes
Cost: €9 (no tolls)

● St Malo ➔ Châteaulin

Suggested Route
Leave St Malo towards Dinard
D168 past the airport
D768 to Lamballe
N12 to Guingamp
D787 to Carhaix-Plouguer
N164 to Châteaulin

Summary
Distance: 72km (122mi)
Time: 3 hours, 5 minutes
Cost: €24 (no tolls)

● St Malo ➔ Rennes

Suggested Route
N137 south out of the town
Continue on N137 to Rennes

Summary
Distance: 69km (43mi)
Time: 1 hour
Cost: €9 (no tolls)

● St Malo ➔ Lorient

Suggested Route
N137 south out of the town
Continue on N137 to Rennes
N24 towards Lorient
N165 into Lorient

Summary
Distance: 214km (134mi)
Time: 2 hours, 15 minutes
Cost: €15 (no tolls)

Tolls & Télépéage

At toll booths (*péage*) there are lanes marked '*CB*' (for *carte bancaire*), which accept British credit cards and are a usually a faster option than a manned kiosk. No signature or PIN are required.

If you travel regularly on French motorways, it's worth considering Télépéage to avoid queuing at toll booths and, in some cases, qualify for discounts. With the standard contract there's no discount on the price per kilometre but the advantage is that you no longer have to queue up to pay, as you can use a dedicated lane. There are various other contracts that give discounts of up to 40 per cent on your journey, but these are primarily for commuters. An invoice is sent out monthly. If you use this system and your average speed between tolls exceeds the limit, you may receive a speeding penalty soon after your monthly bill!

You must pay a deposit of €30 for a disc that fits to your windscreen, then an annual subscription of €20. To sign up you must visit a Télépéage office, which are usually to one side of the toll booths. You will be given an application form and an authorisation request for a direct debit from a French bank account to complete and must provide your bank account details (*relevé d'identité bancaire/RIB*). The disc will be available within around 20 minutes. Alternatively, go to the website (🖳 *www.cofiroute.fr*) and click on 'Télépéage Liber-t'. The same disc can be used at all *péages* across France.

Motorway Information

🖳 *www.autoroutes.fr* – This is a comprehensive site giving weather and traffic conditions; it even shows the level of traffic on various sections of the motorway network. The site is available in English.

🖳 *www.bison-fute.equipement.gouv.fr* – A comprehensive site containing information on roadworks, diversions, congestion and other factors that can affect your journey.

Getting There by Rail

Eurostar   🖳 *www.eurostar.co.uk*   UK   ☎ 08705-186186
                                               France ☎ 08 92 35 35 39

The Eurostar travels from Waterloo (London) and Ashford to both Lille and Paris. There are one or two trains per hour and the journey time to Paris Gare du Nord is around three hours. There are direct trains from Lille to Rennes and from there you can connect to other stations in the region. This is a better option than travelling to Paris and then across the underground (*métro*) with luggage to the connecting station. If you do travel to Paris, you must then take the underground or a bus or taxi to Montparnasse, which serves the following stations:

Destination	Paris Station	Route
Côtes-d'Armor		
Bröons	Montparnasse	Change at Rennes

Guingamp	Montparnasse	Direct
Lannion	Montparnasse	Direct
Loudéac	Montparnasse	Change at St Brieuc
St Brieuc	Montparnasse	Direct
Finistère Brest	Montparnasse	Direct
Carhaix- Plouguer	Montparnasse	Change at Guingamp
Châteaulin	Montparnasse	Change at Quimper
Morlaix	Montparnasse	Direct
Quimper	Montparnasse	Direct
Ille-et-Vilaine Combourg	Montparnasse	Change at Rennes
Fougères	Montparnasse	Change at Laval
Redon	Montparnasse	Direct
Rennes	Montparnasse	Direct
St Malo	Montparnasse	Change at Rennes
Morbihan Lorient	Montparnasse	Direct
Vannes	Montparnasse	Direct

There are no railway stations at Bain-de-Bretagne, Le Faouët or Ploërmel.

For details of mainline train services, contact the SNCF:

SNCF   ☎ 3635
🖥 *www.voyages-sncf.com*
The website has an English option and enables you to look up
and book train travel both to and within France.

Stations no longer have direct dial numbers; the SNCF number above offers information on trains, timetables, booking and other details.

Getting Around

This section covers boats, buses and local trains. For details of taxi services, see page 31. A comprehensive booklet, the *Guide Régional des Transports*, is available from railway and bus stations and provides details of all local transport services, both across the region and within individual towns, including timetables for trains and buses.

Boats

Lorient   Batobus, CTRL, Gare d'Echanges, cours ☎ 02 97 21 28 29
                 de Chazelles
                 🖥 *www.ctrl.fr*
                 Six routes across the estuary connecting Lorient, Locmiquélic,
                 Larmor-Plage and Port-Louis. Boats operate every day, all
                 year. Tickets €1.15, valid for one hour.

Vannes   Navettes   ☎ 02 97 46 46 38
                 Free shuttle boats in July and August (Mondays to Saturdays,
                 except bank holidays) between the large car park at Parc du
                 Golfe and the town centre.

Water Taxis

The following coastal towns are dissected by various inlets and river mouths. As a result, water taxis are available as an alternative to road taxis.

Lorient   Navettes et Taxis Groisillons, 1 rue   ☎ 02 97 65 52 52
                 Yves Montand, Larmor-Plage

Vannes   Le Tac Sea Jaune   ☎ 06 61 87 87 13

Buses

Many buses in the region are primarily to serve the schools and colleges and so the routes pass not only the schools but in many cases railway stations as well. Unfortunately, this also means that there's drastic reduction (if not a total cessation) in services on some routes during school holidays. Timetables are usually displayed at bus stops and can be obtained from tourist offices or the relevant transport company's offices.

General   TAE (Transports Armor Express), 26   ☎ 02 99 26 16 00
                 rue Bignon, Chantepie
                 Buses run across the region, including routes to Rennes,
                 Vannes and Loudéac.

Côtes-d'Armor

General	La Route des Cars, Gare Routière, 6 rue ☎ 02 96 68 31 20 du Combat des Trente, St Brieuc

This is the regional bus service including routes to Lannion, Paimpol, Vannes and Guingamp. Buses depart from the railway stations.

Lannion	Transports Urbains Lannionnais, ☎ 02 96 46 78 33 Mairie, quai Maréchal Foch

There are four routes that cover the town and surrounding areas.

St Brieuc	Tub (Transport Urbain Briochin), place ☎ 02 96 33 47 42 Duguesclin

A local bus service with 19 routes covering the town and the surrounding area. Noctub is an evening bus service that operates Mondays to Saturdays until 11.15pm on routes 3, 5 and 8.

Finistère

General	Gare Routière, place du 19ème RI ☎ 02 98 44 46 73 Bus routes across the department.

Brest	Bibus, 33 avenue Clémenceau ☎ 02 98 80 30 30 💻 *www.bibus.fr*

This is the bus service in and around the town. Tickets costing €1 are valid on all the routes, but for only one hour. Day tickets are valid on all routes from 6am and cost €3. Night buses operate on routes A to D until 10.40pm Sundays to Thursdays and 12.15am Fridays and Saturdays.

There's a regular shuttle bus running between the town centre and the airport; contact the tourist office (☎ 02 98 32 01 00).

Quimper	QUB, 2 quai de l'Odet ☎ 02 98 95 26 27 💻 *www.qub.fr*

Single journey tickets €1, daily tickets €3 and season tickets from a month to a year. An extra service runs to the railway station on Sunday evenings, passing the major schools and colleges that have residential students.

Ille-et-Vilaine

General	Transports Armor Express (TAE), 19 ☎ 02 99 26 16 00 rue Bignon, Chantepie

Bus routes across the department.

Fougères	**Autocars TIV** This bus service operates on various routes across the department, including one from Fougères to Rennes. Timetables available from the bus station, place de la Gare.
	Service Urbain de la Région Fougeraise ☎ 02 99 99 08 77 **(SURF), place de la Gare** A local bus service operating three routes around the town and immediate areas. Separate timetables for school holidays.
Rennes	**Service des Transports de l'Agglomé-** ☎ 02 99 79 37 37 **ration Rennaise (STAR), 12 rue du Pré Botté** 🖳 *www.star.fr*
	Autocars, 16 place de la Gare ☎ 02 99 30 87 80 (next to the railway station)
St Malo	**St Malo Bus, 88 rue de la Hulotais** ☎ 02 99 81 43 29 A local bus service in and around the town.

Morbihan

General	**CTM, 4 rue du Commandant Le Prieur,** ☎ 02 97 87 14 87 **ZI Kéryado, Lorient**
	CTM, 43 rue des Frères Lumière, ☎ 02 97 01 22 01 **Vannes** 🖳 *www.lactm.com* Bus routes across the department.
Lorient	**Compagnie des Transports de la** ☎ 02 97 21 28 29 **Région Lorientaise, cours de Chazelles** 🖳 *www.ctrl.fr* 19 routes in and around the town, including stops at various ports to connect with the islands.
Vannes	**TPV, 45 rue des Frères Lumière** ☎ 02 97 01 22 10 🖳 *www.tpv.com* Bus services in and around Vannes.

Local Trains

General	**Ter Bretagne** ☎ 3635 🖳 *www.ter-sncf.com/bretagne* A local rail network operated in conjunction with the SNCF.
Rennes	**Le VAL, 12 rue du Pré Botté** ☎ 02 99 79 37 37 🖳 *www.star.fr*

Métro is a rail system in Rennes with 15 stations across the city. Trains run from 5.30am to midnight. A single ticket, valid for any length of journey but with a maximum travel time of one hour, costs €1; an all-day ticket is €3.

Kernic   JoTaylor

2

General Information

This chapter lists useful general information in alphabetical order; detailed information relating to each department is contained, under similar headings, in **Chapters 3** to **6**.

Throughout this chapter we give details on how to look up the relevant information in the yellow pages (*pages jaunes*). Alternatively, you can use the internet (🖥 *www.pagesjaunes.fr*). For details see **Telephone Directories** on page 61.

Accommodation

Camping

Many towns have a municipal campsite while seaside locations have many more that are privately run. The majority of tourist office websites have details of local campsites and the yellow pages website (🖥 *www. pagesjaunes.fr*) has a comprehensive list, often with detailed information and links to the campsite's websites. Campsites can be found under *Camping (terrains)* in yellow pages. Below are some websites that give details of campsites in the region.

> 🖥 *www.campingplus.com*
> 🖥 *www.eurocamp.co.uk*
> 🖥 *www.gaf.tm.fr/en/france/campsite/brittany*
> 🖥 *www.haveneurope.com/campsites-in-brittany*
> 🖥 *www.keycamp.co.uk*

Chateaux

> Bienvenue au Château
> 🖥 *www.bienvenue-au-chateau.com*
> This website is available in English and gives details of chateau accommodation in northern and western areas of France.

> Châteaux Country
> 🖥 *www.chateauxcountry.com*
> Information on chateaux across France, including those suitable for large parties and weddings. The website is available in English.

Gîtes and Bed & Breakfast

Tourist offices have details of bed and breakfast facilities (B&B) in the area and may display information in their window. Many tourist office websites have details of *gîtes* and B&B (see **Tourist Offices** in the following chapters). Some communes have *gîtes* available for renting via the *mairie*.

The following websites list *gîte* and B&B accommodation, the majority of which you can book online.

Clévacances	💻 *www.clevacances.fr*
Formules Bretagne	💻 *www.formulesbretagne.com*
Gîtes de France	💻 *www.gites-de-france.com*
Holiday Homes France	💻 *www.holidayhomes-france.co.uk*
Ouest France	💻 *www.ouestfrance-vacances.com*
Pour Les Vacances	💻 *www.pour-les-vacances.com*
Regional tourist office	💻 *www.tourismebretagne.com*

Hotels

Most French hotels charge per room rather than per person. All prices given in the following chapters are per room unless otherwise stated.

Class	Prices From (€)	Comments
Basic	25	Often above a bar or restaurant
Comfortable/ Two-star	40	Independent and chain hotels
Three-star	65	Prices up to €115 per night and suites may be available
Four-star	145	Not many hotels of this standard outside big cities

National Chains

Formule 1	💻 *www.hotelformule1.com*	☎ 08 92 68 56 85
Hôtel de France	💻 *www.hotel-france.com*	☎ 01 41 39 22 23
Hôtels Première Classe/Kyriad/Campanile	💻 *www.envergure.fr*	☎ 08 25 00 30 03

Ibis Hotels   ⌨ *www.ibishotel.com*   ☎ 08 92 68 66 86

Mercure   ⌨ *www.mercure.com*   ☎ 08 25 88 33 33
                                                        UK ☎ 0870-609 0965

Novotel   ⌨ *www.novotel.com*   ☎ 08 25 88 44 44
                                                        UK ☎ 0870-609 0962

Long-term Rentals

If you're coming to France house-hunting and have already sold up in your home country, you may be looking for a property to rent long term. There are many *gîtes* (see page 50) that are empty for long periods, and you may be able to arrange a long let with the owners, even over the summer period, as they may prefer to have a guaranteed income for a long period than unpredictable short-term rentals. Prices are higher near the coast than inland, a three-bedroom house on the coast south of Quimper costing around €675 per month, a similar property inland only €500.

Most large estate agents have properties to rent with contacts from six months upwards. There's a small monthly charge, generally less than 10 per cent of the rent, plus a one-off fee to the estate agent.

Local classified newspapers such as *Le 22 Annonces, Le 56 annonces, Bonjour, Bonjour l'Echo du Golfe, le Carillon, Le Fougerais, Paru Vendu, Petit Quimpérois* and *Pub-Bonjour* have advertisements for properties to rent.

Properties for rent can be found on notice boards in *mairies* or shop windows. *Mairies* may also handle *gîte* accommodation that can be let on a long-term basis.

Villages de vacances are either mobile homes or chalet-type accommodation, often alongside campsite facilities, which can provide inexpensive long-term accommodation. These can be found in the yellow pages under *Villages et clubs de vacances* or via tourist offices. The larger complexes, with indoor pools and comprehensive facilities, accommodate holiday makers all year round, so it's usually the smaller, more basic sites that offer good rates out of season.

Administration

Regional Capital

Rennes   Préfecture de la Région Bretagne, 3 rue   ☎ 02 99 02 10 35
                   Martenot
                   ⌨ *www.bretagne.pref.gouv.fr*

Conseil Régional de Bretagne, Hôtel de   ☎ 02 99 27 10 10
Région, 283 avenue Général Georges Patton
🖳 *www.region-bretagne.fr*

Préfectures

The préfecture is the administrative centre for each department and is located in the department's main town. You may need to contact or visit the préfecture or sous-préfecture (see below) to register ownership of a new car or apply for planning permission.

Côtes-d'Amor	place du Général de Gaulle, St Brieuc 🖳 *www.cotes-darmor.pref.gouv.fr*	☎ 02 96 62 44 22
Finistère	42 boulevard Dupleix, Quimper 🖳 *www.finistere.pref.gouv.fr*	☎ 02 98 76 29 29
Ille-et-Vilaine	3 avenue de la Préfecture, Rennes 🖳 *www.ille-et-vilaine.pref.gouv.fr*	☎ 02 99 02 10 35
Morbihan	place Général de Gaulle, Vannes 🖳 *www.morbihan.pref.gouv.fr*	☎ 02 97 54 84 00

Sous-préfectures

Côtes-d'Amor

Dinan	17 Rue Michel	☎ 02 96 85 55 55
Guingamp	34 rue du Maréchal Joffre	☎ 02 96 44 25 13
Lannion	5 allée du Palais de Justice	☎ 02 96 46 74 56

Finistère

Brest	rue Parmentier	☎ 02 98 00 97 00
Châteaulin	33 rue Amiral Bauguen	☎ 02 98 86 10 17
Morlaix	4 rue Jean-Yves Guillard	☎ 02 98 62 72 72

Ille-et-Vilaine

Fougères	9 avenue François Mitterrand	☎ 02 99 94 56 00
Redon	place Charles de Gaulle	☎ 02 99 71 14 04
St Malo	2 rue Toullier	☎ 02 99 20 22 40

Morbihan

| Lorient | Quai de Rohan | ☎ 02 97 84 40 00 |
| Pontivy | place Aristide Briand | ☎ 02 97 25 00 08 |

Town Halls (Mairies)

All French towns have an *hôtel de ville*, which is the equivalent of a town hall, and most villages have a *mairie*, which has no equivalent in the UK (and certainly isn't a 'village hall'!). To avoid confusion, we have used the French word *mairie* to apply to both town hall and *mairie* unless otherwise specified. The 'mayor' of a town or village is *Monsieur* or *Madame le Maire* (yes, even a female mayor is '*le Maire*'!).

Although *mairies* are usually open Mondays to Fridays, the opening hours vary greatly and in small communes they may be open only two or three times a week, whilst in large towns they may be open also Saturday mornings. There's usually a function room (*une salle des fêtes* or *salle polyvalente*), attached to the town hall/*mairie* or close by. Notice boards at *mairies* are used for formal notices, while local shops usually display a variety of posters for local events.

The *Maire* is the equivalent of a British mayor but is usually more accessible and has more immediate authority in the community. If you buy or rent a property in a small community, you should visit the *mairie* at the earliest opportunity to introduce yourselves to the *Maire*.

Local rules and regulations can be surprisingly strict; some communes can even stipulate the colour you paint your front door. So if you're considering making any alterations to your house or boundaries, it's **essential** to contact the *mairie* **before** undertaking any work or even drawing up plans. Full details of the required procedures are described in *Renovating & Maintaining Your French Home* (see page 379).

The *mairie* should also be your first port of call if you need any advice, as they're a mine of useful information and, if they haven't got what you need, will either get it for you or point you in the right direction.

Embassies & Consulates

British Embassy 35 rue du Faubourg St Honoré, Paris   ☎ 01 44 51 31 00
🖳 *www.britishembassy.gov.uk*
The embassy is open Mondays, Wednesdays, Thursdays and Fridays from 9.30am to 1pm and 2.30 to 6pm, Tuesdays from 9.30am to 4.30pm.

Banks

The majority of French banks close for lunch and are open on Saturday mornings. Banks are rarely open on Mondays and in small towns may be open only in the mornings or even just a few sessions a week. Below are the names of the most commonly found banks, with a web address and a central contact number (if available) to allow you to find the branch closest to you.

Banque de   🖥 *www.bdbretagne.com*   ☎ 08 20 82 08 00
Bretagne   To find your local branch click on 'nos agences' and then on the map.

Banque   🖥 *www.banquepopulaire.fr*
Populaire   To find your local branch click on 'nos agences' and then on the map.

BNP Paribas   🖥 www.bnpparibas.net   ☎ 08 20 82 00 01
     To find your nearest branch click on 'trouver une agence'.

Banque   🖥 *www.tarneaud.fr*   ☎ 08 10 63 28 28
Tarneaud   To find your nearest branch click on 'recherche d'agence'.

Caisse   🖥 *www.caissedepargne.com*
d'Epargne

Crédit   🖥 *www.creditagricole.fr*
Agricole   To find your nearest branch, on the front page of the site use the box in the top right corner with the map of France.

Crédit   🖥 *www.creditlyonnais.fr*
Lyonnais   To find your nearest branch click on 'une agence particuliers'.

Crédit   🖥 *www.cmso.com*   ☎ 08 21 01 10 12
Mutuel   To find your nearest branch click on 'Où nous trouver?'.

Société   🖥 *www.societegenerale.fr*   ☎ 01 42 91 10 00
Générale   To find your nearest branch click on 'trouver une agence'.

English-language Banks

Britline   15 esplanade Brillaud de Laujardière,   ☎ 02 31 55 67 89
14050 Caen
🖥 *www.britline.com*
Britline is a branch of Crédit Agricole and is located in Caen, Lower Normandy. It's an English-language bank with some of its forms in English, although most forms are in French. However, an English-speaking teller always answers the telephone. Note that as this

section of Crédit Agricole is based in Normandy, Crédit Agricole branches locally aren't always familiar with dealing with Britline and you cannot pay in cheques at your local branch. To pay a cheque into your Britline account you must post it to Britline at the above address. Withdrawals, however, are possible from any Crédit Agricole cash machine. As more and more Crédit Agricole branches have English-speaking staff, you may find opening an account locally more advantageous.

Barclays Bank   15 rue Jeanne d'Arc, Rouen   ☎ 02 35 71 70 63
🖳 *www.barclays.fr*
This site has information available in English; go to 'Destination France'. Although this branch isn't in Brittany, it has English-speaking account managers and offers a wide range of packages for international clients living, working or owning property in France. Open Mondays to Fridays 8.30am to 12.25pm and 1.45 to 4.45pm.

General Information

French banking is quite different from banking in the UK. The most noticeable differences are the following:

- French cheques are laid out differently (the amount precedes the payee), and you must state the town where the cheque was written. Note also that, when writing figures, a comma is used in place of a decimal point and a point or space instead of a comma in thousands, e.g. €1.234,56 or €1 234,56.

- You may have to press a button or even enter a code to gain access to a bank.

- Most banks have open-plan desks with receptionists, who handle minimal amounts of cash, most cash transactions are carried out by machine.

- Some banks don't have any cash at the counter. When withdrawing money, you're given a card, which you take to a cash machine to obtain the money. This system doesn't always enable you to withdraw the exact amount you want, e.g. €20 or €40, but not €30.

- Receipts aren't always issued when paying in money without a paying-in slip, so ask for a paying-in book (or simply ask for a receipt – *un reçu*).

- When you open an account, you will be given copies of your *relevé d'identité bancaire* (normally called *un RIB* – pronounced 'reeb'), which contains all your account details. As you will need to provide a *RIB* when setting up a direct debit or an account (e.g. with a shop) and when asking anyone (e.g. an employer) to pay money into your account, it's wise to take extra copies.

● There are no cheque guarantee cards, although many shops now insist on identification with cheques.

● Cheques are guaranteed for payment in France, but if you write a cheque without sufficient funds in your account (unless you have an authorised overdraft facility) it may result in a phone call to your home or a registered letter being sent by the bank demanding that funds are paid into the account within 8 days. If this happens again within 12 months, the account may be closed and you will be unable to hold any account in France for a year and will be blacklisted for three years. You have been warned!

● It's wise to keep at least €30 in your account at all times to cover any unexpected charges. For example, some banks charge to transfer money between accounts of the same bank while others charge each time you access your account online and up to €15 just to accept a letter from you confirming that you have cancelled a direct debit with a third party.

● If your cheque book is lost or stolen, irrespective of which bank you use, call ☎ 08 92 68 32 08 between 8am and 11pm. The loss must be confirmed in writing to your bank immediately.

● If your French credit card is lost or stolen, contact the emergency number for your bank (see page 55) or the national number ☎ 08 92 70 57 05.

● 'Chip and Pin' cards are being introduced by British banks and should have replaced all existing cards by 2006. Until then, many shops and companies in France aren't accepting 'chip and signature' cards, i.e. those that have a microchip but don't yet have a PIN. Despite the card being clearly marked VISA, the equipment at many shops cannot read the card strip or chip. It's possible for the shop keeper to key the card number into the machine but knowledge of this (and willingness to do so) isn't common. If you don't yet have a chip and pin card, ensure that you have another method of payment.

Opening a French bank account will provide many benefits – not least the provision of a debit card (*une carte bleue*), which has a microchip and requires you to enter a four-digit PIN rather than sign a receipt. Such a card enables you to use automated petrol pumps (see **Petrol Stations** on page 80) and will save you embarrassment and hassle in shops where the staff are unfamiliar with UK credit cards or can't accept them (see above) Most *cartes bleues* can be used all over Europe.

Moneo

Moneo is a system designed to eliminate the need to carry small change. A Moneo card has an annual cost of €8 and is then 'charged' with up to €100. It can be used to buy a newspaper, a loaf of bread or even a bar of chocolate in shops, cafés, newsagents and bakeries displaying the 'Mon€o' sign, of which there's an increasing number. The card can be used for purchases up to €30. Cards are ordered from your bank and you must have a French bank account to obtain one.

Business Services

Computer Services

A selection of companies that offer computer services are listed in the relevant chapter and usually include computer repairs, software, accessories and computers built to your requirement. Other companies can be found in yellow pages under *Micro-informatique*

Computer Training

There are many centres offering computer courses: for specific software packages, in website design or simply an introduction to computing. Enquire at libraries and tourist offices for details of local organisations, such as Maison de Jeunes et Culture (MJC) or look in yellow pages under *Formation continue* or *Enseignement commerce, gestion, informatique.*

Employment Agencies

Agence Nationale pour l'Emploi (ANPE)
🖳 *www.anpe.fr*

The main offices of ANPE can be found in the yellow pages under *Administrations du travail et de l'emploi.* Independent companies, **which are only allowed to offer temporary employment**, include the following:

Adecco	🖳 *www.adecco.fr*
Manpower	🖳 *www.manpower.fr*
Vedior Bis	🖳 *www.vediorbis.com*

New Businesses

Agence Pour la Création d'Entreprise
🖳 *www.apce.com*

This is an excellent website for anyone thinking of starting a business in France, and part of the site is available in English. Alternatively, ask at your *mairie* for details of the local Chamber of Commerce, where staff are usually very approachable and keen to help entrepreneurs in their area.

Communications

Telephone

Fixed Line Telephone Services

Telephone installations must be carried out by France Télécom, but telephone services are also available from a number of other operators, some of which are listed below.

France Télécom   🖳 *www.francetelecom.fr*   ☎ 1014
The website has an English option.
France Télécom has a dedicated English-language helpline (☎ 08 00 36 47 75), open Mondays to Fridays 8.30am to 8pm.

One.Tel   🖳 *www.onetel.fr*   ☎ 3238

Primus Telecom   🖳 www.as24telecom.com   ☎ 05 53 05 47 82
An English-speaking company.

Tele2   🖳 *www.tele2.fr*   ☎ 08 05 04 44 44

These companies can prove to be cheaper than France Télécom, especially for international calls, which are often the same tariff day and night, but you should always compare before deciding. France Télécom's standing charge is payable for the line, even if you use another service provider. It's worth noting that some UK non-geographical numbers (e.g. beginning 0870 or 0345) are accessible only via a France Télécom phone call. Some British companies that have free-phone numbers within the UK but are accustomed to receiving phone calls from abroad (e.g. credit card companies and banks) offer a different phone number for overseas callers or a number for you to use with reverse charges.

Mobile Telephones

Mobile phone (*portable* or *mobile*) shops are found in most town centres, and hypermarkets sell a good selection of handsets and connection packages. Reception in rural areas can be poor, some quite large areas having no reception at all. Technology and tariff options are generally behind those offered by UK companies, French companies still charging for calls by the minute rather than by the second.

There are three service providers in France: Bouygues, Orange and SFR. Mobile phone shops can be found in yellow pages under *Téléphonie mobile*. If your mobile phone is lost or stolen, contact the appropriate number below:

Bouygues   🖥 *www.bouyguestelecom.fr*   ☎ 08 00 29 10 00

Orange   🖥 *www.orange.fr*   ☎ 08 25 00 57 00

SFR   🖥 *www.sfr.fr*   ☎ 06 10 00 19 00

Public Telephones

These are located in towns and villages: in railway stations, bars and cafés. The new kiosks are Perspex and usually accept only cards; however, if there's a group of three or more kiosks, one may accept coins. All public phones allow international calls and there's a button with a double flag symbol, which you can press for the telephone display to appear in different languages.

Telephone cards are available from post offices, railway stations, cafés, banks and anywhere you see the sign *Télécarte en vente ici*. Cards don't have a standard design, as they're used for advertising. You usually need a telephone card for internet access at a public facility such as the post office.

The post office sell a rechargeable card (*carte téléphonique*) that charges the caller by the second and can be used to make calls from call boxes and private phones.

Special Rate Phone Numbers

Special rate numbers normally start with 08 or 09 (mobile numbers start 06). Numbers beginning 09 are charged at high rates and are to be avoided if possible. The cost of calls to numbers beginning 08 varies greatly (see below), and you're advised to be wary of numbers for which the charge isn't specified. You should also avoid numbers starting with 00, as calls may be routed via another country. Common 08 prefixes include the following:

- 0800, 0805, 0809 – free call (known as *numéros verts*);

- 0810, 0811 – local call rates (known as *numéros azur*);

- 0836, 0892, 0893, 0898, 0899 – calls vary from free to €1.35 for connection plus up to 75 centimes per minute;

- 0899 79 – €1.35 for connection plus 34 centimes per minute.

Telephone Directories

If you have a fixed line telephone, you will automatically receive the local telephone directory (or directories), which are published in April each year. Directories usually incorporate both yellow pages (*pages jaunes*) and white pages, containing residential listings (*annuaire*), in a single volume, back to back, but there are separate volumes for some large towns. All listings in the residential section are in alphabetical order within each commune, so you need to know the commune where someone lives in order to find their number.

If you don't have a yellow pages or residential directory or would like a copy for a neighbouring department, they can be obtained by phoning ☎ 08 10 81 07 67. There's a recorded message: choose option 2 and you will be put through to an operator. For a different department it will cost €12.50 for just a yellow pages or €25 for both yellow pages and the residential directory.

If you're looking for a company or private number you can also use the internet (🖳 *www.pagesjaunes.fr*). This is an easy to use website that offers many services including:

● A search facility for companies and services, available in English (click on the Union Jack in the top right corner).

● Residential listings. On the front page of the website is a tab for *Pages Blanches*, which is the residential listing.

● Finding an address from a telephone number. If you want to find a company or private address and only have the phone number, go to the header *A qui donc est ce numéro?*. There's a charge of €0.50 for each search.

● Phone numbers abroad. If you want to find a telephone number in another country, click on the header *Annuaires du Monde* and it takes you to telephone directories from all over the world.

● Traffic and weather information. For information on a particular town, call up any page of services for the town e.g. *garages* or *mairie*, listed at the top of the page. For example, you can go to a street map (*Plan*), find out about traffic in the area (*Trafic*), or tune in to a webcam of the town centre or a particular area of interest, if available (*Webcam*). The weather forecast for the town on that day is also given; if you want a forecast for the forthcoming four-day period, click on *Météo*. If there's a website for the *mairie*, it will be accessible from here; click on *Site de la mairie* next to the French flag.

Useful Numbers

French Directory Enquiries   ☎ 12

International Directory Enquiries & dialling information ☎ 3212

BT Direct – for making reverse-charge calls to the UK   ☎ 08 00 99 00 44

Internet

There are a number of internet service providers (*ISP*) in France, and the following websites can help you to choose the best provider for you.

> 💻 *www.club-internet.fr*
> 💻 *www.freesurf.fr*
> 💻 *www.illiclic.com* (operated by La Poste)
> 💻 *www.tiscali.fr*
> 💻 *www.wanadoo.fr* (operated by France Télécom)

The best way to get connected is to go to a public internet access provider (see below) and register an address and obtain the dial-up numbers, etc. so that you can then go online at home. Note that software may need to be installed in your computer. Alternatively, you can register with Wanadoo by phone (☎ 3608), when you will be given all the access codes and phone numbers immediately.

Wanadoo offers a number of dial-up packages, which can work out cheaper than paying for access calls on a per minute basis if you spent more than a certain time online.

Broadband

High-speed lines (*ADSL* or *le haut-débit*) are gradually becoming available in rural areas as well as in towns and cities, and the French government plans to have high-speed lines available throughout the country by 2007. To find out if broadband is currently available where you are, go to 💻 *www. francetelecom.fr* and on left of the front page click on '*Tout sur l'ADSL*, then on the right hand side below *l'ADSL disponible chez vous* enter your phone number and it will tell you straight away if high-speed lines are available to you.

There are various tariffs available for high-speed connections. For example, Wanadoo and France Télécom offer ADSL packages, usually entailing a set fee plus a monthly payment. Offers are changing all the time and are frequently advertised on TV and on the relevant websites. More information can be obtained from 💻 *www.francetelecom.fr* and 💻 *www.adsl-france.org*.

Some companies (including those listed below) offer high-speed internet access via satellites. However they only increase the speed of information coming in; outgoing information, including emails, still goes out via an ordinary telephone line.

⌨ *www.high-speed-internet-access-guide.com*
⌨ *www.satelite-internet.com*
⌨ *www.skycasters.com*

Public Internet Access

All France Télécom shops have internet access, as do many post offices. Public places that offer access usually require a telephone card (see **Public Telephones** on page 60). Some internet cafes offer free internet access to customers and some public facilities such as tourist offices offer free access. Commercial internet access providers such as internet cafes and libraries offer access from ten minutes to an hour and sometimes up to ten hours. Prices start at around €1 for ten minutes and €10 for three hours.

Useful Web Addresses

The following is a selection from the myriad websites accessible:

⌨ *www.voila.fr* – A French search engine.

⌨ *www.pagesjaunes.fr* – Yellow pages. This site has the option at the bottom to convert the site to English.

⌨ *www.meteoconsult.com* – Weather site, available in English.

⌨ *www.service-public.fr* – The official gateway to the French civil service.

⌨ *www.google.com* – Although this is an English-language search engine, when foreign websites are located it gives you the option of translating the web page into English – the results are never less than entertaining!

Television & Radio

Whether your television (TV) set will work in France is dependent on which model you have. Most televisions bought in the UK in the last few years should work in France, as most now have the capability to pick up both Secam and PAL signals. If you buy a television in France, you may find that it's sold without a stand.

If you're learning French, watching French TV with subtitles is a good idea. If subtitles are available, they can be found on Teletext 888. If you have a TV guide, the programme may have a symbol of an ear to show that it has subtitles, which are generally for the hard of hearing but will do just as well for foreigners!

It's possible to get British television in France but a satellite dish is needed and you must ensure that you're aware of the legalities before proceeding. There are various British suppliers and installers of satellite who will give you all the information you need, including the following company, which has a comprehensive website:

Big Dish Satellite, Mouriol, Milhaguet,   ☎ 05 55 78 72 98
87440 Marval
🖳 *www.bigdishsat.com*

Licence

To watch TV in France you need a licence, costing €116.50 for colour and €74.31 for black and white. This fee covers all the television sets that you own in France, even if in different locations such as a caravan or holiday home. As in the UK, when a television set is purchased, the shop must inform the authorities and a television licence bill will duly arrive (unlike the UK, it takes several months!).

If you bring a British TV into France that's capable of receiving French programmes, you should notify the Centre Régional de la Redevance Audiovisuelle within 30 days.

Centre Régional de la Redevance de   ☎ 02 99 85 72 85
l'Audiovisuel, 27 place Colombier, 35000 Rennes

CRRA   ☎ 01 49 70 40 00
🖳 *www.service-public.fr*

Radio

There's a wide variety of local and national stations that can be received in the area, some of which are detailed below.

Station	FM Frequency	Description
Chérie FM	100.2, 102.6	Current chart music
Classique	92.3, 95.0	Primarily classical music
Culture	89.0, 97.8	Primarily talk and intellectual discussion
Europe	102.7, 104.7	A wide variety of music

Europe 2	89.9, 92.4, 96.4, 101.0	Current chart music
France Bleu	93.0, 98.6, 103.3	A wide variety of music and talk radio
France Bleu Armorique	104.5	A wide variety of music and talk radio
Fun Radio	106 9	Current chart music
Hit West	107.1, 106.9	Current chart music
Inter	95.4	Primarily talk radio
Nostalgie	106.2	'Golden oldies'
NRJ	103.5, 106.0	Current chart music
Radio Océane	99.2,104.9	Current chart music
RCF Clarté	100.6	Catholic radio
RTL	97.3, 104.3	A wide variety of music
Skyrock	94.3, 101.6	Current chart music
Trégor FM	96.00	Current chart music.

Domestic Services

Bouncy Castle Hire

Bouncy castles (*gonflables*) can be found in yellow pages under *Location de matériel pour réceptions, pour évènements.*

Clothes Alterations

Shops and workshops can be found in most towns, offering made-to-measure clothes, repairs, alterations and sometimes soft furnishings. Listed in yellow pages under *Couture, retouches.*

Crèches & Nurseries

Children can start nursery from the age of two (as long as they're toilet trained) and most crèches/nurseries (*halte-garderie*) cater for up to three-year-olds. In larger towns there may be a facility for older children.

Opening hours vary from half days to full days all week. Listed in yellow pages under *Halte-garderie* or *Garde d'enfants*.

Equipment & Tool Hire

The larger equipment hire centres offer a wide range including chain saws, ride-on lawn mowers, mini-diggers and diggers, lifting platforms and rotovators. To hire equipment you need to take one piece of identification and proof of address (such as a household bill) and pay a deposit – using a cheque or bank card. Details are given in the following chapters and companies can be found in yellow pages under *Location de matériel pour entrepreneurs*. Some DIY shops hire out basic equipment (see page 104).

Fancy Dress Hire

Fancy dress (*déguisement*) and costume (*costume*) hire shops are few and far between, although garments can often be hired from a specialist party shop. Listed in yellow pages under *Costumiers*.

Garden Services

Listed in the yellow pages under *Jardins et parcs, aménagement, entretien*.

Launderettes

Laundrettes (*laveries*) are more readily available than in the UK, each large town having at least one, although not always listed in the yellow pages. Modern launderettes have a central pay point where you must select the number of the machine (or tumble drier) that you want to use and then pay. Dry cleaners' (*pressing*) are found in town centres and usually offer minor clothes repairs such as hems and zips and sometimes an ironing service.

Marquee Hire

Companies that hire out marquees often also hire chairs, tables, china and cutlery and sometimes offer an outside catering service. Listed in yellow pages under *Location de tentes et chapiteaux* or *Location de matériel pour réceptions, pour évènements*.

Party Services

Sound systems, lighting, karaoke systems and clowns can all be found in yellow pages under *Animation artistique*.

Septic Tank Services

The use of septic tanks (*fosse septique*) is set to diminish as more properties are connected to mains drainage. However, it may be many years until the new legislation has been fully implemented and there will always be some rural houses that aren't connected. Visit the *mairie* to find out whether your property is likely to be put on mains drainage and when, and for information about the latest regulations regarding inspections and any local companies specialising in installation or maintenance.

Companies that clean, unblock and empty septic tanks as well as those that install and maintain them can be found in yellow pages under *Vidange, curage*.

Entertainment

General   Billetterie, Leclerc
Inside the foyer of Leclerc hypermarkets you will find a large board giving details of forthcoming concerts and large events, from Paris to Rennes, including many international acts. Tickets for these events can be bought at the *Billetterie* or *Espace Culturel* within the complex.

Cinemas

Some French cinemas show English-language films in their original version, i.e. in English with French subtitles (*sous-titres français*). These are identified by the letters *VO* (*version originale*) next to the title; *VF* or *version française* indicates that a film has been dubbed into French. Small cinemas that show 'art' and foreign films (*art & essai*) are likely to show more films in English than a large cinema complex. However, occasionally, an English-language film comes out with only French sub-titles and is therefore shown in all cinemas in English. If you go to the website of the major cinema chains, such as ⌨ *www.cinefil.com*, there's an option for *En Version Originale*, which details all the films currently showing in English.

Cinema tickets cost around €5 for adults and €4 for children. Tickets can usually be bought in advance but, if the tickets haven't been collected half an hour before the film starts, they may be re-sold. Tickets can be purchased online, with an additional cost of around €0.50. Some cinemas reduce ticket prices on certain days, such as Mondays or Wednesdays. French films are classified and are advertised as *interdit aux moins de 18 (16,12) ans*.

Note that films shown on television that aren't suitable for under 12s, under 16s, etc. have a small circle in the bottom right corner of the screen with, for example, '-12' for a film not suitable for under 12s. This is on display throughout the entire film.

Large cinema complexes are increasingly found on the outskirts of towns and cities. Cinemas have large, comfortable seats and air-conditioning.

Cinemas and film listings for the main chain cinemas can be found on the following websites:

> 🖥 *www.cgrcinemas.fr*
> 🖥 *www.ugc.fr*
> 🖥 *www.pathe.fr/cinema*

English Books

There are a small number of second-hand English book shops in the region, detailed in the following chapters. Some of the large supermarkets and independent newsagents stock a selection of novels in English. Many libraries (*bibliothèque/mediathèque*) have a small supply of books in English as well as bilingual books (see below).

Festivals

There are many annual festivals in this region, just a small selection of which are listed in this book. Dates vary each year, so just the month has been given. Details can be obtained from the local tourist office.

Libraries

Apart from books, libraries may offer music CDs, videos and children's story books and other media. If a library has no books in English, it may have bilingual books. These are books with the left page in French and the right in English (for example) – an excellent way to help improve your French. Library membership will require one piece of identification and proof of address such as a utility bill. There's a nominal charge per annum for membership to the library.

Theatres

Theatres can be found in all major towns and cities (see following chapters) and in some small towns and villages, where plays and musicals may otherwise be shown at the *Salle des Fêtes*. Listed in yellow pages under *Théâtres et salles de spectacles*.

Video & DVD Hire

DVDs are widely available and are usually viewable in English, but check the back of the case before buying or renting: there will be a Union Jack and/or the words *Sous-titres* (sub-titles) and *Langues* (languages) with '*Anglais*' in the list that follows. Some video shops also hire out DVD players (*lecteurs DVD*). Automatic video and DVD dispensers are more common than video shops, often in the frontage of an old video shop or in supermarket car parks. Payment is made by credit card but not all British cards are accepted (see page 57).

Leisure

Many leisure activities aren't listed in yellow pages. Most towns have at least one of the following: *Amicale Laïque, Centre Culturel, Maison de Jeunesse et de Culture* (*MJC*). These associations organise a diverse range of activities from tea dances to climbing, rollerskating to football and are a good place to start if looking for a specific activity. Alternatively contact the *Maison des Associations*, as they hold details on all the groups and clubs. The *mairie* or tourist office will be able to put you in touch with the relevant association in your town.

If you decide to join a local leisure activity, there will be an annual or, for some groups, per-term (*trimestre*) membership. If it's a physical activity, you will require a licence. The relevant club will have the forms and a medical will be required, which your doctor can carry out as a standard consultation (€20).

Arts & Crafts

All forms of artistic activity from pottery to watercolour painting can be found in yellow pages under *Arts graphiques, arts plastiques*.

Bowling

Bowling alleys (listed in yellow pages under *Bowling*) are usually located in large complexes on the outskirts of major towns, often near a retail park. These usually have a bar and pool tables and serve snack food.

Bridge

Welcome groups (e.g. *Accueil des Villes Françaises* – see page 71) often organise bridge sessions. Not usually listed in yellow pages but may be found in the residential directory for larger towns under '*Bridge Club*'.

Children's Activity Clubs

Maisons de Jeunesse et de Culture (*MJC*) and *Centres de Loisirs* can be found in most towns and organise activities on Wednesdays and during school holidays (except Christmas). In the summer there may be week long trips to the sea, activity camps, horse riding outings, etc. Prices are reasonable: from around €5 for a half-day activity to €250 for a week-long residential camp.

Choral Singing

Choir (*choeur*) groups are organised by music schools and occasionally churches. Enquire at the local *Maison des Associations* or the tourist office. Voice training and singing lessons can be found in yellow pages under *Musique et chant (leçons)*.

Circus Skills & Magic

Circus (*cirque*) and magic skills are popular in France. Private companies or local activity groups run courses.

Dancing

Dancing schools (*école de danse*) can be found in yellow pages under *Danse (salles et leçons)*. There are classes for ballet (*classique*), ballroom and Latin American (*dance de société*), jazz (*jazz*) and tap (*claquettes*). Tea dances (*thé dansant*), often held at a dedicated dance hall (*guinguette*), are popular on Saturday evenings and Sunday afternoons, but don't expect to be served tea! Dance groups are listed in yellow pages under *Théâtre, ballet, danse (troupes, compagnies)*.

Drama

Theatre workshops (*atelier théâtre*) are often attached to theatres or run by local associations. Theatre groups are listed in yellow pages under *Théâtre, ballet, danse (troupes, compagnies)*.

Dress Making

Dress-making classes (*atelier de couture*) may be run locally by associations or private individuals.

Flower Arranging

Flower arranging (*art floral*) classes are usually held monthly.

Gardening

Gardening clubs are arranged by the local horticultural association and may organise flower arranging classes and trips to local public gardens and relevant exhibitions.

Gym

Traditional keep fit and gym classes (*gymnastique volontaire*), including step, cardiac and toning, are often advertised in shop windows and on library and supermarket notice boards. Health clubs (see below) also run a selection of gym classes.

Gyms & Health Clubs

Health clubs (*club de forme*) aren't as widespread as in the UK, for example, but some national chains are starting to develop including *Club Moving* and *Amazon*. They can be found in yellow pages under *Clubs de forme*.

Ice Skating

Ice rinks (*patinoire*) are usually found on the outskirts of large towns near retail parks. Open all year, they offer ice skating, ice hockey and ice dancing. Listed in yellow pages under *Patinoires*.

Music

Individual lessons (*cours particulier*) and group lessons (*cours*) are given by music schools and private individuals. Various music lessons can be found in yellow pages under *Musique et chant (leçons)*. Music shops may run, or have adverts for, local classes as well as hiring out instruments. Pianos can also be hired from specific shops, found in yellow pages under *Pianos: vente, location*. Outlets for other instruments can be found in yellow pages under *Musique: instruments et accessoires (vente, location)* and sheet music shops under *Musique:partitions*.

Photography

Clubs for 35mm photography, digital (*numérique*) and black and white.

Scouts & Guides

Large towns have both local and national groups catering from children from 8 to 19-year-olds. For details, visit ▤ *www.scoutsetguides.fr*.

Social Groups

Town Twinning

The majority of French towns and many villages are twinned (*jumelé*) with towns or villages in at least one other country, sometimes up to six, although not always with one in the UK. Involvement in such a group is a great way to integrate with the French community and meet fellow English speakers. To find details on local town twinning, contact the *mairie* or tourist office.

Welcome Groups

Some towns have a branch of Accueil des Villes Françaises (AVF), a nationwide organisation designed specifically to help newcomers settle into a town or area. To find your nearest group, go to ▤ *www.avf.asso.fr* (available in English) or ▤ *www.perso.wanadoo.fr/avf-bretagne/bretagne/avf-locales*.

Spas

Northern France is popular for spa treatments and thalassotherapy, which is treatments based on the healing properties of the sea and marine products. They usually have accommodation on-site or an arrangement with a nearby hotel and offer a selection of day or short-stay packages. Major spas are listed in the following chapters; details of others can be found in yellow pages under *Thalassothérapie*.

Stamp Collecting

Stamp collecting (*philatélie*) groups, which often also cover postcard collecting, usually meet once a month on Sunday mornings. Specialist shops can be found in yellow pages under *Philatélie*.

Yoga

Although some yoga classes can be found in yellow pages, under *Yoga (leçons)*, they're often advertised locally in shop windows and on library and supermarket notice boards.

Medical Facilities & Emergency Services

Ambulances

In the event of a medical emergency dial ☎ 15 and the medical emergency services will arrive (*Service d'Aide Médical d'Urgence, SAMU*).

Ambulances are privately operated and not for use in an emergency. You would call an ambulance if you needed to go to a clinic but couldn't drive or needed to get to hospital but not urgently. If the journey has been agreed or requested by a doctor or medical establishment, the cost can be reclaimed if you're registered with the French social security system. Otherwise you must pay as you would for a taxi.

As ambulance services are all privately run, there's no single telephone number. Local companies can be found in yellow pages under *Ambulances*. Ambulances are conventional cars, adapted for ambulance use, and are white with distinctive blue crosses. Ambulance companies often operate taxis as well.

Doctors

French doctors have flexible working hours and may have an 'open surgery' during the week, or even at certain times every day, when no appointment is necessary; you just go and wait your turn. A vast majority of doctors work alone and answer the phone themselves, with an answering machine when they're on call or the surgery is closed (they will usually answer the phone when in the middle of a consultation with another patient!).

You don't need to register with a doctor when you arrive in France; simply call when you need an appointment, although you're now required to appoint a 'regular doctor' (*médecin traitant*). There's a charge each time you visit €20. House calls are more expensive and may not be available. The cost is partially reclaimable if you're registered with French social security (€13) or if you're on holiday from the UK and have an E111 form (**in an emergency only; you cannot reclaim the cost of routine treatment**). An E111 is valid from a year up to three years depending on the issuing office. They're free from post offices in the UK, so if you aren't living permanently in France it's advisable to renew yours regularly.

When you go to a doctor or dentist in France, he will give you a form with details of the treatment given, his details and reference number. Ensure that you give your British address if you intend to reclaim these costs with your E111. This form should be attached to your E111 and sent to the Caisse Régionale Assurance Maladie (CRAM – see **Health Authority** on page 76). If you need to reclaim medical costs, remember to keep all receipts, including those of any prescriptions and the labels from any medicines prescribed, to send with your claim. Chemists will usually peel off the labels from the medicines and stick them to the print-out which they give you.

If you intend to be in France for a long period or indefinitely, it's recommended to ask your UK doctor for a print-out of your medical record. He may not be able to give you copies of the actual written records, but should be willing to provide a print-out (although you may be charged), which you should take with you to your French doctor on your first visit.

Emergencies

In the event of an emergency, dial one of the following numbers:

Any medical emergency
SAMU (*Service d'Aide Médical d'Urgence*)   ☎ 15

Police (see page 77)
Gendarmes   ☎ 17

Fire or accident not requiring medical help (see below)
Sapeurs-pompiers   ☎ 18

The *SAMU* are often the first on the scene in the event of an accident. You should call the police first and they will contact the *SAMU*, or you can call them as well.

If you need to call any of the above numbers, you will be asked a series of questions. Below are examples of what you may be asked (with English translations) and a selection of possible responses.

1. Your name and phone number:
    Quel est votre nom et numéro de téléphone?
    [Give your surname first, then your first name, than a contact telephone number]

2. The nature of accident or problem:
    Quelle est la nature de l'accident?
    Il/elle s'est évanoui(e) (S/he has collapsed/fainted
    Il/elle est tombé(e) d'une échelle/un arbre (S/he has fallen off a ladder/tree)
    Il/elle a eu une crise cardiaque (S/he has had a heart attack)

3. Your exact address/position and how to get there:
    Quelle est votre adresse exacte et pouvez-vous me donner des directions?
    au carrefour (at the crossroads)
    au coin (on the corner)
    tournez à droite/gauche (turn right/left)
    tout droit (straight on)
    après/avant (after/before)
    sur votre gauche/droite (on the left/right)

4. How many people are involved:
    Combien de personnes sont impliquées?
    une/deux/trois personnes (one/two/three people)

5. The condition of any injured parties:
    Quels sont les blessures?
    Il/elle est inconscient(e) (S/he is unconscious)
    Il/elle a une hémorragie (S/he is bleeding)
    Il/elle souffre beaucoup (S/he is in a lot of pain)
    Il/elle a une fracture de la jambe/du bras (She has broken a leg/arm)

6. What treatment has been given:
    Quel médicament a été préscrit?
    Aucun (None)
    [name of medication]

A number of other useful emergency numbers are listed below.

Advice

To find a counsellor in your area   ☎ 05 55 60 01 23
💻 *www.find-a-counsellor-in-france.com*

Bank Cards

If your bank card is lost or stolen
    🖳 *www.carte-bleue.com*

Banque Populaire	☎ 08 92 70 57 05
BNP Paribas	☎ 08 20 82 00 02
Banque Tarneaud	☎ 08 25 00 59 59
Caisse d'Epargne	☎ 08 25 39 39 39
Crédit Agricole*	☎ 01 45 67 84 84
Crédit Lyonnaise	☎ 08 21 80 90 90
Crédit Mutuel	☎ 08 92 70 57 05
Société Générale	☎ 08 25 07 00 70
Other banks	☎ 08 92 70 57 05

   * includes Britline (see page 55)

If your cheque book is lost or stolen
    All banks   ☎ 08 92 68 32 08

Once you've reported your card or cheque book stolen by telephone, you must then confirm this in writing to your branch immediately.

Electricity Emergency

Côtes-d'Armor   ☎ 08 10 33 33 22

Finistère   ☎ 08 10 33 33 29

Ille-et-Vilaine   ☎ 08 10 33 33 35

Morbihan   ☎ 08 10 33 33 56

Gas Leak

Côtes-d'Armor   ☎ 08 10 43 30 22

Finistère   ☎ 08 10 43 30 29

Ille-et-Vilaine   ☎ 02 99 35 11 33

Morbihan	Le Faouët	☎ 08 10 43 30 56
	Lorient	☎ 02 97 76 38 68
	Vannes	☎ 02 97 63 37 40

Pest Control (e.g. Termites)

Côtes-d'Armor   ☎ 08 70 27 47 45

Finistère	☎ 02 98 45 75 07
Ille-et-Vilaine	☎ 02 99 60 67 60
Morbihan	☎ 02 97 84 08 44

Poisoning

Centre Anti-Poisons, Rennes	☎ 02 99 59 22 22
Centre Anti-Poisons Animal, Nantes	☎ 02 40 68 77 40

Other emergency numbers and support groups are listed in the front of yellow pages.

Fire Brigade

The fire brigade (*sapeurs-pompiers* or *pompiers*) have a high level of medical training and are one of the first on the scene of any accident, often carrying out medical procedures until the arrival of the *SAMU*. In rural areas, *pompiers* are often 'reserves' and are called to duty by a siren giving three short, very loud blasts.

You can also call the fire brigade if you have a bee or wasp nest in the house or a swarm is presenting an immediate threat. You pay them directly, around €30, for the service.

The fire brigade is listed in yellow pages under *Sapeurs-pompiers*.

Health Authority

The Caisse Régionale Assurance Maladie (CRAM) deals with medical claims and expenses. You must contact CRAM in order to join the French social security system. CRAM representatives pay regular visits to some towns (enquire at the *mairie*), in which case you can meet them in person and ask any questions you may have. Otherwise, you need to contact one of the CRAM or Caisse Primaire Assurance Maladie (CPAM) offices listed in the relevant chapter. The main department offices are given below.

Côtes-d'Armor	CPAM des Côtes-d'Armor, 106 boulevard Hoche, St Brieuc	☎ 08 20 90 41 79
	🖳 *www.saint-brieuc.ameli.fr*	
	The office is open Mondays to Fridays 8am to 5pm.	
Finistère	CPAM, 18 rue de la République, Quimper	☎ 08 20 90 41 99
	🖳 *www.ameli.fr*	

Office open Mondays to Fridays 8.30am to 5pm, Saturdays 8.30am to 12.30pm.

Ille-et-Vilaine   CPAM d'Ille-et-Vilaine, 7 cours des   ☎ 08 20 90 41 74
Alliés, Rennes
🖳 *www.rennes.ameli.fr*
This is also the regional office. Open Mondays to Fridays 8am to 5pm.

Morbihan   CPAM du Morbihan, 73 rue du Général ☎ 08 20 90 41 49
Weygand, Vannes
🖳 *www.cpam56.fr*
This is the main office for the department. Open Mondays to Fridays 8am to 5pm.

Hospitals

The term hospital (*hôpital*) in France covers all medical facilities, including specialist units such as psychiatry, retirement and convalescent homes. Details of all the hospitals in the region are given in the following chapters. Listed in yellow pages under *Hôpitaux*.

Police

There are two main types of police in France: *police nationale* and *gendarmes*.

The *police nationale* is under the control of the Interior Ministry and deals with 'general' crime, mostly in urban or semi-urban areas. They're most commonly seen in towns and are distinguished by the silver buttons on their uniforms. At night and in rain and fog they often wear white caps and capes.

The *gendarmerie nationale* is part of the army and under the control of the Ministry of Defence, although it's also at the service of the Interior Ministry. *Gendarmes* deal with serious crime on a national scale and all crime in rural areas where there's no *police* station. They're also responsible for motorway patrols, air safety, mountain rescue, etc. *Gendarmes* wear blue uniforms and traditional caps (*képis*) although their new uniform includes a baseball cap. Gendarmes include police motorcyclists (*motards*), who patrol in pairs. Some of the smaller *gendarmeries* are being merged and a rural station may be open limited hours, but the local number will always be put through to the station that's on duty.

In addition to the above, most cities and medium-size towns have their own police force, *police municipale* or *corps urbain*, who deal mainly with petty crime, traffic offences and road accidents. They're based at the *mairie* or close by.

All French police are armed with guns.

A full list of gendarmeries can be found in yellow pages under *Gendarmaries* or (in older directories) *Administration de la Défense et des Anciens Combattants.*

If you need to contact the police, below are examples of what you may be asked (with English translations) and a selection of possible responses. **Always remain polite when talking to French police officers!**

1. Your name and phone number:
   Quel est votre nom et numéro de téléphone?
   [Give your surname first, then your first name, then a contact telephone number.]

2. The nature of the incident:
   Quelle est la nature de l'incident?
   On m'a volé mon auto/sac à main/portefeuille (My car/handbag/wallet has been stolen.)

3. When did the incident occur?
   Quand est-ce arrivé?
   Hier soir/ce matin/il y a une heure (last night/this morning/an hour ago.)

4. Where did the incident occur?
   Où a eu lieu cet incident/cet évènement/ce vol?
   [Name the place.]

5. If stopped by the police:
   Puis-je voir vos papiers? (Can I see your papers?)
   Cette auto est-elle à vous? (Is this your car?)
   Vous étiez en excès de vitesse/vous conduisiez trop vite (You were speeding/driving too fast.)
   Venez près de mon auto/ma moto or *avancez jusqu'à mon auto/ma moto* (Pull over by my car/motorbike.)

6. Your address and how to get there:
   Quelle est votre adresse exacte et pouvez-vous me donner des directions?
   au carrefour (at the crossroads)
   au coin (on the corner)
   tournez à droite/gauche (turn right/left)
   tout droit (straight on)
   après/avant (after/before)
   sur votre gauche/droite (on the left/right).

Motoring

Accidents

In the event of an accident involving two or more cars, it's normal for the drivers to complete an accident report form (*constat à l'amiable*), which is provided by French insurance companies. This is completed by all drivers involved, who must agree (more or less) on what happened. You can write in English or any other language and it's important that you check the particulars (e.g. address) of the other driver(s) listed on the form against something official, such as their driving licence. Take care when crossing the relevant boxes (the French use a cross rather than a tick) that the form cannot be added to or changed later and be sure that you're happy that you understand what has been written by the other driver(s). A *constat à l'amiable* isn't mandatory, and you can refuse to complete one if the other driver(s) disagree with your interpretation of what happened.

Breakers' Yards

Found in yellow pages under *Casses automobiles.*

Car Dealers

Car dealerships can be found in yellow pages under *Garages d'automobiles, réparation.* Alternatively, websites for the relevant make of car usually have an option to find the nearest dealership.

Car Insurance

If you're bringing a foreign-registered vehicle to France, it isn't necessary to have an insurance 'green card' (although some insurance companies issue one as a matter of course), but you must notify your insurance company of your dates of travel. Insurance for British-registered cars abroad is becoming more difficult to obtain, as many British insurance companies are reducing the length of time they're allowing a car to be abroad, so check carefully with your insurance company. If you're bringing a car to France permanently, you must check that it can be re-registered there (e.g. it isn't a lease car and hasn't been modified), as you're unlikely to find a French insurance company that will insure it for more than 12 months. Even if you plan to re-register a car in France and need only temporary insurance, **you should read the small print, as cover may apply only for six or three months or even just one month.** The major French car insurers are listed below.

AGF Assurfinance
🖥 *www.agf.fr*

AXA Assurance
💻 *www.axa.fr*

Azur Assurances
💻 *www.azur-assurances.fr*

GAN Assurances
💻 *www.gan.fr*

MAAF Assurances
💻 *www.maaf.fr*

Mutuel du Mans Assurances
💻 *www.mma.fr*

Europ Assistance, 1 promenade de la   ☎ 01 41 85 85 85
Bonnette, 92230 Gennevilliers
💻 *www.europ-assistance.com*
Provides international breakdown cover, health and house
insurance and offer relocation services. The website is
in English.

Car Repairs & Service

Most privately owned petrol stations service and repair cars and some of
the large chains, such as Shell and Esso, have a workshop (*atelier*) attached.
Even small towns will have a repair garage of some description. However,
if your car is damaged, you must contact your insurer **before** having any
repairs carried out, as the insurer may specify certain garages to carry out
the repairs or insist that a loss-adjuster approve the cost of the repair.
Garages that carry out repairs can be found in yellow pages under *Garages
d'automobiles, reparation*.

Petrol Stations

Petrol stations in France are generally open much shorter hours than in the
UK, occasionally 6am to 10pm, but generally 8am to 7pm and very
occasionally 24 hours a day. If a station has a '24/24' sign, this means that
petrol can be bought using automated pumps that will take only a credit or
debit card with a microchip and a four-digit code, such as French bank
cards. See page 57. Listed in yellow pages under *Stations-service*.

Rules & Regulations

When driving in France, you must have the following items in your car at
all times:

- Vehicle registration document or, if you're driving a leased or hired car, a letter of authority and a VE103 Hired Vehicle Certificate from the leasing or hire company;

- Your driving licence;

- Vehicle insurance documents;

- A warning triangle;

- Spare bulbs.

It's also advisable to carry a fire extinguisher and a first-aid kit.

Note also the following general rules and regulations:

- The wearing of seatbelts is compulsory and includes passengers in rear seats when seatbelts are fitted. You (or any of your passengers) can be fined up to €90 for not wearing a seatbelt. Children must be accommodated in approved child seats, and children under ten cannot ride in the front of a vehicle unless it has no back seat.

- Failure to dip your lights when following or approaching another vehicle can cost you up to €750 and a penalty point on your licence, if you have a French licence. (French licenses – *permis de conduire* – work in reverse, with points given with the licence that you can then lose.)

- French traffic lights usually have a small set of lights at eye level, which are handy if you can't see the main lights (there are rarely lights on the far side of a junction). If the amber light (either a normal round light or an arrow shape) is flashing, you may continue (in the direction indicated, if an arrow shape) but must observe any relevant priority signs. If you jump a red light, you can be fined €300 and earn four penalty points!

- There's no green light on traffic lights at road works. Flashing orange means proceed if the road ahead is clear.

- Watch out for a triangular sign with a red border displaying a large black X. This means that you **don't** have priority at the next junction (which may not be a crossroads) but **must** give way to the right, however minor the joining road is.

- Always come to a complete stop at junctions when required to (i.e. by a STOP sign) and ensure that your front wheels are behind the white line. Failing to stop behind the line can cost you €750 and four licence points (as well as being dangerous).

- **Beware of moped riders.** French people are allowed on mopeds from the age of 14, and many youngsters pull out and weave around traffic without looking or indicating; even French motorists give them an extremely wide berth when overtaking!

- The name sign as you enter a village or town marks the start of the urban speed limit (see below) and the name crossed through as you leave marks the end.

- Parking in towns with parking meters is often free between noon and 2pm (times vary).

- All motorists are recommended to use dipped headlights outside towns during the day, October to March, although this isn't a legal requirement – yet.

- Speed cameras are increasing in frequency, warning signs are displayed. However, the police often hide behind hedges or down side roads with speed detecting binoculars and at the very least you will be given an on-the-spot fine.

- Finally, don't assume that a British licence plate will prevent you from being stopped. Tickets for motoring offences such as illegal parking and speeding are now sent for payment to the country in which the car is registered.

Further details of French driving regulations can be found in *Living and Working in France* (see page 379).

Speed Limits

Speed limits in France vary according to road conditions, as shown below. When visibility is below 50m (165ft) for any reason (e.g. rain or fog), you must not exceed 50kph (32mph) on **any** road. Speeds shown are in kilometres per hour with miles-per-hour equivalents in brackets.

Type of Road	Speed Limit	
	Dry Road	**Wet Road**
Motorway	130 (81)	110 (68)
Dual-carriageway	110 (68)	100 (62)
Single-carriageway	90 (56)	80 (50)
Towns	50 (32)	50 (32)

The above limits apply unless otherwise indicated.

If you're caught exceeding a speed limit by 40kph (25mph), your driving licence can be confiscated on the spot.

Tyre & Exhaust Centres

National companies include Feu Vert, Vulco, SiliGom and Point S. These centres not only sell and fit tyres (*pneus*), exhausts (*échappements*), brakes (*freins*) and shock absorbers (*amortisseurs*) but also carry out oil changes (*vidange*). These centres can be found in yellow pages under *Pneus* or *Centres auto, entretien rapide.*

Nightlife

In the following chapters you will find details on late-night bars, nightclubs and discos. Listed in yellow pages under *Discothèques et dancings* and *Cafés, bars, brasseries.*

Pets

General Information

France is a nation of dog-lovers, although French people's attitude towards other pets and animals in general can be alarmingly indifferent (sometimes also to dogs). The following information may be of use to those importing a pet or buying a pet in France.

- Many restaurants will provide food and water for dogs, some even allowing dogs to be seated at the table! Hotels may provide a rate for pets to stay.

- It's common practice to have third party insurance in case your pet bites someone or causes an accident; the majority of household insurance policies include this, but you should check.

- Dogs must be kept on leads in most public parks and gardens in France and there are large fines for dog owners who don't comply.

- In 2004 there were some cases of rabies in France and everyone is strongly advised to have all pets vaccinated. If you intend to put a cat or a dog into kennels or a cattery, it must have had a rabies vaccination.

- Rural French dogs are generally kept more as guard dogs than as pets and often live outdoors. Vicious dogs are (usually) confined or chained, but in a small community other 'pet' dogs may be left to wander around the village or hamlet.

- Dogs aren't welcome on the majority of beaches and, if you're staying on a campsite, they must be vaccinated against rabies and wear a collar at all times.

- On trains, pets under 6kg (13lb) which can be carried in a bag are charged around €5, but larger ones must be on a lead and wear a muzzle and will be charged half the normal second-class fare.

- Some Mercure and Formule 1 hotels accept dogs (see page 51 for contact details).

Dog Hygiene

In towns and cities, a variety of schemes are being implemented to keep the streets free of canine waste. These usually take the form of a bag and scoop or tong dispenser (generally green, with a picture of a dog) and a dedicated bin for the bag to be deposited in. These items sometimes have euphemistic names such as *La Pelle Civique*!

Dog Training

Dog training classes include general obedience, agility (obstacle courses) and puppy training. Some kennels may also offer training classes. Look in yellow pages under *Animaux dressage* or at the advertisements under *Pensions pour chiens, chats.*

Farriers

Farriers (*maréchal-ferrant*) are listed in the following chapters and in yellow pages under *Forgerons*, which also includes forges for iron work. If you have difficulty finding a local farrier, enquire at a horse yard or veterinary clinic.

Horse Dentists

Vets in France don't always deal with horses' teeth and so there are specific equine dentists (*dentiste équine*), who are listed in the following chapters. You're advised to book a few weeks in advance and you will be included in their next circuit.

Horse Feed

The feed you need is obviously dependent on how your horses are used and what their current feeding regime is. In any case, until you've established your new suppliers, it's wise to bring over with you any specific feeds.

Your local agricultural co-operative (look out for huge hoppers, sometimes in the middle of nowhere) will sell sacks of feed and often pony nuts. Some have started selling only 'high-performance' nuts, so check carefully. Maize and barley are often available.

A local farmer may be your best source of feed; grain is normally sold whole or as flour (*farine*), although some farmers will grind grain for you. An alternative for horses that have come from the UK is whole-grain barley soaked for 24 hours. Your local farmer will also be the best source of hay (*foin*) and straw (*paille*).

Spillers
🖳 *www.spillers-feeds.com*
Spillers exports horse feeds to France; to find your nearest supplier visit Spillers' website or contact:

SA Sodiva, 7 rue de la Roberdière,   ☎ 02 99 59 87 05
35000 Rennes
🖳 *www.coopagr-bretagne.fr*

See also **Riding Equipment** on page 87.

Horse Vets

General   Centre Vétérinaire, 12 rue Laennec,   ☎ 02 98 99 71 47
                 Huelgoat
                 (in Finistère, north-west of Carhaix-Plouguer)
                 Raphael Nachtengale at this centre specialises in horses and
                 speaks good English.

Identification

All dogs in France must be tattooed or microchipped with an identity number, enabling owners to quickly find lost pets and also preventing a rabies or other vaccination certificate from being used for more than one dog. Tattoos used to be done inside the ear but may now be done inside the animal's back leg. The costs of the two procedures are similar, although charges aren't fixed and vary considerably according to the veterinary practice – between around €25 and €75 for tattooing and from €35 to €70 for microchipping. The numbers are kept in a central computer by the SPA (see page 87). If you lose your pet, contact the nearest SPA office.

Kennels & Catteries

Kennels and catteries can be combined or separate and more are being run by English-speaking owners. Dog training and breeding are often available at kennels. Listed in yellow pages under *Pensions pour chiens et chats*.

Pet Parlours

Although many dogs are used as guard dogs, there are many that are domestic pets, and a large number of 'pet parlours' are to be found in France. Listed in yellow pages under *Salon de toilettage*.

Pet Travel

Pet Passport Scheme

The Department for Food, Agriculture and Rural Affairs (DEFRA) operates a 'pet passport' scheme (known as PETS) for the benefit of owners wishing to take their pets abroad and bring them back to the UK. Full details of the requirements for re-entry into the UK are available from the DEFRA helpline or website (see below). Alternatively, a company called Dogs Away (see below) offers a free eight-page booklet to guide you through the process.

If applying for a passport for a pet that has been tattooed, always ensure that you have in your possession the *carte de tatouage* before you start the pet passport process, as unless you have this card, which has your name and address as the registered owner, the registration of the microchip (*puce*) will be refused, along with the rabies vaccination, blood test, etc.

DEFRA   ☎ +44 (0)870-241 1710
💻 *www.defra.gov.uk*
The helpline is accessible from both England and France and the lines are open from 8.30am to 5pm (UK time) Mondays to Fridays.

Dogs Away   ☎ +44 (0)20-8441 9311
💻 *www.dogsaway.co.uk*

Paws 4 Travel
💻 *www.paws4travel.co.uk*

Sea Crossings

Crossing the Channel through the Tunnel reduces the possibility of stress for your pets, as you can remain with them. Some ferry companies may allow you to check your pet on the car deck during the crossing, but this isn't always easy and the car decks can be very noisy and cause more stress to the pet. For contact details of the companies listed below, see page 35.

Eurotunnel

The check-in desk for pets at Coquelles is to the right of the check-in lanes. Animals are checked in before entering the Eurotunnel site. A single journey costs £30 per animal; guide dogs for the disabled are free. You can book via the website but are advised to book by phone, as a limited number of pets are allowed per train. You must check in well in advance, as detailed below.

Hoverspeed
Each pet is charged £18 each way. Bookings aren't possible online and must be made by phone.

P&O Ferries
You must check in at least an hour before departure.

Sea France
You must check in at least 45 minutes before departure.

Riding Equipment

Gamm Vert
💻 *www.gammvert.fr*
These garden centres sell horse feed and some basic equipment, depending on the size of the shop. The website gives both location and opening hours of your nearest shop.

Décathlon
💻 *www.decathlon.fr*
These large sports shops carry a wide selection of riding accessories and equipment, including the hire of clippers (*tondeuses*), which are available for half or full days.

SPA

The Société pour la Protection des Animaux (SPA) is an organisation similar to the RSPCA in the UK but it isn't a national scheme, so you must contact your departmental office with any complaints or questions. Details are included in the following chapters.

Veterinary Clinics

Most veterinary surgeries are open Mondays to Saturdays, usually closing for lunch. There are usually several open surgeries during the week, when an appointment is not needed. Many vets will deal with horses and other equines but generally those that are used for riding out rather than expensive eventing or competition horses. Details of a specialist horse vet can be found on page 85.

Places to Visit

This section isn't intended to be a definitive guide but gives a wide range of ideas for places to visit in each department. Prices and opening hours were correct at the time of writing, but it's best to check before travelling long distances.

There's a section at the front of the yellow pages, *les infos Loisirs*, that has details on places to visit, including museums, chateaux, churches, parks and forests.

Animal Parks & Aquariums

Aquariums and zoos are usually open all year while some animal parks are open only from spring to autumn. Listed in yellow pages under *Parcs animaliers, parcs zoologiques*.

Beaches & Leisure Parks

There are many beaches along the Brittany coast; the following chapters list the main beaches and seaside resorts. The region has numerous leisure lakes with sandy beaches and supervised bathing, along with an assortment of watersports. Some lakes may have fishing, a playground, crazy golf and more. There's no charge for entry to the lakeside or for parking. Details of all these lakes are given in the following chapters.

Boat, Train & Wagon Rides

All four departments in the region have coastline and so there's an abundance of boat trips along the coast and across to nearby islands, including dinner cruises.

The only genuine tourist train is in Côtes d'Armor (see page 152). All the other listings under this heading are for rides on wheeled electric 'trains' (known as *petits trains*) that tour the streets of the larger towns, offering commentary along the way.

Calèches are open-sided wagons that offer trips around the countryside.

Details of all three can be found in the following chapters.

Chateaux

Many chateaux are still privately owned and lived in. As a result, admission times and restrictions vary: you may be able to wander around at your leisure, you may have to join a guided tour or you may only be able to admire the chateau from the garden. Gardens may be open longer hours than the chateau.

Churches & Abbeys

Churches of interest are signposted from main roads and motorways and can be easily identified, e.g. *Eglise XIVème Siècle* = 14th century church.

Small churches may be locked when not in use, while others may be open the whole day (except possibly at lunchtimes).

Miscellaneous

This section includes a diverse selection of places to visit, from a planetaria to mazes, race tracks to mines.

Museums, Memorials & Galleries

A limited number of museums can be found in yellow pages under *Musées* and smaller, private galleries under *Galeries d'art.*

Parks, Gardens & Forests

The larger towns often have elaborate gardens around the *hôtel de ville*, and many forests have a visitors' centre with details of walks, cycle rides, wildlife and fauna. Tourist offices have a list of local parks and gardens to visit.

Regional Produce

Cider producers, biscuit manufacturers and local farmers welcome visitors, generally with free tastings and a shop selling their produce.

Standing Stones & Megaliths

Brittany is world famous for its standing stones (*menhirs*) and dolmen (a prehistoric burial chamber constructed from standing stones and earth). There are many locations throughout the region that have a significant, solitary stone or a collection of dozens, hundreds or even thousands.

Professional Services

Accountants

An English-speaking accountant (*expert comptable*) has been given for each department in the following chapters.

Architects & Project Managers

As many architects also offer project management and general building services, they've been listed under **Architects & Project Managers** in the **Tradesmen** sections.

Solicitors & Notaires

A *notaire* is similar to a British solicitor, dealing with house purchases, wills and probate. Listed under *Notaires* in yellow pages. Legal fees for a house purchase are fixed, according to the value of the property. If a matter has to go to court or specialist advice is needed, you deal with an *avocat*, similar to a lawyer (listed in yellow pages under *Avocats*). An English-speaking *notaire* has been given for each department in the following chapters.

Property

Building Plots

These can be found simply by driving around, as many are advertised by a board saying '*à vendre*' on the edge of the land for sale. Many estate agents have land for sale and, increasingly commonly, *mairies* are selling land, either as individual plots or in 'estates' (*lotissement*) of around 5 to 15 plots at the edge of villages in an attempt to revitalise them. Such land can vary considerably in price according to how keen the *mairie* is to boost the local population; it has been known to sell for as little as €1 per square metre.

There are many companies that specialise in building new houses, and the larger ones may have a stock of building plots (listed in yellow pages under *Bâtiment (entreprises)*).

House Hunting

There are many ways of finding homes for sale in France, including the following:

Estate Agents & Notaires

There are many estate agents in Brittany who have English-speaking staff. You will be taken to a property and shown around by the agent or his representative and won't (usually) be given an address and sent off into the wilderness. Many agents will set aside a whole day to spend with you and many offer a comprehensive after-sales services, getting telephone lines, electricity and water supplies transferred for you.

Properties for sale are often listed with several agents and sometimes the sale prices differ. This may simply be because some show the price with fees included, whilst others don't, but check.

Many people are starting property search or selling agencies who aren't actually estate agents themselves but only representatives of estate agents – or should be. If they're legally registered they will have a *carte professionnelle* and will be able to tell you the estate agent that they work with. If in doubt, ask to see their *carte professionnelle* (also referred to as a *carte grise* and not to be confused with a car registration document, which has the same name!) or deal directly with the agent they're working for.

Notaires are the government representatives you must deal with for any property transaction and they often have a supply of property for sale, which can be displayed in their window or on a notice board outside. If you're buying direct from a *notaire*, there's no agency fee but they're allowed to charge a negotiating fee, which is generally lower than an estate agent's fees. Their legal fees are a percentage of the sale price and are fixed by law.

In France it's the purchaser who generally pays the estate agent's fee and you need to allow up to 10 per cent of the purchase price for this and other fees and legal costs.

Internet Sales

There are many sites dedicated to property in Brittany. If you use an English-language search engine such as Google (🖳 *www.google.com*) and type in 'property for sale' and the area or department you're looking for, it will produce a selection of French and English sites.

Private Sales

Many property owners sell privately by putting up a 'for sale' (*à vendre* or *AV*) sign outside the property in order to avoid paying an agent's commission (see **Estate Agents** above).

Property Exhibitions

These exhibitions are held throughout the UK and are packed with almost every English-speaking estate agent from France. Go early, wear comfortable shoes and collect as much information on both estate agents and house buying as you can, to read properly once at home. Many homes that are on display will have been sold by the time you next visit France, but it will give you an immediate picture of what's available, for how much and which agents cover the area you're interested in. For forthcoming shows see 🖳 *www.vivelafrance.co.uk* and the magazine websites listed below.

Magazines

There are many magazines dedicated to French property and living, which contain advertisements by agents and individuals, including the following. They're available in newsagents' unless otherwise stated.

Everything France
🖳 *www.everythingfrancemag.co.uk*

Focus on France
🖳 *www.outboundpublishing.com*

France
🖥 *www.francemag.com*

French Magazine
🖥 *www.frenchmagazine.co.uk*

French Property News (subscription only)
🖥 *www.french-property-news.com*

Living France
🖥 *www.livingfrance.com*

Property Prices

The following information gives an idea of what you can buy within a particular price range. As property prices are constantly changing, these figures should be used only as a guide. Four property categories have been given for each of the towns within the department and the prices were based on property on the market at the end of 2004. These are the **starting** price for properties in each category, in or close to the towns specified. Where an area didn't have any property in a particular category, no price is given. Over €250,000 the variety of property available becomes very broad; for example, a new three-bedroom house can be the same price as an old five-bedroom property with a large plot in the same area. All prices are in euros.

	Ruin or Land	Requiring Renovation	3-bed Modern(ised)	4+-bed with Character or Land
Côtes-d'Armor				
Bröons	44,000	92,000	130,000	180,000
Guingamp	35,000	66,000	110,000	254,000
Lannion	29,000*	88,000 1	65,000	244,000
Loudéac	36,000*	80,000	117,000	276,000
St Brieuc	47,000*	-	145,000	210,000
Finistère				
Brest	39,000*	67,000	135,000	230,000
Carhaix-Plouguer	33,000	65,000	110,000	294,000
Châteaulin	-	115,000	130,000	200,000

Morlaix	30,000	54,000	130,000	195,000
Quimper	42,000*	92,000	140,000	220,000
Ille-et-Vilaine Bain-de- Bretagne	49,000	114,000	190,000	260,000
Combourg	53,000*	75,000	150,000	300,000
Fougères	34,000	84,000	173,000	230,000
Redon	63,000*	140,000	165,000	230,000
Rennes	34,000	75,000	150,000	290,000
St Malo	88,000*	110,000	147,000	318,000
Morbihan Le Faouët	26,000*	76,000	130,000	222,000
Lorient	34,000	83,000	146,000	263,000
Ploërmel	73,000*	135,000	158,000	278,000
Vannes	90,000	124,000	200,000	275,000

*   Land only; prices without an asterisk indicate a ruin or property requiring extensive renovation (*caveat emptor!*).

Property Taxes

As an owner/occupier of French property, you will receive two or three tax bills a year. *Taxe foncière* is a land tax payable by the owner of the property. Even if there are no buildings on the land, this tax will still be due unless the land is being used for agricultural purposes. *Taxe d'habitation* is payable by the occupier of the property on 1st January each year and may include a portion for refuse collection (*ordures*). If not, a separate bill will be issued for this.

For the year during which you buy your property, the vendor will be responsible for paying the *taxe d'habitation,* as he would have been in occupation on 1st January. Even if you become the owner on 2nd January, this tax will still be his responsibility. For *taxe foncière* there's normally an apportionment between the vendor and the seller according to how long they each own the property in that year. This is usually provided for by the *notaire* in the final conveyance deed (*acte de vente*). Although the vendor will be sent the *taxe foncière* bill and must pay it, he will be entitled to immediate reimbursement by the purchaser as soon as he provides proof that he has been billed.

Both *taxe d'habitation* and *taxe foncière* are calculated using the rental value of the property as a base figure. Hence taxes on property in towns and cities are higher than those on properties in small villages. If your property is situated in a tourist area, there may be additional tax included in the *taxe d'habitation* charge for maintaining the area to a higher than normal standard. Also, if there's an exceptional expense, such as improving the sewage system, there may be a separate one-off bill. Note that television licence charges are now included in your *taxe d'habitation* bill.

You should always pay tax bills promptly, as otherwise you may incur penalties. It isn't uncommon for non-resident owners of French property not to receive their tax bills. In this case you should write to the appropriate authority by recorded delivery informing them you haven't received a bill and asking them to send it; otherwise you may have great difficulty convincing them that you aren't liable for the late payment charge.

Purchase Procedure

Once you've found a property, the process to follow in order the complete the purchase is quite straightforward.

There are two forms of standard preliminary contract, a *compromis de vente* and a *promesse de vente*, the former being preferable, as it offers you greater protection. The preliminary contract is usually prepared and signed by the parties, within a week or so of orally agreeing the sale, sometimes on the same day. Before this can occur, however, some specialist reports may have to be obtained, particularly if the property is old. These reports (certifying the presence or absence of asbestos, lead and termites) are usually paid for by the vendor.

You should at this time ensure that any conditions that you want are included in the contract and that you understand (and it's clear) what is and what isn't included in the sale. Upon signature of the preliminary contract, the vendor is fully committed to the sale, but the position is different for the buyer. Under French law the buyer has a 'cooling off' period of seven days after receipt of copies of the signed agreement. During this seven day period, he's free to change his mind and withdraw from the agreement without penalty. At the end of this period, the buyer pays a deposit (normally of 10 per cent of the purchase price) to the *notaire* handling the sale.

Under French law, the transfer deed, called the *acte authentique*, transfers the property to the buyer at completion. This document must be prepared by a *notaire*. The *notaire* can act for both the seller and the buyer, although the buyer will pay his fee. There's nothing to stop you as the seller from instructing your own *notaire*, who will assist the other *notaire* and share the fee with him, although this is rarely necessary. You should remember that the *notaire* doesn't represent the interest of either party in the transaction. He deals with the formalities of checking the title, checking that any loans are paid off and making enquiries of any developments intended in the vicinity of the property. It's common practice for the parties to agree a pre-signature inspection of the property, either on the date of signature, or alternatively the day before.

Buyers need to ensure that their funds are paid into the *notaire*'s account in plenty of time. It's recommended to use a specialist currency dealer in order to change foreign currency to euros. Also, it's essential to have property insurance that's effective on the day of signature – don't rely upon taking over the vendor's policy.

The last part of the sale takes place at the *notaire*'s office, where both parties sign the *acte authentique* and finalise the financial side of the transaction. The keys to the home are yours as soon as the this procedure is completed.

For comprehensive information on the purchase procedure see this book's sister publication **Buying a Home in France** by David Hampshire (Survival Books – see page 379).

Public Holidays

The official French public holidays (*jours fériés*) are listed below. Note, however, that when a holiday falls on a Saturday or Sunday, another day off isn't usually granted 'in lieu', but when a holiday falls on a Tuesday or Thursday, the day before or the day after may also be taken a holiday, either officially or unofficially, to make a four-day weekend; the extra day is called a *pont* (bridge).

Date	Holiday	French
1st January	New Year's Day	*Jour de l'An*
March/April	Easter Monday (1)	*Lundi de Pâques*
1st May	Labour Day	*Fête du Travail*
8th May	VE Day	*Fête de la Libération/Victoire 1945*

May (2)	Ascension Day	*Jour de l'Ascension*
May/June (3)	Whit Monday	*Pentecôte*
14th July	Bastille Day	*Fête Nationale*
15th August	Assumption Day	*Fête de l'Assomption*
1st November	All Saints' Day	*Toussaint*
11th November	Armistice Day	*Fête de l'Armistice*
25th December	Christmas Day	*Noël*

Notes:
1. Good Friday isn't a public holiday in France.

2. Ascension Day is the sixth Thursday after Easter.

3. Whit Monday (*Pentecôte*) is the second Monday after Ascension Day and was officially suppressed in 2004 but continues to be widely observed.

Shrove Tuesday (*Mardi Gras*) in February is given by some businesses as a staff holiday.

Religion

France is unofficially a Catholic country, and most churches and ceremonies are Catholic. Churches can be found in most communities and services in the villages are generally held in rotation with other churches in the parish. Notices are displayed on church doors or just inside giving details of the forthcoming services. In some small villages, the church doesn't have regular services but is used only on special occasions once or twice a year.

Protestant and Evangelical churches, synagogues and places of worship for other faiths exist and can be found in yellow pages under *Eglises*.

Anglican Services in English

English-language church services in Brittany are listed under this heading in the following chapters.

Restaurants

There are so many restaurants in the region that we've been able to give only a selection to get you started on your gastronomic voyage of discovery. We've included restaurants that are open continuously from lunch through to the evenings, as these are quite unusual. Gastronomic and Michelin-starred restaurants have also been given along with any others that have an unusual speciality.

It's usual for restaurants of all types to offer set menus (*menu*), which are dishes put together by the chef that complement each other and may change daily. In smaller restaurants, this may be all that's available, although there's usually a choice of two or three dishes for each course. An average price for a set menu at a traditional restaurant is around €15.

Routiers

These restaurants can be found on main roads and have a circular logo – half red, half blue. They're usually alongside lorry parking areas and provide meals for drivers which have a reputation for being good quality and good value, the restaurants themselves being clean and tidy. You may be seated canteen style and find yourself next to a 'trucker' but you will get a reasonably priced four-course meal, sometimes with wine included in the price (it's the coffee you have to pay extra for!). Prices vary, but around €12 is usual.

Rubbish & Recycling

Dustmen

The collection of household rubbish (*ramassage*) varies not only between departments but also within areas of each department. It may be collected once or twice a week, even daily in some large towns and there may be separate collections (e.g. weekly or fortnightly) for recyclable waste (see **Recycling** on page 98).

In towns, you may find 'wheelie bins' in the street. If so, you're responsible for putting your rubbish sacks in the bins, which are then emptied once or twice a week. If there's more than one type of wheelie bin, the other(s) are for recycling (see **Recycling** on page 98).

Rural areas may also have wheelie bins, usually brown or grey, with one or two for each group of houses. If there are no bins, rubbish should be put in bin bags and left at the edge of the road, although you're advised to hang them up out of reach of marauding dogs, cats and wildlife; **dustmen won't**

go down drives or onto property. Dustmen often come very early, so bags need to be put out the night before. In towns there's usually a specified time before which you cannot put out your rubbish, around 7pm for evening collection or in the early hours for a daytime collection.

If collection day falls on a bank holiday, rubbish is generally collected the day **before** rather than the day after – or the collection may simply be cancelled, although you will usually be notified in advance.

The best way to find out what happens in your commune is to speak to your neighbours or enquire at the *mairie*.

In most areas, separate taxes are payable by homeowners for rubbish collection and many French people are fiercely protective of the services for which they pay. You're therefore strongly advised not to put rubbish into a wheelie bin if you're driving a car registered in another department; the same applies if you try to use a rubbish tip in a different department or even a different commune (see **Rubbish Tips** below).

Metal Collection

If the previous occupiers kindly left their old fridge or bedstead in the garden, your *mairie* should be able to put you in touch with your local 'rag and bone man' or arrange for them to be taken away. In some communes, there's a regular (e.g. quarterly) collection (*récupération des objects encombrants*), the dates of which you should be given in advance. Alternatively, look in yellow pages under *Récuperation, traitement des fers et métaux*.

Recycling

The French are keen on recycling, but systems vary both regionally and locally, some areas having no facilities except a series of containers at a communal point, whilst others collect recyclable waste from outside your house. Whatever the system, the colour coding is always the same, although yellow and blue are sometimes combined.

- **Blue** – Paper and card, including catalogues, old phone directories and junk mail, but not window envelopes.

- **Yellow** – Packaging, cans (including aerosol cans), tins, drinks cartons and plastic milk bottles, but **not** yoghurt pots, oil bottles, plastic bags or the thin plastic that encloses junk mail or six-packs of bottles of water.

- **Green** – All clear and coloured glass, but **not** drinking glasses, medicine bottles, vases or light bulbs and no corks or lids.

Here is a summary of some of the systems currently in place in Brittany:

● Blue and yellow rubbish bags given out free (often by the *mairie*) for collection from outside your property. Glass must be taken to bottle banks.

● Yellow bags given out free for paper, plastic and metal packaging.

● Yellow bags given out free for packaging, plastic, metal and cartons.

● Large mesh/wire crates next to the wheelie bins in the road. These are to put your yellow recycling bags into.

● Paper and cardboard collected from outside your house weekly.

● A series of collection banks, usually for all three categories of recycling, often to be found by football pitches, in car parks or near the *mairie*.

● Wheelie bins in the street with yellow lids for recycling rubbish.

There are many designs of kitchen bin in France that have two or three compartments for the different types of waste. Note that polystyrene cannot be recycled; if you have a large quantity, such as packaging from a household appliance, you can dispose of it at a tip (see below).

Batteries

Batteries can be recycled in most supermarkets, where you can find containers, usually Perspex, in the foyer or by the customer service desk. Car batteries can be recycled at the rubbish tip (see below).

Clothes & Shoes

Recycling containers for clothes and shoes can often be found in supermarket car parks.

Printer Cartridges

Printer ink cartridges can also be recycled, sometimes in supermarket entrance foyers and sometimes via the *mairie* or library. Toner cartridges can be recycled at the rubbish tip.

Rubbish Tips

Every town and many large villages have a rubbish tip (*déchetterie*); even small communes may have a *décharge*, which is primarily for garden rubbish but may also be used for building rubble.

Déchetteries are clearly marked in towns and outlying areas by a symbol of a hand holding three arrows. Here you can dispose of large metal objects, such as bikes and cookers, as well as motor and cooking oil, glass, paper, clothes and batteries, and sometimes garden waste. You aren't allowed to dispose of household rubbish bags, which should be put out for collection at your home.

Some rubbish tips have a maximum quantity of building rubble that they will accept each day from an individual and, if they suspect that you're a tradesman, they will refuse to allow you to deposit at all.

You may have to take proof of a local address when using your rubbish tip, or you may be issued with a pass (available from your *mairie*). If you're driving a car registered in another department (or country), you may be asked where you live or even be prevented from using the tip at all.

Rubbish tips are rarely open on Sundays or bank holidays. Opening hours may be part days throughout the week or similar to shop hours for larger towns, but always closing for lunch.

Schools

If you're planning to put your children into French school, the first place to go is your *mairie*. They will give you details of the relevant school for your child's age, but you may have to ask for details of local private (e.g. Catholic) schools. The school week for junior and infant schools is generally Mondays, Tuesdays, Thursdays and Fridays. Some areas also have lessons on Wednesday mornings, as do most secondary schools (*collèges*). A full list of schools and colleges can be found in yellow pages under *Enseignement*.

Enrolment

To register your children at a school, you must go and see the head teacher, who will tell you whether there are places and the relevant start date. Take the following with you:

● The name and address of the child's last school (if applicable);

● A copy of his last school report and/or any results you have from any academic tests;

● Evidence of school insurance, which is compulsory in France (see below). At your first meeting, it will be sufficient to say that you've applied for the insurance.

- Details of all vaccinations since birth;

- If your child previously attended a French school, a *certificat de radiation*, which is proof that all contact and dealings have terminated with the previous school. A closing report from a UK school is usually sufficient.

French schools don't provide stationery or other equipment and will have a long list of items that you must provide, so ask for a copy at an early stage.

Extra Tuition

If your child wants or needs extra help, but not structured lessons, it's worth contacting the local *collège*, as it may be able to recommend a student who is happy to come to your house and spend time with your child going over class notes or lessons. Not only is this cheaper than a qualified teacher but a younger person may be less daunting for your children.

Holidays

Schools in France are divided into three groups for their holidays so that winter (February/March) and spring (April/May) holidays are staggered, which prevents ski and other resorts from becoming overcrowded. Schools in Brittany are in Group A. Calendars are distributed by a wide variety of organisations giving the school holiday dates for the three groups. Note that neither the winter nor the spring holiday necessarily coincides with Easter. Due to the summer holidays starting around the end of June, there's no half-term break between the spring and summer holidays. If a school operates a four-day week, its holiday dates may vary by a day or two from the 'official' dates to make up the statutory hours per term.

Insurance

All children must have insurance to attend school in France. Insurance is provided by a number of companies, but MAE (see below) is the most popular. The most comprehensive cover costs €26.50 per year and covers your child for all eventualities, both in and out of school. Whichever insurer you use, you must provide the school with a certificate to prove that your child is covered.

MAE	☎ 08 20 00 00 70
💻 *www.mae.fr*	
Central helpline open 8.30am to 8pm Mondays to Fridays and 8.30am to 5pm Saturdays.	

Côtes-d'Armor	18 rue des Champs de Pies, St Brieuc	☎ 02 96 94 10 73
Finistère	70 rue Sébastopol, Brest	☎ 02 98 02 35 36

| Ille-et-Vilaine | 9bis Mail François Mitterrand, Rennes | ☎ 02 99 54 97 97 |
| Morbihan | 2 rue Général Dubail, Lorient | ☎ 02 97 64 53 40 |

Transport

There's a comprehensive network of school buses (*car/bus scolaire*), which collect children in rural areas. An application form for a bus pass can be obtained from the school or the *mairie* and you will need to provide two passport-size photographs. The cost, if any, depends on where you live, how many school-age children there are in the family and what schools they go to.

Shopping

Opening Hours

When available, the opening hours of various shops have been included, but they're liable to change and so it's advisable to check before travelling long distances to any specific shop.

Many small businesses are staffed only by members of a family and as a result you may find that the village shop or even the town co-op may close completely for two weeks while the proprietor goes on holiday.

Shop opening hours can change from summer to winter (normally in September, when school starts). Shops that were open all day (*sans interruption*) and on Sunday mornings may suddenly be closed for two hours at lunchtime and not open on Sundays at all. Other shops may change their lunchtime closure times and close completely on Mondays.

The information in this section relates to shopping in general; details of shops in each department can be found in the following chapters.

Architectural Antiques

Businesses that sell reclaimed building materials are usually situated on main roads, from which their goods are clearly visible. Statues, fireplaces and stone archways in what looks like a field are a clue that there's reclaimed wood, tiles and stonework for sale as well. Listed in yellow pages under *Matériaux de construction anciens*.

When buying reclaimed materials, you should check that they aren't from buildings that could have been restored but have been destroyed by people wanting to make a quick profit.

Bakeries

Bakeries (*boulangeries*) are usually small family-run businesses that close one day a week and often on Sunday afternoons. They also run delivery vans, going through local villages and hamlets from two to seven days per week, depending on the area.

British Groceries

Many supermarkets are now introducing some 'high demand' British produce to their international sections, e.g. Golden Syrup and HP Sauce. Stock varies with demand and the size of the shop, so keep a look out, especially in hypermarkets and popular tourist areas. Shops selling just British groceries are listed in the following chapters.

> Expatdirect.co.uk　　　　　　　☎ +44 (0)113 255 0333
> 🖥 *www.expatdirect.co.uk*
> This company supplies British produce at supermarket prices and delivers anywhere in France: £14.95 for 30kg of goods.

Building Materials

Building yards are normally open early in the morning Mondays to Fridays (closed for lunch) and Saturday mornings. Listed in yellow pages under *Matériaux de construction*.

Chemists'

Even small towns will have a chemist's (*pharmacie*) but they may be open limited hours, such as Tuesdays to Fridays and every other Saturday and Monday. Outside normal opening hours a notice should be displayed giving the address of the nearest duty chemist (*pharmacie de garde*). Alternatively, the *gendarmes* hold a list of duty chemists; dial ☎ 17 or the number of your local *gendarmerie*.

Chemists are trained to give first aid and can also carry out certain routine medical procedures, such as taking blood pressure. They can be asked advice on many ailments and without a prescription can give a wider variety of medicines than are available over the counter in the UK. Chemists are also trained to distinguish between around 50 types of mushroom and toadstool in order to identify edible and poisonous varieties, and to identify local snakes in order to prescribe the correct antidote for poisoning.

Department Stores

There are three main department stores in France: Printemps (🖥 *www.printemps.com*), Nouvelles Galeries and Galeries Lafayette, the last two being part of the same group and sharing a website (💻 *www.galerieslafayette.com*). All the department stores in the region have been listed in the following chapters.

DIY

There are many DIY (*bricolage*) shops in the region, most towns having at least one of the following:

Bricomarché
💻 *www.bricomarche.com*

Castorama
💻 *www.castorama.fr*

Leroy Merlin
💻 *www.leroymerlin.fr*

Mr Bricolage
💻 *www.mr-bricolage.fr*

Weldom
💻 *www.weldom.com*

Dress Making & Crafts

Fabric, art and craft shops can often be found on retail parks. Listed in yellow pages under *Tissu au mètre* for fabrics and *Art graphiques, arts plastiques: matériel et fournitures* for art and craft supplies. Cultura (💻 *www.cultura.fr*) is a national chain of shops that sell music, books and a comprehensive range of art and craft supplies.

Fireplaces & Log Burners

There are some specialist shops for fireplaces (*cheminée*) and log burners (*poêles*), but both can also be found in large DIY stores (see above) and building materials suppliers' (see page 103). Shops are listed in yellow pages under *Cheminées d'intérieur et accessoires* and *Poêles*.

Fishmongers'

There are still fresh fish shops in most towns and some have vans that travel through the villages. Listed in yellow pages under *Poissonneries détail*.

Frozen Food

Some frozen food (*surgelés*) shops also do home deliveries whilst other companies only sell direct, orders being placed by phone, via the internet or with the driver. The two largest companies that have both shops and do home deliveries are:

Picard Surgelés
💻 *www.picard.fr*

Thiriet Glaces
💻 *www.thiriet.com*

Garden Centres

National chains of garden centres (*jardineries*) are given below. Jardiland and Truffaut are generally found on retail parks.

Gamm Vert
💻 *www.gammvert.fr*

Jardiland
💻 *www.jardiland.fr*

Truffaut
💻 *www.truffaut.fr*

Hypermarkets

French hypermarkets (*hypermarchés*) advertise heavily on roadside hoardings, often giving directions and distance in minutes, but note that these directions can just stop, leaving you lost and apparently a great deal more than '5 mins' away from the shop.

Hypermarkets tend to be situated in retail parks on the outskirts of towns and cities and the buildings themselves are usually small shopping precincts with a variety of shops and services. Hypermarkets aren't open on Sundays.

There are four main hypermarket chains in Brittany (listed below). Hypermarkets are listed in yellow pages under *Supermarchés et hypermarchés*. Individual stores are listed in the following chapters.

Hypermarkets are one of the best sources of electrical goods and general household items. There aren't as many specialist electrical shops in France as there are in the UK and it's quite normal to buy your new washing machine from a hypermarket, although prices may be no lower than at a specialist shop and after-sales service will almost certainly be worse.

Due to the damage done to the environment by the thin plastic carrier bags currently given away by some hypermarkets, they're soon to be banned completely. As a result, shops are encouraging shoppers to buy 'long life' bags, which they will replace free when they wear out.

> Auchan
> 🖥 *www.auchan.fr*
>
> Carrefour
> 🖥 *www.carrefour.com*
>
> Géant
> 🖥 *www.geant.fr*
>
> Leclerc
> 🖥 *www.e-leclerc.com*

Carrefour now offers online shopping, with home delivery, via 🖥 *www. ooshop.com*.

Key Cutting & Heel Bars

Key cutting kiosks and heel bars (*cordonneries*) can be found in hypermarket complexes, outside supermarkets and as independent shops in the high street. They also make up vehicle number plates, but you must take your registration document (*carte grise*) with you.

Kitchens & Bathrooms

Specialist shops selling kitchen and bathroom furniture and fittings are often found on retail parks. Large DIY shops and building suppliers also sell kitchens and bathrooms. Specialist shops are listed in yellow pages under *Cuisines vente, installation* and *Salles de bains: équipements*.

Markets

Some markets and fairs take place in the centre of towns and villages and can cause streets to be closed. Parking can become difficult, as they're often situated in car parks. Food markets in France are well worth a visit if you haven't experienced them before (and aren't squeamish), but do check the prices, particularly at indoor markets, which are sometimes higher than you might expect.

Mobile Shops

In rural communities there are various mobile shops, all of which sound their horns loudly as they go through the village. These may include a bakery (*boulangerie*), a butcher's (*boucherie*), a grocery (*épicerie*) and a fishmonger's (*poissonnerie*).

Music

Music shops often advertise lessons and hire out instruments and sometimes run workshops. Listed in yellow pages under *Musique: instruments et accessoires.*

Newsagents'

Many newsagents' (*maison de la presse* or simply *presse*) sell British daily newspapers and even British magazines and paperbacks. They can usually order specific magazines or publications, such as the *TV Times* and *Radio Times*, on request.

Publications

Le 22 Annonces, Le 56 annonces, Bonjour, Bonjour l'Echo du Golfe, le Carillon, Le Fougerais, Paru Vendu, Petit Quimpérois and *Pub-Bonjour* are just some of the local 'classified' newspapers, which include advertisements for local events, items for sale, etc. They're free and can be found in *tabacs*, bakeries and other shops.

The following are English-language newspapers for France and are published monthly.

The Connexion, BP25 06480 La Colle-sur-Loup   ☎ 04 93 32 16 59
💻 *www.connexionfrance.com*

French News, 5 chemin de la Monzie/ BP4042, 24004 Périgueux   ☎ 05 53 06 84 40
💻 *www.brittany-news.net*

The two weekly newspapers listed below are designed and written for expatriates and can be delivered anywhere in the world. An annual subscription costs between £112 and £118.

The Guardian Weekly   UK ☎ 0870-066 0510
💻 *www.guardian.co.uk/guardianweekly/subscribe/*
Condenses the best of *The Guardian, The Observer, Le Monde* and *The Washington Post* and adds bespoke articles.

The Weekly Telegraph   UK ☎ 01454-642464
💻 *www.expat.telegraph.co.uk*
Condenses the best of *The Daily* and *Sunday Telegraph* and adds bespoke articles.

Organic Produce

Organic produce (*produits biologiques/bio*) is widely available in supermarkets and hypermarkets. Organic shops are becoming more popular but have a tendency to come and go. Listed in yellow pages under *Diététique, produits biologiques détail*.

Passport Photos

Kiosks can usually be found in the entrance to supermarkets and in hypermarket centres.

Post Offices

French post offices have a wide range of facilities, including cash machines and internet access. Some have automated postage machines that can operate in English and allow you to pay by 'chip and pin' credit card.

Retail Parks

As in the UK, retail parks tend to be on the outskirts of cities and large towns and in France there's usually a hypermarket in the centre. See also **Hypermarkets** on page 105.

Second-hand Shops

Brocantes are a cross between an antique shop and a second-hand shop and come in all shapes and sizes. You can find them in most towns and along main roads, and they can be a good source of bargains.

Many *brocantes* do house clearance (*débarras*). *Dépôts-vente* are also a good source of second-hand goods, selling on behalf of the public for a commission of around 20 per cent. Listed in yellow pages under the above headings.

Sports Goods

Often found on retails parks, sports shops stock a comprehensive range of equipment from rollerskating and horse riding to climbing and skiing. Two large national chains are Décathlon and Intersport. Listed in yellow pages under *Sports et Loisirs: articles et vêtements détail*.

Supermarkets

The most common supermarkets in this region are listed below; the websites will give you the location of the shop nearest to you.

Champion
💻 *www.champion.fr*

Cora
🖥 *www.cora.fr*

Leclerc
🖥 *www.e-leclerc.com*

Intermarché
🖥 *www.intermarche.com*

Super U
🖥 *www.super-u.com*

Note the following general points regarding supermarket opening times:

- Larger shops may open all day Mondays to Fridays, others only on Fridays and Saturdays, closing for lunch the rest of the week, while the smallest shops closing for lunch every day and possibly Monday mornings.

- Very few supermarkets open on Sundays – occasionally on Sunday mornings but never in the afternoons.

- Opening hours can change from summer to winter, with longer lunchtime closing and later evening opening in the summer.

Supermarkets are listed in yellow pages under *Supermarchés et hypermarchés*. See also **Hypermarkets** on page 105.

Wine & Spirits

There aren't as many off licences (*caves*) in France as in the UK, as hypermarkets and supermarkets sell the majority of alcoholic drinks. Some *caves* sell table wine by the litre, usually starting at just over €1 per litre, but you must take your own container. Suitable containers with taps can be bought at DIY shops or large supermarkets. Listed in yellow pages under *Vins et spiritueux, vente au détail*.

Sports & Outdoor Activities

A selection of the activities available in each department is provided in the following chapters; full details are available from tourist offices and *mairies*. Not surprisingly, large towns have the widest range of facilities.

Note that many 'physical' sports require a licence. The relevant club will have the forms and a medical may be required, which your doctor can carry out as a standard consultation.

Aerial Sports

Ballooning

Ballooning is an ideal way to view the countryside. Trips are dependent on the weather, and distance travelled depends on the wind speed. Each trip lasts around four hours, including inflating, deflating and packing away. Listed in yellow pages under *Montgolfières et dirigeables*.

Flying

At small airports and aerodromes there are often small organisations that offer trial flights (*baptêmes de l'air*) or tourist flights (*vol touristique*) in aeroplanes and helicopters. Flying schools are listed in yellow pages under *Aéroclubs et écoles de pilotage*.

Parachuting

Parachuting (*parachutisme*) clubs can be found at local aerodromes and in yellow pages under *Parachutisme, vol libre*.

Archery

Archery (*tir à l'arc*) is available to children and adults and some clubs have indoor ranges.

Badminton

Badminton (*badminton*) clubs usually meet weekly in term time and sometimes have separate groups for children and adults.

Boules/Pétanque

Almost every town in Brittany has a *boules* or *pétanque* club, which may meet weekly or even daily. Unless fenced off, *boules* courts are open to everyone at all times (unless there's a competition) and there's no charge.

Canoeing & Kayaking

Watersports centres (*centre de nautique, base nautique*) can be on rivers, lakes or the coast. They generally hold weekly sessions from September to June and full week courses during the summer holidays. Individual canoe hire is available as well as accompanied river descents, with a vehicle to bring you back to the base.

Climbing

Artificial climbing (*escalade*) walls and natural sites across the region. The Club Alpin Français organises trips throughout France, with groups in most large towns.

Cycling & Bike Hire

Road cycling (*cyclo tourisme*) is a popular pastime. Clubs have weekly rides, usually on Sunday mornings, all year round. To find your local cycling club ask at the tourist office or *mairie*. Mountain biking (*VTT*) routes are common in forests and woods. Bike hire providers are listed in the following chapters.

Fishing

Maps are available from fishing shops and tourist offices showing local fishing waters. If there's a lake locally, permits will be on sale in nearby *tabacs*, fishing shops and at the *mairie*. There are many shops dedicated to fishing and hunting, and supermarkets have fridges containing live bait alongside the fishing equipment.

Football

Even the smallest town will have a stadium (*stade*) of some description. Football clubs vary in size, many with a range of teams from five-year-olds to veterans and ladies' teams.

Golf

Golf courses are listed in the following chapters and can be found under *Golf (terrains et leçons)* in yellow pages. A comprehensive site providing full details of clubs in and around the region is 🖳 *www.golflounge.com*.

Hockey

There are various types of hockey available, depending on the size of the town and the facilities. Variations include field hockey (*hockey-sur-gazon*), ice hockey (*hockey-sur-glace*), rink hockey and street hockey (*hockey in-line*). The sport is organised locally by groups and clubs; enquire at the tourist offices or *mairie*.

Horse Riding

There are stables (*centre d'équitation* or *centre hippique*) throughout the region, some offering rides along the beach. Stables can be found in yellow pages under *Equitation et centres hippiques.*

Land Yachting

A cross between windsurfing and skateboarding, land yachting (*char à voile*) is popular on the beaches of Brittany, although it isn't for the faint-hearted, as 'yachts' can reach high speeds. Courses are often arranged by sailing and watersports clubs. Enquire at the tourist office or *mairie*.

Motorsports

Cars

Car clubs within the region include rally clubs and touring clubs.

Karts

Karting tracks run courses, hire karts and run group events. Karting centres often have smaller karts specifically for younger children.

Motorbikes

There are motorbike clubs (*club de moto*) for motocross and trial and road biking in many towns and villages.

Quad Bikes

Quad bike (*quad*) centres offer tracks for accompanied or unaccompanied rides through woodland and may have smaller bikes for children to ride around restricted circuits.

Paint Ball

Paint ball centres are usually in woodland areas and, although only open at specific times, usually take group bookings throughout the year.

Rollerskating

Most towns have a skate park suitable for skate boards, BMX bikes and rollerskates. Some organisations take groups of skaters out along paths and through towns (*randonnées*).

Shooting

Firing ranges (*champ de tir*) are usually on the outskirts of towns and allow children and adults to shoot. Ranges can sometimes be found in yellow pages under *Tir (stands de)*.

Squash

Squash (*squash* but bizarrely pronounced 'skwatch') clubs aren't as common as in the UK, but you can usually find courts in large towns. Listed in yellow pages under *Squash (salles et leçons)*.

Swimming

More swimming pools are becoming water complexes with a selection of pools that includes a traditional training pool, Jacuzzi, paddling pools and flumes (*toboggan*). Listed in yellow pages under *Piscines (établissements)*.

Tennis

Details of tennis clubs are found in the following chapters and can occasionally be found in yellow pages under *Tennis (courts et leçons)*. If you want to hire the tennis courts (*terrain de tennis*) in a small town or village, enquire at the *mairie*. If they're closed, the local *tabac* or general store often holds the key and takes payment for the courts.

Tree Climbing

A popular leisure activity in France. Adventure centres have courses for a variety of ages and heights. The height requirement is measured either to the top of your head or to your finger tips when your arms are raised above your head. This is because a lot of the courses require you to hold safety ropes above you. Full safety equipment is provided, but you should wear sensible sports shoes and go prepared for several hours of mental and physical exertion!

Walking & Rambling

Walking/rambling (*randonnée*) is a regular pastime. There are groups in most towns that organise regular half-day or full-day walks. Enquire at the tourist office for details of a local group or a list of dates and departure points. Tourist offices also sell *Topo Guides* which give a selection of walks, of varying length.

Watersports

Rowing

Rowing (*aviron*) centres may be based on lakes but more commonly on rivers.

Sailing

Although sailing (*voile*) is primarily in small dinghies (*dériveur*), some companies offer sailing weekends on board large yachts, either as a passenger or an active crew-member.

Scuba Diving

Scuba diving (*plongée sous-marine*) groups usually train at indoor pools during the winter. In the summer they carry out open-water dives, either along the coast or on organised trips further afield.

Windsurfing

To hire windsurfing equipment (*planche à voile*) and surfboards (*planche de surf*) look in yellow pages under *Location de bateaux, canoës, kayaks et planches à voile*.

Tourist Offices

Tourist offices hold details of local events throughout the year and are a good source of general information and local guide books. Details of relevant regional and departmental offices are given in the following chapters; opening hours are current but may change slightly from year to year.

Comité Régional du Tourisme en Bretagne
⌨ *www.tourismebretagne.com*

The Paris tourist office can provide information for the whole of France.

Office de Tourisme de Paris, 25 rue des   ☎ 08 92 68 30 00
Pyramides, 75001 Paris
⌨ *www.paris-touristoffice.com*

Tradesmen

Almost every commune has a tradesman (*artisan*) of some description, from carpenter (*menuisier*) or builder (*maçon*) to electrician (*électricien*) or plumber (*plombier*). One way to find out what local tradesmen there are is to look through the phone book in the residential listing for your commune; tradesmen will have their profession next to their name and address. The best way, however, is to ask at the *mairie*; it's likely that the *Maire* will even give you a personal introduction.

Using local French tradesmen has the advantage that they know the materials they will be working with, are familiar with the systems in place in your property and, as they live locally, have a reputation to maintain. The increasing influx of Britons and other foreigners to rural France means that more and more French artisans are willing to communicate in a mixture of French and English, drawings and sign language (see also **Translators & Teachers** below).

Registered builders in France have their work guaranteed for ten years and must be fully insured to cover any accident or damage to themselves, you or your property. To check whether a tradesman is registered to work in France, go to ⌨ *www.cofacerating.fr*, click on the Union Jack at the top and under 'For more information on' click on 'A company'; this takes you to a form where you enter the tradesman's telephone number. If he's registered, the company information will appear; a big red cross indicates that he isn't registered.

Should you decide to use an un-registered tradesman – either French or foreign – you should be aware that, if there's an accident, you will be personally and financially liable; you will have no warranty on the work carried out and you won't be able to claim the low VAT rate (5.5 per cent instead of 19.6 per cent) available until the end of 2005 (and possibly longer) for renovation work. You could have additional problems if you need to make an insurance claim involving the work (e.g. in the case of a flood or subsidence).

Note also that a tradesman's insurance doesn't cover them for all work, but only for the skills for which they're registered; for example, your builder may offer to sort out your electrics, but he may not be registered as an electrician and hence not insured for that work.

Just as you would in the UK, ensure that you obtain several quotes, if possible see some work already done and assess whether you will get along with a tradesman before engaging him.

Further details of finding and supervising builders in France can be found in *Renovating and Maintaining Your French Home* (Survival Books – see page 379).

The following website has details on English-speaking tradesmen that are French registered.

🖳 *www.artisan-anglais.com*

Architects & Project Managers

English-speaking architects and project managers are listed in the following chapters. Others can be found in yellow pages under *Architectes* and *Maîtres d'oeuvre en bâtiment*.

Builders

English-speaking builders are listed in the following chapters. General builders are listed in yellow pages under *Maçonnerie, entreprises* and builders for new homes under *Bâtiment, entreprises* and *Constructeurs*.

Carpenters

English-speaking carpenters are listed in the following chapters. Tradesmen for roof carpentry are listed in yellow pages under *Couverture*. A carpenter for furniture and furniture repairs can be found under *Ebénisterie*. For general joinery, windows, etc. look under *Menuiserie*.

Chimney Sweeps

Although you're no longer legally required to have your chimney swept regularly, if you have a chimney fire and are unable to produce a receipt showing that your chimney has been swept recently, you may have difficulty claiming on insurance (check your policy). If using a fire or log burner throughout the winter, you're recommended to have a chimney swept at least once a year anyway.

There are tradesmen who just sweep chimneys (*ramoneur*), but plumbers (see below) frequently do chimney sweeping as well. It costs around €45 to have a chimney swept. To do it yourself, brushes and poles can be bought at DIY shops. DIY shops also sell a product called a *bouchon de ramonage*, which is a slow-burning 'brick' that burns the soot and ash off the inside of a chimney; it doesn't work on thick tar deposits and should be used in addition to, not instead of, a chimney sweep.

Electricians & Plumbers

Although quite different trades, electrics and plumbing are commonly carried out by the same tradesman. Listed in yellow pages under *Electricité générale* and *Plombiers*.

Planning Permission

If you want to make any alterations to your home – even painting the window frames a different colour – you must first visit the *mairie*. There are strict regulations (which vary from commune to commune) governing what can and cannot be done and a strict procedure that must be followed for certain types of work. This is too complex a subject to describe here. For details, refer to **Renovating and Maintaining Your French Home** (Survival Books – see page 379).

Translators & Teachers

French Teachers & Courses

French teachers are listed in the following chapters. See also **Schools** on page 100.

Translations

If you have a small amount of text that you need translated, the Altavista website (🖳 *www.altavista.com*) can translate up to 150 words from a variety of different languages. This isn't an accurate translation and should never be relied on for legal or professional purposes, but it will give you the gist of the information.

Another website that offers translations is 🖳 www.wanadoo.fr – go to '*traduction*' on the left hand side under the heading '*Utile & pratique*'. It can translate both typed-in text and websites.

Translators

Translators are listed in yellow pages under *Traducteurs*. If want a translation of a document to be used in court, you must use a court-approved translator. The court house (*palais de justice*) will be able to give you a list.

Utilities

Electricity

Électricité de France/Gaz de France (EDF/GDF) is one company for the whole of France but operates its gas and electricity divisions separately. The numbers below are for general information; emergency numbers can be found on page 73.

Electricity bills are in two parts: consumption (*consommation*) and a monthly standing charge (*abonnement*). The standing charge is related to how much power (calculated in kilowatts or kW) you have available to you at any time: the more power you have available, the higher the standing charge. Your consumption charge is also related to the amount of power you have available, the charge per unit being higher the more power is available.

Your bill, under '*votre facture en détail*', will tell you what your standing charge is per month (...*€/mois*). Under *montant à prélever* it will give you your existing allowance of kW at any one time, e.g. '*puissance 6kW, code 024*'. If you qualify for cheap rate hours (*heures creuses*), it will also show the relevant times, which are usually from 1 to 7am and from noon to 2pm.

If you use more than the power available, the trip switch is triggered and you will be thrown into darkness and left to fumble for a torch. To prevent repeated 'tripping' of the system, you may need to uprate your supply to cover your expected maximum power consumption at any one time (e.g. running a dishwasher, washing machine and cooker all at once), although this will cost you more.

An alternative is to install a piece of equipment called a *délesteur*, which is a tiny computer wired into your system: when the system is overloaded, it automatically switches off apparatus in order of priority (pre-determined by you, e.g. hot water tank and tumble drier before lights, alarm or plug sockets).

Like most other utility bills, electricity bills are normally issued bi-monthly. As your meter will be outside the property and accessible from the street (you mustn't block access to it), it may be read without your knowing. If a reading hasn't been taken, your electricity bill will be estimated (indicated by an *E* alongside the figures). If the estimate is higher than the actual reading, you can take your bill to your local office (listed in subsequent chapters) and you will be sent an amended bill in the form of a credit to your account.

Gas

Gas (*gaz*) can be 'natural' (from a main supply), butane or propane. If you aren't on mains gas (*gaz de ville*), which is generally available only in larger towns and residential areas, you will need a tank (*citerne*), which provides propane gas, or bottles to provide propane or butane. If you use gas only for cooking, bottles are sufficient; if you have gas central heating, a tank is essential. The main difference between natural and butane or propane gas is that the latter burn much hotter (take care when trying to simmer milk!) and appliances designed for natural gas will need to have the injectors changed to a smaller size. If the appliance is new, it should come with two sizes of injector (the larger size, usually the one that comes fitted, is for natural gas).

If there's already a tank at the property, you will be required to pay a deposit for it and, when it has been filled, the price of a full tank of gas, irrespective of how much was left in it. The gas company will credit the previous owners with what was left in the tank. The deposit can be as much as €1,000 and a tank full of gas as much as €900, so take this into account when considering purchasing the property. Instead of a deposit, you can choose to pay a monthly charge for the tank.

You can monitor your gas consumption using the gauge on a tank and re-order when it drops to the red line. You may find that the gas company will come automatically when they believe you should be due for a refill or phone you if they're going to be in the area to see if you want more gas delivered. The driver will give you a delivery note stating the quantity delivered, the price per kg and the total due. If the bill is large, you may be able to send two cheques, one dated a month after the other, but ask your supplier first.

The first time you buy bottled gas, you must pay a deposit for the bottle plus the price of the gas; when you have a bottle refilled, you pay only for the gas. You don't need to take the paperwork with you for refills, just the empty bottle. The deposit is around €25 but varies slightly according to the gas you choose. Bottles, which don't have gauges but can simply be shaken to ascertain how much gas is left gas, are available from petrol stations and many garden centres, but there are several types (of different colours), so make sure the supplier stocks the one you need before unloading your empty bottle!

Oil

Heating oil (*fioul*) is supplied by independent and national companies and supermarkets. Listings can be found in yellow pages under *Combustibles: fioul*.

Water

Water is supplied by a variety of organisations, from national companies to individual communes – in the latter case with bills sent out by the *mairie*. Listings can be found in yellow pages under *Eaux: distribution, services*.

Wood

To find a local supplier of firewood, ask a neighbour or at the *mairie*, as many farmers in the region supply suitable wood. When ordering wood, you must specify how much you want in an arcane measure called a *stère*, which is roughly 0.6 cubic metres (many people erroneously believe it's one cubic metre) or 500kg of wood. You may also need to specify whether it's for burning now or in a few years and whether it's for a large open fire or a log burner. Wood for log burners is slightly more expensive, as it has to be cut smaller. Depending on the age and type of wood, expect to pay around €20 to €25 per cubic metre.

You can, of course, order the longer length and cut your own wood for a log burner. Electric and petrol chainsaws (*tronçonneuses*) are available from all DIY shops from the autumn onwards and can also be hired from certain outlets.

Six cubic metres (around ten *stères*) should be enough for a winter if you're only using fires and log burners for cold days or in the evenings. If fires are your only source of heating, you will need more, depending of course on how many fires you have and whether you have a wood-burning cooker.

Wood suppliers are listed in yellow pages under *Combustibles: fioul, bois, charbon*.

Wood varies in suitability for use on an open fire. Good and unsuitable woods are listed below.

Good Woods

● Apple (*pommier*) – produces a good scent;

● Ash (*frêne*) – burns well and produces plenty of warmth whether green or brown, wet or dry;

● Beech (*hêtre*) – almost smokeless;

- Chestnut (*châtaignier*) – needs to be aged;

- Oak (*chêne*) – must be old and dry;

- Pear (*poirier*) – produces a good scent.

Unsuitable Woods

- Birch (*bouleau*) – bright and fast burning;

- Elm (*orme*) – doesn't burn well;

- Fir (*sapin*) – bright and fast burning;

- Poplar (*peuplier*) – bright and fast burning, producing a bitter smoke.

Moulin à mer, Île de Bréhat   Jo Taylor

3

Côtes-d'Armor

This chapter provides details of facilities and services in the department of Côtes-d'Armor (22). General information about each subject can be found in **Chapter 2**. All entries are arranged alphabetically by town, except where a service applies over a wide area, in which case it's listed at the beginning of the relevant section under 'General'. A map of Côtes-d'Armor is shown below.

Accommodation

Various tourist office websites have details of campsites, *gîtes*, B&B and hotel accommodation, including the following:

    🖥 *www.baiedesaintbrieuc.com*
    🖥 *www.centrebretagne.com*
    🖥 *www.cotesdarmor.com*
    🖥 *www.dinanhotel.com*
    🖥 *www.tourismebretagne.com*

Camping

Bröons   Camping La Planchette, route de   ☎ 02 96 84 60 03
       Plumaugat
       Two-star campsite alongside a swimming pool and lake.

Dinan   Camping Chateaubriand, 103 rue   ☎ 02 96 39 11 96
       Chateaubriand
       Two-star campsite ten minutes from the town centre.

| Guingamp | Milin Kerhé, Pabu | ☎ 02 96 44 05 79 |

Milin Kerhé, Pabu
(alongside the river north of the town)
Two-star campsite with 80 pitches.
☎ 02 96 44 05 79

Guingamp

Jugon-les-Lacs   Le Bocage   ☎ 02 96 31 60 16
✉ *camping-le-bocage@wanadoo.fr*
Three-star campsite with chalets and mobile homes. Open from
April to October.

Lancieux   Les Mielles, 1 rue de la Mairie   ☎ 02 96 86 22 98
✉ *mairie.lancieux@wanadoo.fr*
(on the coast north of Dinan)
Two-star campsite 100m from the beach.

Lannion   Camping des 2 Rives, rue du Moulin   ☎ 02 96 46 31 40
du Duc
(by the river to the south of the town)
Three-star campsite. Pets allowed and chalets to rent all year.
Campsite open from March to September.

Loudéac   Camping Municipal des Ponts-es-Bigots ☎ 02 96 28 14 92
(south-east of the town towards Rennes)
Two-star campsite. Open from 15th June to 15th September.

Matignon   Le Vallon aux Merlettes, 53 rue Jobert   ☎ 02 96 41 11 61
✉ *giblanchet@wanadoo.fr*
Three-star campsite. Open from April to September.

Pordic   Camping des Madières, Le Vau Madec   ☎ 02 96 79 02 48
🖳 *www.campinglesmadieres.com*
Three-star campsite. Open from April to October.

St Brieuc   Camping des Vallées, Parc de Brézillet,   ☎ 02 96 94 05 05
boulevard Paul Doumer
🖳 *www.mairie-saint-brieuc.fr/services/camping*
Three-star campsite with mobile homes, water complex, tennis
and horse riding. Open from Easter to October.

St Jacut-de-la-   Camping Municipal, rue de la   ☎ 02 96 27 70 33
Mer   Manchette
Two-star campsite. Direct access to the beach and close to
local shops. Open from April to September.

Chateaux

Brélidy   Château de Brélidy   ☎ 02 96 95 69 38
(north of Guingamp)
15th century chateau. Double rooms €91 to €119 per night,
suites from €135 per night. Closed 2nd January to mid-March.

Hillion   Château de Bonabry   ☎ 02 96 32 21 06
     🖳 *www.perso.wanadoo.fr/bonabry*
     (on the coast north-east of St Brieuc)
     A seaside chateau that has been in the same family for 500
     years. There's a dovecote and chapel in the grounds and
     private access to the beach. Suites from €115 to €130. Dogs
     accepted and English spoken.

Plougrescant   Manoir de Kergrec'h, Kergrec'h   ☎ 02 96 92 59 13
     (on the coast directly north of Guingamp)
     An 18th century manor. Double rooms from €100, suites for
     three people from €120.

Gîtes and Bed & Breakfast

General   Gîtes de France Côtes-d'Armor, 7 rue   ☎ 02 96 62 21 73
     St Benoit, St Brieuc
     🖳 *www.gitesdarmor.com*

     Clévacances, Maison du Tourisme des   ☎ 02 96 62 72 00
     Côtes-d'Armor, St Brieuc
     🖳 *www.clevacances.com*

     🖳 *www.cotesdarmor.com*

Hotels

Three hotels are listed in price order for each town, where possible
covering all budgets. Many towns have the national chains such as those
listed on page 51.

Bröons   Le Dav'Ann, 3 avenue de la Libération   ☎ 02 96 84 65 36
     Double rooms from €35 per night.

     Le Relais du Connétable, 15 place   ☎ 02 96 84 62 18
     Duguesclin
     Double rooms from €36 per night.

     Les Dineux Village, Jugon-les-Lacs   ☎ 02 96 84 65 80
     (just north of Bröons on the N12)
     Double rooms from €49 to €80 per night.

Guingamp   Hôtel du Quartz, 3 boulevard Georges   ☎ 02 96 43 73 46
     Clémenceau
     Rooms from €28 per night.

     Armor Hôtel, 44 boulevard Georges   ☎ 02 96 43 76 16
     Clémenceau
     Two-star hotel with rooms from €46 to €60 per night.

Le Relais du Roy, 42 place du Centre   ☎ 02 96 43 76 62
Three-star hotel with rooms from €60 per night.

Lannion   Le Coatilliau, 16 rue Paul Salaun,   ☎ 02 96 47 18 32
Ploubezre
(a few minutes south of the town)
Double rooms from €34 per night.

Arcadia, route de Perros-Guirec   ☎ 02 96 48 45 65
✉ *hotel-arcadia@wanadoo.fr*
Two-star hotel with an indoor pool. Double rooms from €46 to
€58 per night.

Ibis, 30 avenue du Général de Gaulle   ☎ 02 96 37 03 67
💻 *www.ibislannion.com*
(in the centre of town near the railway station and river)
Two-star hotel with double rooms from €47 to €67 per night.

Loudéac   Les Routiers, 7 rue Lavergne   ☎ 02 96 28 01 44
Rooms from €20 per night.

Hôtel le France, place de l'Eglise   ☎ 02 96 66 00 15
✉ *hotel-le-france-loudeac@wanadoo.fr*
Rooms from €30. Closed from Christmas to 1st January.

Les Voyageurs, 10 rue Cadélac   ☎ 02 96 28 00 47
💻 *www.hoteldesvoyageurs.fr*
Two-star hotel with rooms from €45 to €60 per night.

St Brieuc   Le Beau Soleil, 55 rue Docteur Raheul   ☎ 02 96 33 24 68
Double rooms from €28 per night.

Hôtel Ker Izel, 20 rue de Gouët   ☎ 02 96 33 46 29
Double rooms from €50 per night.

Hôtel de Clisson, 36 rue de Gouët   ☎ 02 96 62 19 29
💻 *www.hoteldeclisson.com*
(in the town centre)
Three-star hotel with double rooms from €68 to €90 per night.

Long-term Rentals

See general information on page 52.

Administration

See general information on page 52.

Banks

See general information on page 55.

Business Services

Computer Services

General	M2 Services Informatique, 17 rue St Jean, Moncontour	☎ 02 96 73 46 31

An English-speaking company offering computer repairs, a call-out service and custom-built systems. There's also a recording studio for hire.

Bröons	AEI Services, 13 rue Noé Derval	☎ 02 96 84 64 16

Home repairs and installation, training, accessories and software.

Guingamp	RTW Multimédia, 29 boulevard de la Marne	☎ 02 96 40 17 17

(south of the town centre, on the same road as the post office)
Computers built to order, software and accessories.

Lannion	ICS, 6 bis quai Viarmes	☎ 02 96 46 18 46

💻 *www.ics-web.net*
Sale, maintenance and repair of computers.

Loudéac	Créatis 22 Multimédia, 40 rue Bigrel	☎ 02 96 66 01 10

Repair, installation, sales and hire of PCs and Macs.

St Brieuc	ASAP Informatique, 38 boulevard Pasteur	☎ 02 96 60 85 40

💻 *www.asap-informatique.com*
Maintenance, training, printers, supplies and accessories.

Computer Training

Guingamp	Club Microtel, place du Château	☎ 02 96 40 09 75

✉ *microtel-guingamp@voila.fr*
Courses covering many topics, including email and Publisher and PowerPoint software. Open Mondays to Fridays 2 to 5.30pm, Saturdays 2 to 4pm.

Lannion	Double M, 64 rue Tréguier	☎ 02 96 37 49 44

💻 *www.double-m.net*

St Brieuc	MJC du Plateau, avenue Antoine Mazier	☎ 02 96 61 94 58

Employment Agencies

See general information on page 58.

Communications

Telephone

See also general information on page 59.

Fixed Line Telephone Services

General   France Télécom   ☎ 1014
               💻 *www.francetelecom.fr*
               Local France Télécom shops are listed below.

Guingamp   10 place du Champ au Roy

Lannion   quai d'Aiguillon
               (near the tourist office)

St Brieuc   Espace Commercial de Langueux
               (on the Carrefour retail park off the N12)
               Open Mondays to Saturdays 9.30am to 8pm.

Internet

Broadband

See general information on page 62.

Public Internet Access

Bröons   Médiathèque, place Jean-Louis Labbé   ☎ 02 96 80 00 44
               Open Mondays 2 to 6pm, Wednesdays 10am to noon and 2 to
               6pm, Saturdays 10am to noon and 2 to 5pm.

Guingamp   Médiathèque Municipale, place du   ☎ 02 96 44 06 60
               Champ au Roy
               ✉ *mediatheque.guingamp@wanadoo.fr*
               Free internet access. Open Tuesdays noon to 6pm,
               Wednesdays 10am to noon and 2 to 6pm, Fridays 10am to
               noon and 3 to 7pm, Saturdays 10am to noon and 2 to 6pm.

Lannion   Surf I Médi@, place des Patriotes   ☎ 02 96 37 21 43
               Open Mondays 10am to noon and 3 to 7pm, Tuesdays to
               Fridays 3 to 7pm.

Loudéac   Médiathèque de Loudéac, 66 rue de   ☎ 02 96 28 16 13
               Cadélac

Open Tuesdays 1.30 to 7pm, Wednesdays 10am to noon and 1.30 to 6pm, Fridays 1.30 to 7pm, Saturdays 10am to noon and 1.30 to 5pm.

St Brieuc   Ty Web, 16 rue du 71ème RI   ☎ 02 96 60 47 94
15 computers with high-speed internet access plus scanner, CD writers and printers. Open Mondays to Thursdays 1 to 9pm, Fridays and Saturdays 1 to 11pm, Sundays 2 to 7pm (July and August open every day 3 to 11pm).

Useful Web Addresses

See general information on page 63.

Television & Radio

See general information on page 63.

Domestic Services

Bouncy Castle Hire

See general information on page 65.

Clothes Alterations

Guingamp   Espace Couture, rue St Yves   ☎ 02 96 44 42 67
Open Tuesdays to Saturdays 9am to noon and 1 to 7pm (Saturdays 6pm).

Lannion   Brenda Couture, 6 rue Forlac'h   ☎ 02 96 46 19 79

Loudéac   Rapid' Couture, 22 rue Moncontour   ☎ 02 96 28 66 78

St Brieuc   Espace Couture, 105 rue Gouédic   ☎ 02 96 68 63 58

Crèches & Nurseries

Guingamp   Crèche Associative Pinocchio, 2 rue du   ☎ 02 96 44 37 55
             Manoir
Children from two-and-a-half months to three years old.

Lannion   Crèche des Fontaines, Résidence   ☎ 02 96 37 95 86
             Fontaines

Loudéac   Halte-garderie, 19 rue Pontivy   ☎ 02 96 28 90 05

St Brieuc   Crèche du Point du Jour, 1 rue René   ☎ 02 96 94 53 81
             Yves Creston

Crèche du Plateau, 1 rue Mathurin   ☎ 02 96 33 74 42
Méheust

Equipment & Tool Hire

Guingamp   Locarmor, ZI Grâces, 10 route Porsmin   ☎ 02 96 44 22 22
🖳 *www.locarmor.com*

Lannion   Brémat Location, route Perros-Guirec   ☎ 02 96 05 55 45
🖳 *www.bremat.fr*

Loudéac   Locarmor, rue Henri Ragot   ☎ 02 96 66 06 06

Plusquellec   P Gravener, Kerdual   ☎ 02 96 45 04 43
✉ *p.gravener@tiscali.fr*
English-speaking company.

St Brieuc   Alpha Location, 20 rue Gustave Eiffel,   ☎ 02 96 52 53 54
Langueux
(east of the town)

Loxam, ZI 6 rue Landes, Langueux   ☎ 02 96 33 09 50
🖳 *www.loxam.fr*

St Quay-Perros   Outils Loca-Services, ZA St Méen   ☎ 02 96 91 26 90
✉ *outilslocaservices@tiscali.fr*

Fancy Dress Hire

See general information on page 66.

Garden Services

General   Art Payg', 24 rue de Moncontour,   ☎ 02 96 66 06 63
Loudéac
Garden design and creation, landscaping and swimming pools.
English-speaking. Work throughout the department.

Central Brittany Gardening, Kroas-ar-   ☎ 02 96 29 68 47
Pichon, Paule
Garden maintenance, hedge cutting and tree felling. Covers
south-west Cotes-d'Armor around Rostrenen and Gourin.
English-speaking.

Squire Services, Kerguédalen,   ☎ 06 30 59 34 34
St Caradec-Tregomel
✉ *john@squirearbo.com*
Internationally qualified arborist for all tree, hedge and woodland work. Tree felling and crowns lifted. English-speaking.

Plusquellec   Peter Gravener, Kerdual   ☎ 02 96 45 04 43
              ✉ *p.gravener@tiscali.fr*
              Ground clearance and landscaping. English-speaking.

Langoat   Frédéric Mallo, 3 Goas an Gac   ☎ 06 72 58 84 80
              ✉ *mallo-f@wanadoo.fr*
              (east of Lannion)
              Maintenance, fencing, hedge cutting, ground clearance and
              tree surgery.

Lannion   Joseph Rochelle, 21 chemin Trohillio   ☎ 02 96 48 78 50
              Servel
              ✉ *jo.rochelle@wanadoo.fr*
              Ground clearance, hedge cutting and general garden
              maintenance.

Lanrelas   Triskell Services   ☎ 02 96 86 62 43
              (north-east of Loudéac)
              Garden maintenance including laying lawns, wood cutting and
              ground clearance.

Pléhédel   P. Beauvais, Manoir du Boisgelin   ☎ 02 96 22 32 37
              (near the coast, north-east of Guingamp)
              Grass cutting, hedges, small garden building jobs and general
              garden maintenance.

Launderettes

Guingamp   Le Bateau Lavoir, 12 rue St Michel   ☎ 02 96 44 12 56

Lannion   Lavomatique, 10 rue de Kérampont   ☎ 02 96 23 69 61
              (south of the river)

Loudéac   Laverie Auto Caruhel, 11 rue   ☎ 02 96 28 11 00
              Moncontour

St Brieuc   Lavomatique 2000, 39bis rue Théodule   ☎ 06 08 05 29 84
              Ribot
              (on the main road coming into the town from the west)

Marquee Hire

Guingamp   France Location, ZI de Bellevue   ☎ 02 96 11 87 87
              💻 *www.francelocation.com*
              Marquees, tables, chairs, china and cutlery.

Party Services

General   Anim' Services, Centre d'Affaires   ☎ 08 00 00 13 32
              Eleusis, Plerin

🖳 *www.animservices.fr*
This company can supply and organise events from weddings to festivals, children's entertainment to firework displays.

Night-Fever Sonorisation, Ploufragan   ☎ 02 96 76 12 64
🖳 *www.breizhgames.com*
Karaoke, discos, lighting, giant screens and themed evenings.

Septic Tank Services

Hénansal   Assainissement Robillard, La Planche   ☎ 02 96 31 51 13
                ✉ *nicolas.robillard@wanadoo.fr*
                (east of St Brieuc, north-east of Lamballe)
                Emptying, cleaning and general maintenance of septic tanks.

St Brieuc   C Salaün, 52 rue Ville Grohan, Trégueux ☎ 06 89 10 13 89
                Emptying, unblocking and cleaning of septic tanks.

Entertainment

Cinemas

Guingamp   Les Baladins, rue St Nicolas   ☎ 02 96 43 73 07
                🖳 *www.cinefil.com*

Lannion   Les Baladins, 34 avenue du Général de   ☎ 02 96 37 26 10
                Gaulle
                🖳 *www.cinefil.com*
                (facing the station)

Loudéac   Le Royal, 9 boulevard Victor Etienne   ☎ 02 96 28 05 25
                Art cinema often showing English-language films.

St Brieuc   Le Club 6, 40 boulevard Clémenceau   ☎ 02 96 33 83 25
                🖳 *www.cinefil.com*

English Books

General   Le Chat qui Lit, Pempoulrot, Kergrist- ☎ 02 96 36 59 00
                Moëlou
                🖳 *www.chatquilit.com*
                (north of Rostrenen, in the south-west of the department)
                Second-hand English books. Open Tuesdays to Thursdays
                from 2 to 6pm, Fridays and Saturdays 10am to 6pm.

Festivals

There are many festivals in this department, and just a small selection are detailed here. All events are annual unless otherwise stated. Further information about these and other festivals is available from tourist offices (see page 177).

March	**Bröons**

Bröons
Carnival de Bröons   ☎ 02 96 84 60 03
A large carnival every other year, the second Sunday of March.
The next one will be 2006.

Spring
St Brieuc
Festival Art'rock   ☎ 02 96 68 46 26
🖥 *www.artrock.org*
This festival has been running since 1979 and attracts over
40,000 people over three days. There's music, theatre, dance,
street artists, video and art.

April
Guingamp
Marathon de Guingamp
🖥 *www.marathon-guingamp.com*
A marathon open to all with a pasta party the night before.

Perros-Guirec
Festival de la Bande Dessiné   ☎ 02 96 23 21 15
A cartoon festival around the third weekend of the month.

May
Douvenant, St Brieuc
Moto-cross National   ☎ 02 96 33 32 50
Motocross event.

Plérin, St Brieuc
La Fête du Nautisme   ☎ 02 96 33 32 50
Maritime festival.

St Brieuc
Foire aux Fleurs et aux Plantes   ☎ 02 96 33 32 50
A large plant and flower festival.

June
Gomené
Festival de Jazz
Jazz festival during the second two weeks of June.

Lannion
Fête de la Musique   ☎ 02 96 46 41 00
Music festival.

St Brieuc
Festival of African music and dance   ☎ 02 96 33 32 50
🖥 *www.completmandingue.com*

Summer	**Guingamp** Jeud'his de Guingamp ☎ 02 96 43 73 89 On Thursdays throughout the summer, free street entertainment in the form of shows, music and comedians.

Lannion
Festival d'Orgue et de Musique de   ☎ 02 96 46 41 00
Lannion
Organ and music festival, with concerts held throughout
July and August at various churches and other venues
throughout Lannion.

Plérin, St Brieuc
Mercredis Animés   ☎ 02 96 33 32 50
Every Wednesday afternoon at 3pm there are shows and
children's entertainers at l'Esplanade des Rosaires.

Pontrieux
Vendredis de l'Eté
Free shows and entertainment every Friday during the summer
from 9pm.

St Brieuc
Les Nocturnes   ☎ 02 96 33 32 50
Every Thursday and Friday evening there are street
entertainers in the old quarter of the town.

July

Lannion
Les Tardives   ☎ 02 96 46 41 00
A two-week festival of fairy tales, music and dance.

Lannion
Puces Lannionnaises   ☎ 02 96 46 41 00
Large flea market around the third Sunday of the month.

August

Bourbriac
Quinzaine de la Culture en Pays Plinn   ☎ 02 96 43 46 03
Two weeks of shows, music and traditional bread making.

Guingamp
St Loup   ☎ 02 96 43 73 89
A variety of dance contests and concerts during the third week
of August.

Loudéac
La Fête du Cheval
Horse festival during the first two weeks of August.

Plouguenast
Fête du Pain   ☎ 02 96 26 83 85
Bread festival on the last weekend of August.

November   St Brieuc
                   Jazz dans les Feuilles   ☎ 02 96 33 32 50
                   💻 *www.jazzdanslesfeuilles.com*
                   Jazz festival at the Baie de St Brieuc.

December   St Brieuc
                   Noël en Fête   ☎ 02 96 33 32 50
                   💻 *www.mairie-saint-brieuc.fr*
                   Street entertainment and shows in the run-up to Christmas.

Libraries

Bröons   Médiathèque, place Jean-Louis Labbé   ☎ 02 96 80 00 44
                  Open Mondays 2 to 6pm, Wednesdays 10am to noon and 2 to
                  6pm, Saturdays 10am to noon and 2 to 5pm. This library
                  doesn't currently stock English books but plans to in the
                  near future.

Guingamp   Médiathèque Municipale, place du   ☎ 02 96 44 06 60
                  Champ au Roy
                  ✉ *mediatheque.guingamp@wanadoo.fr*
                  Open Tuesdays noon to 6pm, Wednesdays 10am to noon and
                  2 to 6pm, Fridays 10am to noon and 3 to 7pm, Saturdays 10am
                  to noon and 2 to 6pm. There's a selection of English books at
                  this library.

Lannion   Bibliothèque Municipale, 17 place des   ☎ 02 96 37 68 09
                  Patriotes
                  Open Tuesdays 2.30 to 6pm, Wednesdays 10am to noon and
                  1.30 to 6pm, Fridays 10am to noon and 2.30 to 6pm, Saturdays
                  10am to noon and 2 to 5pm. This library has a selection of
                  English books.

Loudéac   Médiathèque de Loudéac, 66 rue de   ☎ 02 96 28 16 13
                  Cadélac
                  Open Tuesdays 1.30 to 7pm, Wednesdays 10am to noon and
                  1.30 to 6pm, Fridays 1.30 to 7pm, Saturdays 10am to noon and
                  1.30 to 5pm. There are currently no books in English.

St Brieuc   Bibliothèque Municipale, 44 rue du   ☎ 02 96 62 55 19
                  71ème RI
                  Open Tuesdays, Thursdays and Fridays 1.30 to 6.30pm,
                  Wednesdays 10am to noon and 1.30 to 6.30pm, Saturdays
                  10am to noon and 1.30 to 5pm. There's a selection of books
                  in English.

Theatres

Guingamp	Le Théâtre du Champ au Roy, Champ au Roy	☎ 02 96 40 64 45
Lannion	Carré Magique, Centre d'Arts de Lannion, place Ursulines	☎ 02 96 37 19 20
Loudéac	Palais des Congrès, rue Joseph Chapron	☎ 02 96 28 65 50
St Brieuc	La Passerelle, place de la Résistance ▭ *www.lapasserelle.info*	☎ 02 96 68 18 40
	Théâtre du Totem, 4 rue Moulin à Papier	☎ 02 96 61 29 55
	Théâtre Quai Ouest, 6 rue de la Tullaye	☎ 02 96 61 37 29

Video & DVD Hire

See general information on page 68.

Leisure

This section isn't intended to be a definitive guide but gives a wide range of ideas for the department. Prices and opening hours were correct at the time of writing, but it's best to check before travelling long distances.

Arts & Crafts

Guingamp	Ecole Municipale des Arts Plastiques, Centre Culturel, place du Champ au Roy ✉ *celine.larriere@ville-guingamp.com* Various art classes on Wednesdays, Thursdays and Saturdays.	☎ 02 96 43 85 58
Lannion	Ecole Municipale de Dessin et de Peinture, Ursulines et Pavillon du Parc Ste Anne, place des Patriotes (on the third floor of the building) Various art courses from October to June.	☎ 02 96 37 03 95
Loudéac	Atelier Graal Workshops for different age groups covering modelling, painting and drawing, sculpture and ceramics. Contact Mme Le Bouffo.	☎ 02 96 28 07 35
St Brieuc	MJC du Point du Jour, Cité Waron	☎ 02 96 01 51 40

Ecole Municipale des Beaux Arts, 4   ☎ 02 96 62 55 21
boulevard Charner

Bowling

Lannion   Bowling l'Eclipse, ZC Le Lion St Marc   ☎ 02 96 14 14 74
                 🖥 *www.tregor-bowling.com*
                 (south-west of the town off the new ring road)
                 Bowling, restaurant, bar, pool, snooker, squash and a dance
                 floor. Open every day; 11am to 2am during the week, 11am to
                 3am weekends.

St Brieuc   Club Le Cyclope, 14 rue de Paris   ☎ 02 96 61 30 01
                 (south-east of the town centre, just off the N12)

Dinan   Le Belem, 8 rue Tramontane, Taden   ☎ 02 96 87 03 08
                 (just north of the town)
                 Bowling, restaurant, pool, karaoke and darts. Open every day
                 from 11am.

Bridge

Guingamp   Bridge Club de Guingamp, Centre   ☎ 02 96 21 07 62
                 Culturel, place du Champ au Roy
                 Regular tournaments and meetings. Contact Mme Deflassieux.

Lannion   Club de Bridge, 9 rue des Haras   ☎ 02 96 46 47 89
                 Tournaments on Mondays and Thursdays at 2pm and
                 Tuesdays at 8pm; beginners 2pm Wednesdays.

St Brieuc   Bridge Club Briochin, Centre Curie,   ☎ 02 96 33 48 19
                 rue Curie

Children's Activity Clubs

Guingamp   Initiatives Jeunes, Centre Social, rue   ☎ 02 96 43 73 98
                 Hyacinthe Cheval
                 Various activities, including football, and dance and theatre
                 workshops.

Lannion   Centre de Loisirs Municipal, 37 rue   ☎ 02 96 23 21 34
                 Hilda Gélis Didot
                 Activities, workshops and excursions for 3 to 12-year-olds.

Loudéac   Colonie Aventure   ☎ 02 96 28 69 05
                 🖥 *www.perso.wanadoo.fr/colonie-aventure.loudeac*
                 Residential summer holiday camps lasting 11 to 22 days.
                 Contact M. Chevé.

| Plemet | Le Camp Vert, route de St Rumel   ☎ 02 96 25 61 68 |
| | A variety of holiday camps for 10 to 16-year-olds. From weekend to three-week trips, including sailing and horse riding. |

St Brieuc — MJC du Plateau, avenue Antoine   ☎ 02 96 61 94 58
Mazier

Choral Singing

Bröons — Association Culturelle et Musicale du   ☎ 02 96 80 07 28
Canton de Bröons
Contact M. Cendre.

Guingamp — Chorale Arpège, Ecole de Musique,   ☎ 02 96 43 94 41
Centre Culturel, place du Champ au Roy
Adult choir that puts on around ten concerts each year.
Rehearsals on Tuesdays, term time only. Contact M. Berthou.

Lannion — Ecole de Musique du Trégor, Hôtel de   ☎ 02 96 46 53 70
Tonquédec, 40 rue Jean Savidan

Loudéac — Les Chanteurs d'Argoat et du Lié   ☎ 02 96 28 16 54
Groupe Vocal, Salle 102, Bâtiment Vercel,
7 rue Pasteur
Mixed choir on Tuesdays 8.15 to 10.30pm; women's choir
the second Monday of each month 5.30 to 7pm. Contact
Mme Jauffret.

St Brieuc — MJC du Point du Jour, Cité Waron   ☎ 02 9601 51 40

Circus Skills & Magic

Lannion — Le Carré Magique, Parvis des Droits de   ☎ 02 96 37 19 20
l'Homme
This magic circle founded a circus school in 2001. Programme
available from the tourist office.

St Brieuc — MJC du Plateau, avenue Antoine   ☎ 02 96 61 94 58
Mazier

Dancing

Bröons — Amicale Laïque Section Danse   ☎ 02 96 84 61 05
Contact Mme Noel.

Club de l'Amitié   ☎ 02 96 84 67 01
This club organises regular tea dances.

| Guingamp | Studio Danse et Forme, 1 Venelle St Sébastien | ☎ 02 96 44 41 24 |

Ballet, contemporary dance, jazz, tap and salsa.

| Lannion | CDSLT, Maison des Sports, Park Nevez | ☎ 02 96 48 51 79 |

Ballroom and Latin American. The Lannion dance school is also based here, covering ballet and jazz.

| Loudéac | Djembe, l'Ilot des Récollets, Pontivy | ☎ 02 97 25 75 78 |

Courses and shows for contemporary, African and jazz dance. Meetings Thursdays and Saturdays. Contact M. Hennebelle.

Entrechats Danse, Petit Gymnase, route ☎ 02 96 28 92 38
de St Brieuc
Ballet, jazz, contemporary and tap.

| St Brieuc | Ecole Nationale de Musique et de Danse, 4 boulevard Charner | ☎ 02 96 94 21 85 |

Ballet and jazz.

Association de Quartier Ville-Hellio, ☎ 02 96 94 32 33
Quartier Ville-Hellio
Ballroom and Latin American.

Drama

| Guingamp | Ateliers Théâtre, Théâtre du Champ au Roy | ☎ 02 96 40 64 45 |

✉ celine.larriere@ville-guingamp.com

| Loudéac | Amicale Laïque Section Théâtre, Bâtiment Vercel, rue Pasteur | ☎ 02 96 28 32 44 |

Theatre group meeting Wednesday evenings 8pm.

| St Brieuc | Théâtre Folle Pensée, 4 rue Jouallan | ☎ 02 96 33 62 41 |

Dress Making

| Guingamp | CLAP Atelier de Couture, la Bibliothèque, place du Champ au Roy | ☎ 02 96 44 29 21 |

Held in a room above the library. Contact Mme Mahé.

| St Brieuc | AVF St Brieuc, Centre Charner, Bâtiment A, Porte 1, boulevard Charner | ☎ 02 96 78 23 44 |

Flower Arranging

| Bröons | Club de l'Amitié | ☎ 02 96 84 67 01 |

| Guingamp | CLAP Art Floral, le Bibliothèque, place du Champ au Roy | ☎ 02 96 44 29 21 |

Held in a room above the library. Contact Mme Mahé.

| St Brieuc | Comité d'Animation de Robien | ☎ 06 76 71 01 89 |

Gardening

| St Brieuc | Société d'Horticulture et d'Art Floral | ☎ 02 96 94 47 97 |

Gym

| Bröons | Club de l'Amitié, la Maison des Associations | ☎ 02 96 84 67 01 |

Gym class on Tuesdays from 10 to 11am.

| Guingamp | Studio Danse et Forme, 1 Venelle St Sébastien | ☎ 02 96 44 41 24 |

Stretch, step, dance and relaxation classes.

| Lannion | Energy, route de Perros-Guirec | ☎ 02 96 48 15 85 |

Health gym that runs various classes throughout the week.

| Loudéac | Centre Body Form Loudéacien | ☎ 02 96 25 89 80 |

Classes throughout the week including gym, aerobic and step. Contact M. Prouff.

| St Brieuc | Club de Musculation et de Culturisme Curie, 4 rue Félix le Dantec | ☎ 02 96 61 50 88 |

For information and enquiries about current classes call between 5 and 9pm.

Gyms & Health Clubs

| Lannion | Energy, route de Lannion, route de Perros-Guirec | ☎ 02 96 48 15 85 |

Gym, personal training, free weights and group classes.

| Guingamp | Energie, 13bis rue du Four St Sauveur | ☎ 02 96 44 37 46 |

Step classes, free weights and cardio training. Open Mondays to Saturdays.

| St Brieuc | Club de Musculation et de Culturisme Curie, 4 rue Félix le Dantec | ☎ 02 96 61 50 88 |

Gym classes, weights and cardio training.

Ice Skating

| St Brieuc | La Patinoire de St Brieuc, 24 rue du | ☎ 02 96 33 03 08 |

Pont Léon, Espace Commercial de Langueux
(east of the town, on the Carrefour retail park off the N12)
Open all year, including late evening sessions on Saturdays.

Music

Bröons	Association Culturelle et Musicale du Canton de Bröons Contact M. Cendre.	☎ 02 96 80 07 28

Guingamp   Ecole Municipale de Musique, Centre   ☎ 02 96 21 24 38
            Culturel, place du Champ au Roy
            Lessons in a variety of instruments, including drums,
            saxophone, clarinet, piano and guitar.

Lannion   Ecole de Musique du Trégor, Hôtel de   ☎ 02 96 46 53 70
            Tonquédec, 40 rue Jean Savidan

Loudéac   Le Moulin à Sons, Maison de la   ☎ 02 96 28 35 49
            Musique du Pays de Loudéac
            Introduction to music, lessons and various groups including
            jazz, classical and choir.

St Brieuc   Ecole Nationale de Musique et de   ☎ 02 96 94 21 85
            Danse, 4 boulevard Charner

Photography

Loudéac   Club Photo Louvafilm, rue Pasteur   ☎ 02 96 28 10 46
            💻 www.louvafilm22.free.fr
            Contact M. Daniel.

St Brieuc   MJC du Plateau, avenue Antoine   ☎ 02 96 61 94 58
            Mazier

Scouts & Guides

Loudéac   Scouts de France   ☎ 02 97 38 88 40
            Meetings held every fortnight with different age groups and
            summer camps. Contact M. Coulombe.

Social Groups

Town Twinning

Guingamp   Comité de Jumelage   ☎ 02 96 43 93 39
            Twinned with Shannon in Ireland. Contact M. Gauthier.

St Brieuc   Mairie de St Brieuc   ☎ 02 96 62 54 00
            Twinned with Aberystwyth in Wales. Contact M. Armel.

Welcome Groups

Guingamp	Guingamp Accueil, Centre de Pors-an-Quen	☎ 02 96 23 85 14

Part of the AVF network (see page 71). Contact Mme Le Pourhiet.

Lannion	AVF, 32 rue de Tréguier	☎ 02 96 37 24 41

Open every Thursday during term time, 9.30 to 11.30pm.

Loudéac	Loudéac Accueil Loisirs Création, Bâtiment Jules Ferry, rue des Ecoles	☎ 02 96 28 38 79

This organisation isn't part of the AVF network but has the same aim of welcoming newcomers to the town.

St Brieuc	AVF St Brieuc, Centre Charner, Bâtiment A, Porte 1, boulevard Charner	☎ 02 96 78 23 44

Open Mondays to Fridays 2.30 to 5pm.

Spas

Lannion	Le Lagon, route de Perros	☎ 02 96 48 11 01

Jacuzzi, steam rooms, sun beds and an extensive range of treatments including Shiatsu massage.

St Brieuc	Océane, 9 rue Jules Verne, Langueux (east of the town)	☎ 02 96 33 45 88

Large spa with an extensive range of treatments.

Stamp Collecting

Guingamp	Association Philatélique du Pays de Guingamp, Centre de Pors-an-Quen	☎ 02 96 43 72 86

Contact M. Le Lay.

St Brieuc	Club Philatélique Briochin	☎ 02 96 33 16 64

Yoga

Bröons	Gymnastique et Yoga	☎ 02 96 84 64 92

Contact Mme Lucas.

Guingamp	Amicale Laïque de Pabu, Ecole du Croissant, Pabu	☎ 02 96 21 22 97

Classes on Mondays and Wednesdays from 8.15 to 9.15pm. Contact Mme Piedcoq.

Lannion	ASPTT, rue de Broglie and rue de l'Aérodrome	☎ 02 96 05 83 83

Loudéac   Alody   ☎ 02 97 27 94 48
                   This organisation holds courses throughout the week; daytime
                   and evenings. Contact Mme Marchadour-Lorand.

St Brieuc   EPMM, Salle 44, Lycée Curie   ☎ 02 96 61 16 80
                   Contact Mme Boivin.

Medical Facilities & Emergency Services

Ambulances

See general information on page 72.

Doctors

English-speakers may like to contact the following doctors:

Bröons   Groupe Médical, 2 rue Tiphaine de   ☎ 02 96 84 61 47
                   Raguenel

Guingamp   Dr Grard, 8 boulevard Clémenceau   ☎ 02 96 43 70 36

Lannion   Dr Vernusset, rue Buttes   ☎ 02 96 37 42 52

Loudéac   Groupe Médical, 4 rue Ecoles   ☎ 02 96 28 01 57

St Brieuc   Cabinet Médical, 3 rue Trois Frères   ☎ 02 96 61 73 54
                   Merlin

Emergencies

See general information on page 73.

Fire Brigade

See general information on page 76.

Health Authority

General   CPAM des Côtes-d'Armor, 106   ☎ 08 20 90 41 79
                   boulevard Hoche, St Brieuc
                   💻 www.saint-brieuc.ameli.fr
                   This is the main office and website for the department. Office
                   open Mondays to Fridays 8am to 5pm.

Bröons   Maison du Développement, route de Dinan
                   A CPAM representative here on Fridays from 10.45am to noon.

Guingamp	CPAM, 3 place Champ au Roy
Lannion	CPAM, 2 avenue de Park Nevez
Loudéac	CPAM, 1 rue St Yves

Hospitals

All the following hospitals have an emergency department unless otherwise stated.

Dinan	Centre Hospitalier René Pleven, rue Chateaubriand	☎ 02 96 85 72 85
Guingamp	Centre Hospitalier de Guingamp, 17 rue de l'Armor, Pabu (north-east of the town)	☎ 02 96 44 56 56
Lannion	Centre Hospitalier Pierre Damany, rue Kergomar (south of the town, past the railway station)	☎ 02 96 05 71 11
Loudéac	Centre Hospitalier, rue Chesnaie (in the town centre)	☎ 02 96 25 32 25
Paimpol	Centre Hospitalier de Paimpol, chemin Malabry	☎ 02 96 55 60 00
Plémet	Centre Hospitalier du Centre Bretagne, Bodiffé This hospital covers the Loudéac area. There's no emergency department.	☎ 02 96 66 31 31
St Brieuc	Centre Hospitalier Yves le Foll, rue Marcel Proust 🖥 www.ch-stbrieuc.fr	☎ 02 96 01 71 23

Police

See general information on page 77.

Motoring

See general information on page 79.

Nightlife

This section isn't intended to be a definitive guide but gives a range of ideas for the department. Prices and opening hours were correct at the time of writing, but it's best to check before travelling long distances.

Bourbriac   Nil's Club, 34 rue de l'Armor   ☎ 02 96 43 60 69
(south of Guingamp)
Bar/disco with a themed evening on Thursdays.

Bröons   E Louis, 27 rue Moulin   ☎ 02 96 84 67 56
Disco.

Fréhel   Casino des Sables d'Or, boulevard Mer   ☎ 02 96 41 49 05
Sables d'Or Les Pins
Gaming machines, shows and concerts, restaurant, bar,
roulette and blackjack. Open every day from 10pm to 4am,
gaming machines open from 10am.

Guingamp   Le Bouk@n, 42 rue de la Trinité   ☎ 02 96 43 72 47
Cyber café that usually holds a concert every Saturday. Open
Thursdays to Saturdays from 2pm to 3am.

Le Caméléon, 32 rue de la Trinité   ☎ 02 96 40 07 38
Bar with themed evenings, cocktails and fast food. Open
Mondays to Fridays from 7.15am to 1am, Saturdays and
Sundays 11am to 1am.

Campbell's Pub, place St Michel   ☎ 02 96 43 85 32
Late bar with cocktails and concerts two or three times a
month. Open Mondays to Saturdays until 3am, Sundays 2am.

Le Galopin, 20 rue St Nicolas   ☎ 02 96 21 15 85
Weekly concerts from September to June.

Le Green's Pub, Chemin de Cadolan   ☎ 02 96 43 88 69
Disco open from 10.30pm to 5am.

Nosey Parker, 8 rue de la Trinité   ☎ 02 96 44 04 61
Lively late bar.

La Plantation, route de Tréguier,   ☎ 02 96 43 97 24
Plouisy
(north-west of the town)
Disco open from 10pm to 5am Fridays, Saturdays and bank
holidays. €10 entry. Tea dances every Sunday afternoon.

Le Starway, Pont Ezer, Plouisy   ☎ 02 96 44 38 79
(north-west of the town)

Disco open 10pm to 5am Wednesdays to Sundays. Free entry.

Le White Bird, rue St Michel   ☎ 02 96 21 00 92
A late bar with an American atmosphere. Open every day
until 1am.

Lannion   L'Atmosphère, 11 rue des Chapeliers   ☎ 02 96 46 67 32
Cocktail bar open from 2pm to 2am (Thursdays to Saturdays
until 3am).

Bowling l'Eclipse, ZC Le Lion St Marc   ☎ 02 96 14 14 74
💻 *www.tregor-bowling.com*
(south-west of the town, off the new ring road)
Bowling, pool, snooker, squash and dancing, with a restaurant
and bar. Open every day: 11am to 2am during the week, 11am
to 3am at weekends.

La Brasserie, 20 rue des Chapeliers   ☎ 02 96 37 43 00
Bar-brasserie with a terrace offering a large choice of beers,
plus darts and pool. Open Mondays to Saturdays from 11am to
1am (May to September until 2am).

Happy Days, 4 rue du Marchallac'h   ☎ 02 96 37 08 52
Late bar with an extensive selection of rums. Open Mondays
to Wednesdays from 5pm to 2am, Thursdays to Saturdays
2pm to 3am.

Loudéac   La Lannionnaise, 31 place du Général   ☎ 02 96 46 74 79
Leclerc
Wine bar also serving local beers and snacks. Open from 8am
to 1am (2am at weekends; in July and August 8am to 2am
every day).

Perros-Guirec   Casino de Perros et Côte Granit Rose,   ☎ 02 96 49 80 80
place de Trestraou
Gaming machines and tables, bar and restaurant overlooking
the sea. Open from 11am to 3am.

Pleneuf-val-   Casino du Val André, 1 rue Winston   ☎ 02 96 72 85 06
André   Churchill
💻 *www.casino-val-andre.com*
(east of St Brieuc)
Gaming machines, blackjack and roulette, cinema,
terrace café and shows. Restaurant open for lunch and
dinner every day. The casino is open from 11am to 3am
all year.

St Brieuc   Chez Rolais, rue du Général Leclerc   ☎ 02 96 61 23 03
Wine bar.

Le Clémenceau, 42 boulevard Georges   ☎ 02 96 33 89 63
Clémenceau
Pool and snooker club open every day from 3pm to 2am.
There's an open tournament on Thursdays from 8.30pm.

Cotton Bar, 3 rue Gouédic   ☎ 02 96 33 32 77
Programme of events, including jazz evenings, all year.

Le Mayflower, 7 place du Chai   ☎ 02 96 68 50 00
Late bar with dancing.

O'Kenny Irish Pub, 10 rue Mireille   ☎ 02 96 61 37 36
Christosome
Irish bar.

Le Piano Bleu, 4 rue Fardel   ☎ 02 96 33 41 62
Café/theatre with various performers throughout the year.

St Hervé	Le Rancard, la Gare d'Uzel	☎ 02 96 26 26 22
St Quay-Portrieux	Casino St Quay-Portrieux, 6 boulevard Général de Gaulle Gaming machines, bar and restaurant.	☎ 02 96 70 40 36

Pets

Dog Hygiene

See general information on page 84.

Dog Training

See general information on page 84.

Farriers

General	Bruno Gaudin, Plérin	☎ 06 07 34 25 62
	Pierre-Yves Le Clech'h, Traou-Goaziou, Gommenec'h	☎ 02 96 52 34 65

Horse Dentists

See general information on page 84.

Horse Feed

General	Joe Denham, la Garenne, Langonnet	☎ 02 97 23 91 65

✉ *lagarenne2004@yahoo.co.uk*
Quality hay and haylage (preserved hay with a slightly higher protein/energy content). English-speaking.

Horse Vets

See general information on page 85.

Identification

See general information on page 85.

Kennels & Catteries

See general information on page 85.

Pet Parlours

See general information on page 86.

Pet Travel

See general information on page 86.

Riding Equipment

Dinan   Sellerie l'Ecurie, 8 rue Lainerie   ☎ 02 96 39 17 73

SPA

St Brieuc   SPA La Briochine, chemin Courses   ☎ 02 96 61 26 89

Veterinary Clinics

See general information on page 87.

Places to Visit

This section isn't intended to be a definitive guide but gives a wide range of ideas for the department. Prices and opening hours were correct at the time of writing, but it's best to check before travelling long distances.

Animal Parks & Aquariums

Belle-Isle-en-   L'Aquarium des Curieux de Nature   ☎ 02 96 43 08 39
Terre   This is the regional centre for all things aquatic with various
                 water-themed exhibitions. Open from March to November on
                 Wednesdays and Sundays from 2 to 6pm; Easter and autumn
                 half term Tuesdays to Sundays 2 to 6pm; July and August
                 Tuesdays to Sundays 10am to noon and 2 to 6pm.

Trégastel   Aquarium Marin de Trégastel,   ☎ 02 96 23 48 58
                     boulevard du Coz Pors
                     💻 *www.aquarium-tregastel.com*
                     (on the coast north of Lannion)
                     Marine animals including sea scorpions, small sharks and fish
                     local to the area. Open every day from April to 1st November
                     and during the winter school holidays. Family ticket for two
                     adults and two children €12.50.

Plouagat   Terrarium de Kerdanet   ☎ 02 96 32 64 49
                     💻 *www.perso.wanadoo.fr/terrarium*
                     (between Guingamp and St Brieuc)
                     Vipers, toads and tortoises are just some of the creatures on
                     show as well as grass snakes and boa constrictors. Open from
                     May to September on Wednesdays, Saturdays and Sundays
                     from 2 to 5.30pm; July and August Wednesdays, Saturdays
                     and Sundays 10 to 11.30am and 2 to 5.30pm. Under 12s
                     €3.80, others €4.50.

Les Sept Iles   (off the coast north of Lannion)
                     This group of seven small islands is the most important bird
                     reserve in France, with over 20,000 pairs and 27 species. Open
                     from February to November with boats leaving from Trestraou
                     and Ploumanac'h (see **Boat Rides** on page 151).

St Brieuc   La Maison de la Baie, Site de l'Etoile, ☎ 02 96 32 27 98
                     Hillion
                     💻 *www.reservebaiedesaintbrieuc.com*
                     Nature reserve organising walks, courses and exhibitions
                     based on the wildlife and fauna of the area.

Beaches & Leisure Parks

General   Seaside resorts along the coast include Erquey, Pléneuf-Val-
                     André and St Jacut-de-la-Mer, all with beaches, swimming
                     and watersports.

Allineuc   Plan d'Eau, Bosméléac
                     (north-west of Loudéac)
                     Fishing, camping, walks, picnic area, beach and swimming (no
                     lifeguard), playground, bike hire and *crêperie*.

Bégard   Armoripark, Bégard   ☎ 02 96 45 36 36
                     💻 *www.tregorgoelo.com/armoripark*
                     (north-west of Guingamp)
                     This adventure park has indoor and outdoor heated pools,
                     three giant toboggans (including a 130m slide), outdoor
                     bowling, pedalos, bouncy castles, pedal karts, 18-hole crazy
                     golf and trampolines. Open from April to mid-June from 11am to
                     7pm on Wednesdays, weekends and bank holidays; mid-June
                     to mid-September 11am to 7pm every day.

Jugon-les-Lacs These lakes have various lakeside facilities including swimming, canoeing and a watersports centre.

Lannion Although Lannion isn't on the coast, there are many beaches to the north and east. The largest beaches can be found at Landes-de-Keravel, Pors-Mabo, Tresmeur, Goas-Triez, Landrellec, Grève-Blanche, Trestraou and Trestrignel and on the Ile Grande and Ile Renote, 'islands' that can be reached by road.

Merdrignac Val de Landrouet
Fishing, walks, picnic area, crazy golf, tennis, beach and swimming pool, *boules* court and playground.

St Brieuc There are many beaches around St Brieuc, Pordic and Hillion, plus seven at Plérin.

Club de Plage des Rosaires, Esplanade ☎ 02 96 94 43 45
des Rosaires
Runs children's clubs during July and August with a full calendar of activities.

St Cast This seaside resort has seven beaches.

Trégor Trégor Loisirs, ZA de Ploumilliau ☎ 02 96 54 40 50
This leisure park includes an 18-hole crazy golf course, giant basket ball, toboggan and ball pool. Open from April to June and September on Wednesdays, weekends, bank holidays and school holidays from 2 to 7pm; July and August every day 11am to 7pm.

Boat, Train & Wagon Rides

Boat Trips

Perros-Guirec Port Miniature, Bassin du Linkin ☎ 02 96 91 06 11
(near the marina)
A miniature port with a variety of model boats for children (and adults) to captain. Open from April to June during school holidays and long weekends from 2.30 to 6pm; July and August every day 10.45am to 7.30pm. €4 per person.

Trestraou Armor Découverte, Gare Maritime, ☎ 02 96 91 10 00
place de Trestraou
Boat trips to the Archipel des Sept Iles from February to November. Trips last from an hour and a quarter to two-and-a-half hours. 3 to 12-year-olds €8 to €10, over 12s €13 to €16.

Fillao 'Morskoul', Centre Nautique, ☎ 02 96 49 81 21
Plage de Trestraou

A modern vessel taking up to 12 people along the coast: from two-hour to day trips. From €12.50 to €22.50 (day trip); free for under threes.

St Brieuc   Le Grand Lejon, 8 quai Gabriel Péri,   ☎ 02 96 52 17 66
                 Plérin
                 🖥 *www.le-grand-lejon.com*
                 Excursions into the Bay of St Brieuc on a replica sailing vessel from the late 19th century. Day and weekend trips.

Perros-Guirec   Croisière Azuro   ☎ 08 10 12 22 12
                  This motor yacht is available to hire, with skipper, for a day, weekend or week. The Sebauro is 14.5m (50ft) long and has a maximum speed of 31 knots (57kph). There's a fly bridge with seats and table and, below decks, a fitted kitchen, salon with plasma TV, three bedrooms and two bathrooms. The yacht can accommodate up to ten people plus crew. Fees from €1,350 to €1,500 per day (the rate decreases the longer the period of hire).

Train Rides

Lannion   Train Touristique, quai d'Aiguillon   ☎ 02 96 46 41 00
                 (in front of the EDF building)
                 This 'train' drives through the centre of Lannion giving a commentary as you pass places of interest. Operates from the second week in July to the end of August, with five departures daily. Tickets purchased on board. Under 12s free, others €3.

Pontrieux   Train à Vapeur, Gare de Paimpol,   ☎ 02 96 20 52 06
                 avenue du Général de Gaulle
                 Steam train that runs between Paimpol and Pontrieux. Stops possible at Manoir de Traou-Nez for tastings of local products. Open mid-June to the end of September. Reservations needed. Horse-drawn carriage rides possible from the station back to the town centre. 4 to 11-year-olds €6.50 to €10.50, over 11s €13 to €21 (price dependent on journey type, i.e. single or return and with or without a stop).

Wagon Rides

See general information on page 88.

Chateaux

Erquy   Château de Bienassis   ☎ 02 96 72 22 03
                 A fortified chateau built in the 15th century and restored in the 17th century after being damaged in the League Wars. During the Revolution it was a prison before reverting to a private residence in 1880. There's a moat, courtyard and formal gardens outside. Inside, there's a guard room, dining and drawing rooms (furnished and used by the current owners) and

chapel. Open from mid-June to mid-September Mondays to Saturdays from 10.30am to 12.30pm and 2 to 6.30pm, Sundays 2 to 6.30pm.

Kergrist	Le Château de Kergrist	☎ 02 96 38 91 44

(15km south of Lannion)
15th and 18th century chateau known as La Perle du Trégor. A typically Breton interior courtyard and traditional French gardens. Open in April and May, weekends and bank holidays from 2 to 6pm; June and September every day 2 to 6pm; July and August every day 11am to 6.30pm. Entry €5 for the gardens, €7 for gardens and chateau.

Lannion   Le Château de Cruguil, route de   ☎ 02 96 48 42 26
             Louannec
(north of the town going out towards St Quay-Perros)
A 15th century chateau. Traditional French garden and some rooms open to the public with a guided tour. Open from Mondays to Fridays in July and August, from 2.30 to 6pm (closed bank holidays). Admission €4 for over 18s.

Churches & Abbeys

See general information on page 88.

Miscellaneous

Guingamp   Hippodrome du Bel Orme   ☎ 02 96 43 81 31
              Trotting, flat racing and steeplechase.

Lannion   Visite Historique de Lannion   ☎ 02 96 46 41 00
Throughout the year there are guided tours at 2.30pm from the tourist office through the streets and squares, past churches and timber-framed houses. Adults €5. Booking required.

Promenade Historique Nocture
In July and August there's a tour of the town from 9 to 10.30pm departing from the car park of the Eglise de Brélévenez. Price €5. Booking required.

Journées Terroir & Patrimoine   ☎ 02 96 46 41 00
'Heritage days', including lunch (or dinner) at a restaurant, where you will be served traditional local cuisine, an afternoon at the large regional market and an evening tour of the town. Meet at the tourist office, where you will be given an itinerary. €25 per person.

Loudéac   Hippodrome de Calouet   ☎ 02 96 28 08 42
              Trotting, flat racing and steeplechase.

Paimpol   Labyrinthe Végétal de Paimpol

(on the coast north-east of Guingamp, off the D786, west of the D15)
An enormous maze made out of six-foot-high corn. Open in July and August Tuesdays to Sundays from 1.30 to 8pm.

Perros-Guirec

Maison du Littoral, chemin du Phare   ☎ 02 96 91 62 77
Ploumanac'h
(on the coast north of Lannion)
An exhibition about the Côte de Granit Rose: its geology and rock formations, uses of the granite extracted from the quarries, and the local wildlife. Open from mid-June to mid-September from 10am to 1pm and 2 to 6pm (during school holidays Tuesdays to Sundays 2 to 5pm). Free entry.

Pleumeur-Bodou

Planétarium de Bretagne, Site de   ☎ 02 96 15 80 30
Cosmopolis
(north-west of Lannion)
This is the largest digital planetarium in Europe, with 3D images to guide you through the constellations and planets. Sessions for children from five years old. Open every day in the school holidays; closed Saturdays during term time (and Wednesdays in November, December, February and March) and for the whole of January. Entry €6.75.

Le Radôme et Musée des Télécoms,   ☎ 02 96 46 63 80
Site de Cosmopolis
🖳 *www.leradome.com*
Museum of telecommunications: from the first underwater cables to the internet and the future. Afternoon shows. Open from February to December. Adults €7, children €5.60.

St Brieuc

Expositions du Château de St Ilan,   ☎ 02 96 72 60 37
Languez, 6 avenue Achille de Clézieux
A permanent exhibition on electric trains (full-size ones). The shop has model trains and cars for sale. Open during the Easter and Christmas holidays every day from 2 to 6.30pm; July and August Mondays to Saturdays 2 to 6.30pm. Admission €3 in summer, €4 at Christmas.

L'Hippodrome de la Baie, rue St   ☎ 02 96 72 77 51
Laurent, Yffiniac
2005 is the 200th anniversary of this race track, which has a full calendar of events including trotting, flat racing and steeplechase.

St Thélo

Maison des Toiles, le Bourg   ☎ 02 96 56 38 26
(12km north-west of Loudéac)
This exhibition centre celebrates the tiny blue flax flower, the source of Brittany's famous linen cloth. The exhibition traces the story of flax from seed to weave, with demonstrations by textile craftsmen every day during the summer. Open from

June to September every day from 10am to 1pm and 2 to
6.30pm; October, April and May every day 2 to 6pm; November
to March Sundays and bank holidays 2 to 6pm. Adults €3,
children €1.50.

Trégastel   Moulin à Marée, Chaussée du Port   ☎ 02 96 23 47 48
                 This restored mill still has all its original machinery. Open from
                 mid-June to mid-September. Free entry.

Museums, Memorials & Galleries

La Chèze   Musée Régional des Métiers, 1 rue du   ☎ 02 96 26 63 16
                 Moulin
                 (south-east of Loudéac)
                 This museum covers the many traditional trades of the area
                 with exhibitions, films, guided tours and demonstrations.
                 Specific areas show the work of slate craftsmen, printers and
                 blacksmiths. Open May, June and September Sundays to
                 Fridays from 2 to 6pm; July and August Mondays to Saturdays
                 9am to noon and 2 to 6pm, Sundays 2 to 6pm; October to April
                 by appointment.

Dinan   Musée du Rail, place 11 Novembre   ☎ 02 96 39 81 33
                 (to the side of the main railway station)
                 💻 www.museedurail-dinan.com
                 Railway museum open from June to mid-September every day
                 from 2 to 6pm. Entry €3.80.

                 Musée Remember, le Pont de la Haye,   ☎ 02 96 39 65 89
                 Lehon
                 (opposite the hospital)
                 An exhibition of military uniforms, helmets, equipment and
                 tanks, including some items belonging to the SAS. Open every
                 day during school holidays and on bank holidays from 10am to
                 noon and 1.30 to 6.30pm.

Guingamp   Musée de la Boule Bretonne, place du   ☎ 02 96 43 73 89
                 Champ au Roy
                 The history and evolution of *boules*, from granite to synthetic.

Perros-Guirec   Musée de Cire, 51 boulevard du Linkin ☎ 02 96 91 23 45
                 (on the coast north of Lannion)
                 Waxwork museum displaying the history and traditions of the
                 region with ten exhibition rooms. Open April, May and
                 September from 10am to 12.15pm and 2 to 6pm; June to
                 August 9.30am to 6.30pm. Adults €3, children €1.50.

Pleudihen-sur-   Musée de la Pomme et du Cidre,   ☎ 02 96 83 20 78
Rance   la Ville Hervy
                 (at the mouth of the river Rance, north-east of Dinan)

Cider and apple museum and working farm. Open mid-March to mid-October 2 to 7pm; July and August 10am to 7pm. Adults €3.50, children €2.

St Brieuc   La Briqueterie, rue de la Briqueterie,   ☎ 02 96 63 36 66
Les Grèves, Langueux
On the site of an old brick factory, an exhibition centre dedicated to the activities of the people of the Bay of St Brieuc, including fishermen and market gardeners. Displays include a reconstructed railway wagon and engine. Open in June and September Wednesdays and Fridays to Sundays from 11am to 6.30pm; July and August Mondays and Wednesdays to Sundays 11am to 6.30pm; October to May Wednesdays and Fridays to Sundays 2 to 6pm. 6 to 12-year-olds €2.50, over 12s €4.

Parks, Gardens & Forests

La Chapelle-   Jardin de Plantes Médicinales, Centre   ☎ 02 96 21 60 20
Neuve   Forêt Bocage
✉ centre-foret-bocage@wanadoo.fr
(just off the D787, mid-way between Guingamp and Carhaix Plouguer)
A garden dedicated to herbal and medicinal plants, labelled with both their scientific and French names and an exhibition of their different uses. Open May to September from Mondays to Fridays (closed bank holidays). Free entry.

Loudéac   Forêt de Loudéac
(north-east of the town)
This forest is 2,500ha (6,250 acres) of ideal walking terrain (no cycling or riding allowed) and is home to large numbers of stags, roe-deer and wild boar.

Pleumeur-   Bois de Lann-ar-Waremm
Bodou   (north-west of Lannion)
This is a 300ha (750-acre) forest with many walking, horse riding and cycling routes.

Marais du Quellen
These wet-lands have water all year round, plentiful wildlife, a rich assortment of plants and vegetation and Camargue horses grazing the land.

Ploëzal   Parc et Jardins du Château de la Roche   ☎ 02 96 95 62 35
Jagu
(directly north of Guingamp)
The chateau is surrounded by 55ha (140 acres) of parkland with modern interpretations of medieval gardens, as well as palm trees, water features and a collection of camellia. Open all

year with guided tours available daily in July and August. In the summer various shows are held in the grounds.

St Brieuc   Parc des Promenades
                   A large park in the centre of the town that offers a variety
                   of walks.

Regional Produce

Asnelles-   La Côtes d'Armorienne, Chemin des   ☎ 02 31 21 33 52
Meuvaines   Roquettes
                   (near the coast north-east of Bröons)
                   Oyster farm where you can see and learn about the breeding
                   and preparation of oysters for the table.

Belle-Isle-en-   Sabotier, place de l'Eglise   ☎ 02 96 43 30 13
Terre   Workshop producing traditional Breton clogs (*sabot*). Open
                   every Tuesday in July from 5 to 7pm. Clogs are for sale in the
                   shop. Free entry.

Cohiniac   P. Gautier, le Moulin aux Moines   ☎ 02 96 73 89 18
                   Apiculture centre, where you can see the bees and sample the
                   various products made. Open every Saturday from 2.30 to
                   6.30pm. Free admission.

Lannion   Distillerie Warengham, route de   ☎ 02 96 37 00 08
                   Guingamp
                   🖳 *www.distillerie-warenghem.com*
                   Breton whisky distillery. Open from mid-June to the end of
                   August, Mondays from 3 to 6pm, Tuesdays to Fridays 10am to
                   noon and 3 to 6pm, Saturdays 10am to noon. Free entry;
                   guided tours only.

Quemper-   JF Guégan, Ferme de Kermenguy   ☎ 02 96 95 08 71
Guezennec   Pig and poultry farm open all year for visits and tastings, by
                   appointment. Farm products for sale.

Trégastel   Biscuiterie des Iles, Belle-Isle-en-Terre   ☎ 02 96 23 40 22
                   (on the N12)
                   Biscuit factory. See the various biscuits being made and a
                   video explaining the manufacturing process. Open all year
                   Mondays to Saturdays from 10am to 5pm (July and August
                   from 11am). Free entry.

Standing Stones & Megaliths

Beg Léguer   Vallée de Goaslagorn
                   (west of Lannion)

Boquého   Menhir de Pré-Suzon and Menhir de Kergoff

Bourbriac	Tumulus de Tanouédou
	Dolmen and menhir.
Le Gouray	La Roche aux Fées and La Table Margot
Ile Grande	(north-west of Lannion)
Pédernec	Menhir de Minhir
Pledran	Allée couverte de la Roche Camio
	Standing stones and tables.
Ploufragan	la Couette, l'Argantel and la Vallée
	Three alleys of standing stones.
St Vran	Menhirs du Perfaux
Trégastel	Site de Kerguntuil
Trégon	Dolmens and menhirs.

Professional Services

The following offices have an English-speaking professional.

Accountants

St Brieuc   Cabinet Crémault et Associés, 10 rue   ☎ 02 96 61 45 45
              Caquinerie

Architects & Project Managers

See page 178.

Solicitors & Notaires

St Brieuc   Maître Duchâteau, 54 rue 71ème RI   ☎ 02 96 60 84 00

Property

See general information on page 90.

Public Holidays

See general information on page 95.

Religion

Anglican Services in English

Guerlesquin   La Chapelle St Jean, Le Bourg   ☎ 02 98 78 11 01
(directly west of Guingamp on the border with Finistère)
English-language services every Sunday at 10.30am.

Catholic Churches

See **Religion** on page 96.

Restaurants

Brélidy   Château de Brélidy   ☎ 02 96 95 69 38
💻 *www.chateau-brelidy.com*
(north of Guingamp, near the D8)
Within a 16th century chateau, the restaurant offers set menus
from €26 per person and *à la carte*.

Guingamp   L'Hermine, 1 boulevard Clémenceau   ☎ 02 96 21 02 56
💻 *www.hermine-guingamp.com*
Lunch menu €10 and *à la carte*. Open lunchtimes Mondays to
Fridays and evenings every day until 11pm.

La Pierre à Feu, 34 rue de la Trinité   ☎ 02 96 40 67 56
Grills and *pierrades* (a stone hotplate that you cook on at your
table). €24 set menu plus salads and grills. Meat or fish
pierrade €16.

Lannion   L'Hacienda, 6 rue Turquet de   ☎ 02 96 37 48 96
Beauregard
Mexican food. Take-away service available. Open Mondays to
Saturdays until 11pm (midnight on Saturdays).

La Gourmandine, 23 rue Cie Roger   ☎ 02 96 46 40 55
Barbé
Grills over a wood fire and regional specialities. Set menus €11
(lunchtimes only) to €28 plus *à la carte*. Closed Mondays,
Saturday lunchtimes and all day Sundays.

L'Odyssée, 24 rue St Marc   ☎ 02 96 14 02 15
Traditional and innovative cuisine, all based on regional
products. Shaded terrace in the summer. Lunchtime menus
from €8.50 to €13.50, evening menus €19 to €36. Closed
Wednesdays and Sunday lunchtimes all year (September to
June also closed Tuesday evenings).

Le Serpolet, 1 rue Félix le Dantec ☎ 02 96 46 50 23
(off rue de Viames, opposite the tourist office)
One-star Michelin restaurant, traditional and creative cuisine.
Set menus from €18 to €31. Closed Saturday lunchtimes,
Sunday evenings and all day Mondays. Closed the last week of
June, the first week of October, the last week of December and
the first week of January.

Loudéac   Thinh Phat, boulevard Victor Etienne ☎ 02 96 66 04 84
Chinese restaurant with take-away service. Open Tuesdays
to Sundays.

St Brieuc   Aux Pesked, 59 rue du Légué ☎ 02 96 33 34 65
💻 *www.auxpesked.com*
Three-star Michelin restaurant, *art déco* interior, extensive fine
wine and cigar list. Shaded terrace with a panoramic view over
the Gouët valley. Set menus from €20 to €90 per person.
Closed Mondays, Saturday lunchtimes and Sunday evenings,
and the first two weeks of January and the first week of May
and September.

Manoir le 4 Saisons, 61 chemin des ☎ 02 96 33 20 38
Courses, Cesson
💻 *www.manoirquatresaisons.fr*
Gastronomic restaurant with set menus from €18 to €60.

Trébeurden   Ti-al-Lannec, Allée de Mézo Guen ☎ 02 96 15 01 01
💻 *www.tiallannec.com*
(near the coast north-west of Lannion)
Within a three-star hotel, the restaurant has views of the sea.
Open lunchtimes and evenings every day. Monday to Friday
menus from €21, other menus available all week from €34 to
€66. Open March to mid-November.

Rubbish & Recycling

See general information on page 97.

Schools

See general information on page 100.

Shopping

When available, the opening hours of shops have been included, but it's
advisable to check before travelling long distances to a specific shop.

Architectural Antiques

Maël-Carhaix   Jacques Venner, Kergicquel-Hamon   ☎ 02 96 24 65 35
(south-east of Guingamp, near the border of the department)
Reclaimed fireplaces and stonework including staircases,
fountains and statues.

Bakeries

See general information on page 103.

British Groceries

Caurel   Chez Winnie, 70 rue Roch'ell   ☎ 02 96 26 34 93
(by the lake on the southern border of the department, west of
Loudéac)
Open Mondays, Tuesdays and Thursdays to Saturdays from
9am to noon and 2 to 8pm.

Glomel   MacCormick's, 8 Grande Rue   ☎ 02 96 29 88 05
(in the south-west corner of the department, west of Rostrenen)
British and French foods. Open Mondays, Tuesdays and
Thursdays to Saturdays from 9.30am to 1pm and 2 to 6pm.

Building Materials

See general information on page 103.

Chemists'

See general information on page 103.

Department Stores

See general information on page 103.

DIY

See general information on page 104.

Dress Making & Crafts

Lannion   Chic Tissues, Rond-point St Marc   ☎ 02 96 37 45 89
Fabric for dress making, curtains and furnishings.

St Brieuc   Self Tissues, 13 rue Ambroise Paré,   ☎ 02 96 33 43 46
Langueux
💻 www.self-tissus.fr
(by the car park of Leroy Merlin)
Fabric for dress making, curtains and furnishings.

Fireplaces & Log Burners

See general information on page 104.

Fishmongers'

See general information on page 104.

Frozen Food

Lannion	Picard, route Perros-Guirec 🖳 *www.picard.fr*	☎ 02 96 48 96 54
Loudéac	Argel Ouest, ZA Le Bourgeon, rue Bourgeon	☎ 02 96 28 92 63
Quévert	Picard, Les Quatre Routes	☎ 02 96 39 31 23
St Brieuc	Picard, 22 rue Gouédic	☎ 02 96 61 64 55
Trégueux	Thiriet, 7 rue Jean Monnet	☎ 02 96 78 14 51

Garden Centres

See general information on page 105.

Hypermarkets

See **Retail Parks** on page 164 and general information on pages 105 and 108.

Key Cutting & Heel Bars

See general information on page 106.

Kitchens & Bathrooms

See general information on page 106.

Markets

Belle-Isle-en-Terre	Wednesday mornings
Bröons	Wednesday mornings with a fair the first Wednesday of each month
Guingamp	Friday mornings, place du Vally Saturdays all day, place du Centre

Sunday mornings at Grâces (south-east of the town centre)

Lannion	A very large regional market all day Thursdays at quai d'Aiguillon and across the town centre

Tuesdays to Saturdays (and Sunday mornings in July and August) in the covered market halls from 8am to 1pm

Small local market on Sunday mornings, Quartier de Ker Uhel

Loudéac	Main market on Saturday mornings, with a small local produce market on Thursdays from 5 to 8pm in July and August
Merdrignac	Wednesday mornings
Perros-Guirec	Friday mornings
Pontrieux	Monday mornings
Trébeurden	Tuesday mornings
Trégastel	Monday mornings
St Brieuc	Wednesday and Saturday mornings

Mobile Shops

See general information on page 106.

Music

See general information on page 107.

Newsagents'

See general information on page 107.

Organic Produce

Guingamp	Nature 2000, 3 place du Vally ☎ 02 96 43 72 27 Open Tuesdays to Saturdays from 9am to 12.15pm and 2.15 to 7pm.
Lannion	Biocoop Traou-an-Douar, rue Jean Paul ☎ 02 96 48 90 74 Sartre, Kerligonan

(north-west of the town centre, off rue de Trébeurden in the Ker-Uhel area)
Open Mondays to Saturdays from 9am to 7pm.

Loudéac   Santé Nature, 12 boulevard Victor   ☎ 02 96 28 35 81
                 Etienne

St Brieuc   La Gambille, 10 rue de Robien   ☎ 02 96 75 12 85
                 Open Mondays from 3 to 7pm, Tuesdays to Saturdays 9.30am
                 to 7pm.

Passport Photos

See general information on page 108.

Post Offices

See general information on page 108.

Retail Parks

Guingamp   Carrefour, Rond-point Kennedy   ☎ 02 96 40 17 50
                 💻 *www.carrefour.fr*
                 (west of the town on the road to Brest)
                 The surrounding complex has a chemist's, flower shop, dry
                 cleaner's and photo booth. Open Mondays to Saturdays from
                 9am to 8pm (Fridays till 9.30pm).

Lannion   Centre Commercial Géant
                 (north of the town centre along avenue de la Résistance)
                 There are over 30 shops in the complex, including:
                 ● Décathlon – sports goods;
                 ● Géant – hypermarket   ☎ 02 96 05 84 00
                   💻 *www.geant.fr*
                   Open Mondays to Thursdays from 9am to 8pm, Fridays and
                   Saturdays 9am to 8.30pm (July and August 9am to 8.30pm
                   every day). This hypermarket has a photo booth, jeweller's
                   and restaurant.
                 ● Mr Bricolage – DIY.

St Brieuc   Le Plateau Centre Commercial, Plérin
                 (north of the town, off the N12)
                 Shops include:
                 ● Bébé 9 – baby goods;
                 ● Buffalo Grill – steak house-style restaurant;
                 ● Conforama – furniture and electrical goods;
                 ● Cuisines Schmidt – kitchens;
                 ● Fly – furniture and household accessories;
                 ● Gémo – clothes;
                 ● Leclerc – hypermarket   ☎ 02 96 78 86 86

- Leroy Merlin – DIY;
- Magasin Vert – garden centre;
- McDonald's;
- Monsieur Meuble – furniture;
- Réseau Pro – building materials;
- Saint Maclou – wallpaper and paints;
- Super Sport – sports goods.

Carrefour, Centre Commercial,   ☎ 02 96 62 51 51
Langueux
Open Mondays to Saturdays 8.30am to 9.30pm. Within the complex there's a newsagent's, shoe and clothes shops, dry cleaner's, optician's, jeweller's, florist's, heel bar and hairdresser's.

Second-hand Shops

See general information on page 108.

Sports Goods

See general information on page 108.

Supermarkets

See general information on page 108.

Wine & Spirits

See general information on page 109.

Sports & Outdoor Activities

The following is just a selection of the activities available, the large towns having a wide range of sports facilities. Full details are available from the tourist office or the *mairie*.

Aerial Sports

Ballooning

St Brieuc   Montgolfière Bretagne, 4 chemin de la   ☎ 02 96 79 80 69
Fournière, Plérin
🖳 *www.montgolfiere-bretagne.com*
Flights over the bay of St Brieuc and nearby islands.
Passengers can help in the preparation of the balloons. Up to €200 per person depending on the number of passengers.

Flying

General	Aéro Loc	☎ 06 13 82 27 31

Helicopter for hire for trips along the coastline. Full or half days.

Lannion   Survol de la Côte de Granit Rose   ☎ 02 96 46 41 00
15-minute trial flights from the Ile Grande at Perros-Guirec and
half-hour aerial sight-seeing trips from Trébeurden at Port
Blanc. Book at the tourist office.

St Brieuc   Aéro Club de St Brieuc, Aéroport de St   ☎ 02 96 94 97 04
Brieuc-Armor, Tremuson
(north-west of the town)

Parachuting

St Brieuc   Para Club Armor   ☎ 02 96 91 27 07
🖳 *www.parachutisme-bretagne.com*

Archery

Guingamp   Arc-en-Ciel, Salle des Sports de St   ☎ 02 96 44 97 71
Agathon
✉ *raymond.legallou@wanadoo.fr*

Lannion   Archers du Trégor, Maison des Sports,   ☎ 02 96 38 00 30
Park Nevez
(part of the sports complex east of the town centre)

Loudéac   Archers du Pays de Loudéac, Salle   ☎ 02 96 28 11 36
Souvestre, rue Pasteur
Indoor and outdoor training on Tuesdays, Wednesdays and
Saturdays. Contact M. Garandel.

St Brieuc   La Compagnie des Archers, MJC du   ☎ 02 96 01 51 40
Point du Jour, Cité Waron

Badminton

Bröons   Bröonnaise Volantes   ☎ 02 96 84 68 13
Contact M. Turbin.

Lannion   Atout Volant, Maison des Sports, Parc   ☎ 02 96 14 05 20
Nevez

Loudéac   Badminton Club Loudéac   ☎ 02 96 66 46 83
Courses for all ages from seven years old. Contact
Mme Volard.

St Brieuc   Amicale Laïque St Brieuc, 24 boulevard   ☎ 02 96 94 32 82
                   Charner

Boules/Pétanque

Guingamp   Association Bouliste Guingampaise,   ☎ 02 96 21 33 14
                   Parc de Kergoz, Pabu

Lannion   La Boule du Trégor, Boulodrome du   ☎ 02 96 37 00 63
                   Rusket, Rusket
                   (on the north side of town, next to the Salle Polyvalente)
                   Indoor and outdoor courts.

Loudéac   Pétanque Club Loudéacien   ☎ 02 96 28 69 13
                   Contact M. Udo.

St Brieuc   Pétanque Club VJ, 37 rue Coquelin   ☎ 02 96 94 18 19

Climbing

Guingamp   Armor Escrime Guingamp, Pors-an-   ☎ 02 96 21 17 54
                   Quen
                   ✉ gerald.creel@wanadoo.fr
                   Contact M. Creel after 6.30pm.

Loudéac   Escal'Armor   ☎ 06 23 64 72 10
                   Training on an indoor climbing wall and trips to outdoor sites.
                   Contact M. Poulichot.

St Brieuc   Les Grimpeurs Briochins, 2 rue de la   ☎ 06 61 83 57 81
                   Pérouse, Pordic
                   Contact M. Devémy (evenings).

Cycling & Bike Hire

Bröons   Entente Cyclo-Sportive VTT   ☎ 02 96 84 63 42
                   Road cycling and mountain biking. Contact M. Carfantan.

Guingamp   A guide, *Entre Armor et Argoat*, is available from the
                   tourist office giving details of two mountain bike trails
                   departing from the Salle Omnisport at Ploumagoar.

                   VTT Ploumagoar   ☎ 02 96 44 98 31
                   💻 www.ploumvtt.mutimania.com
                   A mountain biking group. Contact M. Mahé.

                   Lancien, 4 rue Cadolan   ☎ 02 96 44 21 58
                   Bike hire. Open from Mondays to Fridays, weekends by
                   arrangement (every day in summer).

Lannion   A free guide, *Côte de Granit Rose*, is available from the tourist office giving details of five local cycle routes.

ASPTT   ☎ 02 96 48 02 95
Road cycling group.

Loudéac   Amicale Cyclo Loudéac   ☎ 02 96 28 34 66
Rides on Saturdays and Sundays all year round, including road racing and mountain biking in the Loudéac forest. Contact M. Visdeloup.

St Brieuc   Vélo Sport Briochin Avenir Ginglinais,   ☎ 02 96 52 63 39
4 rue Félic le Dantec, Centre Curie
Contact M. Tachen.

St Brieuc VTT'As   ☎ 02 96 61 41 80
Mountain biking club. Contact M. Picard.

A mountain biking guide is available from the tourist office for €10; alternatively contact:
Confédération Départementale du   ☎ 02 96 94 16 08
VTT 22
💻 *www.perso.wanadoo.fr/confederation.vtt.22*

Fishing

Maps are available from fishing shops and tourist offices showing local fishing waters. If there's a lake locally, permits will be on sale in nearby *tabacs* and fishing shops and at the *mairie*.

Bröons   Société de Pêche   ☎ 02 96 84 61 02
Contact M. Berhault.

Guingamp   Association Agréée pour la Pêche et la   ☎ 02 96 44 14 74
Protection du Milieu Aquatique, Grand
Café, place du Centre
Annual fishing permits and local fishing information. Contact M. Coquet.

Lannion   Ecole de Pêche, rue de Roud-ar-Roc'h   ☎ 02 96 37 70 18
Open all year.

Le Léguer
This is one of the best salmon fishing rivers in Brittany. For trout fishermen there are 400km (250mi) of Category 1 waterways and more than 60km (37mi) suitable for fly fishing. Open for salmon fishing from March to the end of July and September to October. Trout fishing from March to October.

From the Pont Ste Anne to the sea the river is classed as maritime but upstream of the bridge fishing permits are needed.

Loudéac   Association de la Pêche de Loudéac   ☎ 02 96 28 65 34
Fishing school for all ages. Contact M. Le Guevel.

Maison des Pécheurs, Etang de Pont-es- ☎ 06 85 77 62 08
Bigot
(south-east of the town)
This lakeside centre organises introductory fishing sessions, classes and courses for everyone from six-year-olds upwards. Fishing permits by the day, week or season on sale.

Plougonver   Les Etangs du Moulin Blanc   ☎ 02 96 21 60 81
(south-west of Guingamp)
Carp and trout lakes, playground, snack bar and campsite.

St Brieuc   Barrage de St Barthélemy, Plan d'Eau
Fishing at the lake formed by the dam.

Other lakes near St Brieuc include the Etang de Douvenant, the Etang de l'Ecluse at Yffiniac and the Barrage de Pont Rolland at Hillion.

Football

Guingamp   SCB Section Foot   ☎ 02 96 43 71 91
✉ *joseph.amourda@tele2.fr*
Contact M. Amourda.

Lannion   Lannion Football Club   ☎ 02 96 37 53 93

Loudéac   Football Club de St Bugan, le Stade, ☎ 02 96 28 38 50
St Bugan
(in the north of the town near the tennis courts and cycle track)
Training on Friday nights at 7pm. Contact M. Remin.

St Brieuc   St Brieuc Football Ouest   ☎ 02 96 94 50 76
✉ *sbfootballouest@club-internet.fr*

Stade Briochin, rue Joseph le Brix   ☎ 02 96 61 86 45
Stadium of the town football team.

St Brieuc Football Féminin   ☎ 02 96 78 47 00
Women's team. Contact Mme Le Boulch.

Golf

Bégard   Golf de Bégard, route de Prat   ☎ 02 96 45 32 64

9-hole course, par 34, 2,217m. Driving range, club house and bar. Green fees €20 to €25. Open to players of any handicap. Clubs, trolleys and buggies for hire.

Morieux   Golf Club Crinière, Manoir de la Ville ☎ 02 96 32 72 60
                 Gourio
                 💻 *www.golfarmor.com*
                 (directly east of St Brieuc, just in from the coast)
                 9-hole course, par 36, 2,964m. Golf school for youngsters; individual and group lessons for all. Restaurant/pizzeria and accommodation available in the manor house.

Pleumeur-   Golf de St Samson, route de Kérénoc   ☎ 02 96 23 87 34
                 Bodou
                 18-hole course, 5,895m. Individual and group lessons and junior courses in the school holidays.

Hockey

Loudéac   Skate Club Loudéac   ☎ 02 96 28 66 51
                 ✉ *mmoisan@tele2.fr*
                 Roller hockey and free skating. Contact M. Moisan.

St Brieuc   Les Korrigans Hockey Club, Patinoire ☎ 02 96 33 03 08
                 d'Armor, 24 rue du Pont Léon, Langueux
                 Ice hockey.

                 Roller Armor Club   ☎ 02 96 33 67 29
                 Rink hockey (on rollerskates). Contact Mme Poulouin.

Horse Riding

Guingamp   Centre Equestre de Kernilien, Lycée   ☎ 02 96 21 25 91
                 Agricole de Kernilien, Plouisy

Loudéac   Centre Equestre de St Guillaume, St   ☎ 02 96 28 95 54
                 Guillaume
                 Dressage, jumping and hacks. Closed on Mondays.

Pleumeur-   Equitation de St Samson, route du Golf ☎ 02 96 23 40 14
Bodou   (north-west of Lannion)
                 Riding school and holiday club.

St Brieuc   Centre Equestre de Brézillet, Stade   ☎ 02 96 9419 19
                 Equestre de Brézillet
                 (in the south of the town near the campsite)
                 Open all year for everyone from four-year-olds upwards. Horses and ponies, a pony club and rides along the beach.

Land Yachting

See general information on page 111.

Motorsports

Cars

General   Brittany British Car Club, Automobile   ☎ 02 99 68 35 53
                   House, Le Tuberie, Ercé-près-Liffré
                   An organisation that brings together owners, collectors and
                   enthusiasts of British cars. Regular meetings, rallies and
                   factory visits.

Guingamp   3e Courte Argoat Tout Terrain   ☎ 06 07 80 11 63
                   Introduction to driving all-terrain (4x4) vehicles, shows and
                   outings. Contact M. Foezon.

Lannion   L'Ecurie Rouge, 8bis route de Ploubezre ☎ 02 96 37 06 25
                   Test drive or ride in a Ferrari Testarossa. Shop selling Ferrari
                   clothes and accessories.

St Brieuc   4x4 Les Ecureuils de la Baie, la Ville   ☎ 06 10 28 08 38
                   Guinvray, Pledran
                   (south of the town)

Karts

Cohiniac   Les Kartings du Leff   ☎ 02 96 73 82 49
                   (a small village west of St Brieuc)
                   Outdoor 800m track, kart hire and competitions. Open from
                   mid-June to mid-September every day from 2 to 8pm; mid-
                   September to mid-June Fridays to Mondays from 2.30pm.

St Brieuc   Kart'Indoor, 14 rue Jules Léquier   ☎ 02 96 74 50 40
                   (take the Rosaires exit at Plérin-sur-Mer)
                   Indoor karting with a 450m circuit. Open Tuesdays to Fridays
                   from 4pm to midnight, Saturdays 2pm to 1am, Sundays 2 to
                   8pm (during school holidays every day from 2pm to midnight).

Motorbikes

Bröons   Moto Club Les Chevaliers de l'Asphalte ☎ 02 96 84 60 74
                   Contact M. Pacheu.

Loudéac   Coyote 164 Moto Club, rue Jacquart   ☎ 02 96 28 28 76
                   Outings once a month, meetings on Sundays at 2pm and the
                   last Friday of each month at 8.30pm. Organised trips to race
                   meetings such as Le Mans. Contact M. Congar.

St Brieuc   Moto Club Birochin, Centre Social Croix ☎ 02 96 78 30 91

St Lambert, rue G. Apollinaire
Motocross.

Quad Bikes

See general information on page 112.

Paint Ball

Dinan   Air Game Paintball   ☎ 06 63 29 17 65
(on the east side of the department)

Guingamp   Manoir de Kerizac, Plouisy   ☎ 02 96 40 06 74
Open all year Wednesdays and weekends; other times by
appointment. From 14-year-olds upwards.

Rollerskating

Guingamp   RS Ploumagoar   ☎ 02 96 44 17 60
Competitions are held at Hall Dulac, Kergoz while beginners'
and adult skating sessions are held at Salle de Ploumagoar.
Contact Martine Leuranguer.

Lannion   Skate park, rue des Cordiers
(near the swimming pool, east of the town centre)

Loudéac   Skate Club Loudéac   ☎ 02 96 28 66 51
✉ mmoisan@tele2.fr
Roller hockey and free skating. Contact M. Moisan.

St Brieuc   Roller Armor Club   ☎ 02 96 33 67 29
Contact Mme Poulouin.

Skate park, Quartier Brézillet   ☎ 02 96 79 82 07
Free access.

Shooting

Guingamp   Association Sportive de Tir de l'Argoat, ☎ 02 96 20 25 37
Carrière de Kergré, Ploumagoar
✉ marcbreizh@club-internet.fr
Contact M. Venga.

Lannion   Tir Sportif du Trégor, Maison des ☎ 02 96 23 25 59
Sports, Park Nevez

St Brieuc   Tir Sportif Briochin, 15 rue Jeanne ☎ 02 96 70 45 45
d'Arc, St Quay Portrieux
Contact M. Gervaise.

Squash

| Lannion | Bowling l'Eclipse, Zone Commerciale, | ☎ 02 96 14 14 74 |

Lannion Bowling l'Eclipse, Zone Commerciale, ☎ 02 96 14 14 74
Le Lion de St Marc
Part of the bowling complex.

St Brieuc Hotel Restaurant au Chêne Vert, 2 rue ☎ 02 96 79 80 20
Croix Lormel, Plérin
💻 *www.hotel-au-chene-vert.com*
(on the north-east side of the town)
Squash courts open to non-residents.

Swimming

Bröons Piscine Municipale, route de Plumaugat ☎ 02 96 84 70 01
An outdoor pool open in July and August.

Guingamp La Piscine, rue François Luzel ☎ 02 96 13 50 00
Diving pool, paddling pools and conventional swimming pool,
water cannons and flume, lessons and aqua-gym classes.
Open every day except bank holidays.

Lannion Piscine Municipale, rue Cordiers ☎ 02 96 37 96 52
Indoor pool. Open September to June with swimming classes,
synchronised swimming and diving.

Loudéac Les Aquatides, route de St Brieuc ☎ 02 96 66 14 40
A selection of pools, 70m flume, lazy river, Jacuzzi and
water fountains. Open all year every day except Monday
mornings.

St Brieuc Aquabaie, rue Pierre de Coubertin, ☎ 02 96 75 67 56
Espace Brézillet
(on the south side of the town, just inside the ring road)
A variety of swimming pools for training or leisure, including
diving, aqua-gym classes, swimming lessons, fitness centre
and restaurant.

Piscine Hélène Boucher, 68 rue Pinot ☎ 02 96 78 26 15
Duclos

Piscine Gernugan, 17 rue Gernugan ☎ 02 96 61 05 54

Trégastel Forum de Trégastel, Plage du Coz-Pors ☎ 02 96 15 30 44
💻 *www.forum-tregastel.com*
(on the coast north of Lannion, near the aquarium)
Water jets, lazy river, sauna, Jacuzzi, swimming lessons,
aqua-gym and weights room.

Tennis

Bröons   Tennis Club de Bröons   ☎ 02 96 84 65 03
Contact M. Duval.

There are outdoor courts off rue de la Chapelle and indoor courts by the swimming pool on rue de Plumaugat.

Guingamp   Tennis Club Guingamp, Espace Sportif
de La Madeleine   ☎ 02 96 43 98 99
(just off place St Michel, to the west of the town centre)

Lannion   Tennis Club Lannionnaise, Park Nevez   ☎ 02 96 37 60 99
(part of a large sports complex east of the town centre)
Three indoor courts.

Loudéac   Association Tennis de Loudéac, St Bugan ☎ 02 96 28 10 46
(in the north of the town near the stadium)
Three indoor courts and a clubhouse. Men's, women's and children's teams, and court hire. Contact M. Daniel.

St Brieuc   Centre de Tennis, rue Pierre de   ☎ 02 96 78 54 45
Coubertin, Parc de Brézillet
(on the south side of the town, just inside the ring road)

Tree Climbing

Dinan   L'Ecureuil, 1 rue du Roquet   ☎ 02 96 85 05 02
Tree-top adventure with full security equipment provided.
Minimum group of eight people.

Walking & Rambling

General   Ancienne Ligne de Chemin de Fer
This is an old railway line between la Brohinière and Carhaix-Plouguer that ceased operating in 1952 and has now been made into a long walking and cycling route.

Bröons   Walks organised Mondays and Fridays departing from the Foyer Rural at 2pm.

There are four marked walks departing from the Super U supermarket ranging from 5km (3mi) to 14km (9mi). Details available from the *mairie*.

Guingamp   A guide, *Balades en Argoat*, is available from the tourist office detailing four routes from 2km (1.2mi) to 10km (6mi) around Guingamp and the surrounding area.

Amicale Laïque de Pabu, Mairie, Pabu   ☎ 02 96 43 89 42
Regular walks organised on Tuesdays and Sundays every
fortnight. Contact Mme Geslin for the calendar.

Lannion   A free guide, *Côte de Granit Rose*, is available from the
                 tourist office detailing 15 walks around Lannion and the
                 surrounding area.

Loudéac   Les Randonneurs Loudéaciens   ☎ 02 96 28 36 77
                 This club organises a three-hour walk departing from the
                 Champ de Foire at 8.30am on Sundays, a two-hour walk
                 departing at 1.45pm on Wednesdays, and a full day walk
                 leaving at 8am on the first Sunday of the month. Contact
                 Mme Daniel.

St Brieuc   ASPTT St Brieuc   ☎ 02 96 79 95 95
                 💻 *www.asptt-stbrieuc.com*

                 The tourist office has a selection of maps detailing walks
                 around the area priced from €1 to €3.

Watersports

Canoeing & Kayaking

Guingamp   Canoë Kayak Club Guingampais, le   ☎ 02 96 40 01 98
                 Trieux, Moulin de la Ville
                 ✉ *brunoj.jegou@laposte.net*
                 Nine-year-olds and over. Must be able to swim.

Lannion   Club de Kayak, 8 rue de Kermaria   ☎ 02 96 37 43 90
                 Courses and trips on the sea and up the river; by the hour, half
                 day or full day. In the summer the club operates from rue St
                 Christophe. Alongside Allée du Palais de Justice there's a
                 purpose-built slalom course. Canoes and kayaks for hire, €6.70
                 per hour to €21.60 per day.

Loudéac   Canoë Club du Lié   ☎ 02 96 25 98 01
                 💻 *www.multimania.com/canoeclubdulie*
                 The canoeing centre is open from September to June on
                 Wednesday and Saturday afternoons; booking is required
                 for trips up the river and introductory sessions. During July
                 and August the centre is open every day for trips up the
                 river, individual and group lessons and courses. Contact
                 M. Mainguy.

St Brieuc   Centre de Canoë Kayak, rue du Moulin ☎ 02 96 61 97 39
                 à Papier

Rowing

St Brieuc   Aviron Club du Gouët, le Pont Noir,   ☎ 02 96 78 55 84
                 Plougragan
                 🖳 *www.multimania.com/avirongouet*

Sailing

Plouha   Centre d'Activités Nautiques du Goëlo- ☎ 02 96 22 62 66
                Argoat
                🖳 *www.cangoeloargoat.asso.fr*
                (near the coast, north-east of Guingamp)
                Kayaking on the sea and rivers, windsurfing and sailing. Out of
                season the centre operates from just up the coast at Bréhec on
                Wednesday afternoons and Saturdays only.

St Brieuc   Centre Municipal de Voile, boulevard ☎ 02 96 74 51 59
                 de Cornouaille, Rosaires, Plérin

Trébeurden   Ecole de Voile de Trébeurden, 3 route ☎ 02 96 23 51 35
                de Traou-Meur
                ✉ *asso.evt@wanadoo.fr*
                (on the coast 10km north-west of Lannion)
                Sailing courses, catamaran hire and windsurfing.

Scuba Diving

Guingamp   Club Subaquatic   ☎ 02 96 91 38 42
                Training at the swimming pool at Guingamp and sea dives.
                Contact M. Bielkiewicz.

Lannion   GISSACG, Piscine Municipale, rue   ☎ 02 96 48 13 67
                Cordiers
                Training at the pool from December to March, dives from April
                to November at Ploumanac'h.

Loudéac   Club de Plongée Loudéac, Piscine de   ☎ 02 96 28 25 58
                Loudéac, rue des Livaudières
                Training at the swimming pool on Wednesdays from 8 to 10pm
                and sea dives. Contact Mme Pavec.

St Brieuc   EPAVE Club de Plongée, MJC du   ☎ 06 82 99 00 26
                Plateau, avenue Antoine Mazier6
                ✉ *club.epave@voila.fr*

Windsurfing

Plouha   Centre d'Activités Nautiques du Goëlo- ☎ 02 96 22 62 66
                Argoat

(near the coast, north-east of Guingamp)
Windsurfing from April to August (booking required on
weekdays from April to June). Equipment for hire and
courses available.

St Brieuc   Centre Municipal de Voile de St Brieuc   ☎ 02 96 74 51 59
                  Contact M. Gaubert.

St Launeuc   Etang de la Hardouinais, Val-de-   ☎ 02 96 28 47 98
                  Landrouët
                  (east of Loudéac)
                  Open April to mid-September.

Trébeurden   Ecole de Voile de Trébeurden, 3 route   ☎ 02 96 23 51 35
                  de Traou-Meur
                  ✉ *asso.evt@wanadoo.fr*
                  (on the coast 10km north-west of Lannion)

Tourist Offices

General   Comité Départemental du Tourisme   ☎ 02 96 62 72 00
                  des Côtes-d'Armor, 7 rue St Benoît
                  💻 *www.cotesdarmor.com*

Bröons   There's no tourist office at Bröons but the *mairie* holds a
                  lot of local information. In the summer there's a tourist
                  information office, but the venue and opening hours
                  change annually.

Guingamp   place du Champ au Roy   ☎ 02 96 43 73 89
                  💻 *www.ot-guingamp.org*
                  Open from June and September daily from 10.15am to noon
                  and 2.15 to 6pm; March to May and October to February
                  Tuesdays, Thursdays to Saturdays 10.15am to noon and
                  2.15pm to 5.30pm.

Lannion   2 quai d'Aiguillon   ☎ 02 96 46 41 00
                  💻 *www.ot-lannion.fr*
                  💻 *www.cotedegranitrose.com*
                  Open from September to June Mondays to Saturdays from
                  9.30am to 12.30pm and 2 to 6pm; July and August Mondays
                  to Saturdays 9am to 7pm, Sundays and bank holidays 10am
                  to 1pm.

Loudéac   1 rue St Joseph   ☎ 02 96 28 25 17
                  💻 *www.ville-loudeac.fr*
                  💻 *www.centrebretagne.com*

Open Mondays to Fridays from 9am to 12.30pm and
1.30 to 6pm, Saturdays 10am to 12.30pm (closed
bank holidays).

St Brieuc   7 rue St Gouéno   ☎ 02 96 33 32 50
                   💻 *www.baiedesaintbrieuc.com*
                   Open from October to June, Mondays to Saturdays from
                   9.30am to 12.30pm and 1.30 to 6pm; July to September
                   Mondays to Saturdays 10am to 7pm, Sundays and bank
                   holidays 10am to 1pm. Closed 1st May, 25th December
                   and 1st January.

Tradesmen

Architects & Project Managers

General   Burrows-Hutchinson, Ploerdut   ☎ 02 97 39 45 53
                   ✉ *burrowhutch@aol.com*
                   English-speaking architectural practice offering interior
                   design, project management, building surveys and reports.

                   Max Lenglet, Plérin   ☎ 02 96 74 49 22
                   English-speaking project manager for building and
                   renovation work, specialising in 'green' and eco-friendly
                   buildings and materials.

                   Mike McCoy, Pen-ar-Vern, Bourbriac   ☎ 02 96 43 44 23
                   ✉ *therealmccoy999@aol.com*
                   Bi-lingual draughtsman for architectural design and planning,
                   renovations and septic tank applications.

                   View Brittany, Le Kanveze, Remungol   ☎ 02 97 60 94 57
                   ✉ *vb.caro@wanadoo.fr*
                   New builds, renovation, surveys and project management.
                   English-speaking.

Builders

General   Artiis – Renovation Solutions   ☎ 06 80 38 19 17
                   💻 *www.artiis.fr*
                   French and English-speaking company with tradesmen for
                   renovations, electrics and plumbing.

                   View Brittany, Le Kanveze, Remungol   ☎ 02 97 60 94 57
                   ✉ *vb.caro@wanadoo.fr*
                   New builds, renovation, surveys and project management.
                   English-speaking.

Carpenters

See general information on page 115.

Chimney Sweeps

See general information on page 115.

Electricians & Plumbers

General   T Electrics, 5 Kerroc'h, Plougonver   ☎ 02 96 21 67 11
                ✉ *electrics@tiscali.fr*
                English-speaking electrician. Large and small jobs and 24-hour
                emergency call-out.

                Hommes au Travail, 10 place de   ☎ 02 96 29 72 89
                l'Eglise, Ste Trephine
                ✉ *nigelradcliffe460@msn.com*
                English-speaking electricians and plumbers.

Planning Permission

See general information on page 116.

Translators & Teachers

French Teachers & Courses

Guingamp   TBS, ZI de Grâces   ☎ 02 96 44 43 40

Lannion   Greta, Lycée Lélix le Dantec, rue des   ☎ 02 96 46 40 74
                Cordiers
                💻 *www.tregor-goelo.greta.fr*

St Brieuc   Greta Côtes-d'Armor, 19 bis boulevard ☎ 02 96 61 48 54
                Lamartine
                💻 *www.greta-bretagne.ac-rennes.fr*

Kergrist-Moëlou Peter Mickelborough, Pempoulrot   ☎ 02 96 36 59 00
                💻 *www.chatquilit.com*
                (in the south-west corner of the department, just north of
                Rostrenen)
                French classes for beginners and improvers.

Translations

See general information on page 116.

Translators

See general information on page 117.

Utilities

See general information on page 117.

Men-Brial   JoTaylor

4

Finistère

This chapter provides details of facilities and services in the department of Finistère (29). General information about each subject can be found in **Chapter 2**. All entries are arranged alphabetically by town, except where a service applies over a wide area, in which case it's listed at the beginning of the relevant section under 'General'. A map of Finistère is shown below.

Accommodation

Various tourist office websites have details of camping, B&B, *gîtes* and hotel accommodation, including the following:

- 🖳 *www.tourismebretagne.com*
- 🖳 *www.finisteretourism.com*
- 🖳 *www.mairie-brest.fr*
- 🖳 *www.chateaulin.fr* – hotels only
- 🖳 *www.morlaixtourisme.fr*
- 🖳 *www.quimper-tourisme.com*

Camping

Bénodet   Camping Sunêlia La Pointe St Gilles,   ☎ 02 98 57 05 37
                 Corniche-de-la-Mer

🖥 *www.camping-stgilles.fr*
Four-star campsite. Open from May to mid-September. Mobile
homes for rent.

Camping du Port de Plaisance, 7 route   ☎ 02 98 57 02 38
de Quimper
🖥 *www.camping.benodet.fr*
Four-star campsite. Open from April to September. Mobile
homes and chalets for rent.

Brest

Camping du Goulet, Ste Anne du   ☎ 02 98 45 86 84
Portzic
✉ *campingdugoulet@wanadoo*
Open all year. Pets allowed.

Camping St Jean, Plougastel-Daoulas   ☎ 02 98 40 32 90
🖥 *www.campingsaintjean.com*
Three-star campsite with indoor pool. Chalets and mobile
homes for rent.

Carhaix-
Plouguer

Camping Municipal de la Vallée de   ☎ 02 98 99 10 58
l'Hyères, Vallée de l'Hyères
Two-star campsite. Open from June to September. Bikes and
canoes for hire and mobile homes for rent. Contact the *mairie*
out of season.

Châteaulin

Camping de Rodaven, Rocade de Parc   ☎ 02 98 86 32 93
Bihan
(just south of the town centre, within the loop of the river)

Chateauneuf-
du-Faou

Camping de Penn-ar-Pont   ☎ 02 98 81 81 25
Two-star campsite. Open from mid-May to mid-September.

Cleden-Poher

Camping du Moulin Vert, Pratulo-Mell-   ☎ 02 98 93 82 05
Glaz
Three-star campsite. Open from June to August.

Carantec

Les Mouettes, La Grande Grève   ☎ 02 98 67 02 46
🖥 *www.les-mouettes.com*
Four-star campsite with indoor swimming pool, outdoor water
park, crazy golf, groceries and take-away food. Open from May
to mid-September.

Douarnenez

Camping de Kerleyou, Tréboul   ☎ 02 98 74 13 03
🖥 *www.camping-kerleyou.com*
Three-star campsite. Open from May to September. Mobile
homes and chalets for rent.

Fouesnant   Camping Sunêlia l'Atlantique,   ☎ 02 98 56 14 44
             Mousterlin
             🖥 *www.latlantique.fr*
             Four-star campsite. Open from May to mid-September. Mobile
             homes and chalets for rent.

Huelgoat   Camping de la Rivière d'Argent   ☎ 02 98 99 90 61
             🖥 *www.campriviere.com*
             Two-star campsite with mobile homes for rent. Take-away food,
             games room, bike hire, swimming pool and tennis. Open from
             mid-April to the end of September.

Penmarc'h   Camping Domaine de la Joie, St   ☎ 02 98 58 63 24
             Guénolé
             🖥 *www.domainedelajoie.com*
             Three-star campsite. Open from April to mid-September.
             Caravans, mobile homes and chalets for rent.

Plomeur   Camping de la Torche, Roz-An-Tremen ☎ 02 98 58 62 82
             🖥 *www.campingdelatorche.fr*
             Three-star campsite. Open from April to September. Caravans,
             mobile homes and chalets for rent.

Plonévez-   Camping de Tréguer Plage, Palud   ☎ 02 98 92 53 52
Porzay   🖥 *www.camping-treguer-plage.com*
             Two-star campsite. Open from mid-June to mid-September.

Quimper   Castel l'Orangerie de Lanniron,   ☎ 02 98 90 62 02
             Château de Lanniron
             🖥 *www.lanniron.com*
             (west of the town)
             Four-star campsite. Open from mid-May to mid-September.
             Shopping and restaurant on site.

Roscoff   Aux Quatre Saisons, Perharidy   ☎ 02 98 69 70 86
             🖥 *www.camping-aux4saisons.com*
             Mobile homes and chalets for rent. Crazy golf, evening events
             and direct access to the beach.

Trégunc   Camping de la Pommeraie, Kerdalidec- ☎ 02 98 50 02 73
             St-Philibert
             🖥 *www.campingdelapommeraie.com*
             Four-star campsite. Open from April to September.

Chateaux

Landudec   Château de Guilguiffin   ☎ 02 98 91 52 11
             🖥 *www.au-chateau.com/guilguiffin*

A large, family-owned 18th century chateau situated in vast parkland offering double rooms and suites from €130 and €170 (respectively) per night. Open all year; booking required during the winter. English spoken.

Quimperlé   Château de Kerlarec, Arzano   ☎ 02 98 71 75 06
               ✉ *chateau-de-kerlarec@wanadoo.fr*
               (east of Quimper)
               A striking late 19th century chateau with square corner towers.
               Double rooms from €80 to €110. Credit cards not accepted.

Gîtes and Bed & Breakfast

General   Gîtes de France Finistère, 5 allée Sully,   ☎ 02 98 64 20 20
               Quimper
               💻 *www.gites-finistere.com*

               Clévacances, 11 rue Théodore Le Hars,   ☎ 02 98 76 20 70
               Quimper
               💻 *www.clevacances.com*

Hotels

Three hotel suggestions are given in price order for each town, where possible covering all budgets. Many towns have the national chains such as those listed on page 51.

Brest   Astoria, 9 rue Traverse   ☎ 02 98 80 19 10
               Rooms from €26 to €50 per night.

               Hôtel de la Rade, 6 rue de Siam   ☎ 02 98 44 47 76
               💻 *www.hoteldelarade.com*
               (opposite the military port and the maritime museum)
               Double rooms from €41 to €51 per night.

               Relais Mercure Voyageurs, 2 rue Yves   ☎ 02 98 80 31 80
               Collet
               Rooms from €68 to €102 per night.

Carhaix-   Hôtel d'Ahes, rue Ferdinand Lancien   ☎ 02 98 93 00 09
Plouguer   Double rooms from €36 to €40 per night.

               Le Paradis, 2 boulevard de la   ☎ 02 98 93 39 75
               République
               Double rooms from €42 per night.

               Noz Vad, 12 boulevard de la   ☎ 02 98 99 12 12
               République

⌨ *www.nozvad.com*
Double rooms from €49 to €67 per night.

Châteaulin   Hôtel de France, 11 quai Cosmao   ☎ 02 98 86 11 26
Double rooms €36 per night.

Au Bon Accueil, avenue Louison Bobet   ☎ 02 98 86 15 77
⌨ *www.bon-accueil.com*
Rooms from €35 to €54 per night.

Le Chrismas, 33 Grand Rue   ☎ 02 98 86 01 24
Double rooms from €45 to €55

Morlaix   Hôtel Fontaine, ZA la Boissière,   ☎ 02 98 62 09 55
(on the outskirts of the town near *Mr Bricolage* DIY store)
Double rooms from €43 to €48.

Hôtel du Port, 3 quai de Léon   ☎ 02 98 88 07 54
Double rooms from €49 to €59 per night.

Hôtel de l'Europe, 1 rue Aiguillon   ☎ 02 98 62 11 99
⌨ *www.hotel-europe-com.fr*
An elegant hotel in the centre of town. Double rooms from €63
to €100, suites from €150 to €250.

Quimper   Nuit d'Hôtel, ZA de Créac'h-Gwen, 6   ☎ 02 98 10 12 55
allée Jolivet
Rooms from €30 per night.

B&B City, 131 route de Bénodet   ☎ 02 98 90 95 95
⌨ *www.hotel-bb.com*
Rooms from €40 per night.

Hôtel Gradlon, 30 rue de Brest   ☎ 02 98 95 04 39
⌨ *www.hotel-gradlon.com*
Three-star hotel with rooms from €69 to €116 and suites from
€128 per night.

Long-term Rentals

See general information on page 52.

Administration

See general information on page 52

Banks

See general information on page 55.

Business Services

Computer Services

General   Apple Mac Assistance, 22 rue Franklin   ☎ 02 98 19 40 82
Roosevelt, Plouescat
💻 *www.macaider.com*
English-speaking business for Apple Mac troubleshooting
and training.

Brest   Ordi Ouest, 29 rue 2ème DB   ☎ 02 98 44 04 44
✉ *ordi-ouest@club-internet.fr*
Computers sold off the shelf and built to order; maintenance
and repair of all makes.

Carhaix-   Link Multimédia, 6 place de la Mairie   ☎ 02 98 99 26 40
Plouguer   ✉ *link-multimedia@wanadoo.fr*
(in front of the *mairie*, in a square set back off the main road)
Computer repairs, sales, accessories and software. Open
Tuesdays to Fridays from 9.15am to noon and 2 to 7pm,
Saturdays 9.30am to noon and 2 to 6pm.

Châteaulin   Atelier Informatique, 46 quai Charles de ☎ 02 98 86 31 13
Gaulle
Computer sales, assembly and repairs, internet, software,
consumables and accessories.

Morlaix   Arobase Informatique, 25 place de   ☎ 02 98 88 28 61
Gaulle
Computers built to order and repairs. Open Mondays from
2 to 7.30pm, Tuesdays to Saturdays 9.30am to 12.30pm and
2 to 7.30pm.

Quimper   L'Astrolabe, 6 place de Locronan   ☎ 02 98 53 71 25
(north-west side of the city centre)
Internet access, printers, scanners and computer workshops.

Computer Training

Brest   Maisons Pour Tous, 39 avenue Georges ☎ 02 98 44 71 85
Clémenceau
Groups for children and adults.

Carhaix- Plouguer	Centre Multimédia, Espace du Château Rouge, 40 rue des Martyres	☎ 02 98 93 79 79

✉ *cybercommune@ville-carhaix.com*
Courses in Word, Excel and Windows software.

Châteaulin   Polysonnance Association, 5 quai   ☎ 02 98 86 13 11
Robert Alba
🖥 *www.polysonnance.free.fr*
Introduction to the internet and general computer courses.

Quimper   Info Center Quimper, 18 avenue Ti   ☎ 02 98 52 00 00
Douar
🖥 *www.icqfrance.com*

Employment Agencies

See general information on page 58.

Communications

Telephone

See also general information on page 59.

Fixed Line Telephone Services

General   France Télécom   ☎ 1014
🖥 *www.francetelecom.fr*
Local France Télécom shops are listed below.

Brest   83 rue Jean Jaurès
(in the centre of town, on the east side of the river)

Centre Commercial Carrefour, Iroise
(off the D789, boulevard de Plymouth, west of the town)

Carhaix-   rue Raymond Poincaré
Plouguer   (tucked away in the far right corner of the place du Champ de
Foire, as you come down into the square from the main road)
Open Tuesdays from 9.30am to 12.30pm and 2.30 to 6.30pm,
Wednesdays to Saturdays 9.30am to 12.30pm and 2 to
6.30pm, Saturdays 9.15am to 1pm.

Morlaix   Centre Commercial Bretagnia, St Martin-des-Champs

Quimper   26 place St Corentin
Open Mondays to Saturdays from 9.30am to 12.30pm and 1.30
to 6.45pm (Tuesdays from 9am).

Internet

Broadband

See general information on page 62.

Public Internet Access

Brest   Net@rena, 30 rue Yves Collet   ☎ 02 98 33 61 11
                   Open Mondays to Saturdays from noon to 1am, Sundays and
                   bank holidays 2 to 11pm.

Carhaix-   Link Multimédia, 6 place de la Mairie   ☎ 02 98 99 26 40
Plouguer   ✉ *link-multimedia@wanadoo.fr*
                   (in front of the *mairie*, in a square set back off the main road)
                   Open Tuesdays to Fridays from 9.15am to noon and 2 to 7pm,
                   Saturdays 9.30am to noon and 2 to 6pm.

Châteaulin   L'Espace Multimédia, 5 quai Robert   ☎ 02 98 86 13 11
                   Alba
                   💻 *www.polysonnance.free.fr*
                   Open Mondays to Saturdays.

Morlaix   Café de l'Aurore, 17 rue Traverse   ☎ 02 98 88 03 05
                   💻 *www.aurorecafe.com*
                   Conventional internet cafe with free internet access for
                   customers. Open Mondays to Saturdays from 8am (for
                   breakfast) to 1am.

Quimper   Eixxos, 10 boulevard Dupleix   ☎ 02 98 64 40 56
                   (in the centre of the city, across the river from *La Poste*)
                   Mondays to Saturday 1pm to 10pm. English spoken.

Useful Web Addresses

See general information on page 63.

Television & Radio

See general information on page 63.

Domestic Services

Bouncy Castle Hire

Concarneau   Star Light Evènement, 12bis avenue du   ☎ 02 98 50 94 06
                   Docteur Nicolas
                   💻 *www.starlight29.com*
                   (south-east of Quimper)

Clothes Alterations

Brest   Créafil, 41 rue d'Aiguillon   ☎ 02 98 43 69 38

Carhaix-   Françoise Kerharo, 9 avenue du   ☎ 02 98 93 70 22
Plouguer   Général de Gaulle

Châteaulin   Rapid' Couture, 3 place de la Résistance ☎ 02 98 86 18 80

Morlaix   Retouches et Mode, rue de Brest   ☎ 02 98 63 33 95
                        (on the first floor)
                        Clothes and furnishings made and altered. Open Mondays
                        from 2.45 to 6pm, Tuesdays, Wednesdays and Fridays 9.30am
                        to noon and 2.45 to 6pm, Saturdays 9.30am to noon.

Quimper   Au fil du Temps, Galerie Géant, route   ☎ 02 98 90 55 30
                        Bénodet

Crèches & Nurseries

Brest   Cavale Blanche, 10 rue Hegel   ☎ 02 98 45 86 43
                        Babysitting service.

                        Halte-garderie Frimousse, 13 rue   ☎ 02 98 43 40 49
                        Graveran

Carhaix-   Culture Loisirs Animation Jeunesse,   ☎ 02 98 93 18 77
Plouguer   Espace du Château Rouge, rue Anatole Le Braz
                        ▣ www.claj.free.fr
                        Babysitting available.

Châteaulin   Polysonnance Association, 5 quai   ☎ 02 98 86 13 11
                        Robert Alba
                        ▣ www.polysonnance.free.fr
                        Babysitting available.

                        Crèche le Nid de Coucous, Résidence   ☎ 02 98 86 27 72
                        Jean Bart, Quimill

Morlaix   Crèche Halte-garderie La Sarabande, 17 ☎ 02 98 88 78 43
                        rue Kerfraval

                        Crèche Familiale Municipale, 29 rue   ☎ 02 98 88 00 25
                        Brest

Quimper   Les Petits Mousses, 1 boulevard de   ☎ 02 98 55 25 33
                        Bretagne

Town centre, Fougères
© Roger Moss
www.picturefrance.com

▲ *Fishing fleet, Concarneau*
© Roger Moss *www.picturefrance.com*

▼ *Harbour, Trégastel*
© Roger Moss
www.picturefrance.com

▲ *Quiberon Peninsula, Côte Sauvage*
© Roger Moss *www.picturefrance.com*

▼ *Dawn mist, Forêt du Cranou*
© Roger Moss *www.picturefrance.com*

▲ Port of Pont Aven
© Roger Moss www.picturefrance.com

▶

Breton figure, Quimper
© Roger Moss www.picturefrance.com

© Survival Books

▲ Café-bookshop, Guimaëc
© Roger Moss www.picturefrance.com

▼ Market, Quiberon
© Roger Moss www.picturefrance.com

© Survival Books

◀

Standing stones, Carnac
© Roger Moss www.picturefrance.com

▼ *Port Haliguen, Quiberon*
© Roger Moss
www.picturefrance.com

▲ *Quimper*
© Roger Moss www.picturefrance.com

© Roger Moss www.picturefrance.com

▲ Laval castle
© Survival Books

▼ Medieval quarter, Quimper
© Roger Moss www.picturefrance.com

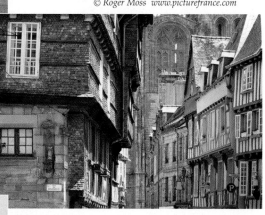

▲ Sand yachting, St Efflam
© Roger Moss
www.picturefrance.com

◄
Quayside, Morlaix
© Roger Moss www.picturefrance.com

▼ Diners in the old port, Roscoff
© Roger Moss www.picturefrance.com

Le Baby Sitting, Centre Social de
Kermoysan
Holds a list of babysitters.

☎ 02 98 55 05 50

Equipment & Tool Hire

Brest

Perramant, Rond-point du Carpont,
Gouesnou
🖳 *www.pro.pagesjaunes.fr/Perramant*
(north side of the town)

☎ 02 98 37 92 92

Carhaix-
Plouguer

Cadiou Location, route Rostrenen, La
Limite

☎ 02 98 99 27 50

Chateaulin

Saint Segal Location, Croix Rodoc, St
Segal
(north-east of the town)
Hire and repair of garden and building equipment. Open
Mondays to Saturdays from 8am to noon and 1.30 to 6pm.

☎ 02 98 73 05 72

Morlaix

Loxam, route Lannion, Coat-Menguy
🖳 *www.loxam.fr*

☎ 02 98 88 09 45

Quimper

Loxam, Centre Gourvily
(north of the town on the Leclerc hypermarket complex)

☎ 02 98 95 97 54

Fancy Dress Hire

Brest

Coud-Coud, 34 rue Aiguillon

☎ 02 98 80 38 30

Garden Services

General

Squire Services, Kerguédalen, St
Caradec Tregomel
✉ *john@squirearbo.com*
Internationally qualified arborist for all tree, hedge and
woodland work. Tree felling and crowns lifted. English
speaking.

☎ 06 30 59 34 34

R. Herrington, Le Vieux Tronc,
Huelgoat
✉ *dawn.collinson@wanadoo.fr*
(north-west of Carhaix-Plouguer)
Land management, heavy garden work and landscaping.
English speaking.

☎ 02 98 99 72 16

Brest

Paysages k'Iroise, route du Conquet,
Pouzané
Garden design and maintenance, fencing and tree cutting.

☎ 02 98 45 89 37

Châteaulin   Genêts d'Or Ateliers, le Vieux Bourg   ☎ 02 98 16 10 97
                    Design and maintenance, ground clearance, tree surgery and
                    garden related stone work.

Launderettes

Brest   Point Bleu, 7 rue de Siam   ☎ 06 07 33 03 53

Carhaix-   Laverie d'Aiguillon, 5 place d'Aiguillon ☎ 02 98 93 76 00
Plouguer   Open every day from 7am to 9pm.

Châteaulin   Laverie Plein Soleil, 14 avenue de   ☎ 06 07 74 07 16
                    Quimper
                    Open every day from 7am to 9pm.

Morlaix   Laverie, 25 place de Gaulle   ☎ 02 98 88 04 72
                    Open every day from 8am to 8.30pm.

Quimper   Lavoir de Kerfeunteun, avenue de la   ☎ 02 98 64 23 05
                    France Libre
                    Open every day from 7.30am to 9pm.

Marquee Hire

Briec   Loca Briec, 2 chemin de Prat Hir   ☎ 02 98 57 77 70
                    Marquees and crockery for hire.

Concarneau   Star Light Evènement, 12bis avenue du ☎ 02 98 50 94 06
                    Docteur Nicolas
                    🖳 *www.starlight29.com*
                    (south-east of Quimper)

Party Services

See general information on page 66.

Septic Tank Services

Carhaix-   Le Vidangeur Breton, ZA de Kerampuil   ☎ 02 98 99 55 27
Plouguer   ✉ *levidangeurbreton@wanadoo.fr*

Bénodet   Hydroservices de l'Ouest, route   ☎ 02 98 56 12 67
                    Fouesnant
                    (south of Quimper)

Lanmeur   Milon Père et Fils, 2 rue Madeleine   ☎ 02 98 67 65 40
                    (north-east of Morlaix)

Entertainment

Cinemas

| Brest | Le Celtic, 187 rue Jean Jaurès | ☎ 02 98 80 34 55 |

www.cinefil.com

Le Studio, 4 rue Paul Masson ☎ 02 98 46 25 58
Art cinema (frequent English language films).

Club 7 Cinémas, 136 rue Jean Jaurès ☎ 02 98 44 00 73

Carhaix-   Le Grand Bleu, rue Jean Monnet ☎ 02 98 93 12 44
Plouguer   (on north-east side of town, set back from the road on its own)
Art cinema frequently showing films in English.

Châteaulin   Cinéma l'Agora, 5 place de la Résistance ☎ 02 98 86 18 55

Morlaix   Cinéma Rialto, 3 rue de l'Hospice ☎ 02 98 88 05 05
www.cinefil.com

La Salamandre, rue Eugène Pottier ☎ 02 98 62 15 14

Quimper   Cinéma Arcades Odet, 36 boulevard ☎ 02 98 90 26 26
Dupleix
www.cinefil.com

Le Bretagne, 5 allée François Truffaut ☎ 02 98 53 23 11

Le Chapeau Rouge, 1 rue du Paradis ☎ 02 98 53 60 75
Art cinema frequently showing films in English.

English Books

General   Le Chat qui Lit, Pempoulrot, Kergrist- ☎ 02 96 36 59 00
Moëlou
www.chatquilit.com
(directly east of Carhaix-Plouguer, just over the border into
Côtes d'Armor)
Second-hand English books. Open Tuesdays to Thursdays
from 2 to 6pm, Fridays and Saturdays 10am to 6pm.

Festivals

There are many festivals in this department, and just a small selection of
the annual events are detailed here. Further details are available from
tourist offices.

March

St Goazec
Festival du Camélia, Château de   ☎ 02 98 26 82 79
Trévarez
Camellia flower festival.

April

Carhaix-Plouguer
Festival du Théâtre Amateur   ☎ 02 98 93 04 42
Amateur drama festival.

May

Brest
Fête du Nautisme   ☎ 02 98 34 64 64
Nautical festival.

Summer

Quimper
Les Jeudis de l'Evêché, les Jardins de   ☎ 02 98 55 03 86
l'Evêché
From mid-June to mid-September there's entertainment every
Thursday in the gardens. Under 12s free, others €4.

July

Kergloff
Fête de la Moto Ancienne   ☎ 02 98 93 40 43
Vintage motorbike show.

Quimper
Festival de Cornouaille   ☎ 02 98 55 53 53
💻 www.festival-cornouaille.com
This festival, which has been running more than 75 years, is
aimed at preserving the arts and traditions of the region and
features many artists and shows, music, concerts and
theatrical performances.

August

Spézet
Fête du Cercle Celtique   ☎ 02 98 93 91 18
Celtic dancing festival.

Autumn

Châteaulin
Les Boucles de l'Aulne   ☎ 02 98 86 02 11
A cycling event that draws professional cyclists from around
the world.

September

Gouézec   ☎ 02 98 73 30 06
Descente VTT de la Roche du Feu
Mountain bike descent of the Roche du Feu, a peak in the
Black Mountains offering a fine view of the bay.

October

St Rivoal
Fête de la Pomme et du Champignon   ☎ 02 98 81 40 54
Apple and mushroom festival.

November	Brest
	Festival Européen du Film Court de ☎ 02 98 44 03 94
	Brest

📠 *www.film-festival.brest.com*
A week long short-film festival that has been held at Brest for
20 years.

Libraries

Brest   Place Jack London   ☎ 02 98 05 54 00
📠 *www.mairie-brest.fr/biblio*
Open Tuesdays and Fridays from 10am to noon and 1.30 to
6.30pm, Wednesdays 10am to noon and 1.30 to 6pm,
Thursdays 1.30 to 6.30pm, Saturdays 10am to noon and 1.30
to 5pm. This library does not currently hold any English books.

Carhaix-   Espace du Château Rouge, 40 rue des   ☎ 02 98 93 37 34
Plouguer   Martyrs
📠 *www.bibliocob.com*
Open Tuesdays from 1.30 to 7pm, Wednesdays 10am to noon
and 1.30 to 6.30pm, Thursdays 4 to 6.30pm, Fridays 1.30 to
6.30pm, Saturdays 10am to noon and 1.30 to 6pm. This library
has a selection of English books.

Châteaulin   quai Robert Alba   ☎ 02 98 86 16 12
Open Tuesdays from 4 to 5.30pm, Wednesdays 10am to noon
and 1.30 to 7pm, Thursdays 4 to 7pm, Fridays 1.30 to 7pm,
Saturdays 10am to noon and 1.30 to 6pm. This library has a
small selection of English books.

Morlaix   Les Ailes du Temps, 5 rue Gambetta   ☎ 02 98 15 20 60
Open Tuesdays from 1.30 to 8pm, Wednesdays and Fridays
10am to noon and 1.30 to 6pm and Saturdays 10am to 5pm.
This library has a selection of English books.

Quimper   Bibliothèque Municipale, 9 rue Toul-al-   ☎ 02 98 95 77 82
Laer
Open Tuesdays, Thursdays and Fridays from noon to 6pm,
Wednesdays 10am to 6pm, Saturdays 10am to noon and 1.30
to 5pm. This library has a selection of English books.

Theatres

Brest   Le Quartz, Scène Nationale de Brest,   ☎ 02 98 33 95 00
2 avenue Clémenceau
📠 *www.lequartz.com*
Theatre, dance, international artists and exhibitions.

Carhaix-   Théâtre du Kreiz Brefzh, ZA   ☎ 02 98 99 37 50
Plouguer   Kerampuilh

Morlaix	Théâtre du Pays de Morlaix, 20 rue Gambetta	☎ 02 98 15 22 77
Quimper	Théâtre Max Jacob, 2 boulevard Dupleix ▭ *www.theatrequimper.asso.fr*	☎ 02 98 55 98 55
	Théâtre de Cornouaille, 1 esplanade François Mitterrand	☎ 02 98 55 98 55

Video & DVD Hire

See general information on page 68.

Leisure

This section isn't intended to be a definitive guide but gives a wide range of ideas for the department. Prices and opening hours were correct at the time of writing, but it's best to check before travelling long distances.

Arts & Crafts

Brest	Maisons Pour Tous, 39 avenue Georges Clémenceau A variety of art and craft courses.	☎ 02 98 44 71 85
Carhaix-Plouguer	L'Atelier Polychrome, boulevard de la République Art courses including pencil, pastels, watercolours and acrylics for all levels.	☎ 02 96 36 64 67
Châteaulin	Polysonnance Association, 5 quai Robert Alba ▭ *www.polysonnance.free.fr* Courses in painting, drawing and cartoons.	☎ 02 98 86 13 11
Loctudy	Centre d'Eveil aux Arts Plastiques, 49 rue Sébastien Guiziou, Domaine-de-la-Fort (on the coast south of Quimper and south-east of Pont l'Abbé) Centre specialising in art workshops.	☎ 02 98 66 51 31
Morlaix	Le Patio, Centre d'Initiation aux Arts, 29bis rue Camille Langevin	☎ 02 98 88 26 85

Bowling

Quimper	Le Master, 59 rue Prés Sadate 12 bowling alleys, pool, *crêperie* and grill.	☎ 02 98 53 09 59

Bridge

Brest
AVF Brest, 4 rue du Colonel Fonferrier   ☎ 02 98 44 49 20
The office is open Mondays to Fridays from 10am to noon and
2 to 5pm.

Morlaix
Bridge Club Morlaix, rue Yves Prigent,   ☎ 02 98 88 75 50
La Boissière
✉ *bc.morlaix@wanadoo.fr*
Tournaments and lessons.

Quimper
AVF Quimper, 5 rue Frederic Le   ☎ 02 98 95 79 78
Guyader
(in the town centre near place de la Tourbie)

Children's Activity Clubs

Brest
Maisons Pour Tous, 39 avenue Georges   ☎ 02 98 44 71 85
Clémenceau
Activities organised during the school holidays and regular
toddler groups for music and dance.

Carhaix-
Plouguer
Culture Loisirs Animation Jeunesse,   ☎ 02 98 93 18 77
Espace du Château Rouge, rue Anatole Le Braz
🖥 *www.claj.free.fr*
Youth club, holiday courses and activities.

Châteaulin
Association Polysonnance, 5 quai   ☎ 02 98 86 13 11
Robert Alba
🖥 *www.polysonnance.free.fr*
Activities organised for 4 to 16-year-olds.

Morlaix
Morlaix Animation Jeunesse, rue   ☎ 02 98 88 04 87
Eugène Pottier
✉ *la-maj@wanadoo.fr*
Activities for 7 to 18-year-olds.

Quimper
Zone de l'Hippo, 5 rue du Docteur   ☎ 02 98 53 08 65
Piquenard, ZI de l'Hippodrome
Indoor adventure playground for babies to 12-year-olds.

Choral Singing

Brest
Maisons Pour Tous, Guelmeur, place   ☎ 02 98 44 71 85
André Jézéquel

Carhaix-
Plouguer
Ecole de Musique Municipale Paul Le   ☎ 02 98 93 78 71
Flem, Espace du Château Rouge, 40 rue des Martyrs
Choir for adults and children.

| Châteaulin | Polysonnance Association, 5 quai Robert Alba | ☎ 02 98 86 13 11 |
| | 🖳 *www.polysonnance.free.fr* | |

| Morlaix | Bab Singers, 4 place du Calvaire | ☎ 02 98 63 21 40 |
| | ✉ *arthepaut@aol.com* | |

Circus Skills & Magic

| Brest | Maisons Pour Tous, 39 avenue Georges Clémenceau | ☎ 02 98 44 71 85 |

| | Kahero, 9 rue Boussingault | ☎ 02 98 44 16 22 |
| | 🖳 *www.jonglerie.fr* | |

Jugglers meet the first and third Tuesday of each month at 9pm at 54 rue de Glasgow. Monocycles and a wide range of juggling equipment for sale. The website has details of informal meetings and groups across the town.

| Morlaix | Association Protectrice de l'Imaginaire, 7 rue Germain Martin | ☎ 02 98 63 21 29 |
| | ✉ *gaston.blutt@wanadoo.fr* | |

Classes in the art of clowning.

Dancing

| Brest | Maisons Pour Tous, Kérinou, rue Somme Py | ☎ 02 98 44 32 10 |

Ballroom, Latin American and country dancing.

| | Pen-ar-Créac'h, 13 rue Professeur Chrétien | ☎ 02 98 02 18 56 |

Tea dances.

| Carhaix-Plouguer | CLAP, Salle Polyvalente, Plounèvèzel | ☎ 02 97 23 51 25 |

Rock, country, salsa, ballroom and Latin American dancing. Contact M. Martin.

| Châteaulin | Polysonnance Association, 5 quai Robert Alba | ☎ 02 98 86 13 11 |
| | 🖳 *www.polysonnance.free.fr* | |

Ballroom, Latin American, jazz and tap dancing.

| Morlaix | Ecole de Danse, 47 rue de la Mairie | ☎ 02 98 21 55 73 |

All levels of dance taught, including jazz and contemporary.

| Quimper | Ecole de Danse Danièle et Francis Regeffe, 11bis rue Stang-ar-c'Hoat | ☎ 02 98 95 34 50 |

Drama

Brest	Maisons Pour Tous, 39 avenue Georges Clémenceau Groups for children and adults.	☎ 02 98 44 71 85
Carhaix-Plouguer	Compagnie Faltazia, Salle Cinédix Courses run for children and adults, September to June. Contact M. Quesseveur.	☎ 02 98 93 93 51
Châteaulin	Théâtre du Miroir, Espace Coatigrac'h, rue de Coatigrac'h	☎ 02 98 86 06 85
Morlaix	Théâtre de la Corniche, MJC, 7 place du Dossen 🖳 *www.theatre-corniche.com*	☎ 02 98 63 42 14
Quimper	Compagnie Patrick Le Doaré, 21 rue Pen-ar-Steïr	☎ 02 98 95 14 00

Dress Making

Brest	Maisons Pour Tous, Kérinou, rue Somme Py	☎ 02 98 44 32 10

Flower Arranging

Brest	Maisons Pour Tous, Kérinou, rue Somme Py	☎ 02 98 44 32 10
Quimper	AVF Quimper, 5 rue Frédéric le Guyader (in the town centre near place de la Tourbie)	☎ 02 98 95 79 78

Gardening

Carhaix-Plouguer	Société d'Horticulture et de Sylviculture de Carhaix et du Poher, Salle Justice de Paix, Mairie de Carhaix, place de la Mairie This group meets on the second Monday of the month at 8.30pm. Contact M. Charles.	☎ 02 98 93 26 70

Gym

Brest	Maisons Pour Tous, 39 avenue Georges Clémenceau A variety of classes including step and general fitness.	☎ 02 98 44 71 85
Carhaix-	Gym-Form, Moulin du Roy	☎ 02 98 99 29 14

| Plouguer | ✉ *gymformcarhaix@wanadoo.fr* |
| | Classes throughout the week including cardio and keep fit. |

| Châteaulin | Gymnastique Féminine, Gymnase H. ☎ 02 98 86 03 37 |
| | Mao, rue Tristan Corbière |

Quimper	Moving Club de Locmarie, 19 allée ☎ 02 98 53 18 20
	Banellou
	💻 *www.centerform.fr*

Gyms & Health Clubs

| Brest | Vital Club, 42 rue Glasgow ☎ 02 98 43 09 78 |
| | The gym is open every day with exercise classes and individual training. |

Morlaix	Energie Sport, 2 bis Voie d'Accès au ☎ 02 98 88 84 84
	Port
	Weights, cardio and personalised training programmes.

Quimper	Moving Club de Locmarie, 19 allée ☎ 02 98 53 18 20
	Banellou
	💻 *www.centerform.fr*
	Squash courts, indoor swimming pool, aqua-gym, weights, exercise classes and cardio training.

Ice Skating

Brest	Patinoire de Brest, Cub Rïnkla Stadium, ☎ 02 98 03 01 30
	place Napoléon III
	💻 *www.rinkla-stadium.com*
	The rink is open from Tuesdays to Sundays in term time, every day in the school holidays.

Music

Brest	Maisons Pour Tous, Guelmeur, place ☎ 02 98 44 71 85
	André Jézéquel
	Piano and guitar lessons.

| | Ecole Nationale de Musique, 16 rue du ☎ 02 98 00 87 04 |
| | Château |

Carhaix-	Ecole de Musique Municipale Paul Le ☎ 02 98 93 78 71
Plouguer	Flem, Espace du Château Rouge, 40 rue
	des Martyrs
	Full range of instruments taught.

| Châteaulin | Polysonnance Association, 5 quai Robert Alba
🖳 *www.polysonnance.free.fr*
Guitar, flute, clarinet, accordion and choir. | ☎ 02 98 86 13 11 |

| | Ecole Municipale de Musique, Ecole Marie Curie, rue Raoul Anthony | ☎ 02 98 86 10 05 |

| Morlaix | Le Patio, Centre d'Initiation aux Arts, 29bis rue Camille Langevin | ☎ 02 98 88 26 85 |

Photography

| Brest | Maisons Pour Tous, 39 avenue Georges Clémenceau | ☎ 02 98 44 71 85 |

| Carhaix-Plouguer | 36e Vue
Amateur and professional photographers welcome. Contact M. Legret. | ☎ 02 98 93 05 74 |

| Châteaulin | Polysonnance Association, 5 quai Robert Alba
🖳 *www.polysonnance.free.fr* | ☎ 02 98 86 13 11 |

| Morlaix | Delphoto, MAJ, 7 rue Eugène Pottier | ☎ 06 79 58 80 26 |

Scouts & Guides

| Brest | Scouts de France, 22 avenue Louis Pasteur
✉ *sdf-finistere@wanadoo.fr* | ☎ 02 98 44 45 75 |

| Quimper | Scouts Unitaires de France, 21 rue Créach Allan | ☎ 02 98 95 47 52 |

Social Groups

Town Twinning

| Brest | Brest Jumelages, ABJCI, 1 rue de l'Harteloire
Brest is twinned with nine towns across the world, including Plymouth in England. | ☎ 02 98 46 51 52 |

| Carhaix-Plouguer | Comité de Jumelage
Twinned with Carrickmacross in Ireland. Contact Mme Hiban. | ☎ 02 98 93 15 98 |

Comité de Jumelage   ☎ 02 98 93 30 56
Twinned with Dawlish in Devon. Contact M. Abeguilé.

Morlaix   Comité de Jumelage Morlaix/Truro,   ☎ 02 98 67 30 80
                 place Onésime Krébel
                 ✉ *paul.catherine@wanadoo.fr*
                 Twinned with Truro in Cornwall.

Welcome Groups

General   Union Régionale des AVF de Bretagne,   ☎ 06 84 16 92 67
                 Crozon
                 ✉ *nicole.garnier.ur.avf@wanadoo.fr*
                 This is the departmental office of the AVF.

Brest   AVF Brest, 4 rue du Colonel Fonferrier   ☎ 02 98 44 49 20
                 The office is open Mondays to Fridays from 10am to noon and
                 2 to 5pm. Various groups organised, including patchwork, yoga
                 and bridge.

Morlaix   Morlaix Accueil, rue Jean Moulin   ☎ 02 98 63 30 54

Quimper   AVF Quimper, 5 rue Frederic le   ☎ 02 98 95 79 78
                 Guyader
                 (in the town centre near place de la Tourbie)
                 Office open Mondays, Tuesdays, Thursdays and Fridays from 2
                 to 4pm. Groups for bridge, French, flower arranging and yoga.

Spas

Douarnenez   Thalasso de Douarnenez, Tréboul Plage   ☎ 08 25 00 42 30

Roscoff   Thalasso Roscoff, Rockroum   ☎ 02 98 29 20 00
                 🖥 *www.thalasso.com*
                 Seawater swimming pool, Jacuzzi and sauna. Aqua-gym.

Stamp Collecting

Brest   Maisons Pour Tous, Guelmeur, place   ☎ 02 98 44 71 85
                 André Jézéquel

Carhaix-   Association Philatélique du Pher,   ☎ 02 98 93 23 28
Plouguer   boulevard de la République
                 Meets on the second Sunday of the month at 10am.

Châteaulin   Polysonnance Association, 5 quai   ☎ 02 98 86 13 11
                 Robert Alba
                 🖥 *www.polysonnance.free.fr*

| Morlaix | Cercle Philatélique Morlaix, route de St Sève, St Martin-des-Champs | ☎ 06 60 23 47 46 |
| | 🖳 www.philmxstmartin.free.fr | |

Yoga

| Brest | Maisons Pour Tous, 39 avenue Georges Clémenceau | ☎ 02 98 44 71 85 |

| Carhaix-Plouguer | Carhaix Yoga, Salle 205, Office des Sports, boulevard de la République | ☎ 02 96 47 23 42 |
| | Sessions held on Tuesdays. Contact Mme Gubry. | |

Châteaulin	Polysonnance Association, 5 quai Robert Alba	☎ 02 98 86 13 11
	🖳 www.polysonnance.free.fr	
	Sessions held Tuesday evenings at Salle Bibliothèque and Friday evenings rue de l'Eglise.	

| Morlaix | JM Creismeas, 20 place des Otages | ☎ 06 26 35 26 65 |
| | Held on the second floor. Courses Mondays and Wednesdays. | |

| Quimper | AVF Quimper, 5 rue Frederic le Guyader | ☎ 02 98 95 79 78 |
| | (in the town centre near place de la Tourbie) | |

Medical Facilities & Emergency Services

Ambulances

See general information on page 72.

Doctors

English-speakers may like to contact the following doctors:

| Brest | Groupe Médical, 38 rue Albert Louppe | ☎ 02 98 02 42 88 |
| | Duty doctor | ☎ 02 98 44 55 55 |

| Carhaix-Plouguer | Maison Médicale, 13 rue Aqueduc Romain | ☎ 02 98 93 02 03 |

| Châteaulin | Groupe Médical, 18 Grand Rue | ☎ 02 98 86 02 52 |

| Morlaix | Groupe Médical de la Boissière, 19 rue Léonard de Vinci | ☎ 02 98 88 49 54 |

| Quimper | Groupe Médical, 3 rue Trédern-de-Lézérec | ☎ 02 98 90 27 74 |
| | *Duty doctor* | ☎ 08 25 00 06 12 |

Emergencies

See general information on page 73.

Fire Brigade

See general information on page 76.

Health Authority

| Brest | CPAM de Brest, rue de Savoie | ☎ 08 20 90 41 98 |

🖳 *www.brest.ameli.fr*
Office open Mondays to Fridays from 8am to 5pm.

| Carhaix-Plouguer | 12 rue Brizeux | ☎ 08 20 90 41 99 |

| Châteaulin | Centre d'Information, 40 Grande Rue | ☎ 02 98 76 41 41 |

There's a CPAM representative here Wednesdays 9am to noon and 1.30 to 4pm.

| Morlaix | 36 rue de Brest | ☎ 02 98 88 38 67 |

Office open Mondays to Fridays from 8am to 6pm, by appointment only.

| Quimper | CPAM de Quimper, 18 rue de la République | ☎ 08 20 90 41 99 |

🖳 *www.ameli.fr*
Office open Mondays to Fridays from 8.30am to 5pm, Saturdays 8.30am to 12.30pm.

Hospitals

All the following hospitals have an emergency department unless otherwise stated.

| Brest | Centre Hospitalier Universitaire, 2 avenue Foch | ☎ 02 98 22 33 33 |

🖳 *www.chu-brest.fr*

| Carhaix-Plouguer | Centre Hospitalier, rue Docteur Menguy | ☎ 02 98 99 20 20 |

| Châteaulin | There are various clinics here and a children's annex of Quimper hospital, but no general hospital or emergency department. | |

Landerneau	Centre Hospitalier Ferdinand Grall, route Pencran	☎ 02 98 21 80 00
Morlaix	Centre Hospitalier des Pays de Morlaix, 15 rue Kersaint Gilly 💻 *www.ch-morlaix.fr*	☎ 02 98 62 61 60
Pont l'Abbé	Hôtel Dieu, rue Roger Signor	☎ 02 98 82 40 40
Quimper	Centre Hospitalier de Cornouaille, 14 avenue Yves Thépôt	☎ 02 98 52 60 60

Police

See general information on page 77.

Motoring

See general information on page 79.

Nightlife

This section isn't intended to be a definitive guide but gives a wide range of ideas for the department. Prices and opening hours were correct at the time of writing, but it's best to check before travelling long distances.

| Bénodet | Casino de Bénodet, Corniche de la Plage | ☎ 02 98 66 27 27 |

Games machines, English roulette, blackjack, bar and restaurant. Open daily from 10am to 3am (4am on Saturdays).

| Brest | Pub Hamilton, 2 rue de la 2ème DB | ☎ 02 98 43 32 32 |

Giant television screen, snooker and karaoke.

| | Le Sinclair, 14 rue Kéréon | ☎ 02 98 43 43 63 |

Disco.

| | Soul Food Cafe, 77 rue Auguste Kervern | ☎ 02 98 46 37 88 |

Music bar with live music every Friday and the first Saturday of the month from 9.30pm.

| | Tara Inn, Port de Commerce | ☎ 02 98 80 36 07 |

Irish pub open every day. Irish music on Tuesday evenings from 10pm and food at lunchtimes mid-week.

Le Tour du Monde, Port de Plaisance   ☎ 02 98 41 93 65
Moulin Blanc
(by the marina, just past Océanopolis)
Late bar open 11am to 1am every day.

Carhaix-   La Bohème, place du Champ de Foire   ☎ 02 98 93 31 66
Plouguer   Late bar with pool tables. Open until 1am at weekends.

Joe Sheridan's, 23 rue des Martyrs   ☎ 02 98 99 46 18
Irish bar. Open Tuesdays to Thursdays from 4pm to 3am,
Fridays 4pm to 4am, Saturdays 3pm to 4am, Sundays 5pm to
3am. Karaoke on the last Friday of each month from 10pm.

Le P'tit Bar, 26 rue des Martyrs   ☎ 02 98 93 05 43
Late bar open Tuesdays to Sundays from 11am to 1am.

Locmaria-   Restoshow, 89 route de Kerfily   ☎ 02 98 48 58 91
Plouzané   (just west of Brest)
             ✉ restoshow@wanadoo.fr
             Dinner dances and cabarets.

Morlaix   Le Dimple, Croix Rouge, Plouigneau   ☎ 02 98 63 44 16
             (directly east of the town)
             Disco open from 10pm to 5am.

Le Flash, 41 rue de Paris   ☎ 02 98 88 30 56
Disco.

Plouescat   Casino, 100 rue de Brest   ☎ 02 98 69 63 41
             Gaming machines, roulette and blackjack, bars, shows every
             weekend and restaurant open every day. Casino open from
             10am to 4am (5am Saturdays).

Quimper   Les 40èmes, 7 avenue Georges   ☎ 02 98 64 76 40
             Pompidou
             Disco.

Café des Arts, 4 rue Ste Catherine   ☎ 02 98 90 32 06
Late bar open Mondays to Fridays from 11.30am to 1am,
Saturdays and Sundays 3.30pm to 1am.

Roscoff   Casino de Roscoff, Port de Bloscon   ☎ 02 98 69 75 84
             Blackjack, roulette, games machines and restaurant. Open
             every day from 10am.

Scaër   Le Kendo, Coadigou   ☎ 02 98 57 64 25
             (on the D782, south-west of the town)
             Disco/bar.

Pets

Dog Hygiene

See general information on page 84.

Dog Training

Morlaix	Club Morlaisien du Chien d'Utilité, 75 route de Pont-Pol, Plouring-lès-Morlaix	☎ 02 98 88 29 34
Quimper	Club Canin de l'Odet, 67 chemin Toulven	☎ 02 98 54 82 26

Farriers

General	Erwan Derrien, 36ter rue Aristide Briand, Quimper	☎ 06 85 13 85 53
	Maurice Legros, Kerdianou, Moëlan-sur-Mer (based in the south-east of Quimper)	☎ 02 98 71 03 85

Horse Dentists

See general information on page 84.

Horse Feed

General	Joe Denham, la Garenne, Langonnet ✉ *lagarenne2004@yahoo.co.uk* Quality hay and haylage (preserved hay with a slightly higher protein/energy content). English speaking.	☎ 02 97 23 91 65

Horse Vets

See general information on page 85.

Identification

See general information on page 85.

Kennels & Catteries

See general information on page 85.

Pet Parlours

See general information on page 86.

Pet Travel

See general information on page 86.

Riding Equipment

Brest	Sellerie du Ponant, 4 place de la Liberté Equipment for horse and rider.	☎ 02 98 44 59 10
Kerhuon	Le Sport, Centre Commercial Leclerc	☎ 02 98 28 60 28
Morlaix	Al Likorn, 21 rue Brest ✉ *al.likorn@wanadoo.fr*	☎ 02 98 63 93 47
Quimper	Sellerie de l'Odet, 6 place 118ème RI Equipment for horse and rider.	☎ 02 98 55 08 24

SPA

Plouzané	SPA du Léon, Minou (west of Brest, near the Minou lighthouse) Open from 2 to 6pm.	☎ 02 98 48 44 06

Veterinary Clinics

See general information on page 87.

Places to Visit

This section isn't intended to be a definitive guide but gives a wide range of ideas for the department. Prices and opening hours were correct at the time of writing, but it's best to check before travelling long distances.

Animal Parks & Aquariums

Audierne	L'Aquashow d'Audierne, rue du Goyen ☎ 02 98 70 03 03 (on the coast west of Quimper, towards Pointe-du-Raz) Large aquariums with shows involving sea birds, including cormorants fishing underwater, and a 3D cinema. Open April to September daily from 10am to 7pm.	
Brest	Océanopolis, Port de Plaisance du ☎ 02 98 34 40 40 Moulin Blanc 💻 *www.oceanopolis.com* (on the coast to the east of the town) Unique in Europe, this marine complex has three zones – temperate, polar and tropical – where there are 1,000 different species and over 10,000 animals. Allow a whole day for the visit. Open April to August every day from 9am to 6pm;	

September to March Tuesdays to Saturdays from 10am to 5pm, Sundays and bank holidays from 10am to 6pm (open Mondays in the school holidays). 4- to 17-year-olds €10.50, over 17s €10; free entrance if visiting just the shops and restaurants.

Beaches & Leisure Parks

There are few beaches on the north coast of Finistère, which is predominantly rocky, although there's a small, protected bay near Brignogan (see below).

Audierne	Baie d'Audierne (south of the town) There are beaches all round this bay.
Bénodet	(directly south of Quimper) Beaches, marina, sea-front promenade and sailing school.
Brignogan	Plage des Chardons Bleus, Brignogan-Plage & Plage du Lividic (on the north coast, north-east of Brest) Across the small bay are the beaches of Pors-Meur amd Pors-Guen.
Concarneau	(south-east of Quimper) There are a number of beaches along the bays around Corncarneau.
Douarnenez	Beuzec-Cap (west of the town, towards Pointe-du-Raz) Several beaches.
La Forêt-Fouesnant	Port-la-Forêt (south of Quimper, east of Bénodet) Beach, watersports centre, playground and a marina.
Fouesnant	Mousterlin, Beg-Meil and Cap-Coz (south of Quimper, east of Bénodet) Large, fine sandy beaches.
Guilvinec	(south-west of Quimper) Beach.
Milizac	La Récré des Trois Curés, Parc de Loisirs ☎ 02 98 07 95 59 🖳 *www.larecredes3cures.fr* (north-west of Brest) A leisure park set around a lake with a miniature railway, go-karts, dodgem boats, giant water slides, a bar and snackbar

and an indoor play area. Open May and September
Wednesdays and weekends from 11am to 6.30pm; June to
August every day 11am to 7pm; rest of the year Wednesdays
and weekends 2 to 6pm. Open every day during school
holidays. Entry €9, free for those under 1m in height.

Le Pouldu   (west of Lorient)
                  Beach.

Quimper   Parc de Loisirs de Créac'h-Gwen
                  (five minutes south of the town centre towards Bénodet)
                  Lake, skate park, footpaths, playground, miniature port, water
                  complex and tennis courts.

Raguenès   (between Quimper and Lorient)
                  Beach.

Boat, Train & Wagon Rides

Boat Trips

Bénodet   Vedettes de l'Odet, 2 avenue de l'Odet,   ☎ 02 98 57 00 58
                  Vieux Port
                  🖳 www.vedettes-odet.com
                  (off the coast south of Quimper)
                  Boat trips to Iles Glénan, along the river l'Odet, sea fishing,
                  lunch cruises and trips on boats with underwater viewing
                  galleries. Cruises start at €22; lunch cruises €22 plus the meal
                  (chosen from an à la carte menu); sea fishing from €28.

Brest   Société Maritime Azenor, Port de   ☎ 02 98 41 46 23
                  Plaisance du Moulin Blanc
                  🖳 www.azenor.com
                  Boat trips around the military port and harbour and across to Le
                  Fret. Trip around the port, one and a half hours; dinner cruise
                  three and a half hours. Lunch and dinner cruises need to be
                  booked.

Chateauneuf-   Aulne Loisirs Plaisance, Site de Penn-   ☎ 02 98 73 28 63
du-Faou   ar-Pont
                  🖳 www.aulneloisirs.com
                  (south-west of Carhaix-Plouguer)
                  Electric- and petrol-engine boats for hire.

Le Conquet   Aquafaune, Le Port   ☎ 02 98 89 14 13
                  (west of Brest on the western tip of the peninsular)
                  Glass-bottomed boat making trips out to sea. Operates from
                  February to October. Tickets on sale at tourist offices in Brest
                  and Le Conquet.

Compagnie Maritime Penn-ar-Bed,   ☎ 02 98 80 80 80
Port de Commerce
🖳 *www.pennarbed.fr*
Ouessant is a small inhabited island with a *mairie* and
aerodrome. Boats depart to the island every morning. Return
crossings leave the island at 9.45am daily but at least twice a
week there's an afternoon or evening departure and there are
places to stay on the island if you miss the return!

Train Rides

Roscoff

Le Petit Train Touristique, Vieux Port   ☎ 02 98 61 12 13
A small 'train' that runs through the old streets of Roscoff, with
a commentary on buildings of interest. The trip lasts half an
hour and operates mornings and afternoons from June to
August.

Quimper

Le Petit Train de Quimper   ☎ 02 98 97 25 82
Guided tours of the town aboard this road-rolling 'train'.
Commentary available in English.

Wagon Rides

Ile d'Ouessant

Calèches du Ponant, Le Goubars   ☎ 02 98 48 89 29
(a small island just off the coast, east of Brest)
Horse-drawn rides around the island. From €12.80 per person
per hour, for four people. (See above for details of boat trips to
the island.)

Locmaria-
Berrien

Roulottes et Calèches de Bretagne,   ☎ 02 98 99 73 28
La Gare
(north-west of Carhaix-Plouguer)
Horse-drawn caravans for weekend or short week trips through
the north Finistère countryside. From €245 for a weekend.

Quimper

Calèche Promenade, 12 rue G. Sand   ☎ 02 98 95 19 69
Horse-drawn open carriage rides through the old town.

Chateaux

Concarneau

Château de Kériolet, rue de Kériolet   ☎ 02 98 97 36 50
The chateau was originally built in the 15th century but has
been added to over the centuries. Left to fall into ruin, it has
been restored since 1988. Open June to September daily from
10.30am to 1pm and 2 to 6pm (closed Saturday afternoons). 7
to 15-year-olds €3, over 15s €5.

St Vougay

Château de Kerjean   ☎ 02 98 69 93 69
🖳 *www.chateau-de-kerjean.com*
(west of Morlaix)

Chateau and park open April to mid-June Mondays and Wednesdays to Sundays from 2 to 6pm; last two weeks of June Mondays and Wednesdays to Sundays 10am to 6pm. 7 to 17-year-olds €1, over 17s €5. Guided tours available.

Trévarez   Château de Trévarez, St Goazec   ☎ 02 98 26 82 79
💻 *www.trevarez.com*
(south-east of Châteaulin)
A medieval-style chateau built in 1893 with turrets, steep slate roofs and red brick facade. Now owned by the department of Finistère. There are currently only two rooms open to the public: the library and the dining room. The old stables hold art exhibitions and various flower festivals. Set in parkland and gardens of 85ha (210 acres). Open in March Wednesdays and weekends from 2 to 5.30pm; April to June and September every day 1 to 6pm; July and August every day 11am to 6.30pm. Over 25s €4.30, 12 to 25-year-olds €3.35, under 12s free.

Churches & Abbeys

Quimper   La Cathédrale St Corentin
Open May to October daily from 9.30am to noon and 1.30 to 6.30pm; November to April 9am to noon and 1.30 to 6.30pm (closed Sunday mornings).

Miscellaneous

Carhaix-   Hippodrome de Penalan   ☎ 02 98 93 26 35
Plouguer   Trotting and steeplechase.

Morlaix   Hippodrome de Langolvas   ☎ 02 98 62 19 92
Trotting, flat racing and steeplechase.

Les Iles   A group of small islands off the western coast of Finistère
d'Ouessant-   and surrounded by reefs and strong currents. Ouessant is
et-Molène   an island of character, stone houses with painted shutters, sheep breeding and five lighthouses. There are regular boat crossing to the island (see **Boat Trips** on page 212).

Quimper   Port Miniature, boulevard de Créac'h-   ☎ 02 98 10 17 03
Gwen
Miniature port with scaled-down electric boats for children to navigate.

Museums, Memorials & Galleries

Brest   Centre d'Art Passerelle, 4 rue Charles   ☎ 02 98 43 34 95
Berthelot

This is a centre of contemporary art with exhibitions of paintings, sculptures, photographs and videos. Open Tuesdays to Saturdays from 2 to 6pm (Tuesdays until 8pm).

Le Musée des Beaux Arts, 24 rue   ☎ 02 98 00 87 96
Traverse
(in the centre of town between the river and the Hôtel de Ville)
An art gallery housing paintings from Flemish, Italian and French artists from the 17th to 20th centuries. Open Mondays and Wednesdays to Saturdays from 10am to noon and 2 to 6pm, Sundays 10am to noon. Adults €4, children free.

Musée National de la Marine, Château   ☎ 02 98 22 12 09
de Brest
🖳 www.musee-marine.fr
(in the chateau overlooking the harbour)
A maritime collection including model shops, paintings and sculptures. Open April to mid-September daily from 10am to 6.30pm; mid-September to the end of March 10am to noon and 2 to 6pm (closed Tuesdays). Adults €4.60, children €3.

Quimper   Centre d'Art Contemporain, rue du   ☎ 02 98 55 55 77
Couedic
🖳 www.le-quartier.net
Contemporary art gallery. Entry €1.50 (free on Sundays).

Musée des Beaux Arts, 40, place Saint-   ☎ 02 98 95 45 20
Corentin
🖳 www.mairie-quimper.fr/musee
A large collection of art from the 17th and 18th centuries including works by Corot and Boudin. Regular special exhibitions. Open April to mid-July and September to October Mondays and Wednesdays to Saturdays 10am to noon and 2 to 6pm; mid-July to August every day 10am to 7pm; November to March Mondays and Wednesdays to Saturdays 10am to noon and 2 to 6pm, Sundays 2 to 6pm. Closed bank holidays. Adults €4, children €2.50.

Musée de la Faïence de Quimper, 14   ☎ 02 98 90 12 72
rue JB Bousquet
🖳 www.quimper-faiences.com
Museum of earthenware and painted china. Open mid-April to mid-October Mondays to Saturdays from 10am to 6pm. 7 to 17-year-olds €2.30, over 17s €4.

Trégarvan   Musée de l'Ecole Rurale   ☎ 02 98 81 90 08
✉ musee.ecole.bretagne@wanadoo.fr
(north-west of Châteaulin)

This school was opened in 1907 and eventually closed in 1974 with only five pupils. It's now a museum with wooden benches, slate boards and an exhibitions showing the teaching methods at the beginning of the 20th century.

Parks, Gardens & Forests

General

Montagnes Noires
The 'Black Mountains' are in the centre of the department and are surrounded by wild areas and forests ideal for walking, climbing and exploring.

Parc Naturel Régional d'Armorique　☎ 02 98 68 86 33
🖳 pnr-armorique.fr
🖳 www.argol.fr.st
This regional park stretches from the coast at Camaret to Bolazec in the east. There's a discovery centre at Sizun with a renovated mill, exhibitions, aquariums, picnic area and discovery paths through the woods. Menez-Meur has an animal park with domestic and wild animals, a forest with marked trails, a picnic area, playground and tasting of regional produce. Argol has a traditional craft heritage centre including clog and basket making, spinning and wood turning. Demonstrations throughout the year include butter making and linen making.

Brest

Le Jardin des Explorateurs, rue de la Pointe
(Quartier de Recouvrance, alongside the military port)
This garden contains plant species from the four corners of the world brought back by explorers from the town. A good vantage point for views over the harbour and up to the chateau. Open mid-May to mid-September from 9am to 10pm; the remainder of the year 9am to 6pm.

Conservatoire Botanique National du　☎ 02 98 02 46 00
Stang-Alar, la route de Quimper
(alongside the route de Quimper; the entrance is south of the garden)
One of the most prestigious botanical gardens in the world with some of the rarest plants on the planet. Gardens open daily from 9am to 6pm (until 8pm in the summer). Greenhouses open July to mid-September Sundays to Thursdays from 2 to 5.30pm; mid-September to June Sundays guided tour at 4.30pm (meet at the Point Accueil).

Carhaix-
Plouguer

Parc de la Vallée de l'Hyères
Lake, arboretum (tree collection), bird observatory and playground.

Huelgoat

Arboretum du Poerop et Jardin de　☎ 02 98 99 95 90
l'Argoat, 55 rue des Cieux
🖳 www.arboretum-huelgoat.com

One of the most important botanical garden in Brittany, with trees and bushes from five continents and more than 3,000 varieties. Open Easter to mid-October every day from 10am to 6pm; rest of the year Mondays to Saturdays 10am to 5pm. Closed bank holidays.

Ploujean   Château de Suscinio   ☎ 02 98 72 05 86
✉ *efk.parcsuscinio@wanadoo.fr*
Botanical garden in the grounds of the chateau. Open January, November and December daily from 10am to noon and 2 to 5pm; February, March and October 10am to noon and 2 to 6pm; April to September every day 10am to 7pm. Closed Wednesdays in term time October to March. Adults €5, children eight and over €2, under eights free.

Roscoff   Jardin Exotique de Roscoff   ☎ 02 98 61 29 19
(on the coast north-west of Morlaix)
This garden concentrates on plants from the southern hemisphere, primarily Australia, Chile and South Africa. There are nearly 2,000 plant varieties and panoramic views over the bay of Morlaix. Open April to June, September and October every day 10.30am to 12.30pm and 2 to 6pm; July and August every day 10am to 7pm.

St Goazec   Parc et Château de Trévarez   ☎ 02 98 26 82 79
(north-east of Quimper, south-east of Châteaulin)
The parkland and formal gardens surrounding this chateau cover 85ha (210 acres) and have an exceptional collection of plants and flowers. The gardens include 400 varieties of camellia and 1,000 varieties of rhododendron and azalea. There are fountains, waterfalls, a lake, chapel and stables. The chateau is currently being restored. Open April to June and September every day from 1 to 6.30pm; July and August every day 11am to 7pm; October to March weekends, bank holidays and every day in the school holidays 2 to 6pm.

Trévarez   Château de Trévarez, St Goazec   ☎ 02 98 26 82 79
💻 *www.trevarez.com*
(south-east of Châteaulin)
A beautiful red brick turreted chateau in parkland and gardens of 85ha (210 acres). There are water gardens, animal sculptures and modern garden designs. The front of the chateau looks out over formal gardens. The old stables hold art exhibitions and various flower festivals. Open Wednesdays and weekends in March from 2 to 5.30pm; April to June and September every day 1 to 6pm; July and August every day 11am to 6.30pm. Over 25s €4.30, 12 to 25-year-olds €3.35, under 12s free.

Regional Produce

Coray   Biscuiterie Jos Peron, route de Quimper   ☎ 02 98 59 36 35

This company has been making biscuits since 1916. There's a tour and free tastings. Open March to June, September and October Mondays to Fridays for guided tours at 11am, 2pm and 3.30pm; July and August 10am, 11am, and hourly from 2pm to 5pm; November to February 11am and 2pm.

Huelgoat	Ferme de Kerohou	☎ 02 98 99 93 45

Bread making with flour milled at the farm and cooked in a wood burning bread oven. Tours on Wednesdays and Fridays at 4pm and Saturdays 6pm.

Pleyben	Chocolaterie Châtillon, 46 place Charles de Gaulle	☎ 02 98 26 63 77

See the production of fine chocolates, Florentines and biscuits. Open every day from 9am to 12.30pm and 2 to 7pm (closed Sundays November to Easter).

Plonéis	Cidre Paul Coïc, route d'Audierne, Kerscouedic	☎ 02 98 91 14 11

(just outside Quimper)
Harvesting of fruit and production and tastings of apple juice, *Pommeau*, cider and apple and rhubarb juice. Open daily.

Standing Stones & Megaliths

Brasparts	Alignement des Noces de Pierres
Brennilis	Dolmen Ti ar Boudiged
Chateauneuf-du-Faou	Tumulus d'Ar Blazennou
Pont-Menhir	Les Trois Menhirs de Pont-Menhir
St Goazec	Allée couverte de Castel Ruffel

Professional Services

The following offices have an English-speaking professional.

Accountants

Châteaulin	Fiduciaire de France, Penmez	☎ 02 98 16 14 60

Architects & Project Managers

See page 238.

Solicitors & Notaires

Carhaix-
Plouguer
Maître le Gohic, 32 bis rue des Martyrs   ☎ 02 98 93 00 50
✉ *romuald@legohic@notaires.fr*

Quimper
Maître Gautier, 3 rue Mairie   ☎ 02 98 95 01 73

Property

See general information on page 90.

Public Holidays

See general information on page 95.

Religion

Anglican Services in English

Guerlesquin
La Chapelle St Jean, Le Bourg   ☎ 02 98 78 11 01
(south-east of Morlaix on the border with Côtes-d'Armor)
English language services every Sunday at 10.30pm.

Catholic Churches

See **Religion** on page 96.

Restaurants

Brest
Délices de l'Orient, 6 rue des 11 Martyrs ☎ 02 98 43 42 28
Oriental cuisine Monday to Saturday lunchtimes, Friday and
Saturday evenings. Open Monday to Thursday evenings if
booked. Closed throughout August.

La Fleur de Sel, 15bis rue de Lyon   ☎ 02 98 44 38 65
A formal restaurant with gastronomic cuisine; menus from €19
to €35. Open Mondays to Fridays and Saturday evenings.

La Menara, 6 rue Kerfautras   ☎ 02 98 43 21 03
Moroccan and oriental cuisine. Set menu lunchtimes only,
couscous take-away lunch and evenings. Dancing shows at
weekends.

Le Taverne de Maître Kanter, 15 avenue ☎ 02 98 80 25 73
Clémenceau

Brasserie/restaurant that specialises in seafood. Open every day with service continuous from noon to midnight.

La Vatel, 23 rue Fautras   ☎ 02 98 44 51 02
💻 *www.le-vatel.com*
Gastronomic restaurant with regional cuisine and seafood. Set menus from €14 to €50 per person.

Aux Vieux Gréements, 40 quai de la   ☎ 02 98 43 20 48
Douane
(on the commercial port, just to the east of the chateau)
Speciality seafood restaurant with menus from €19.50 to €33.
Closed Sunday evenings.

Wazobanan, 6 rue Louis Pasteur   ☎ 02 98 43 61 17
Indian restaurant open every day. Take-away available.

Carhaix-
Plouguer
La Perle d'Asie, 24 avenue Victor Hugo ☎ 02 98 93 76 51
Chinese restaurant.

Châteaulin
Au Bon Accueil, avenue Louison Bobet ☎ 02 98 86 15 77
💻 *www.bon-accueil.com*
Part of a hotel, this restaurant has set menus from €14 to €42.
Regional cuisine that changes according to the season.

Morlaix
Indochine, 31 de Gaulle   ☎ 02 98 63 20 74
Indian restaurant. €8.50 lunch menu, €14 set menu and *à la carte*. Closed Tuesdays.

La Marée Bleue, 3 rampe St Melaine   ☎ 02 98 63 24 21
(off the main road through the town centre)
A small restaurant specialising in seafood with a fine wine list.
Set menus from €14 to €36.50.

Le Saïgon, 4 Venelle au Son   ☎ 02 98 62 18 03
Vietnamese and Chinese cuisine. Set menus €10 and €14.
Closed Wednesdays.

Le Sterne, Port de Plaisance, quai de   ☎ 02 98 15 12 12
Léon
(on the left hand side of the marina as you go out of the town)
A restaurant boat moored at the quay just along from the town centre specialising in seafood. No set menus; average main course €13.

Ploudalmézeau   Le Château d'Eau   ☎ 02 98 48 15 88
💻 *www.lechateaudeau.com*
(20 minutes north-west of Brest, near the coast)
Spectacular views from this bar and *crêperie* at the top of a former water tower. There's a lift and so it's accessible to

everyone. Open mid-February to mid-November daily serving continuously from noon to 10pm; rest of the year weekends and school holidays only.

Quimper   Auberge Ti Coz, 4 Hent Coz ☎ 02 98 94 50 02
Fine cuisine. Set menus from €17 to €53. Open lunchtime Sundays, Tuesdays and Wednesdays and all day Thursdays to Saturdays (all week in July and August).

Les Épices du Monde, 44 rue St Mathieu ☎ 02 98 55 30 14
Restaurant with an international wine list and cuisine.

Le Mandarin, 12bis avenue de la ☎ 02 98 90 41 84
Libération
Asian cuisine. Open every day, lunchtimes and evenings.

La Taverne de Maître Kanter, Les Halles ☎ 02 98 95 30 05
St François, 14 quai du Steir
Brasserie and seafood restaurant serving continuously from noon to midnight every day.

Rubbish & Recycling

See general information on page 97.

Schools

See general information on page 100.

Shopping

When available, the opening hours of shops have been included, but these are liable to change and so it's advisable to check before travelling long distances to a specific shop.

Architectural Antiques

Landivisiau   Nedelec, Le Drennec ☎ 02 98 68 10 69
(south-west of Morlaix)
Company specialising in the sale of reclaimed building materials.

Bakeries

See general information on page 103.

British Groceries

Carhaix-Plouguer
The Little English Shop, 21 Felix Faure   ☎ 02 98 93 61 38
Open Mondays to Saturdays from 9am to noon and 2 to 6pm.

Glomel
MacCormick's, 8 Grande Rue   ☎ 02 96 29 88 05
(just over the border into Côtes-d'Armor, east of Carhaix-Plouguer)
British and French foods. Open Mondays, Tuesdays and Thursdays to Saturdays from 9.30am to 1pm and 2 to 6pm.

Building Materials

See general information on page 103.

Chemists'

See general information on page 103.

Department Stores

Brest
Printemps, 59 rue Jean Jaurès   ☎ 02 98 44 65 65
🖥 *www.printemps.com*
Open Mondays to Saturdays from 9.30am to 7pm.

DIY

See general information on page 104.

Dress Making & Crafts

Brest
Self Tissus, Rond-point Kergaradec,   ☎ 02 98 42 19 34
ZAC Hermitage
Curtain, clothing and furnishing fabrics, craft supplies and haberdashery.

Châteaulin
Guérin, 7 rue Eglise   ☎ 02 98 86 23 90
Singer shop also selling fabric and haberdashery.

Morlaix
Aux Etoffes Morlaisiennes, 32 rue   ☎ 02 98 88 05 67
Aiguillon
Curtain and furnishing fabrics.

Kertiss, Zone Artisanale Launay,   ☎ 02 98 15 12 03
St Martin-des-Champs

Quimper
Self Tissus, ZI Hippodrome, 6 allée   ☎ 02 98 64 75 0
Docteur Piquenard6
Curtain, clothing and furnishing fabrics, craft supplies and haberdashery.

Fireplaces & Log Burners

See general information on page 104.

Fishmongers'

See general information on page 104.

Frozen Food

Brest	Picard, rue Gouesnou 🖳 *www.picard.fr*	☎ 02 98 02 12 03
	Picard, boulevard Plymouth	☎ 02 98 05 53 66
Carhaix- Plouguer	Argel Ouest, boulevard Jean Moulin	☎ 02 98 93 39 73
Quimper	Picard, 3 allée Tréqueffelec	☎ 02 98 64 35 17
	Thiriet, Centre Commercial Hyper Carrefour 🖳 *www.thiriet.fr* (by Carrefour hypermarket)	☎ 02 98 52 00 12

Garden Centres

See general information on page 105.

Hypermarkets

See **Retail Parks** on page 226 and general information on pages 105 and 108.

Key Cutting & Heel Bars

See general information on page 106.

Kitchens & Bathrooms

See general information on page 106.

Markets

Audierne	Saturday mornings
Brest	Daily market at Les Halles St Louis from 7am to 1pm and 4 to 7.30pm, Sundays 7am to 1pm
	Daily morning market Les Halles St Martin

Organic market at Les Halles de Kérinou Tuesdays from 4 to 7pm and Saturdays 8am to noon

Camaret	All-day market the third Tuesday of each month
Carhaix-Plouguer	All-day market on Saturdays
Châteaulin	All-day market on Thursdays
Cléder	All-day market on Fridays
Concarneau	Morning market on Mondays and Fridays
Douarnenez	All-day market on Mondays and Fridays
Le Faou	Tuesdays, Fridays and the last Saturday of the month
Guerlesquin	All-day market Mondays
Kerlouan	Thursday mornings, in summer only
Landerneau	All-day market on Tuesdays, Fridays and Saturdays
Landivisiau	All-day market on Wednesdays
Lannilis	All-day market on Wednesdays
Lesneven	All-day market on Mondays
Morlaix	All-day market on Saturdays
Plonévez-du-Faou	All-day market the second Friday of each month
Plougasnou	Tuesday mornings, summer only
Pont l'Abbé	All-day market on Thursdays
Quimper	There's a covered market in the centre of the town, open all year Mondays to Saturdays until 8pm, Sundays until 1pm. The market extends outside on Wednesdays and Saturdays.

Saturday morning market at Ursulines

Organic market at Kerfeunteun on Fridays from 3 to 7.30pm

Quimperlé	All-day market on Fridays
Rosscoff	Wednesday mornings at quai d'Auxerre
Scaër	Saturday mornings
St Guénolé	Friday mornings
St Pol-de-Léon	All-day market on Tuesdays
Trégunc	Wednesday mornings

Mobile Shops

See general information on page 106.

Music

See general information on page 107.

Newsagents'

See general information on page 107.

Organic Produce

Brest	Biocoop Kerbio, 3 rue Kerfautras	☎ 02 98 46 45 81
Carhaix-Plouguer	le Coop Bio, 4 rue Charles le Goff (on the right going out of the town, immediately before Intermarché) Open Tuesdays to Saturdays from 9am to 12.30pm and 2.30 to 7pm.	☎ 02 98 99 44 96

There's an organic stall in the market on Saturday mornings.

Châteaulin	Vie Nature, 4bis Grand Rue	☎ 02 98 86 37 10
Morlaix	Votre Santé Diététique, 10 place Jacobins	☎ 02 98 88 00 59
Quimper	Brin d'Avoine, 5 allée Kernénez, ZAC Créac'h-Gwen ✉ *brin.avoine@wanadoo.fr*	☎ 02 98 10 13 50

Open Mondays from 2 to 7pm, Tuesdays to Saturdays 9am to 7pm.

Passport Photos

See general information on page 108.

Post Offices

See general information on page 108.

Retail Parks

Brest

ZA Kergaradec
(on the north-east side of the town)
Shops include:
- Conforama – household electrical and furniture;
- Décathlon – sports goods;
- Leclerc – hypermarket.

Centre Iroise
(off the D789, boulevard de Plymouth, west of the town)
Shops include:
- Carrefour hypermarket   ☎ 02 98 31 77 00
  Open Mondays to Thursdays from 9am to 9pm, Fridays 9am to 10pm, Saturdays 9am to 8pm.

Morlaix

St Martin-des-Champs
(on the west side of the town)
Shops include:
- Décathlon – sports goods;
- Fabrichaise – beds and chairs;
- Géant – hypermarket;
- Joué Club – toys;
- Mondécor – carpets and furnishings;
- Les Tissus du Launay – fabric.

Quimper

Centre Gourvily
(north of the town)
Shops include:
- L'Auto Leclerc – tyre and exhaust centre;
- Chantemur – wallpaper and paint;
- Connexion – electrical goods;
- Darty – electrical goods;
- Fly – furniture and household accessories;
- Halle aux Chaussures – shoes;
- Leclerc – hypermarket   ☎ 02 98 98 50 50
  Open Mondays to Fridays from 8.30am to 8.30pm (Fridays till 9pm). The centre includes a dry cleaner's, picture framing, café, optician's, chemist's, travel agent's, instant photo developing, photo booth and heel bar.
- Loxam – equipment hire;

- Maison de la Literie – beds;
- Monsieur Meubles – furniture;
- Le Sport – sports goods;

Centre Commercial Carrefour
(south of the town centre, off boulevard Louis le Guennac)
Shops include:
- Carrefour – hypermarket   ☎ 02 98 64 16 64
  Open Mondays to Saturdays from 9am to 9pm (Fridays till
  10pm). The complex surrounding the hypermarket has 35
  shops including photography, luggage and clothes: open
  Mondays to Saturdays from 9am to 8pm.
- Feu-Vert – tyre and exhaust centre.

Second-hand Shops

See general information on page 108.

Sports Goods

See general information on page 108.

Supermarkets

See general information on page 108.

Wine & Spirits

See general information on page 109.

Sports & Outdoor Activities

The following is just a selection of the activities available, the large towns
having a wide range of sports facilities. Full details are available from the
tourist office or the *mairie*.

Aerial Sports

Ballooning

See general information on page 110.

Flying

Morlaix   Aéro Club de Morlaix, Aéroport de   ☎ 02 98 88 32 80
                   Morlaix
                   🖳 *www.morlaix.cci.fr*
                   Trial flights and flying lessons.

| Quimper | Baptêmes de l'Air | ☎ 02 98 53 04 05 |

www.quimper-tourisme.com
The tourist office organises a series of sightseeing flights over
the area. There are several options and routes with flights
available daily from May to September.

Parachuting

| General | Para Club du Nord Finistère | ☎ 02 97 60 78 69 |

Archery

| Brest | Les Archers d'Iroise, Salle Traon | ☎ 02 98 48 26 47 |

Quizac, rue A. Thomas
All welcome from eight-year-olds upwards. Contact
Mme Perrot.

| Carhaix-Plouguer | Archers du Poher, Gymnase de | ☎ 02 98 93 10 68 |

Kerampuilh, boulevard de la République
Training on Fridays from 8.30 to 10pm (first three sessions
free). Contact M. Vessier.

| Quimper | Archers de l'Odet, Penvillers Hall D, | ☎ 02 98 95 66 58 |

Parc Penvillers

Badminton

| Brest | Patronage Laïque Municipal, | ☎ 02 98 45 86 43 |

Omnisport de la Cavale Blanche, avenue
de la Libération
Contact M. Larvor.

| Carhaix-Plouguer | Club Carhaisien de Badminton, Salle | ☎ 02 98 93 73 15 |

Omnisports, Lycée, avenue de Waldkappel
Sessions throughout the week. Contact Mme Le Troadec.

| Châteaulin | Polysonnance Association, Gymnase | ☎ 02 98 86 13 11 |

Marie Curie, rue Raoul Anthony
www.polysonnance.free.fr

| Morlaix | Badminton Club des Pays de Morlaix | ☎ 02 98 88 69 64 |

✉ *tristanb@bouygtel.fr*

Boules/Pétanque

| Brest | Amicale des Pétanqueurs de Pen-ar-Créac'h, rue St Marc | ☎ 02 98 41 76 98 |

Contact M. Floch.

| Carhaix-Plouguer | Pétanque Loisirs, rue Renan | ☎ 02 98 93 26 15 |

Tuesdays and Saturdays from 2pm.

| Châteaulin | Pétanque Châteaulinoise, Terrain de Lostang | ☎ 02 98 86 13 62 |

(north of the town centre, on the west side of the river)
The club meets on Saturday mornings from 9.30 to 11.30am.

| Morlaix | Amicale Bouliste Morlaisienne, Vallée du Ty-Dour | ☎ 02 98 63 39 70 |

Climbing

| Brest | Club Omnisport Populaire Brestois, Kérichen, rue Prince de Joinville | ☎ 02 98 47 07 07 |

This club has an artificial climbing wall.

| Carhaix-Plouguer | Centre Nautique et de Plein Air du Kreiz-Breizh | ☎ 02 96 29 65 01 |

✉ *cnpakb@free.fr*

| Morlaix | Les Danseurs de Roc , Club d'Escalade du Pays de Morlaix | ☎ 02 98 72 53 04 |

✉ *anpaul@wanadoo.fr*

| St Thois | ULAMIR Aulne | ☎ 02 98 73 20 76 |

Natural and artificial climbing sites.

Cycling & Bike Hire

| Brest | Brest Iroise Cyclisme 2000 | ☎ 02 98 41 44 95 |

Road and mountain biking. Contact M. Boudinot.

| | Torche VTT, 93 boulevard Montaigne | ☎ 02 98 46 06 07 |

Bike hire.

| Carhaix-Plouguer | Union Cycliste Carhaisienne, boulevard de la République | ☎ 02 98 93 09 69 |

Cycling school for 6- to 12-year-olds and cycling groups for all
ages. Contact M. Le Guet.

| | Carhaix VTT Club | ☎ 06 74 33 65 42 |

Sunday morning mountain bike rides, departing at 9am.
Departure points change each week. Contact M. Corre.

| Châteaulin | Cyclotouristes de l'Aulne, Maison du Vélo, rue Raoul Anthony | ☎ 02 98 86 12 93 |

Rides leave from the Maison du Vélo or the tourist office.

| Chateauneuf-du-Faou | Aulne Loisirs Plaisance, Site de Penn-ar-Pont | ☎ 02 98 73 28 63 |

⌨ *www.aulneloisirs.com*
(south-west of Carhaix-Plouguer)
Traditional and mountain bikes to hire.

| Morlaix | Club Cycliste Morlaisien, St Didy, Plouigneau | ☎ 06 81 20 64 85 |

Road cycling.

| | La Bicyclette, place de l'Eglise | ☎ 02 98 48 81 34 |

Bikes for hire.

| Quimper | Cyclos et Randonneurs de Cornouaille | ☎ 02 98 64 26 57 |

Organised bike rides.

| | Torch VTT, 58 rue de la Providence | ☎ 02 98 53 84 41 |

Mountain bike hire.

Fishing

Maps are available from fishing shops and tourist offices showing local fishing waters. If there's a lake locally, permits will be on sale in nearby *tabacs* and fishing shops and at the *mairie*.

| General | Fédération Départementale de Pêche, 4 allée Loeiz Herrieu, Quimper | ☎ 02 98 10 34 20 |

This office has details of all fishing facilities in the department.

| Carhaix-Plouguer | La Gaule Carhaisienne, Kergalet | ☎ 02 98 93 03 16 |

Fishing school for beginners and those who want to develop their skills. All ages welcome. Contact M. Guenver.

| Morlaix | Club des Pêcheurs à la Mouche du Pays de Morlaix | ☎ 02 98 79 66 31 |

⌨ *www.club.bdway.com/cfly*

Football

| Brest | Football Club du Bergot, Kérédern, rue de Kergrach | ☎ 02 98 04 96 11 |

Men's and women's teams.

| | Tonnerre de Brest, Stade Petit Kerzu, rue J. Lesven | ☎ 06 61 75 72 60 |

American football club. Contact M. Deudon.

| Carhaix-Plouguer | Dernières Cartouches Carhaix, Stade Charles Pinson, 10 rue Docteur Menguy | ☎ 02 98 93 02 52 |

Teams for all ages from five-year-olds to veterans. Contact
M. Penvern.

| Châteaulin | Châteaulin Football Club, Stade | ☎ 02 98 86 38 91 |

Municipal, Juvénat, rue de Ty Carre
Training held at the stadium and Gymnase St Louis off rue de
Ty Carre.

| Morlaix | Morlaix Football Club, Stade de | ☎ 02 98 88 45 33 |

Coatserho, rue de Porsmoguer

Golf

| La Forêt-
Fousenant | Golf de Cornouaille, Manoir du | ☎ 02 98 56 97 09 |

Mesmeur
🖳 *www.golfdecornouaille.com*
(near the coast, south of Quimper)
18 holes, par 71, 5,625m. Lessons, pro shop, bar and
restaurant. Green fees €33 to €47 for 18 holes.

| Plouarzel | Golf de Brest des Abers, Kerhoaden | ☎ 02 98 89 68 33 |

🖳 *www.abersgolf.com*
(near the coast, west of Brest)
18 holes, par 70, 5,103m. Golf equipment and buggies for hire
and a driving range. Green fees from €24 to €34 for 18 holes.

Hockey

| Brest | Hockey Club 29, Espace Foucauld, rue | ☎ 02 98 47 49 25 |

de Quimper
Outdoor and indoor hockey. Contact M. Costiou.

Brest Albatros, Rinkla Stadium, place   ☎ 06 87 19 24 78
Napoléon III
Ice hockey club open to all from four-year-olds upwards.
Contact Mme Bounoure.

Patronage Laïque Guerin, Gymnase   ☎ 02 98 80 08 42
Tissot, rue Tissot
Rink and street hockey (on rollerskates).

| Carhaix-
Plouguer | Carhaix Hockey Club, Salle | ☎ 02 98 93 32 05 |

Omnisports, Lycée, avenue de Waldkappel
Roller hockey for six-year-olds and upwards. Contact
M. Hamonou.

Horse Riding

| Brest | Centre Equestre de Brest, le Questel, | ☎ 02 98 49 27 30 |

rue Pont Audemar

Riding school with dressage, indoor riding school, cross-country course and jumping ring.

Carhaix-Plouguer	Centre Equestre de Kerniguez, Vallée de l'Hyères Indoor and outdoor riding school.	☎ 02 98 93 35 44
Châteaulin	Centre Equestre du Vieux Bourg (to the west of the town centre)	☎ 02 98 16 12 49
Morlaix	Ecurie de Kerozal, Taulé (north-west of Morlaix) Lessons, pony club and hacks from one hour to full days.	☎ 02 98 72 42 23
Quimper	Centre Equestre de Kerfeunteun, 61 chemin de Penhoat Riding school, pony club, cross-country and show jumping.	☎ 02 98 64 39 38

Land Yachting

See general information on page 111.

Motorsports

Cars

General	Brittany British Car Club, Automobile House, Le Tuberie, Ercé-près-Liffré An organisation that brings together owners, collectors and enthusiasts of British cars. Regular meetings, rallies and factory visits.	☎ 02 99 68 35 53
Brest	Automobile Course de Côte Rally club. Competitors must be 18 or over, co-drivers 16 or over. Contact M. Chausson.	☎ 02 98 45 95 55

Karts

Ploumoguer	AS Karting du Finistère, Piste de Karting de Ploumoguer (near the coast west of Brest)	☎ 02 98 89 34 40
Quimper	Kart West, ZI de l'Hippdrome (opposite the Stade de Kerheuel on the east side of the town) Indoor karting on a 350m circuit. Adults' and children's karts. Open every day.	☎ 02 98 53 03 03

Motorbikes

Brest	Moto Club des Abers, Le Fouden	☎ 02 98 05 18 97

(between St Renan and Lanrivoaré)
Motocross for all ages. Contact M. Gouriou.

Carhaix-Plouguer	Moto Club des Montagnes Noire, Base de Loisirs de St Hernin Motocross and karting. Contact M. Morvan.	☎ 02 98 93 45 07
Châteaulin	Moto Club de l'Aulne, Terrain de Lein-ar-Voguer, Dinéault (west of the town)	☎ 02 98 91 86 33
Morlaix	Moto Club de la Baie de Morlaix, 8 rue Waldeck Rousseau 💻 *www.mcbm.free.fr*	☎ 02 98 63 84 43
St Hernin	Moto Club des Montagnes Noires, Pont Kervran Motocross for 6 to 18-year-olds. Office open on Tuesdays, Wednesdays, Fridays and Saturdays from 10am to noon.	☎ 02 98 93 26 95

Quad Bikes

See general information on page 112.

Paint Ball

Quimper	Quimper Paintball, 20 chemin Keraudren	☎ 02 98 52 82 27

Rollerskating

Brest	Patronage Laïque Guerin, Gymnase Tissot, rue Tissot Rink and street hockey (on rollerskates).	☎ 02 98 80 08 42
Carhaix-Plouguer	Skate park, rue St Antoine	
Châteaulin	Patinage, Gymnase Marie Curie, rue Raoul Anthony Contact M. Rouxel.	☎ 02 98 86 25 63
Morlaix	Oxyd' Roller, 46 rue des Brebis	☎ 06 60 93 40 06
	Bongo Riding Fighta, MAJ, rue Eugène Pottier Skateboarding.	☎ 02 98 88 47 10

Quimper   Parc de Loisirs de Créac'h-Gwen
                 (five minutes south of the town, towards Bénodet)
                 Skate park.

Shooting

Brest   Avenir de Brest, rue Bugeaud   ☎ 02 98 46 24 69
                 Contact M. Venn.

Carhaix-   Club de Tir du Poher, Kerborgnès   ☎ 02 98 99 13 08
Plouguer   Open Sundays from 10am to 12.30pm. Contact M. Guélard.

Squash

Brest   Squash Club de Brest, 108 rue Hoche   ☎ 02 98 02 31 64

Quimper   Moving Club de Locmarie, 19 allée   ☎ 02 98 53 18 20
                 Banellou
                 🖳 *www.centerform.fr*
                 Squash courts, indoor swimming pool, aqua-gym, weights,
                 exercise classes and cardio training.

Swimming

Brest   There are five indoor pools at Brest, all using the same
                 telephone number   ☎ 02 98 33 21 90
                 Piscine de l'Avenue Foch, avenue Foch
                 Piscine de Kerhallet, rue du Maine
                 Piscine de Recouvrance, rue de Maissin
                 Piscine de St Marc, route de Quimper
                 Piscine Ferdinand Buisson, rue Coëtlogon

Carhaix-   Espace Aqualudique du Pher, rue la   ☎ 02 98 99 39 50
Plouguer   Piscine
                 Leisure, training and paddling pools, Jacuzzi, flumes and water
                 cannons. Open every day.

Châteaulin   Piscine Municipale, Rodaven Parc   ☎ 02 98 86 06 55
                 Bilhan
                 Swimming lessons, aqua-gym and sauna. The indoor pool is
                 open from Tuesdays to Saturdays all year round (closed
                 bank holidays).

Landerneau   Aqualorn, rue Calvaire   ☎ 02 98 85 18 89
                 🖳 *www.pays-landerneau-daoulas.fr/aqualorn*
                 Water complex open every day. Indoor and outdoor pools (nine
                 in total), summer bar, garden and therapy pools.

Morlaix   Piscine Municipale, rue Eugène Pottier ☎ 02 98 88 48 70

| Quimper | Aquarive, route de Kerogan, 19 boulevard de Créac'h-Gwen | ☎ 02 98 52 00 15 |

Water complex including training pool and flume.

Tennis

| Brest | Brest Iroise Tennis Club, Centre Omnisport de la Cavale Blanche, avenue de la Libération | ☎ 02 98 45 74 16 |

Junior tennis school and competitions, all players welcome. Contact M. Lescop.

| Carhaix-Plouguer | Complexe Charles Pinson, 10 rue Docteur Menguy |

Two indoor courts.

| | Tennis Club Carhaisien, 10 rue du Docteur Menguy | ☎ 02 98 93 76 09 |

Courses Mondays to Saturdays and competitions at weekends.

| Châteaulin | Tennis Club de Châteaulin, Salle de Tennis, Grand Rue | ☎ 06 77 78 14 89 |

(behind the Stade E. Piriou, near the supermarket)

| Morlaix | Tennis Club de Morlaix, Parc des Expositions de Langolvas | ☎ 02 98 62 04 76 |

| Quimper | Tennis Municipaux, 131 boulevard de Créac'h-Gwen | ☎ 02 98 90 49 55 |

Indoor and outdoor courts.

Tree Climbing

| Brest | Arbreizh Aventure, Bois de Kéroual, Guilers | ☎ 02 98 33 18 51 |

🖥 *www.arbreizh.com*
(on the north-west side of the town)
Tree-top adventure with full safety equipment provided. There are various routes that include monkey bridges, aerial runways and rope swings. A head for heights is needed, as the routes are up to 15m (50ft) from the ground. Open weekends (every day in the school holidays) 10am to 6pm. *Crêperie* and picnic area. 4 to 6-year-olds €5, 7 to 13-year-olds €10, over 13s €15.

| Quimper | Bonobo Parc, 59 rue du Président Sadate | ☎ 02 98 53 09 59 |

Three routes including aerial runways, monkey bridges and Tarzan ropes for all the family from four-year-olds upwards. Open June to September and school holidays every day, Wednesdays and bank holidays in term time.

Walking & Rambling

Brest Patronage Laïque Cavale Blanche ☎ 02 98 85 46 43
Regular walks organised.

Carhaix- Les Marcheurs du Poher ☎ 02 98 93 70 04
Plouguer Regular walks organised including a full day walk on Sundays.
Contact Mme Le Berre.

Morlaix Association des Courses Pédestres St ☎ 02 98 88 40 35
Pol Morlaix
⌨ *www.saintpolmorlaix.com*

Quimper Cyclos et Randonneurs de Cornouaille ☎ 02 98 64 26 57
Organised walks.

Watersports

Canoeing & Kayaking

Brest Canoë Kayak Brestois, Centre Nautique ☎ 02 98 41 69 40
de Moulin Blanc, Port de Plaisance
Canoeing on the river and sea. Groups for all ages from eight-
year-olds upwards.

USAM Voile, Centre Nautique du ☎ 02 98 02 36 73
Moulin Blanc, Port de Plaisance
✉ *usamvoilebrest@wanadoo.fr*
Canoe and kayak hire.

Carhaix- Centre Nautique et de Plein Air du ☎ 02 96 29 65 01
Plouguer Kreiz-Breizh
✉ *cnpakb@free.fr*
Courses, canoe hire and rafting.

Châteaulin Kayak Club Kastellin, quai Alba ☎ 02 98 86 51 80
Training on the canal and sea.

Quimper Club de Canoë Kayak, rue du Chanoine ☎ 02 98 53 19 99
Moreau
Introductory sessions, courses and canoe hire.

Rowing

Châteaulin Aviron Châteaulinois, Coatigaor, rue ☎ 02 98 86 33 25
de Coatigaor
✉ *aviron.chateaulin@wanadoo.fr*
(north-east of the town along the west bank of the river)
Training held at Canal Bief, Port Launay.

| Quimper | Club d'Aviron de l'Odet, Base Nautique de Locmarie, 1 rue Chanoine Moreau | ☎ 02 98 90 64 16 |

Sailing

Brest   USAM Voile, Centre Nautique, rue Eugène Berest, le Moulin Blanc   ☎ 02 98 02 36 73
💻 *www.asso.ffv.fr/usam-brest*
Yacht hire and courses for individuals; sailing school from five-year-olds upwards, competitions from eight-year-olds upwards.

Fouesnant   Centre Nautique de Fouesnant-Cornouaille, 1 chemin de Kersentic   ☎ 02 98 56 01 05
(on the coast directly south of Quimper)
Sailing for all ages.

Morlaix   La Poterne du Château du Taureau, 25 rue des Fontaines   ☎ 02 98 88 57 04

Quimper   Nautisme en Finistère, 11 rue Théodore Le Hars   ☎ 02 98 76 21 31
💻 *www.nautisme-finistere.com*

Scuba Diving

Brest   Groupe Manche Atlantique Plongée, Piscine Foch, avenue Foch   ☎ 02 98 43 15 11
✉ *gmap@wanadoo.fr*

Châteaulin   Plongée, Piscine Municipale, Rodaven Parc Bilhan   ☎ 02 98 73 61 22
Meetings on Thursdays at 8pm. From 14-year-olds upwards. Contact Mme Briand.

Morlaix   Groupe Subaquatique Morlaix Trégor, 18 route de Kernéhélen, Plouézoch   ☎ 02 98 79 50 95
✉ *plongee.gsmt@free.fr*

Windsurfing

Brest   Breizh Kite, 14 rue Henri Dunant   ☎ 02 98 47 66 54

Tourist Offices

General   Comité Départemental du Tourisme du Finistère, 11 rue Théodore Le Hars   ☎ 02 98 76 20 70
💻 *www.finisteretourisme.com*

Brest

place de la Liberté   ☎ 02 98 44 24 96
💻 *www.cub-brest.fr*
💻 *www.mairie-brest.fr*
Open mid-June to mid-September Mondays to Saturdays from
9.30am to 7pm, Sundays and bank holidays 10am to noon;
mid-September to mid-June Mondays to Saturdays 9.30am to
12.30pm and 2 to 6pm (closed bank holidays).

Carhaix-
Plouguer

4 rue Brizeux   ☎ 02 98 93 04 42
💻 *www.ville-carhaix.com* 💻 *www.poher.com*
Open September to June Tuesdays to Saturdays from 10am to
noon and 2 to 5.30pm (closed Thursday mornings); July and
August Mondays to Saturdays 9am to 12.30pm and 1.30 to
7pm, Sundays and bank holidays 10am to 1pm.

The tourist office at Carhaix-Plouguer has someone who
deals with problems encountered by newcomers to the
town or area. This is part of a recent initiative in the area
and several local tourist offices are participating.

Châteaulin

Quai Cosmao   ☎ 02 98 86 02 11
                        out of season   ☎ 02 98 86 10 05
💻 *www.chateaulin.fr*
💻 *www.villedechateaulin.free.fr*
Open February to May and September to December on
Wednesdays from 2.30 to 6.30pm and Saturdays mornings;
June to August Mondays to Saturdays 2.30 to 6.30pm. These
hours are currently under review.

Morlaix

place des Otages   ☎ 02 98 62 14 94
✉ *officetourisme.morlaix@wanadoo.fr*
Open Mondays to Saturdays from 10am to noon and 2 to 6pm.

Quimper

place de la Résistance   ☎ 02 98 53 04 05
💻 *www.quimper-tourisme.com*
Open mid-March to June and September Mondays to
Saturdays from 9.30am to 12.30pm and 1.30 to 6.30pm; July
and August Mondays to Saturdays 9am to 7pm; October to
mid-March Mondays to Fridays 9.30am to 12.30pm and 1.30 to
6pm. Also open on Sundays and bank holidays in June and the
first two weeks of September from 10am to 12.45pm; July and
August 10am to 12.45pm and 3 to 5.45pm.

Tradesmen

Architects & Project Managers

General

Burrows-Hutchinson, Ploerdut   ☎ 02 97 39 45 53
✉ *burrowhutch@aol.com*

English-speaking architectural practice offering interior design, project management, building surveys and reports.

Max Lenglet, Plérin   ☎ 02 96 74 49 22
English-speaking project manager for building and renovation work, specialising in 'green' and eco-friendly buildings and materials.

Mike McCoy, Pen-ar-Vern, Bourbriac   ☎ 02 96 43 44 23
✉ *therealmccoy999@aol.com*
Bi-lingual draughtsman for architectural design and planning, renovations and septic tank applications.

View Brittany, Le Kanveze, Remungol   ☎ 02 97 60 94 57
✉ *vb.caro@wanadoo.fr*
New builds, renovation, surveys and project management. English-speaking.

Builders

General   View Brittany, Le Kanveze, Remungol   ☎ 02 97 60 94 57
✉ *vb.caro@wanadoo.fr*
New builds, renovation, surveys and project management. English-speaking.

Carpenters

See general information on page 115.

Chimney Sweeps

See general information on page 115.

Electricians & Plumbers

General   T Electrics, 5 Kerroc'h, Plougonver   ☎ 02 96 21 67 11
✉ *electrics@tiscali.fr*
English-speaking electrician. Large and small jobs and 24-hour emergency call-out.

Planning Permission

See general information on page 116.

Translators & Teachers

French Teachers & Courses

Brest   ABAAFE, 6 rue Nattier   ☎ 02 98 42 51 41
✉ *abaafe@wanadoo.fr*

(just off boulevard de l'Europe)
This organisation specialises in teaching French as a foreign language. Daytime and evening courses.

Carhaix-Plouguer	Greta, avenue de Waldkappel	☎ 02 98 93 75 77

Alison Wall   ☎ 02 98 93 77 00
✉ *alison.wall@wanadoo.fr*
Individual and group lessons held locally.

Morlaix   Eurolangue, 1 Venelle-au-Son   ☎ 02 98 88 88 09

Quimper   AVF Quimper, 5 rue Frederic le   ☎ 02 98 95 79 78
Guyader
(in the town centre near place de la Tourbie)
Office open Mondays, Tuesdays, Thursdays and Fridays from 2 to 4pm.

Collège Max Jacob, 2 rue Kerjestin-   ☎ 02 98 95 55 12
Penhars
Mixed group Mondays and Thursdays from 10am to noon, ladies' group Mondays and Thursdays from 2 to 4pm. Contact Mme Clément.

Translations

See general information on page 116.

Translators

See general information on page 117.

Utilities

See general information on page 117.

Combourg

JoTaylor

5

Ille-et-Vilaine

This chapter provides details of facilities and services in the department of Ille-et-Vilaine (35). General information about each subject can be found in **Chapter 2**. All entries are arranged alphabetically by town, except where a service applies over a wide area, in which case it's listed at the beginning of the relevant section under 'General'. A map of Ille-et-Vilaine is shown below.

Accommodation

Various tourist office websites have details of camping, B&B, *gîte* and hotel accommodation, including the following:

🖳 *www.bretagne35.com*
🖳 *www.tourisme-pays-redon.com*
🖳 *www.asteria.fr/bretagne-tourisme*
🖳 *www.bretagne-fougeres.com*

Camping

| Bain-de-Bretagne | Camping Municipal du Lac, route de Launay | ☎ 02 99 43 85 67 |

(on the east side of the lake)
Open from mid-June to September.

Combourg	Camping Municipal, le Vieux Châtel, avenue de Waldmünchen	☎ 02 99 73 07 03

Two-star campsite. Open from June to August.

Fougères	route de la Chapelle-Janson	☎ 02 99 99 40 81

(on the east of the town near the sports complex)
Open from April to October.

Redon	La Goule d'Eau	☎ 02 99 71 08 10

(south-west of the town, alongside the Vilaine river)
Open from the end of June to the first weekend in September.

Rennes	Camping Municipal des Gayeulles, rue du Professeur Maurice Audin	☎ 02 99 36 91 22

🖥 *www.camping-rennes.com*
(north-east of the city, part of a large leisure and sports area)
Three-star campsite.

St Briac-sur-Mer	Le Pont Laurin, La Vallée Gatorge	☎ 02 99 88 34 64

🖥 *www.ouest-camping.com*
Close to the town centre. Open from April to November

St Lunaire	Camping La Touesse, 171 rue Ville Géhan	☎ 02 99 46 61 13

🖥 *www.saint-malo-camping.com*
Three-star campsite next to a beach. Bar and restaurant.
Mobile homes for rent. Open from April to September.

St Malo	Camping de la Fontaine, 49 rue Fontaine aux Pélerins	☎ 02 99 81 62 62

🖥 *www.campinglafontaine.com*
Two-star campsite. Open all year. Chalets for rent.

Chateaux

St Rémy-du-Plain	Château de la Haye-d'Irée	☎ 02 99 73 62 07

🖥 *www.chateaubreton.com*
(south-east of Combourg)
An 18th century chateau, offering four bedrooms with the
possibility of side rooms for children. There's an outdoor
swimming pool, large park, fishing lake and snooker room.
Double rooms from €80. Open from Easter to October.

Le Chatellier	Château de la Foltière	☎ 02 99 95 48 32

🖥 *www.parcfloralbretagne.com*
(just north-west of Fougères)

Spacious bedrooms offering panoramic views over the
gardens. The chateau has a lift for ease of access to the
bedrooms. Double rooms from €138 per night.

Gîtes and Bed & Breakfast

General   Gîtes de France Ille et Vilaine, 107   ☎ 02 99 22 68 68
                    avenue Henri Fréville, Rennes
                    🖳 *www.gitesdefrance35.com*

                    Clévacances
                    🖳 *www.clevacances.com*

Hotels

Three hotel suggestions are listed in price order for each town, where
possible covering all budgets. Many towns have the national chains such
as those given on page 51.

Bain-de-   There are currently only two hotels in the town, listed
Bretagne   below.

                    Le Point du Jour, 55 rue Henri Fillioux   ☎ 02 99 43 85 13
                    Rooms from €35 to €42 per night.

                    La Croix Verte, 10 place Henri IV   ☎ 02 99 43 71 55
                    🖳 *www.lacroixverte.com*
                    Rooms from €41 per night. English spoken, pets accepted.
                    Closed between Christmas and the New Year.

Combourg   There are currently only two hotels in the town.

                    Aux Berges du Canal, 93 rue Nationale,   ☎ 02 99 45 21 65
                    St Domineuc
                    (10km west of the town along the D13)
                    Double rooms from €21 to €29 per night. Closed September.

                    Hôtel du Lac, 2 place Chateaubriand   ☎ 02 99 73 05 65
                    🖳 *www.hotel-restaurant-du-lac.com*
                    A two-star hotel by the lake at the foot of the chateau. Double
                    rooms from €45 to €67. Pets allowed and English spoken.
                    Closed the last two weeks in January.

                    Hôtel du Château, 1 place   ☎ 02 99 73 00 38
                    Chateaubriand
                    🖳 *www.hotelduchateau.com*
                    A three-star hotel at the foot of the Combourg chateau. Double
                    rooms from €52 to €154 per night. The hotel has a gastronomic
                    restaurant. Pets allowed.

Fougères	Hôtel de Bretagne, 7 place de la République Double rooms from €24 per night. English spoken.	☎ 02 99 99 31 68
	Le Balzac, 15 rue Nationale 🖥 *www.balzachotel.com* Double rooms from €38 to €52 per night. English spoken.	☎ 02 99 99 42 46
	Hôtel du Commerce, 3 place de l'Europe ✉ *tmk.fougeres@wanadoo.fr* Double rooms from €59 per night.	☎ 02 99 94 40 40
Redon	L'Auberge du Courée, route de Malestroit-Ploërmel Rooms from €28 per night. Closed between Christmas and New Year and the first three weeks of August.	☎ 02 99 71 22 51
	Marmotte, route de Rennes 🖥 *www.marmotte.fr* Rooms from €36 per night.	☎ 02 99 72 71 71
	JM Chandouineau, 1 rue Thiers Two-star hotel with rooms from €62 to €74 per night.	☎ 02 99 71 02 04
Rennes	Ibis, 1 boulevard Solférino Rooms from €47 to €61 per night.	☎ 02 99 67 31 12
	Novotel Rennes Alma, avenue du Canada Three-star hotel. Double rooms from €78 to €112 per night.	☎ 02 99 86 14 14
	Lecoq Gadby, 156 rue d'Antrain 🖥 *www.lecoqu-gadby.com* Four-star hotel. Double rooms from €145 to €165 per night.	☎ 02 99 38 05 55
St Malo	Le Nautilus, 9 rue de la Corne-de-Cerf 🖥 *www.lenautilus.com* Double rooms from €40 to €56 per night.	☎ 02 99 40 42 27
	Hôtel du Louvre, 2 rue des Marins 🖥 *www.hoteldulouvre-saintmalo.com* Three-star hotel. Double rooms from €73 to €107.	☎ 02 99 40 86 62
	Ajoncs d'Or, 10 rue des Forgeurs 🖥 *www.st-malo-hotel-ajoncs-dor.com* Three-star hotel. Double rooms from €95 to €115 per night.	☎ 02 99 40 85 03

Long-term Rentals

See general information on page 52.

Administration

See general information on page 52.

Banks

See general information on page 55.

Business Services

Computer Services

Bain-de-Bretagne	Services Informatique Bainais, 14 place Henri IV	☎ 02 99 43 86 94

Open Tuesdays to Saturdays from 10am to 12.30pm and 2.30 to 7pm (Saturdays till 5.30pm).

Combourg	Webcommunicom, 29 boulevard du Mail	☎ 02 99 73 13 55

Computer repairs and supplies including services at your home.

Fougères	VD Ordi, 3 rue des Feuteries	☎ 02 99 99 88 50

🖳 *www.fougeres-web.com/vd-ordi*
Software, accessories and sale and repair of computers, printers and scanners. Open Mondays 2 to 7pm, Tuesdays to Saturdays 9am to noon and 2 to 7pm.

Redon	Sigma Informatique, 6 quai de Brest	☎ 02 99 72 49 13

🖳 *www.sigma-info.com*
Computers made to order; software, advice, repairs, accessories and consumables.

Rennes	Bogbusters Rennes, 100 avenue Sergent Maginot	☎ 02 23 21 03 86

🖳 *www.bogbustersrennes.free.fr*
Computers built and sold, home repairs, consumables and accessories.

St Malo	New-Tek Informatique, 39 rue Georges Clémenceau, St Servan	☎ 02 23 52 29 60

🖳 *www.newtekinfo.com*

Computer Training

Bain-de-Bretagne	Esp@ce Multimédi@, 39bis avenue Guillotin de Corson ✉ *cybercommunebain@wanadoo.fr* (a pre-fabricated building near the swimming pool)	☎ 02 99 44 82 03

Combourg | Espace Multimédia de Combourg, place Piquette
✉ *cybercombourg@wanadoo.fr*
Training sessions on Tuesdays and Thursdays. | ☎ 02 99 73 56 38

Fougères | Point Cyb Espace Jeune Numérique, 12 rue Baron
Training for a variety of software packages and introduction to the internet. | ☎ 02 99 99 63 73

Redon | Les Mulots, 35 rue Notre-Dame
🖳 *www.lesmulots.free.fr*
Workshops twice a week for all levels. Sessions last one and a half hours, four to six people in a group. Contact M. Boureux. | ☎ 02 99 70 50 60

Rennes | Microcam, 19 rue du Pré Perché
✉ *microcam@wanadoo.fr*
Classes for youngsters and adults, beginners and intermediates. | ☎ 02 99 03 34 58

St Malo | La Souris Verte, 10 rue Val
✉ *lasouris.verte@laposte.net* | ☎ 02 99 82 50 47

Employment Agencies

See general information on page 58.

Communications

Telephone

See also general information on page 59.

Fixed Line Telephone Services

General	France Télécom 🖳 *www.francetelecom.fr* Local France Télécom shops are listed below.	☎ 1014

Fougères | Centre Commercial Carrefour, 39 boulevard de Groslay

Redon	50 Grande Rue Open Mondays from 9am to 12.30pm and 2 to 6pm, Tuesdays 9am to 12.30pm and 2.30 to 6pm, Wednesdays to Saturdays 9am to 12.30pm and 2 to 6pm.
Rennes	9bis rue le Bastard
	Centre Alma (within the Carrefour hypermarket complex, south of Rennes) Open Mondays to Fridays from 9.30am to 8.30pm, Saturdays 9am to 8pm.
	place de la République
St Malo	Centre Commercial la Madeleine (on the south-west side of town)

Internet

Broadband

See general information on page 62.

Public Internet Access

Bain-de- Bretagne	Esp@ce Multimédi@, 39bis avenue Guillotin de Corson	☎ 02 99 44 82 03
Combourg	Espace Multimédia de Combourg, place Piquette ✉ *cybercombourg@wanadoo.fr* Open Mondays from 2 to 6pm, Wednesdays 9.30am to noon, Thursdays 2 to 6pm, Fridays 9.30am to noon.	☎ 02 99 73 56 38
Fougères	Point Cyb Espace Jeune Numérique, 12 rue Baron	☎ 02 99 99 63 73
Redon	Micro Family, 5 rue Notre Dame Open Mondays to Saturdays from 9.30am to 12.30pm and 2 to 10pm.	☎ 02 99 72 35 52
Rennes	Cybernet Online, 22 rue St Georges 💻 *www.cybernetonline.com* Open Mondays from 2 to 8pm, Tuesdays to Fridays 10.30am to 8pm.	☎ 02 99 36 37 41
	Cyber Ian, 20 rue esplanade du Champ de Mars	☎ 02 99 31 71 43

✉ *cyberlan2@wanadoo.fr*
Open Mondays to Fridays from 10am to 1am, Saturdays noon
to 1am, Sundays 2.30pm to 1am.

St Malo   Cyber' Com, 26bis boulevard des   ☎ 02 99 56 05 83
             Talards
             🖥 *www.cybermalo.com*
             (near the railway station in the town centre)
             Open Mondays from 2 to 6pm, Tuesdays, Wednesdays and
             Fridays 9am to noon and 2 to 6pm, Thursdays 2 to 9pm,
             Saturdays 9am to noon and 2 to 5.30pm.

Useful Web Addresses

See general information on page 63.

Television & Radio

See general information on page 63.

Domestic Services

Bouncy Castle Hire

St Malo   LDC Animations, quai Duguay-Trouin   ☎ 02 23 52 02 59
             🖥 *www.ldcanimations.com*
             An enormous selection of inflatables (*gonflables*) for hire,
             including sumo wrestling suits, gladiator courts and children's
             play structures.

Clothes Alterations

Bain-de-   Gisel' Boutique, 1 place de la   ☎ 02 99 43 78 92
Bretagne   République

Combourg   Aux Doigts de Fée, rue Chateaubriand   ☎ 06 60 16 17 47
             Sewing, ironing and clothes made to measure. Open
             Tuesdays from 2.30 to 7pm, Wednesdays, Fridays and
             Saturdays 2 to 7pm.

Fougères   Rapid' Couture, 3 rue de l'Hospice   ☎ 02 99 94 34 56
             Repairs and alterations on fabrics and leather. Open from
             Tuesdays to Saturdays.

Redon   De Fil en Aiguille, 31 rue Notre Dame   ☎ 02 99 72 15 57
             Clothes made to measure, altered and repaired.

Rennes   Pressim Couture, 1 place Maréchal Juin   ☎ 02 99 30 50 03

Clothes repaired and altered. Open from Mondays to
Saturdays.

St Malo   Couture Service, 2 rue Danycan   ☎ 02 99 82 66 62

Crèches & Nurseries

Bain-de-   Halte-garderie, 22 rue de la Bodais   ☎ 02 99 44 80 38
Bretagne   Crèche for children from three months to six years old. Open
                  Mondays, Tuesdays and Fridays from 9am to 6pm. Contact
                  Mme Mulvet.

Combourg   Halte-garderie, 41 rue des Champs   ☎ 02 99 73 52 15

Fougères   Les Petits Lutin, 1 boulevard de Groslay ☎ 02 99 94 45 22
                  Crèche for children from three months to three years old. Open
                  Tuesdays, Thursdays and Fridays from 8.30am to noon and
                  1.30 to 5.30pm.

                  Point Infos Jeunesse, 12 rue Baron   ☎ 02 99 99 63 73
                  Baby-sitting.

Redon   Halte-garderie, Centre Social, 5 rue   ☎ 02 99 71 44 57
                  Guy Pabois
                  ✉ *cs.redon@wanadoo.fr*
                  Open Mondays from 9am to 5.30pm, Tuesdays and Fridays
                  1.30 to 5.30pm. Children from three months to three years old.

Rennes   Crèche Parentale au Clair de la Lune, 6 ☎ 02 99 14 14 71
                  avenue Gaston Berger

                  Crèche Municipale Alain Bouchart, 41 ☎ 02 99 53 90 37
                  rue Alain Bouchart

St Malo   Crèche Les Cottages, 12 avenue   ☎ 02 23 18 37 13
                  Cottages

                  Halte-garderie, 20 rue Bel Air   ☎ 02 99 19 73 47

                  Horizons Nouveaux, 2 rue Henri Barbot ☎ 06 08 68 01 81
                  Baby-sitting.

Equipment & Tool Hire

Bain-de-   B2F Location, ZA Château Gaillard   ☎ 02 99 44 80 63
Bretagne

Fougères   Matériel BTP, 16 rue des Français Libres ☎ 02 99 17 00 99
                  Sale, hire and maintenance.

| Redon | Loxam, ZI Portuaire, 108 rue de Vannes ☎ 02 99 72 12 36
💻 *www.loxam.fr* |
| Rennes | Slevmi, 22 rue Retardais, ZI route Lorient ☎ 02 99 59 14 99
💻 *www.slevmi.fr*
Full list of equipment available on the website. |
| St Malo | Loca-Mat, 22 avenue du Général Ferrié, ZI Sud ☎ 02 99 81 13 74 |
| Vezin-le- | Kiloutou, route Lorient, ZA 3 Marches Coquet ☎ 02 99 14 68 68
💻 *www.kiloutou.fr* |

Fancy Dress Hire

See general information on page 65.

Garden Services

| General | Squire Services, Kerguédalen, St Caradec-Tregomel ☎ 06 30 59 34 34
✉ *john@squirearbo.com*
Internationally qualified, English-speaking arborist for all tree, hedge and woodland work. Tree felling and crowns lifted. |
| | Jardins 35, Le Bas Courget, 35560 Noyal-sous-Bazouges ☎ 02 23 16 12 61
✉ *jardins35@wanadoo.fr*
General garden maintenance, hedge cutting and planting. English speaking. |
| Bain-de-Bretagne | Planchais Paysages, 733 rue du Tertre Gris ☎ 02 99 43 87 43 |
| Bains-sur-Oust | Bucheron Paysagiste, la Croix Verte ☎ 02 99 71 00 08
(just north of Redon)
Garden design and maintenance, tree surgery, fences and walls. Annual maintenance contracts negotiable. |
| St Aubin-du-Cormier | Les Jardins du Couesnon, ZA de Chédeville ☎ 06 81 43 99 76
(mid-way between Fougères and Rennes) |

Launderettes

| Combourg | Lavomatique, rue des Sports ☎ 02 99 73 13 07
Open every day from 9.30am to 7pm. |

Redon	Le Lavoir Breton, 8 place Charles de Gaulle Open every day from 7am to 10pm.	☎ 02 99 72 38 97
Rennes	156 rue Fougères Open every day. Machines take up to 16kg.	☎ 06 09 66 43 72
St Malo	Agramatic, 19 rue Bas Sablons	☎ 02 99 82 14 08

Marquee Hire

Le Rheu	Rance Chapiteaux, 36bis Route Nationale (on the west side of Rennes) Marquees and furniture for hire.	☎ 02 99 14 63 70
St Malo	Loca-Mat, 22 avenue Général Ferrié, ZI Sud 💻 www.loca-mat.com Marquees, furniture, dinner services, etc.	☎ 02 99 81 13 74

Party Services

See general information on page 66.

Septic Tank Services

Bain-de-Bretagne	Arnaud Guiheux, rue Hippolyte Fillioux	☎ 06 03 57 20 76
Redon	Ent. Havard, Les Chesnaux, St Nicolas-de-Redon	☎ 02 99 72 75 93
St Brice-en-Cogles	SAVB, Le Grand Frontigné Empting, unblocking and cleaning of septic tanks.	☎ 02 99 98 69 69

Entertainment

Cinemas

Bain-de-Bretagne	Cinéma, avenue Guillotin de Corson Films shown at 9pm from Fridays to Sundays.	☎ 02 99 43 97 87
Combourg	Cinéma Chateaubriand, rue Malouas 💻 www.cine35.com	☎ 02 99 73 23 41
Fougères	Le Club, 12 rue de Bonabry	☎ 02 99 99 01 79

Redon	Cinéfil Manivel Cinéma, rue Thiers	☎ 02 99 72 28 20

💻 *www.cinemanivel.fr*
(facing the old port)

Rennes There are 11 cinemas in the city, including:

	Cinéma Gaumont, 8 quai Duguay Trouin	☎ 02 99 31 57 92

💻 *www.gaumont.fr*

Cinéma l'Arvor, 29 rue d'Antrain ☎ 02 99 38 78 04
💻 *www.cine35.com*
Art cinema frequently showing films in English.

St Malo Le Vauban, 10 boulevard de la Tour ☎ 08 92 68 69 21
d'Auvergne, Rocabey
💻 *www.cine35.com*
Five-screen cinema.

English Books

See **Libraries** on page 258 and general information on page 68.

Festivals

There are many festivals in this department, and just a small selection is detailed here. Further details are available from tourist offices. All events are annual unless otherwise stated.

April Le Chatellier
Festival du Printemps, Parc Floral de ☎ 02 99 95 48 32
Haute-Bretagne
Flower festival; rhododendrons and other hardy plants.

May St Malo
Marché aux Fleurs ☎ 08 25 16 02 00
Two day flower festival and market. Held around the middle of May.

St Malo
Fête du Nautisme ☎ 08 25 16 02 00
💻 *www.station-nautisme-saint-malo.com*
Nautical festival.

June Le Chatellier
Festival d'Eté, Parc Floral de Haute- ☎ 02 99 95 48 32
Bretagne
Summer flower festival.

Combourg
Fête de la Musique   ☎ 02 99 73 13 93
Music festival.

Summer   Redon
Les Mercredis du Grand Site Naturel   ☎ 02 99 91 23 52
Every Wednesday throughout July and August there are
concerts, films, musicals and fairy-tale recitals.

Rennes
Les Festivales de l'Orgue   ☎ 02 99 67 11 11
A series of concerts and organ recitals throughout July
and August.

Rennes
Quartiers d'Eté   ☎ 02 99 67 11 11
Festival of concerts, films, games and shows for youngsters.

July   Bains-sur-Oust   ☎ 02 99 91 68 01
Fête de l'Ile aux Pies
Walking and boat races, firework displays, evening dances,
boules competitions and food.

Fougères
Festival Voix des Pays   ☎ 02 99 94 41 39
Held in Château Fougères. Concerts by artists from around
the world.

Redon
Les Vendredis du Port   ☎ 02 99 71 06 04
Entertainment at the old port on Friday evenings at the end
of July.

Redon
Festival des Folliards   ☎ 02 99 72 17 46
A weekend of concerts, theatre, street entertainment
and games.

Rennes
Cesson-Sévigné   ☎ 02 99 67 11 11
International dance festival at the beginning of July.

Rennes
Les Soirées du Thabor   ☎ 02 99 67 11 11
Shows and concerts of traditional Breton music and
dance. Wednesday evenings in July and the beginning
of August.

St Malo
Folklores du Monde   ☎ 02 99 40 42 50
International folk festival.

August   Combourg
              Semi-Marathon   ☎ 02 99 73 13 93

              Grand Fougeray
              Fête Médiévale   ☎ 02 99 08 40 19
              A medieval festival held at the Duguesclin tower. Includes
              jugglers, musicians, flame throwers, horsemen and
              military camps.

              Louvigne-de-Bais   ☎ 02 99 49 00 20
              La Fête du Cheval et du Chien
              Horse and dog festival.

              Martigné Ferchaud
              Les Etincelles Aquatiques   ☎ 02 99 47 83 83
              A spectacular firework display on the Etang de la Forge.

Autumn   Rennes
              Fête des Confitures, La Chapelle des   ☎ 02 99 67 11 11
              Fougeretz
              Festival of jam and preserves.

              Rennes
              Fête du Jardinage   ☎ 02 99 67 11 11
              Gardening show.

September   Fougères
              Les Angevines   ☎ 02 99 94 12 20
              Large festival held the first weekend of September. Fun fair,
              procession of flower decked floats, waiter race, cycle race
              and fireworks.

October   Fougères
              Le Pommé   ☎ 02 99 94 12 20
              The making of the local apple- and cider-based jam. All the
              locals meet to help in the production, which simmers in large
              copper pans for 24 hours. The opportunity is used to party, eat
              and drink.

              Peillac
              Fête des Fruits de l'Automne   ☎ 02 99 91 27 06
              A festival to celebrate the harvest and the fruits of the season.
              Food and traditional music.

Redon
Foire Teillouse et Bogue d'Or   ☎ 02 99 71 45 40
Festival of music, singing and folklore traditions.

St Malo
Quai des Bulles   ☎ 08 25 16 02 00
🖳 *www.quaidesbulles.com*
Cartoon festival at the end of the month.

November   Rennes
                Jazz à l'Ouest   ☎ 02 99 67 11 11
                Jazz festival involving European and American performers.

Libraries

Bain-de-   Médiathèque Municipale, 19 rue de   ☎ 02 99 44 86 55
Bretagne   l'Hôtel de Ville
                Open Mondays and Saturdays from 10am to 12.30pm,
                Wednesdays 10am to noon and 2.30 to 6pm, Thursdays 4 to
                6pm (5.30pm in July), Fridays 4 to 6.30pm (5.30pm in July).
                Closed the first two weeks of August. This library has a
                selection of English books.

Combourg   Place Piquette   ☎ 02 23 16 47 73
                Open Tuesdays from 4.30 to 6.30pm, Wednesdays 10am to
                noon and 2 to 6.30pm, Fridays 4 to 5.30pm, Saturdays 2 to
                6pm. There's a small selection of English books.

Fougères   Bibliothèque, 2 rue Pommereul   ☎ 02 99 94 88 50
                Open from September to June Mondays and Tuesdays from 2
                to 6.30pm, Wednesdays and Fridays 10am to noon and 2 to
                6.30pm, Saturdays 10am to 12.30pm and 2 to 5pm; July and
                August Mondays to Wednesdays and Fridays 2 to 6.30pm,
                Saturdays 10am to 12.30pm. This library has a selection of
                English and bilingual books.

Redon   Bibliothèque Municipale, rue Etats   ☎ 02 99 71 29 38
                Open Tuesdays and Thursdays from 4 to 6pm, Wednesdays
                10am to noon and 2 to 6pm, Fridays 4 to 7pm, Saturdays 10am
                to 1pm and 2 to 6pm. This library has a few shelves of English
                books under the heading '400, Langue'.

Rennes   There are 14 libraries in the city; the following library has
                some English books.

                Bibliothèque Municipale, 1 rue de la   ☎ 02 99 87 98 98
                Borderie
                🖳 *www.bm.rennes.fr*

Open Mondays, Tuesdays, Thursdays and Fridays from 1.30 to 6.30pm, Wednesdays and Saturdays 10.30am to 12.30pm and 1.30 to 6.30pm.

St Malo   Bibliothèque, 5 rue André Désilles   ☎ 02 99 40 90 93
Open Tuesdays, Wednesdays and Fridays from 10am to noon and 2 to 6pm, Saturdays 10am to noon and 2 to 5pm. There's a small selection of English books.

Theatres

Redon   Théâtre du Pays de Redon, place du   ☎ 02 99 71 09 50
            Parlement
This theatre has a full calendar of events including plays, dance shows, films and concerts.

Rennes   Opéra de Rennes, place de la Mairie   ☎ 02 99 78 48 78
            💻 *www.opera-rennes.fr*

            Théâtre National de Bretagne, 1 rue St   ☎ 02 99 31 12 31
            Hélier
            💻 *www.theatre-national-bretagne.fr*
Temporarily transferred to14 rue Guy Ropartz during building work.

St Malo   Le Théâtre, 6 place Bouvet, St Servan   ☎ 02 99 81 62 61
            💻 *www.theatresaintmalo.com*

Video & DVD Hire

See general information on page 68.

Leisure

This section isn't intended to be a definitive guide but gives a wide range of ideas for the department. Prices and opening hours were correct at the time of writing, but it's best to check before travelling long distances.

Arts & Crafts

Bain-de-   Familles Rurales, 22 rue de la Bodais   ☎ 02 99 43 75 98
Bretagne   Courses for adults and teenagers.

Combourg   Lynn Benson, la Quévinaye, Bonnemain ☎ 02 23 16 04 16
            (just outside the town)
            British lady who gives individual lessons and gives advice and guidance on work done.

Fougères	Ecole de Dessin et d'Arts Plastiques ☎ 02 99 94 11 13 Fougères Communauté, Ecole de Dessin Couvent des Urbanistes, rue des Urbanistes (on the north side of the town centre, opposite the cemetery) 18 courses and workshops for children and adults.
Redon	Amicale Laïque, 1 cours Clémenceau ☎ 02 99 71 46 16 Classes on Tuesdays and Thursdays from 2 to 5.30pm. Contact Mme d'Hocker. Quilt en Pays de Redon ☎ 02 99 72 54 05 Patchwork group. Contact Mme Trochet.
Rennes	MJC, 18 rue des Plantes ☎ 02 99 87 49 49 🖳 *www.grand-cordel.com* Various courses for all ages, from young children.
St Méloir-des- Ondes	Atelier du Verre, 4 rue Radegonde ☎ 02 99 89 18 10 🖳 *www.idverre.net/durand-gasselin* (just inland, directly east across the peninsula from St Malo) Glass blowing workshop with demonstrations and courses available.
St Malo	Atelier d'Arts Plastiques et Décoratifs, ☎ 02 99 56 20 79 9 avenue Roger Salengro Drawing, painting and sculpture. Open all year with courses on Wednesdays and Saturdays.

Bowling

Rennes	Bowling Alma Loisirs, avenue Canada ☎ 02 99 50 65 53 (on the retail park south of the city at the junction of the N136 and N137) Bar, pool tables and bowling. Open Mondays from 2pm to 2am, Tuesdays and Wednesdays 11am to 2am, Thursdays 11am to 3am, Fridays 11am to 4am, Saturdays 2pm to 4am and Sundays 3pm to 1am.

Bridge

Combourg	Centre Culturel, place Piquette ☎ 02 99 73 32 80 Contact Mme Hubert.
Fougères	Bridge Club Fougères, 7bis rue le ☎ 02 99 99 23 81 Bouteiller Sessions on Thursdays and Fridays from 2pm, tournaments Mondays 1.45pm and Wednesdays 8.15pm.
Redon	L'Amical Laïque, 1 cours Clémenceau ☎ 02 99 71 20 93 Contact M. Landais.

| Rennes | AVF Rennes, 45 rue de St Malo | ☎ 02 99 31 80 37 |

Children's Activity Clubs

| Bain-de-Bretagne | Espace Jeux, Familles Rurales, 22 rue de la Bodais | ☎ 02 99 43 99 98 |

Play group for children from three months to six years old on Wednesdays from 9.30am to noon. Contact Mme Dudouet.

| Fougères | Le Rencontre, 38 avenue de Normandie | ☎ 02 99 99 03 26 |

This is a type of youth club where 11 to 20-year-olds are welcome to play table football, pool, table tennis and other games. There's an area to do homework and various games and activities are organised. Open during term time every day from 4pm (2pm on Wednesdays), Saturdays 2 to 7pm; during school holidays Mondays to Saturdays from 2pm (Fridays 4pm).

| Redon | Centre de Loisirs, Maison de l'Enfance, rue Guy Pabois | ☎ 02 99 71 44 96 |

Activities organised for 2 to 12-year-olds after school, all day on Wednesdays and during the school holidays.

| Rennes | Auberge de Jeunesse, 10 Canal St Martin | ☎ 02 99 33 22 33 |

💻 *www.fuaj.org*
Website available in English.

| St Malo | Centre de Vacances de l'Aurore, Manoir de la Goëletrie | ☎ 02 99 81 91 23 |

💻 *www.cva-asso.com*
Activities all year.

Choral Singing

| Bain-de-Bretagne | Le Chœur du Lac | ☎ 02 99 43 96 04 |

Contact Mme Blouin.

| Combourg | Chorale Paroissiale, Sainte Cécile | ☎ 02 99 73 08 21 |

Parish choir. Contact M. Alexandre.

| Fougères | Espérance de Fougères, 1bis rue Lebouteiller | ☎ 02 99 94 50 05 |

Voice workshops. Contact M. Bodereau.

| Redon | L'Amicale Laïque, 1 cours Clémenceau | ☎ 02 99 71 16 00 |

Women's and junior choirs.

| Rennes | Mille et Une Voix, 25 rue Gallouëdec | ☎ 02 99 38 53 20 |

✉ *milletunevoix@wanadoo.fr*
Group for 12 to 25-year-olds.

Circus Skills & Magic

Fougères   Espérance de Fougères, 1bis rue   ☎ 02 99 99 25 81
Lebouteiller
Open to all ages from six-year-olds upwards. Skills include acrobatics, juggling, clowning and monocycle riding. Contact Mme Houdusse.

Rennes   Centre des Arts du Cirque "Bing Bang   ☎ 02 99 32 45 24
Circus", 12bis rue Bernard Palissy
✉ *bingbang.circus@free.fr*
Circus skills for all ages.

Dancing

Combourg   Centre Culturel, place Piquette   ☎ 02 99 73 34 70
Various dance classes.

Ecole de Danse Classique Coppélia,   ☎ 06 87 30 13 26
Centre Culturel, place Piquette
Ballet.

Fougères   Espérance de Fougères, 1bis rue   ☎ 02 99 94 40 11
Lebouteiller
Modern dance, ballroom and Latin American, rock, African, Brazilian, country and tap.

Redon   Centre de Danse, 20 rue Guichardaie   ☎ 02 99 72 70 43
Ballet, jazz and keep-fit lessons. Contact Mme Paindessour.

Rennes   Académie de Danse Art Corps, Jeune   ☎ 02 99 30 20 54
Ballet de Bretagne, 15 rue St Hélier
✉ *lydiadewismes@hotmail.com*
Ballet and jazz for five-year-olds to adults.

Maison de Quartier Francisco Ferrer, 40   ☎ 02 99 22 22 60
rue Montaigne
✉ *mqff@wanadoo.fr*
Ballroom and Latin American dancing.

St Malo   Tempo Danse, 39 rue Argenteuil   ☎ 02 99 81 90 57
Individual or group lessons in rock, salsa and Latin American.

Drama

Bain-de-   Les Troubadours   ☎ 06 62 14 92 85

Bretagne — Theatre group for the over 15s. Rehearsals once a week for modern and traditional productions. Also opportunities for those interested in set design, costumes and lighting. Contact Mme Guillaume.

Combourg — La Chateaubriand, Section Théâtre ☎ 02 23 16 14 67
Contact Mme Duval.

Fougères — Ath'Liv Atelier du Livre Vivant, 38 rue ☎ 02 99 99 49 10
des Jardins
Groups for children, teenagers and adults.

Redon — Théâtre la Mouette ☎ 02 99 72 70 69
Amateur drama group. Contact Mme Ouvrard.

Rennes — Compagnie Légitime Folie, 135bis ☎ 02 99 51 99 29
boulevard Jacques Cartier
✉ *legitime-folie@wanadoo.fr*
Drama groups for all ages.

St Malo — Productions du Dauphin, 6 rue Grout ☎ 02 99 40 18 30
de St Georges

Dress Making

Bain-de-
Bretagne — Familles Rurales, 22 rue de la Bodais ☎ 02 99 43 80 19
This organisation runs workshops once or twice a month.
Contact Mme Briand.

Fougères — Centre Social, 1 boulevard de Groslay ☎ 02 99 94 45 22
🖳 *www.facsfougeres-centresocial.org*
Dress making, knitting and embroidery.

Redon — Les Ciseaux Magiques ☎ 02 99 72 30 13
Contact Mme Martel.

Rennes — Atelier de Marine, 10 rue Garigliano ☎ 02 23 30 87 02

Flower Arranging

Bain-de-
Bretagne — Espace Véréal, avenue du Général ☎ 02 99 43 92 56
Patton
Group meets one a month, beginners welcome. Contact
Mme Bouvet.

Fougères — Espérance de Fougères, 1bis rue ☎ 02 99 99 25 81
Lebouteiller
Contact Mme Houdusse.

Redon	Société d'Horticulture du Pays de Redon Contact M. Youinou.	☎ 02 99 71 34 81
Rennes	Centre Socio-Culturel des Longs Prés, rue des Longs Prés ✉ *leslongspres@free.fr* Two-hour classes once a month (term time only).	☎ 02 99 38 43 86

Gardening

Redon	Société d'Horticulture du Pays de Redon ☎ 02 99 71 34 81 Meetings, exchanges, visits to natural sites and a flower arranging group. Contact M. Youinou.	
Rennes	Société d'Horticulture d'Ille et Vilaine, 6 rue du Général Nicolet	☎ 02 99 50 90 00

Gym

Bain-de-Bretagne	Gymnastique Volontaire, Salle Omnisports, rue du Semnon Classes on Mondays and Thursdays. Contact Mme Gahier (after 6pm).	☎ 02 99 43 96 40
Combourg	Gymnastique Volontaire Contact M. Chevalier.	☎ 02 99 73 33 30
Fougères	Sylphide Forme Step, aerobic, stretching, cardio and toning classes. Held at Cosec de la Chattière, boulevard des Déportées and Salle Raoul II, place Raoul II. Contact Mme Gilles.	☎ 02 99 94 03 47
Redon	Gym pour les Femmes Women's classes held at Salle des Chaffauds, Ecole Primaire, 13 avenue du Pèlerin. Men's classes held at Salle Lucien Poulard, rue Lucien Poulard. Contact Mme Lucas.	☎ 02 99 71 10 47
Rennes	Club Moving, 36 boulevard de la Liberté 🖳 *www.moving-rennes.fr*	☎ 02 99 78 30 31
St Malo	Côte d'Emeraude, 9 rue de Tourville Contact Mme Pelloille.	☎ 02 99 56 42 91

Gyms & Health Clubs

Bain-de-Bretagne	Cabinet de Kinésithérapie, rue du Pavé Part of the physiotherapy clinic.	☎ 02 99 43 78 13

Fougères	Energym, 158 rue de Laval ☎ 02 99 94 92 75

Weights, cardio training, gym classes and sauna. Open Mondays, Tuesdays, Thursdays and Fridays from 9.30am to 1.30pm and 3 to 8pm, Wednesdays 3 to 9pm, Saturdays 9.30am to 12.30pm.

Rennes	Club Moving, 36 boulevard Liberté ☎ 02 99 78 30 31

💻 *www.moving-rennes.fr*

Cardio, weights, exercise classes, swimming pool, aqua-gym, beauty salon and sauna. Open every day.

St Malo	Thermes Marins, Grande Plage du ☎ 02 99 40 75 33

Sillon, 100 boulevard Hébert

💻 *www.thalassotherapie.com*

An assortment of water treatments, aqua-gym, weights, cardio-training and fitness centre.

Ice Skating

Rennes	Le Blizz, 8 avenue Gayeulles ☎ 02 99 36 28 10

(north-east of the city centre)

Under 16-year-olds €5.80, others €6.90, inclusive of skate hire.

Music

Bain-de-Bretagne	Ecole de Musique Intercommunale, ☎ 02 99 43 83 37

Centre Culturel du Clos Loisel, rue Hippolyte Filliouse

Individual lessons adapted to each pupil and an extensive range of instruments taught.

Combourg	Syndicat Intercommunal de Musique ☎ 02 99 68 08 80

Contact M. Delarose.

Fougères	Ecole de Musique du Pays de Fougères, ☎ 02 99 94 37 92

Centre Culturel des Urbanistes, rue des Urbanistes

Introduction to music, workshops and individual instruction. Over 20 instruments taught and five orchestras.

Redon	Ecole de Musique du Pays de Redon, ☎ 02 99 71 11 99

boulevard Bonne Nouvelle

Various workshops for adults and youngsters including jazz, African percussion, choir and instruments such as violin, clarinet, guitar and flute.

Rennes	Studio Variétés et Spectacles, 118 ☎ 02 99 63 07 56

boulevard de Metz

Piano and guitar; group and individual classes.

| St Malo | Ecole de Musique de la Côte d'Emeraude, 94 boulevard St Michel des Sablons | ☎ 02 99 89 41 91 |

Photography

| Bain-de-Bretagne | Atelier Photo, Messac | ☎ 02 99 34 74 44 |

| Fougères | Fougères Déclic Photo, 12 rue de Bonabry | ☎ 02 99 99 67 58 |

Meetings every Tuesday from 8.30 to 10.30pm. Contact M. Brandily.

| Rennes | Maison de Quartier de Villejean, 2 rue de Bourgogne | ☎ 02 99 59 04 02 |

✉ *mq.villejean@wanadoo.fr*

Scouts & Guides

| Redon | Scouts et Guides de France du Pays de Redon | ☎ 02 99 71 84 51 |

✉ *hmh.degres@libertysurf.fr*
Meetings every fortnight. Open to boys and girls from 8 to 19. Contact M. & Mme Degrés.

| Rennes | Scouts et Guides de France, 45 rue de Brest | ☎ 02 99 14 35 35 |

Social Groups

Town Twinning

| Fougères | Comité de Jumelage, la Mairie, 2 rue Porte Léonard | ☎ 02 99 94 88 00 |

Twinned with Ashford in England.

| Redon | Comité de Jumelage de Redon | ☎ 02 99 71 41 37 |

✉ *comite.jumelage-redon@laposte*
Twinned with Andover in England. Contact M. Couannault.

| Rennes | Comité de Jumelage | ☎ 02 99 28 55 55 |

Twinned with Exeter in England.

Welcome Groups

| Redon | La Maison d'Accueil du Pays de Redon | ☎ 02 99 72 14 39 |

| Rennes | AVF Rennes, 45 rue de St Malo | ☎ 02 99 31 80 37 |

| St Malo | AVF, Salle du Cavalier, place du Québec | ☎ 02 99 40 97 41 |

💻 *www.avfsaintmalo.info*
(in the Intra Muros area on the northern tip of the town)
Open Mondays to Fridays in the afternoon. Closed during school holidays.

Spas

| Bain-de-Bretagne | SPA de Balleroy, 6 rue Verdun | ☎ 02 31 21 61 37 |

Health club with sauna, cardio, beauty treatments, pools, Jacuzzi. €18 entry, swimming hats compulsory. Open Mondays, Tuesdays, Thursdays and Fridays from 9am to 9pm, Wednesdays 10am to 9pm, weekends 10am to 7pm.

| St Grégoire | Aquatonic, route de St Malo | ☎ 02 99 23 78 77 |

💻 *www.aquatonic-rennes.com*
Thalassotherapy is treatment using the healing properties of seawater to regenerate, tone and re-balance the body's system. Various packages include fitness, aerobics and aqua-gym courses. Standard admission is to the Turkish baths, spa pool and Jacuzzi.

| St Malo | Thermes Marins, Grande Plage du Sillon, 100 boulevard Hébert | ☎ 02 99 40 75 33 |

💻 *www.thalassotherapie.com*
An assortment of water treatments, with six swimming pools, 80 treatment rooms and fully qualified staff to give a variety of beauty and health treatments.

Stamp Collecting

| Fougères | Club Philatélique du Pays de Fougères, Centre Culturel des Urbanistes, rue des Urbanistes | ☎ 02 99 97 80 09 |

Meetings held the second Sunday of the month from 9.30 to 11.30am. Contact M. Garnier.

| Redon | La Timb'al, l' L'Amicale Laïque, 1 cours Clémenceau | ☎ 02 99 71 24 67 |

Meetings on the second Sunday of each month. Contact M. Michel.

| Rennes | Société Philatélique de Rennes, 22 rue de Brest | ☎ 02 99 33 07 44 |

💻 *www.spr.asso.fr*

Yoga

| Bain-de-Bretagne | Association Bainaise, Salle de Danse, avenue Guillotin de Corson | ☎ 02 99 43 96 96 |

	Group classes afternoons and evenings. Contact Mme Dezier.	
Combourg	Yoga & Sophrologie Contact Mme Erussard.	☎ 02 99 73 03 09
Fougères	Bleu Soleil, Salle Raoul II, place Raoul II Groups for youngsters, beginners, expectant mothers and athletes. Contact Mme Gaigne.	☎ 02 99 99 90 48
Redon	Union Redonnaise de Yoga Contact Mme Le Grin.	☎ 02 99 71 47 67
Rennes	Ecole de Yoga de la Tour d'Auvergne, 8 passage du Couëdic ✉ *j.leboucher@netcourrier.com*	☎ 02 99 55 02 25
St Malo	AS Jeanne d'Arc, 17 boulevard Gouazon	☎ 02 99 19 82 19

Medical Facilities & Emergency Services

Ambulances

See general information on page 72.

Doctors

English-speakers may like to contact the following doctors:

Bain-de- Bretagne	Maison Médicale, 17 rue Croix de Pierre	☎ 02 99 43 70 19
	Duty doctor evenings and weekends	☎ 02 99 92 36 94
	Duty doctor after midnight	☎ 15
Combourg	Dr Gilles Fouillen, 12 rue de la Mairie	☎ 02 99 73 07 65
Fougères	Groupe Médical Ambroise Paré, 3 rue Albert Durand	☎ 02 99 94 57 57
	Duty doctor	☎ 02 99 94 17 17
Redon	Dr Hassib-Pison, 22 avenue Gare	☎ 02 99 71 11 39
Rennes	Maison Médicale, 9 rue Frédéric Mistral	☎ 02 99 50 60 58
	Duty doctor evenings and weekends	☎ 02 23 30 33 33
St Malo	Groupe Médical Charcot, 36 rue Le Pomellec	☎ 02 99 81 61 14

Emergencies

See general information on page 73.

Fire Brigade

See general information on page 76.

Health Authority

Bain-de-Bretagne	La Mairie, 21 rue Hôtel de Ville There's a CPAM representative here on Tuesdays from 9am to noon and 2 to 3pm.	
Fougères	3 avenue François Mitterrand	☎ 02 99 94 59 70
Redon	CPAM, rue Chaffauds	☎ 08 20 90 41 74
Rennes	CPAM d'Ille et Vilaine, 7 cours des Alliés 🖥 *www.rennes.ameli.fr* The regional office. Open Mondays to Fridays from 8am to 5pm.	☎ 08 20 90 41 74
	CPAM, Centre Renée Prévert, 15 rue Renée Prévert There's a CPAM representative here the third Wednesday of the month from 2 to 3.30pm; appointments only.	
	CPAM, 108 avenue Général Leclerc There's a CPAM representative here on Mondays, Wednesdays and Thursdays from 9.30am to noon.	☎ 02 99 33 39 00
St Malo	CPAM, 10 avenue Jean Jaurès	☎ 08 20 90 41 74

Hospitals

All the following hospitals have an emergency department unless otherwise stated.

Bain-de-Bretagne	Hôpital St Thomas de Villeneuve, 2 rue Hippolyte Fillioux No emergency department.	☎ 02 99 43 71 40
Dinard	Hôpital Arthur Gardiner, 1 rue Henri Dunant No emergency department.	☎ 02 99 16 88 88
Fougères	Centre Hospitalier, 133 rue de la Forêt	☎ 02 99 17 70 00

Redon	Centre Hospitalier de Redon, 8 avenue Etienne Gascon	☎ 02 99 71 71 71
Rennes	Centre Hospitalier Régional et Universitaire (CHRU), Hôpital Pontchaillou, 2 rue Henri Le Guilloux	☎ 02 99 28 43 21
St Malo	Centre Hospitalier Brussais, 1 rue de la Marne	☎ 02 99 21 21 21
Vitré	Hôpital, 30 route de Rennes	☎ 02 99 74 14 14

Police

See general information on page 77.

Motoring

See general information on page 79.

Nightlife

This section isn't intended to be a definitive guide but gives a wide range of ideas for the department. Prices and opening hours were correct at the time of writing, but it's best to check before travelling long distances.

| Combourg | Come Back Café, 6 place des Déportés | ☎ 02 99 73 33 90 |

Games room and pool tables. Open until around midnight.

| Fougères | Le Cactus, 51 boulevard Jean Jaurès | ☎ 02 99 94 51 82 |

(just off the place de la République)
Open Tuesdays to Saturdays from 11am to 1am. Themed evenings throughout the year and karaoke the first Sunday of the month from 5pm.

Le Coquelicot, 18 rue de Vitré ☎ 02 99 99 82 11
Cafe/concert bar open from Tuesdays to Saturdays.

Kesington Club, 7 rue des Feuteries ☎ 02 99 94 34 54
Pool and snooker tables, video games and a giant screen.

Le Saxo, 164 rue Laval ☎ 02 99 99 19 43
Disco open Fridays, Saturdays and bank holidays from 11.30pm to 5am. Free entry for women.

Les Vins et Une Fourchette – Les ☎ 02 99 94 55 88

Oubliettes, 1 rue de la Fourchette
(next to the chateau, north-west of the town centre)
A rum bar that has various performers and concerts.

Landéan
Moulin de St François   ☎ 02 99 94 47 69
✉ *thierry.vaissade@worldonline.fr*
(just north of Fougères on the D177)
Bar/disco that has a 'happy hour' from 11pm to 1.30am.

Redon
O'Shannon Pub, Quartier du Vieux Port ☎ 02 99 71 48 28
(by the quay, opposite the Le France hotel)
An Irish pub that holds a variety of evening events. Open
until 1am.

Rennes
There are two monthly publications giving details of
nightlife and events in Rennes: *le Rennais* and *l'Info
Métropole*.

Due to recent disturbances in the city, it's now illegal to be
seen carrying any form of alcohol in public on Thursday
evenings (this may be extended to other evenings).

Le Batchi, 34 rue Vasselot   ☎ 02 99 79 62 27
Disco.

Bowling Alma Loisirs, avenue Canada   ☎ 02 99 50 65 53
(on the retail park south of the city, at the junction of the N136
and N137)
Bar, pool tables and bowling. Open Mondays from 2pm to 2am,
Tuesdays and Wednesdays 11am to 2am, Thursdays 11am to
3am, Fridays 11am to 4am, Saturdays 2pm to 4am, Sundays
3pm to 1am.

Havana Café, rue de l'Arsenal   ☎ 02 99 67 24 15
French and South American concerts and bands.

Ile de Rhodes, 26bis rue du Docteur   ☎ 02 99 30 22 60
Francis Joly
Disco.

Le Jardin Moderne, 11 rue Manoir   ☎ 02 99 14 04 68
Servigné
Cafe/bar with disco and bands.

Café Leffe, 12 place de la Gare   ☎ 02 99 30 29 87
Bar/cafe with regular karaoke nights.

Le Museum Café, 12 rue Duhamel   ☎ 02 99 67 54 57

💻 *www.lestridesters.com*
Comedy night Friday evenings.

Le Platinuim, avenue du Chêne Vert,   ☎ 02 99 14 62 62
Le Rheu
Disco.

Le Sax Café, 4 rue St Thomas   ☎ 02 99 79 00 69
Jazz cafe.

Le Zola, 2 boulevard de la Liberté   ☎ 02 99 30 73 17
Bar/cafe with regular karaoke nights.

St Dolay   Club 80s, Le Pont de Cran, St Dolay   ☎ 02 99 90 11 02
Disco with '80s music. 'Happy hour' every Sunday.

St Malo   Le 109, 3 rue des Cordiers   ☎ 02 99 56 81 09
💻 *www.le-109.com*
(in the Intra Muros area on the northernmost tip of St Malo)
Disco, bar, cocktails and pool tables. Open 10pm to 3am.

Le Café du Coin… la Java, 3 rue Ste   ☎ 02 99 56 41 90
Barbe
(in the Intra Muros area on the northernmost tip of the town)
Piano bar serving cocktails and an extensive range of beers.
Open every day from 8am to 2am.

Le Cancalais, 1 quai Solidor, St Servan ☎ 02 99 81 15 79
Cafe/snack bar with concerts and internet access. Closed on
Mondays out of season.

La Caravelle, 95 boulevard de   ☎ 02 99 56 39 83
Rochebonne
Cocktail bar with sea view and concerts. Open all year from
4pm to 4am.

Le Casino Barrière de Saint Malo, 2   ☎ 02 99 40 64 00
Chaussée du Sillon
💻 *www.casinosbarriere.com*
Gaming machines, concerts, shows and bar. Open 10am to
2am Mondays to Thursdays, 10am to 4am Fridays and
Saturdays, 10am to 3am Sundays.

Le Cutty Sark, 20 rue de la Herse   ☎ 02 99 40 85 70
(in the Intra Muros area on the northernmost tip of the town)
Late bar with karaoke and concerts. Open from 6pm to 3am.

L'Escalier, la Buzardière   ☎ 02 99 81 65 56

🖥 *www.escalier.fr*
(south-east of the town centre)
Disco, bar and cocktails. Open from midnight to 5am.

Hiss & Oh, 7 rue de Chartres   ☎ 02 23 18 17 21
Cafe and rum bar. Open from 3pm to 1am (till 2am in the
summer).

JJ Murphy's & Co Little Castle, 3 rue   ☎ 02 99 40 89 32
Garangeau
(in the Intra Muros area on the northernmost tip of the town)
Irish pub with snack food available until midnight. Open 5pm
to 2am.

Pets

Dog Hygiene

See general information on page 84.

Dog Training

See general information on page 84.

Farriers

General   Jean-Claude Monneuse, Bringnerault-   ☎ 02 99 45 50 38
                 Bazouges, Hédé
                 (north-west of Rennes)

                 David Rouxel, 75 rue de Dinan, Dol-de- ☎ 06 83 55 82 15
                 Bretagne
                 (just in from the coast, directly north of Rennes)

                 André Boutemy, 2 allée Sorbiers,   ☎ 02 99 49 76 98
                 Marpire
                 (east of Rennes)

Horse Dentists

See general information on page 84.

Horse Feed

General   Joe Denham, La Garenne, Langonnet   ☎ 02 97 23 91 65
                 ✉ *lagarenne2004@yahoo.co.uk*
                 Quality hay and haylage (preserved hay with a slightly higher
                 protein/energy content). English speaking.

Horse Vets

See general information on page 85.

Identification

See general information on page 85.

Kennels & Catteries

See general information on page 85.

Pet Parlours

See general information on page 86.

Pet Travel

See general information on page 86.

Riding Equipment

| Bédée | La Chevauchée, Centre Commercial La Bastille, place Lieutenant Louéssard (north-west of Rennes, off the N12) | ☎ 02 99 61 22 87 |
| Rennes | Horse Wood, ZA Ribourdière, Cesson-Sévigné 💻 *www.horsewood.com* (east side of the town) | ☎ 02 99 83 31 49 |

SPA

Chateaubourg	chemin Goulgatière	☎ 02 99 62 32 65
Rennes	route Lorient, ZI des 3 Marches	☎ 02 99 59 32 74
Ste Marie	La Verdière	☎ 02 99 72 40 97

Veterinary Clinics

See general information on page 87.

Places to Visit

This section isn't intended to be a definitive guide but gives a wide range of ideas for the department. Prices and opening hours were correct at the time of writing, but it's best to check before travelling long distances.

Animal Parks & Aquariums

Bruz   Parc Ornithologique, 53 boulevard   ☎ 02 99 52 68 57
Pasteur
(just south-west of Rennes)
A bird centre within a botanical garden. There are 250 species
and over 1,000 exotic birds. Open mid-February to March and
October to mid-November Sundays from 2 to 6pm; April to
June and September every day 2 to 7pm; July and August
every day 10am to noon and 2 to 7pm. Adults €6.20,
children €3.80.

Goven   Ferme du Tessonnet   ☎ 02 99 42 02 55
Animal park with more than 50 breeds of domestic animal.
Open mid-April to June and September Sundays and bank
holidays from 2 to 7pm; July and August Sundays to Fridays
from 2 to 7pm. Adults €3.50, children €2.50.

Langon   La Maison du Naturaliste, Le Patis-Vert ☎ 02 99 08 62 07
(on the southern border of the department, east of Redon)
On the edge of the river Vilaine are reptiles and native
amphibians in their natural habitat. Open April to September
Wednesdays to Sundays from 2 to 7pm (July and August every
day). €3 entry with a guided tour.

Noyal-sur-   la Vallée des Canards, la Heurtelais,   ☎ 02 99 00 65 66
Vilaine   route de Châteaugiron
(just to the east of Rennes, alongside the N157)
Bird park specialising in water birds. More than 125 species
including ornamental ducks, herons, flamingos and cranes.
Open March to October from 9.30am to noon and 2 to 7pm;
November to February 2 to 5.30pm. Under ten-year-olds €3,
others €5.50.

Pleugueneuc   Parc Zoologique de la Bourbansais   ☎ 02 99 69 40 07
🖳 www.labourbansais.com
(directly west of Combourg)
The zoo has exotic and domestic animals from all over the
world. In the park there are demonstrations by falconers and
huntsmen (mounted and on foot) with a pack of 50 hunting
dogs. There's a play area, bouncy castles, snack bar and
tourist train. From the beginning of July to the end of
September there's a large maze grown from corn. The classic
French gardens and chateau are listed historic monuments with
guided tours of some furnished rooms. The zoo and gardens
are open April to September from 10am to 7pm; October to
March 2 to 6pm. Guided tours of the chateau April to
September at 11.15am, 2.30pm, 3.30pm and 5.40pm (June to
August an additional tour at 1.15pm); October to March 3.30pm
and 4.30pm. Entry to the gardens, zoo and shows €13 for
adults, €9.50 for children; admission to the chateau €4 for
adults, €2 for children.

St Malo   Grand Aquarium, avenue du Général   ☎ 02 99 21 19 00
Patton
🖥 *www.aquarium-st-malo.com*
A large aquarium with trips aboard a submarine to see marine life in its natural habitat. There are collections of sharks and tropical fish, a bar/restaurant, shop and 3D cinema. Open January to March and October to December from 10am to 6pm; April to June and September 10am to 7pm; first two weeks of July and the last two weeks of August 9.30 to 8pm; last two weeks of July and first two weeks of August 9.30am to 10pm. Closed for three weeks in January and Mondays to Fridays for two weeks in November. 4 to 14-year-olds €9.80, others €13.50.

Tinteniac   Le Grand Parc de Quebriac, Quebriac   ☎ 02 99 68 10 22
🖥 *www.zooloisirs.com*
(north-west of Rennes, just off the N137)
An animal and adventure park containing emus, parrots, bison and kangaroos, plus toboggans, suspension bridges, adventure playground and bouncy castles. Magic shows. Open daily April to mid-November from 10.30am to 6pm (water park open only in summer). Adults €10/€12, children €8/€10 depending on time of year.

Beaches & Leisure Parks

La Chapelle-   Plan d'Eau de la Haute Vilaine   ☎ 02 99 75 04 46
Erbrée   (on the border, south of Fougères)
Lake for swimming, fishing and watersports. Footpaths, mountain biking trrails, horse riding paths and picnic areas.

Dinard   La Plage de l'Ecluse
Large beach with various activities, parades and competitions throughout the summer.

Landéan   Base de Loisirs de Chênedet   ☎ 02 99 97 35 46
(in the Fougères forest, north of the town)
Beaches, mountain bike routes, canoeing and horse riding.

Redon   L'Etang Aumée, St Nicolas-de-Redon   ☎ 02 99 72 12 67
Based around a large lake, where there's windsurfing, sailing and pedalos, the park offers a sandy beach, volleyball court, picnic area and footpath.

Rennes   L'Etang de la Prévalaye, chemin Rural
72 du Moulin d'Apigné
(south-west of the town)
Sandy beach, fishing, windsurfing, picnic areas and restaurants.

St Malo   Plage du Havre and Plage de Rochebonne
           Two beaches on the coast by St Malo.

Boat, Train & Wagon Rides

Boat Trips

Bazouges-la-   Port Miniature de Villecartier, Base de   ☎ 02 99 98 37 24
Pérouse   Loisirs
                (east of Combourg)
                A collection of replica boats, scaled down to a size suitable
                for young children to play 'captain' on the lake. Snack bar,
                fishing and pedalos. Open April to September weekends and
                bank holidays from 2 to 7pm; July and August every day 11am
                to 7pm. Under threes free, three to ten-year-olds €3, over
                tens €4.

Dinard   Croisières Chateaubriand, Barrage de la   ☎ 02 99 46 44 40
          Rance, Gare Maritime
          🖳 www.chateaubriand.com
          Cruises with bar and brasserie or take your own picnic. For a
          cruise only there are two options: one-and-a-half hours or three
          hours; restaurant cruises all last three hours. Cruise only,
          adults €16/€27, 13 to 18-year-olds €13/€23, under 13s €9/€18;
          dinner cruises, over 13-year-olds €40 to €58 depending on
          menu chosen, under 13s €25.50.

Redon   Bretagne Croisières, 75 rue de Vannes   ☎ 02 99 71 08 05
         🖳 www.bretagnecroisieres.com
         Fully equipped boats for hire, 2 to 12 people, no licence
         required. Available for weekends or a week.

St Malo   Condor Ferries, Gare Maritime de la   ☎ 08 25 13 51 35
           Bourse
           🖳 www.condorferries.com
           Trips to Jersey and Guernsey for a day, weekend or longer.

           Emeraude Jersey Ferries, Terminal   ☎ 08 25 13 51 80
           Ferry du Naye
           🖳 www.emeraude.co.uk
           Trips to Jersey on a modern catamaran. Crossing time one
           hour ten minutes.

           Club Croisières Alet, 44 rue Dauphine,   ☎ 02 99 82 07 48
           St Servan
           🖳 www.clubcroisieres.fr.st
           Hire of sailing and motor boats.

           Compagnie Corsaire, Cale de Dinan   ☎ 08 25 13 80 35
           🖳 www.compagniecorsaire.com

Boat trips to the Iles Chausey, Granville in Normandy and various points along the coast of St Malo bay and sea fishing trips.

Train Rides

Cherrueix   Le Train Marin, Gare St Michel, centre   ☎ 02 99 48 84 88
                Bourg
                🖳 *www.train-marin.com*
                (west of Mont St Michel)
                This 'train' is tractor-powered and takes you on a 5km (3mi) journey along the water's edge, to discover the mussel breeding grounds and traditional fishing methods from the 11th century. Times are dependent on the tide. 4 to 11-year-olds €7.50, over 11s €10.

Fougères   Petit Train de Fougères, place Raoul II   ☎ 02 99 99 71 72
                A 40-minute 'train' tour of the old town. 4 to 12-year-olds €3, over 12s €5.

St Malo   Le Petit Train de St Malo, Porte St   ☎ 02 99 40 49 49
                Vincent
                🖳 *www.lepetittrain-saintmalo.com*
                Guided tours aboard a 'train' that travels around the town. Operates from April to November. The journey takes half an hour and the commentary is available in English. Under ten-year-olds €3.50, others €5.

Wagon Rides

See general information on page 88.

Chateaux

Combourg   Château du Combourg   ☎ 02 99 73 22 95
                🖳 *www.combourg.net*
                (entrance off rue des Princes)
                This medieval fortress has four massive towers. Built between the 12th and 15th centuries, it's still privately owned by the Chateaubriand family. The park is open from April to October Sundays to Fridays from 9am to noon and 2 to 5.30pm (July and August also open Saturdays). The chateau is open for guided tours in the afternoons.

Fougère   Château de Fougères, place Pierre   ☎ 02 99 99 79 59
                Symon
                🖳 *www.ot-fougeres.fr*
                A fine example of military architecture, with various displays of defensive techniques used between the 11th and 15th centuries. Open from February to December (closed Christmas Day). €3.55 for a guided tour.

Grand-Fougeray Tour du Guesclin   ☎ 02 99 08 40 19
(on the southern border of the department, east of Redon)
A 14th century circular keep, topped by a parapet walkway. The
surrounding gardens have some of the finest trees in the
department. Guided tours of the tower in July and August
between 3 and 7pm. The gardens are free to visit all year.

Churches & Abbeys

Dol-de-   Cathédraloscope, place de la   ☎ 02 99 48 35 30
Bretagne   Cathédrale
               ✉ *cathedraloscope@wanadoo.fr*
               (south-east of St Malo)
               A centre dedicated to understanding cathedrals; their
               architecture, construction and art. Open every day from the end
               of March to the end of October from 10am to 7pm. Adults
               €7.50, children €4.90.

St Malo   La Cathédrale St Vincent
               Built from the 12th to 18th centuries and partially destroyed
               during the Second World War. Interesting stained glass
               windows and church furniture.

Miscellaneous

Fougères   Hippodrome de la Grande Marche   ☎ 02 99 99 53 87
               (south of the town, off the D798)
               Trotting, flat racing and steeplechase.

Lanhélin   Cobac Parc   ☎ 02 99 73 80 16
               🖳 *www.cobac-parc.fr*
               (just north-west of Combourg)
               Activities for all ages in natural surroundings. Pool area with
               water slides, little train, crazy golf, pedal karting, century-old
               carrousel, snack bar and picnic area. Open from the end of
               April to the end of June, weekends, bank holidays and school
               holidays from 10.30am to 6pm; July to mid-September daily
               10.30am to 6pm. Under 15s €11, others €13.

Maure-de-   Hippodrome des Bruyèes   ☎ 02 99 34 91 63
Bretagne   (north of Redon)
               This race track has ten meetings a year: trotting, flat racing and
               steeplechase. Panoramic restaurant and children's playground.

Médréac   Vélo Rail, place de la Gare   ☎ 02 99 07 30 48
               ✉ *lagaredemedreac@wanadoo.fr*
               (on the border of the department, north-west of Rennes)
               Specially designed 'platforms' run along a disused railway track
               over bridges and viaducts and through the Val du Néal. Two
               adults pedal and there's space for two children (under eight)
               behind. Booking is recommended and you need to arrive 15

minutes before your booking time. The 6km (4mi) route takes around one hour and costs €8 per 'platform' plus €2 per child under eight. The 14km (9mi) route takes around two hours and costs €12.50 plus €2 per child. Open April, May and October Sundays and bank holidays from 2 to 6pm; June to September every day 10am to 6pm.

Redon

Hippodrome de la Rive, route de Vannes   ☎ 02 99 71 28 88
Trotting and flat racing.

Rennes

Hôtel de Ville, place de la Mairie   ☎ 02 99 67 11 11
A magnificent 18th century building open for guided tours from mid-July to mid-August Mondays to Fridays at 11am, 2pm and 5pm.

St Malo

Fort National   ☎ 02 99 85 34 33
(on the beach facing the chateau)
A historic monument constructed of granite in 1689. Open June to September – opening hours dependent on the tides.

Fort du Petit Bé   ☎ 06 08 27 51 20
🖳 *www.petitbe.com*
(off the Plage de Bon Secours on the northernmost tip of St Malo)
This fort, offering superb views across the bay and over the town, houses an exhibition of 17th, 18th and 19th century plans for fortifications.

Hippodrome de Marville, avenue de Triquerville   ☎ 02 99 56 19 58
✉ *hippodrome.st-malo@wanadoo.fr*
There are 17 meetings a year, from April to October; trotting, flat racing and steeplechase.

Labyrinthe du Corsaire, 20 rue de la Goëletterie   ☎ 02 99 81 17 23
🖳 *www.labyrintheducorsaire.com*
An enormous maze which you can explore via four routes, depending on your sense of adventure! There are numerous activities along the way, including bouncy castles, an obstacle course, a miniature farm and even a mechanical rodeo bull and a game of 'human' baby football. More than 10km (6mi) of paths. Open the first two weeks of July, last week of August and first week of September from 11am to 7pm; last two weeks of July and first three weeks of August 10.30am to 7.30pm (open until midnight on some days in summer). €6.80 entry (credit cards aren't accepted).

St Méloire-des-Ondes

L'Atelier du Verre, 4 rue de Radegonde ☎ 02 99 89 18 10
(just east of St Malo)
🖥 *www.idverre.net/durand-gasselin*
Glass workshop with glass blowing demonstrations and 15-minute trial sessions through to full week courses. Open Tuesdays to Saturdays (every day in July and August). Free entry.

Teillay

Mines de Fer, La Brutz ☎ 02 99 44 27 73
Part of this iron mine ceased production in 1950 and has since been revived for visitors. Adults €4, children €2.50. Guided tours available.

Treffendel

Parc de Treffendel 'Cirque Métropole', ☎ 02 99 61 04 21
Le Gué Charet
(south-west of Rennes along the N24)
A leisure park, animal park and circus with exotic animals and circus activities in a natural wooded site of 10ha (25 acres). The park offers visitors of all ages workshops and courses to learn the arts of circus performing. A day at the circus includes a workshop, tour of the park and performance. Open from April to October Tuesdays to Sundays from 11am to 7pm (closed Saturday mornings). Three to nine-year-olds €8.50, over nines €11.

Vieux-Vy-sur-Couesnon

Le Moulin-de-Bray ☎ 02 99 39 52 76
(directly west of Fougères)
A 19th century water mill run as a trout farm with fishing, a grill and a *crêperie*. Open every day from March to October.

Museums, Memorials & Galleries

Campel

Secrets de Soie ☎ 02 99 34 93 93
🖥 *www.secretsdesoie.fr*
This silk museum explains the process of silk making from silk worms to designer fashions. There's a guided tour taking around 90 minutes, permanent and temporary exhibitions, a shop and a garden. Open from mid-April to the end of May, September and October 2 to 6pm; June to August 10am to noon and 2 to 6pm. Guided tours every day (except Saturdays in April, September and October). Adults €6, children €4.

Fougères

Atelier Musée de l'Horlogerie, 37 rue ☎ 02 99 99 40 98
Nationale
Watch and clock workshop and museum. Open mid-June to the end of the third week in August Tuesdays to Saturdays from 9am to noon and 2 to 7pm, Sundays and Mondays 2 to 6.30pm; September to mid-June Tuesdays to Saturdays 9am to noon and 2 to 7pm. Adults €4.20, 11 to 18-year-olds €3.50.

Lohéac

Le Manoir d'Auto, La Cour Neuve   ☎ 02 99 34 02 32
More than 400 cars including Ferraris, Lamborghinis, rally cars,
vintage cars and 18 Formula 1 cars. Open Tuesdays to
Sundays from 10am to 1pm and 2 to 7pm. 10 to 16-year-olds
€7, over 16s €8.50.

La Richardais

L'Atelier Manoli, 9 rue du Suet   ☎ 02 99 88 55 53
🖥 *www.manoli.org*
(just west of St Malo, across the estuary)
Sculpture museum and workshops with around 400 works on
display. Guided tours on request. Open April to October
weekends and bank holidays from 3 to 7pm; July and August
10.30am to noon and 3 to 7pm. Under 12s free, others €4.

Redon

Musée de la Batellerie de l'Ouest, Quai   ☎ 02 99 72 30 95
Jean Bart
This permanent exhibition is dedicated to the Breton canals
and to the men and their families who lived and worked on the
barges. Open every day mid-June to mid-September from
10am to noon and 3 to 6pm; rest of the year Saturdays,
Sundays, Mondays and Wednesdays 2 to 6pm. Adults €2,
children €0.99.

Rennes

Eco Musée, route de Noyal, Chatillon-   ☎ 02 99 51 38 15
sur-Seiche
(south of the city)
Located south of Rennes, this museum covers five centuries of
history in one of the most beautiful farms in the region. A
signposted tour with 19 varieties of rare farm animal illustrating
Breton agriculture. Open April to September Tuesdays to
Sundays from 9am to 6pm; October to March Tuesdays to
Fridays 9am to noon and 2 to 6pm, Saturdays 2 to 6pm,
Sundays 2 to 7pm. Picnic area open April to September. 6 to
14-year-olds €2.30, over 14s €4.60.

Musée des Beaux Arts, 20 quai Emile   ☎ 02 99 28 55 85
Zola
🖥 *www.mbar.org*
This museum of fine art has works from the 14th to the 21st
centuries, including paintings by Picasso and Rubens, plus
sculptures, statues and archaeological collections relating to
the Egyptian and Greco-Roman civilisations. Open Tuesdays to
Sundays from 10am to noon and 2 to 6pm (closed bank
holidays). Adults €4.05 (€5.10 if an exhibition is on),
children free.

Musée de Bretagne 20 quai Emile Zola   ☎ 02 99 28 55 84
🖥 *www.musee-bretagne.fr*
Open Tuesdays to Sundays from 10am to noon and 2 to 6pm
(closed bank holidays). At the end of 2005 the museum will

move to a new building in Les Champs Libres, near the
railway station.

St Malo	Musée International du Long Cours ☎ 02 99 40 71 58 Cap-Hornier, quai Sébastopol, St Servan A museum dedicated to sailing ships from the 19th and 20th centuries. Open November to March Tuesdays to Sundays from 10am to noon and 2 to 6pm; April to October open every day 10am to noon and 2 to 6pm. Adults €4.90, children €2.50.
	Musée Jacques Cartier, rue David ☎ 02 99 40 97 73 MacDonald Stewart, Limoëlou, Rothéneuf 💻 *musee-jacques-cartier.com* (east of the town centre, between Le Lévy-St-Ideuc and Rotheneuf) Jacques Cartier was one of the most famous European explorers of the 16th century. The manor house of Limoëlou was his home and has been carefully restored. Open June and September, Mondays to Saturdays from 10 to 11.30am and 2.30 to 6pm; July and August every day 10 to 11.30am and 2.30 to 6pm; October to May, Mondays to Saturdays for visits at 10am and 3pm. Adults €4, children €3.
Vitré	Musée de l'Abeille Vivante, 18 rue de la ☎ 02 99 75 09 01 Briqueterie 💻 *www.l-abeille-de-vitre.com* Bee museum with five active colonies, guided tours, tasting of products from the bee hives and the possibility of helping with the extraction of honey. Guided tours in July and August, Mondays to Saturdays between 2 and 6pm. Adults €3.20, children free if accompanied by an adult.

Parks, Gardens & Forests

Bazouges-la- Pérouse	Jardins Baroques du Château de la ☎ 02 99 97 47 86 Ballue 💻 *www.la-ballue.com* (north-east of Combourg) Baroque gardens with some elaborate topiary and over 5,000 trees. Listed among the 80 most beautiful gardens in France. Open May to September, Fridays, weekends and bank holidays 1 to 5.30pm (every day from mid-July to the end of August). Under 13s €4, others €8.
Le Chatellier	Parc Floral de Haute Bretagne, Château ☎ 02 99 95 48 32 de la Foltière 💻 *www.parcfloralbretagne.com* (just north-west of Fougères) Large private gardens, including a botanical garden, secret garden, various water features and rose gardens. Open to the

public from March to mid-November with a number of festivals throughout the year. Adults €8, 13 to 18-year-olds €6.90, 4 to 12-year-olds €5.

Combourg   Parc du Château, 23 rue des Princes   ☎ 02 99 73 22 95
💻 *www.combourg.net*
Park and grounds surrounding the chateau. The park is open from April to October Sundays to Fridays from 9am to noon and 2 to 5.30pm. Under tens free, others €2.

Ercée-en-Lamée Parc Marcel Boisnard   ☎ 02 99 43 98 69
A large collection of rhododendrons, pergolas and a water garden.

Fougères   Forêt de Fougères
A large forest of beech and oak trees, ideal for walking and cycling.

There are also forests at St Aubin-du-Cormier and Bazouges-la-Pérouse.

Langon   Le Jardin Anglais du Manoir de la   ☎ 02 99 08 64 41
Chaussée, Port de Roche
💻 *www.le-manoir.info*
(north-east of Redon)
Whatever route you take around the garden there's a view of the 14th century manor, which has retained much of its medieval charm. The gardens, designed by an English landscape gardener, are among the finest private gardens in France. There are more than 10,000 varied and rare plants, a rose garden, Mediterranean garden, water features and modern structures. Open from May to November Wednesdays and weekends from 2 to 7pm. Under sevens free, others €6; 'passport' for four visits €16.

Piré-sur-Seiche Le Parc du Château des Pères   ☎ 02 99 02 36 82
(south-east of Rennes)
In the grounds of the chateau, this park has some formal areas, statues and flower gardens. A 3km (2mi) footpath takes you through parkland, past Highland cattle, woodland and orchards. For details of this walk ask at tourist offices for *Carte IGN, Plein-Air Ille-et-Vilaine No. 8*. Free entry.

Pleugueneuc   Jardins et Parc du Château de la   ☎ 02 99 69 40 07
Bourbansais
💻 *www.labourbansais.com*
(west of Combourg)
The chateau was constructed in the 16th century and the gardens were designed in the 18th century. The zoo has exotic and domestic animals from all over the world. In the park there

are demonstrations by huntsmen (mounted and on foot) with a pack of 50 hunting dogs (see page 275). Open every day April to September from 10am to 7pm; October to March 2 to 6pm. Adults €12, children €8.50 for admission to zoo and gardens.

Redon

Ile aux Pies
A series of small islands on the Oust river that are a wildlife haven. The area can be explored from marked footpaths along both sides of the river.

Rennes

Parc du Thabor, place St Melaine
The gardens of St Melaine abbey were designed by the Büuhler brothers, famous garden designers of the 19th century. Ten hectares (25 acres) of garden, over 700 varieties of rose, a botanical garden, cave, waterfall, *orangerie* and music pavilion. Open from 7.30am to 8.30pm in the summer, 7.30am to 6.30pm in the winter. On Wednesdays during the summer there are various shows in the park. Free entry; dogs must be on a lead.

Parc des Gayeulles, avenue des ☎ 02 99 87 20 02
Gayeulles
(north-east of the city centre)
A 100ha (250-acre) site that includes three lakes, an ice rink, roller skating rink, swimming pool and pedalos for hire (daily from June to August and weekends September to November). Also crazy golf, tennis, camping, a shooting range, sports complex and restaurants. Areas that have restricted access are open from 8am to 8pm in the summer, 8am to 5.45pm in the winter. Free entry; dogs not permitted.

St Malo

La Cacteraie de la Malounière du Puits ☎ 02 99 82 22 48
Sauvage, Hameau-de-St-Etienne
This garden holds a large collection of cacti and similar plants. A 19th century greenhouse holds more than 800 varieties, originally from South America, Madagascar and Australia. Open in June and September at weekends from 2 to 6pm; July and August every day 2 to 6pm. Under ten-year-olds free, others €5.

Vitré

Parc et Jardin Français du Château des ☎ 02 99 75 04 54
Rochers Sévigné, route d'Argentré du Plessis
(enter the French garden by the Musée des Rochers Sévigné)
Originally designed in the 17th century, this garden was restored in 1980. It features ornate designs on the lawns and formal gardens surrounding the chateau. Open April to June every day from 10am to noon and 2 to 5.30pm; July to September every day 10am to 6pm; October to March Wednesdays to Fridays 10am to noon and 2 to 5.30pm, Saturdays to Mondays 2 to 5.30pm. Adults €4.

Regional Produce

Argentré-du-Plessis	Pain à la Ferme de la Branchette, La Branchette	☎ 02 99 49 49 54

(east of Rennes, along the N157 near the border of the department)
Organic bread and pastries, cooked in a wood burning bread oven dating back 250 years. Visitors welcome to taste the farm produce, which includes cider, apple juice and organic dairy products. Open all year on Fridays and Saturdays (plus Mondays in July and August).

Essé	Earl Texier, La Couesnerie	☎ 02 99 47 06 14

(south-east of Rennes, north-east of Bain-de-Bretagne)
This farm produces a variety of dairy products including milk, butter and cheese. Open every day during evening milking.

Maure-de-Bretagne	La Ferme du Luguen	☎ 02 99 34 08 65

Foie gras and other home-made products can be tasted and bought. Open Tuesdays to Fridays from 10am to 12.30pm and 3 to 6pm, Saturdays 4 to 6pm.

Messac	Champignons de Bretagne, 27 rue Cawiezel	☎ 02 99 34 60 71

Discover the methods of cultivation of the Shii-take mushroom and how to use it. Free guided tours by appointment Mondays to Fridays 8.30am to 12.30pm and 2 to 5pm.

Parigné	Sabots Levacher, 41 rue de la Mairie	☎ 02 99 97 22 15

Traditional Breton clog workshop founded in 1938. Open from Mondays to Saturdays.

Renac	Tisquin, Village-de-Guzt	☎ 06 89 33 93 42

Various aperitifs made from apples, quince and local honey on sale. Visits all year by appointment. Contact Abraham Bertrand.

St Jean-sur-Couesnon	Cidre Bouché Semery, Montchevron	☎ 02 99 39 11 04

(south-west of Fougères)
Production of cider. Open for sales on Saturdays from 10am to 6pm, other days by appointment.

Le Theil-de-Bretagne	La Cordière Tradition Fermière, La Cordière	☎ 02 99 47 77 59

🖳 *www.roche-aux-fees.com*
(south-east of Rennes, north-east of Bain-de-Bretagne)
A pig farm that produces a variety of pork-based products including slicing sausages and black pudding (*boudin*). Open Fridays and Saturdays.

Standing Stones & Megaliths

Champeaux	Megaliths (east of Rennes)
Esse	Megaliths (south-east of Rennes, near Janzé)
Janzé	Megaliths (south-east of Rennes)
Noyal-sous-Bazouges	Le Menhir de Pierre-Longue
Poce-les-Bois	Megaliths (east of Rennes, near Vitré)
Retiers	Megaliths (north-east of Bain-de-Bretagne)
St Just	Le Site Mégalithique de St Just This site extends over 6km (4mi) into the nature reserve and boasts many dolmens, and alleys and lines of standing stones.
Le Sel-de-Bretagne	Megaliths (north-east of Bain-de-Bretagne)

Professional Services

The following offices have an English-speaking professional.

Accountants

Bain-de-Bretagne	Cabinet Lehembre, 3 place St Martin	☎ 02 99 43 74 66

Architects & Project Managers

See page 313.

Solicitors & Notaires

Rennes	Maître Gentilhomme, 14 avenue Jean Janvier	☎ 02 99 29 61 29

Property

See general information on page 90.

Public Holidays

See general information on page 95.

Religion

Anglican Services in English

Dinard   St Bartholomew's Anglican Church,   ☎ 02 99 46 77 00
              rue Faber
              ✉ *sybil.fagg@libertysurf.fr*
              English-language services every Sunday at 11am. All
              denominations welcome.

Catholic Churches

See **Religion** on page 96.

Restaurants

Bain-de-   La Croix Verte, 10 place Henri IV   ☎ 02 99 43 71 55
Bretagne   🖥 *www.lacroixverte.com*
              Traditional and innovative cuisine based on local produce. Set
              menus from €17.50 to €42 plus a large *à la carte* menu. Open
              from Monday evenings to Sunday lunchtimes (closed Friday
              evenings and between Christmas and the New Year).

              Les Gazelles, 9 rue des Frères Hémery   ☎ 02 99 43 75 36
              Tunisian cuisine with couscous on Saturday evenings (if
              booked in advance) and oriental dancing once a month. Open
              lunchtimes only.

              L'Ecrivain, 1 place St Gilduin   ☎ 02 99 73 01 61
              This restaurant won a tourism trophy in 2004. Set menus from
              €14.60 to €35. Closed Wednesday evenings, Thursdays and
              Sunday evenings (mid-July to mid-August closed Thursday
              evenings only).

              Restaurant du Château, 1 place   ☎ 02 99 73 00 38
              Chateaubriand
              Within a three-star hotel, this restaurant offers set menus from
              €20 to €51 per person and an *à la carte* menu. Out of season

closed Sunday evenings and Mondays and closed annually the last two weeks of December and the first two weeks of January. English spoken.

Restaurant du Lac, 2 place ☎ 02 99 73 05 65
Chateaubriand
🖥 *www.hotel-restaurant-du-lac.com*
Within a two-star hotel, this restaurant looks directly across the lake. Set menus from €17.50 during the week and from €24 to €52 at weekends. Lunch menu €9.50. Closed Fridays and Sunday evenings.

Dinard

Croisières Chateaubriand, Barrage de la ☎ 02 99 46 44 40
Rance, Gare Maritime
🖥 *www.chateaubriand.com*
Three-hour restaurant cruise. €40 to €58 depending on menu chosen (under 13s €25.50).

Fougères

Le Haute-Sève, 37 boulevard Jean Jaurès ☎ 02 99 94 23 39
Gastronomic restaurant with set menus from €19 to €38 plus *à la carte*. Open Tuesdays to Saturdays and Sunday lunchtimes. Closed the first week of January, ten days in February and three weeks at the end of July and beginning of August.

Le Pékin, 68 rue de la Pinterie ☎ 02 99 99 73 08
Chinese restaurant.

Le P'tit Bouchon, 13 rue Chateaubriand ☎ 02 99 99 75 98
Traditional cuisine including *raclettes* and *fondues*. Booking required Saturday evenings and Sundays. Set menus from €10 to €18.

Le Samsara, 70 rue de la Pinterie ☎ 02 99 99 68 62
Indian restaurant with set menus from €7 to €18 and vegetarian options. Closed Mondays out of season.

Redon

La Bogue, 3 rue des Etats ☎ 02 99 71 12 95
(opposite the library in the centre of town)
Specialities of fish and regional cuisine that change according to the season. Set menus from €16 to €54 plus *à la carte*.

JM Chandouineau, 1 rue Thiers ☎ 02 99 71 02 04
(up the hill from the tourist office towards the hospital)
Gastronomic cuisine with set menus from €22 to €60. Closed Saturdays (except bank holidays).

Le Moulin de Via, route de la Gacilly ☎ 02 99 71 05 16
Menus using seasonal and local market produce. Set menus from €20 to €60. Open from Wednesdays to Sunday lunchtimes.

Rennes

L'Assiette Créole, 8 rue de St Malo   ☎ 02 99 79 04 40
Cuisine from Reunion. Set menus from €6 to €13. Open from
Tuesdays to Saturdays.

El Popoca, 14 rue Nantaise   ☎ 02 99 30 22 41
South American cuisine. Open from Mondays to Saturdays.

Le Four à Ban, 4 rue St Melaine   ☎ 02 99 38 72 85
✉ *fouraban@wanadoo.fr*
Gastronomic cuisine and regional French menus using local
produce. Set menus from €17 to €45. Closed Monday evenings
and all day Sundays.

Le Marrakech, 75 boulevard de la Tour   ☎ 02 99 30 84 70
d'Auvergne
💻 *www.lemarrakech.com*
Moroccan cuisine, including *couscous* and *tagines*, and *paella*.
Open every day.

Le Parc à Moules, 8 rue Georges Dottin   ☎ 02 99 31 44 28
Fish restaurant. Free home delivery of mussel dishes. Open
Tuesdays to Saturdays.

Restaurant India, 41 rue St Georges   ☎ 02 99 87 09 01
Indian restaurant open every day. Set menus €6 to €16.

St Malo

A la Duchesse Anne, 5 place Guy La   ☎ 02 99 40 85 33
Chambre
(in the Intra Muros area on the northernmost tip of St Malo)
One-star Michelin restaurant, gastronomic cuisine using market
produce and seafood. Set menus from €47 to €57. Closed
Monday lunchtimes and Wednesdays.

Aux Vieilles Pierres, 9 rue Thévenard   ☎ 02 99 56 46 80
(in the Intra Muros area on the northernmost tip of St Malo)
Gastronomic seafood restaurant. Set menus €21 to €37.
Closed lunchtimes Mondays to Saturdays out of season.

Le Cap Horn, 100 boulevard Hébert   ☎ 02 99 40 75 40
💻 *www.thalassotherapie.com*
Within a health spa, this restaurant uses local produce in
traditional cuisine. Set menus from €27 to €53. Sea views.

Le Penjab, 3 rue des Lauriers   ☎ 02 99 56 80 12
Indian restaurant with vegetarian menus and take-away
service. Closed Monday lunchtimes.

Le Sampan, 4 rue Amiral Magon, St   ☎ 02 99 19 59 26
Servan

Thai restaurant. Set menus €4.90 to €26.90. Closed Mondays; non-smoking.

Taverne de Maître Kanter, 6 boulevard ☎ 02 99 56 05 50
des Talards
Meat and fish grills, fish a speciality. Service continuous from lunchtime to midnight. Set menus from €10.85 to €30. Open every day.

Rubbish & Recycling

See general information on page 97.

Schools

See general information on page 100.

Shopping

When available, the opening hours of various shops have been included, but these are liable to change and so it's advisable to check before travelling long distances to a specific shop.

Architectural Antiques

La Mezière   Les Matériaux d'Antan, ZA La   ☎ 02 99 66 56 66
Montgervalaise 1
Salvage yard dealing with fireplaces, doors and various reclaimed woodwork.

Bakeries

See general information on page 103.

British Groceries

See general information on page 103.

Building Materials

See general information on page 103.

Chemists'

See general information on page 103.

Department Stores

Rennes   Printemps, Centre Commercial Alma   ☎ 02 99 32 57 70
              🖳 *www.printemps.com*
              (on the retail park south of Rennes, at the junction of the N136
              and N137)
              Open Mondays to Fridays from 9.30am to 8.30pm, Saturdays
              9am to 8pm.

              Galeries Lafayette, 2 rue Rohan   ☎ 02 99 78 49 49
              Open Mondays to Saturdays from 9am to 7.30pm.

DIY

See general information on page 104.

Dress Making & Crafts

Chantepie   Myrtille Tissus, 4 rue Vieux Jardin   ☎ 02 99 41 63 43
              🖳 *www.tissus-myrtille.fr.st*
              Fabric for clothes, curtains and furnishings.

Redon   Florimont Textile, 3 rue Thiers   ☎ 02 99 72 29 65
              Clothes and fabrics. Specialises in clothes for large and tall
              people.

Rennes   Ecolaines, rue Manoir de Servigné, ZI   ☎ 02 99 14 69 27
              Ouest
              ✉ *ecolaine@wanadoo.fr*
              Extensive range of wool and fabric for clothes and furnishings.

St Malo   La Malo Tissus, 77 avenue Moka   ☎ 02 99 40 95 89

              Cultura, avenue Flaudaie   ☎ 02 99 21 34 00
              🖳 *www.cultura.fr*
              Large selection of art and craft supplies.

Fireplaces & Log Burners

See general information on page 104.

Fishmongers'

See general information on page 104.

Frozen Food

Fougères   Thiriet, boulevard de Groslay   ☎ 02 99 94 10 66
              🖳 *www.thiriet.com*

	Picard, Forum de la Gare, rue Sévigné 💻 *www.picard.fr*	☎ 02 99 94 24 63
Rennes	Picard, 95 boulevard Emile Combes	☎ 02 99 32 00 17
	Thiriet, 1 avenue Peupliers, Cesson-Sévigné	☎ 02 99 83 46 06
St Malo	Picard, avenue Launay Breton	☎ 02 99 19 57 96

Garden Centres

See general information on page 105.

Hypermarkets

See **Retail Parks** on page 295 and general information on pages 105 and 108.

Key Cutting & Heel Bars

See general information on page 106.

Kitchens & Bathrooms

See general information on page 106.

Markets

Bain-de-Bretagne	Monday mornings
Combourg	Monday mornings
Fougères	Saturday mornings in the town centre, Thursday mornings at Quartier des Cotterêts and Friday afternoons at Beaucé
La Gacilly	Saturday mornings
Grand-Fougeray	Saturday mornings
Guichen	General market Tuesday mornings, organic market Thursday mornings
Janzé	Wednesday mornings

Maure-de-Bretagne	Sunday mornings
Redon	Mondays, Fridays and Saturdays in the town centre, Sunday mornings at St Nicolas-de-Redon
Rennes	There are 17 market locations throughout the city, including those given below.

Boulevard de la Liberté, antique and second-hand market Thursdays until 4pm

Place des Lices, the third-largest outdoor food and flower market in France, Saturdays from 7am to 1pm

Place Honoré Commeurec, food market Mondays to Saturdays from 7am to 7pm, Sundays 9.30am to 12.30pm

Place Zagreb in Le Blosne, market Tuesday and Saturday mornings

St Malo	Monday, Thursday and Saturday mornings at Rocabey

Tuesday and Friday mornings at Intra Muros and St Servan

Wednesday and Saturday mornings at Paramé

Vitré	Monday mornings, rue Notre Dame; Saturday mornings rue Porterie.

Mobile Shops

See general information on page 106.

Music

See general information on page 107.

Newsagents'

See general information on page 107.

Organic Produce

Bain-de-Bretagne	Santé Nature, 15 rue Hippolyte Filloux ☎ 02 99 43 99 38 Open Mondays from 1.30 to 7pm, Tuesdays to Saturdays 9am to 12.30pm and 1.30 to 7pm.

Combourg	Le Chat Biotté, 19 rue des Princes	☎ 02 23 16 40 97

Open Mondays from 9.30am to 1pm, Tuesdays to Saturdays
9.30am to 1 and 3 to 7pm.

Fougères	Nature et Santé Diététique, 5 boulevard	☎ 02 99 99 16 99
	Maréchal Leclerc	

Redon	Le Héron Bleu, 51 rue de la	☎ 02 99 72 21 08
	Châtaigneraie	

(signposted at the roadside in an otherwise residential area)
A large organic store. Open Mondays from 9.30am to 1pm,
Tuesdays to Fridays 9.30am to 1pm and 2.30 to 7pm,
Saturdays 9.30am to 5pm.

Rennes	La Vie Claire, 7 rue Poullain Duparc	☎ 02 99 79 18 30
	🖳.www.lavieclaire.com	

St Malo	Biocoop, ZAC de la Grassinaise	☎ 02 99 81 41 28

(south-west of the town towards St Jouan-des-Guérets)
Open Mondays to Saturdays.

Passport Photos

See general information on page 108.

Post Offices

See general information on page 108.

Retail Parks

Fougères	Carrefour, boulevard de Groslay	☎ 02 99 94 74 00
	🖳 www.carrefour.fr	

(south-east of the town, near the park)
Open Mondays to Saturdays 9am to 8pm (Fridays 9pm).

Rennes   Centre Commercial Carrefour, Cesson-Sévigné
(east of the city, from the south ring road take exit no.2, Porte
de la Rigourdière)
● Carrefour – hypermarket   ☎ 02 99 83 96 96
   Open Mondays to Saturdays from 8.30am to 9.30pm
   (Fridays till 10pm).

Centre Commercial Alma
(south of the town, at the junction of the N136 and N137)
Shops include:
● Carrefour – hypermarket   ☎ 02 99 26 55 55
   🖳 www.centre-alma.com
   (south of city, from the ring road take exit no.6, Porte de
   Nantes)

A large complex including clothes, shoe, jewellery and mobile phone shops, a Crédit Agricole bank, travel agent's, hairdresser's, heel bar, optician's, dry cleaner's, newsagent's and a bar. Carrefour is open Mondays to Thursdays from 8.30am to 9.30pm, Fridays 8.30am to 10pm, Saturdays 8.30am to 9pm.

- Conforama – furniture and electrical goods;
- King Jouet – toy shop;
- McDonald's;
- Printemps – department store;
- Super Sport – sports goods;
- Truffaut – garden centre.

Centre Commercial Géant
(north of the town on the junction of the N136 and N137)
Shops include:

- Brico Depot – building materials;
- Darty – electrical goods;
- Géant – hypermarket   ☎ 02 99 59 10 12
  🖳 www.geant.fr
- La Halle – clothes;
- Mondial Moquette Déco – carpets and decorating materials;
- Office Dépôt – office supplies and stationery;
- Univers Pêche Marine – fishing equipment.

St Malo

La Madeleine Centre Commercial
(south-west of the town)
Shops include:

- Bébé 9 – baby goods;
- Carrefour – hypermarket   ☎ 02 99 21 10 10
  Open Mondays to Saturdays from 8.30am to 9pm.
- Cultura – music, books, craft and art supplies.

Second-hand Shops

See general information on page 108.

Sports Goods

See general information on page 108.

Supermarkets

See general information on page 108.

Wine & Spirits

See general information on page 109.

Sports & Outdoor Activities

The following is just a selection of the activities available, the large towns having a wide range of sports facilities.

Aerial Sports

Ballooning

Le Minihic-sur-Rance   Emeraude Montgolfières   ☎ 02 99 88 64 42

Flying

Dinard   Aéroclub de la Côte d'Emeraude,   ☎ 02 99 88 23 42
                Aéroport Dinard-Pleurtuit
                💻 *www.ulm-mont-saint-michel.com*
                (south of Dinard)
                Sight-seeing flights over St Malo and the surrounding area.
                Introduction flights, lessons and courses.

Redon   Aéro Club Redonnais, Aérodrome de   ☎ 02 99 71 00 59
                Bains-sur-Oust, route de Rennes

Rennes   Les Passagers du Vent, 74 rue de la   ☎ 02 99 38 22 77
                Motte Brulon
                ✉ *monica.pavy@wanadoo.fr*
                A paragliding group.

Parachuting

General   Comité Départemental du   ☎ 02 99 52 60 81
                Parachutisme Sportif, 26 rue Ravel, Bruz
                ✉ *claire.le-boucher@wanadoo.fr*

Rennes   Association Sportive des Cheminots   ☎ 02 99 51 15 87
                Rennais

Archery

Fougères   Archers de Coigny, 58bis Duguesclin   ☎ 02 99 94 12 99
                Groups at all levels (beginners welcome September to
                December). September to March at rue Duguesclin; April to
                August at Stade Manfredi.

Redon   La Redonnaise Tir à l'Arc, Complexe   ☎ 02 99 71 31 84
                des Chapelets, route de la Gacilly
                Tuesdays from 6 to 8pm, Fridays 6.30 to 8pm and Saturdays
                10am to noon. Contact M. Serot.

| Rennes | Compagnie d'Archers de Rennes, 4 avenue des Gayeulles | ☎ 02 23 20 31 27 |

💻 *www.archersderennes.fr.st*
From eight-year-olds upwards.

| St Malo | 1ère Compagnie d'Arc Côte d'Emeraude | ☎ 02 99 40 19 88 |

✉ *delorainemichele@yahoo.fr*

Badminton

| Bain-de-Bretagne | USB Section Badminton, Salle Omnisports, rue du Semnon | ☎ 02 99 43 38 53 |

✉ *an.morin@wanadoo.fr*
Leisure and competitive badminton, teams or individuals. Various sessions throughout the week according to age and level. Contact M. Morin.

| Combourg | Association Badminton | ☎ 02 99 73 31 33 |

Contact M. Cavret.

| Fougères | Badminton Club du Pays de Fougères, Salle de Sport, Collège Jeanne d'Arc, rue Jeanne d'Arc | ☎ 02 99 94 15 08 |

Activities for juniors and adults, leisure and competitive. Contact M. Hardy.

| Redon | L'Amicale Laïque, Salle Lucien Poulard | ☎ 02 23 30 72 99 |

Open to adults and children, with a junior badminton school on Saturday mornings. Contact M. Robinne.

| Rennes | Centres d'Initiation Sportive, Palais St Georges, 2 rue Gambetta | ☎ 02 99 78 09 40 |

✉ *ds@wille-rennes.fr*

| St Malo | AS Jacques Cartier, Salle Jacques Cartier, 5 avenue de la Borderie | ☎ 02 99 56 54 86 |

Boules/Pétanque

| Combourg | L'Amicale Bouliste, avenue de Waldmünchen | ☎ 02 99 73 19 74 |

(by the campsite on the south side of the lake)
Contact M. Gingat.

| Fougères | Espérance de Fougères, boulevard de Rennes | ☎ 02 99 94 19 92 |

This group meets at the boulodrome on Tuesdays and Fridays from 2.15 to 5pm.

| Redon | La Pétanque Redonnaise | ☎ 02 99 71 14 03 |

💻 *www.tanqueredonnaise.ifrance.com*
This club has an indoor boulodrome with 50 courts and is the largest in Brittany. There's also an outdoor, shaded boulodrome on cours Clémenceau in the centre of town between the *mairie* and the railway line, open to everyone.

| Rennes | Maison de Quartier, 5 rue du Morbihan | ☎ 02 99 27 21 10 |

💻 *www.labellangerais.org*

| St Malo | Union Bouliste Servannaise, Parc de Bel Air | ☎ 02 99 81 12 93 |

Climbing

| Dol-de-Bretagne | Horizon Vertical, 1 rue des Stuarts | ☎ 06 83 16 94 02 |

✉ *horizon.vertical@free.fr*
(south-east of St Malo)
Outdoor activity centre, including mountain biking, orienteering and climbing.

| Fougères | Club Alpin Français de Fougères, 11 allée de la Pierre Blanche | ☎ 02 99 99 24 94 |

All levels welcome with groups for different ages from ten-year-olds upwards. Training at Gymnase des Cotterêts and natural sites across the region. Contact M. Henri.

| Redon | Grimp' Attitude | ☎ 02 99 71 31 63 |

✉ *michele.guiheneuf@cegetel.net*
Contact Mme Guiheneuf-Labenne.

Natural climbing sites near the campsite at Bains-sur-Oust and another at St Vincent-sur-Oust.

| Rennes | Club Alpin Français de Rennes, 13 rue de Lorraine | ☎ 02 99 59 28 76 |

💻 *www.cafrennes.free.fr*

| St Malo | Roc et Mer, 9 boulevard de la République | ☎ 02 99 20 18 98 |

✉ *rocetmer@wanadoo.fr*

Cycling & Bike Hire

| General | A *Topoguide VTT* is available from tourist offices detailing 37 routes suitable for mountain biking (€9). They cover 800km (496mi) and a variety of levels and distances. |

The Ille-et-Rance canal has some long sections of path alongside, ideal for cycling e.g. Tréverien to Chevaigné (44km/27mi) and Chevaigné to Rennes (17km/11mi).

Bain-de-Bretagne	Amicale Cycliste ☎ 02 99 43 75 01 Road cycling and mountain biking. Contact M. Gledel.	

Combourg   VTT Tintenlac/Combourg   ☎ 02 99 68 14 38
Mountain biking group. Contact M. Rescamps.

Amicale Cyclotourisme   ☎ 02 99 73 05 95
Road cycling group. Contact M. Gautier.

The tourist office has a leaflet, *Balade à Vélo*, giving details of a 23km (14mi) cycle route around the area.

Dol-de-Bretagne   Horizon Vertical, 1 rue des Stuarts   ☎ 06 83 16 94 02
✉ *horizon.vertical@free.fr*
(south-east of St Malo)
Outdoor activity centre, including mountain biking, orientation and climbing.

Fougères   ASPTT Fougères   ☎ 02 99 94 25 24
Road cycling for adults only. Contact M. Belloir for the calendar of rides.

Iffendic   Base VTT-VTC, Trémelin, Forêt de   ☎ 02 99 09 73 79
Brocéliande
🖥 *www.domaine-de-tremelin.fr*
Mountain bike centre. Half days, weekends and full week activities. Mountain bikes for hire.

Centre Initiation aux Activités de Plein   ☎ 02 99 97 35 46
Air, La Ferme de Chênedet, Landéan
(just north of the town)
Mountain bikes for hire and rides organised.

Redon   Redon Vélos Loisirs   ☎ 02 99 72 13 20
Contact Mme Lecomte.

Nicolas Chedaleux, 44 Notre Dame   ☎ 02 99 72 19 95
Mountain bikes for hire. €8 half day, €11 full day, €45 week.

Rennes   Cycles Guédard, 13 boulevard   ☎ 02 99 30 43 78
Beaumont
Bicycles loaned for up to seven hours.

ARRS, 61 rue Papu   ☎ 02 99 54 73 65
Adult road-cycling group. Contact Mme Guyot.

Bretagne Vélo Tout Terrain, 1 rue   ☎ 02 99 50 92 56
d'Andorre
💻 *www.bretagnevtt.free.fr*
Mountain biking club.

St Malo   Les Vélos Bleus, 19 rue Alphonse   ☎ 02 99 40 31 63
Thébault
💻 *www.velos-bleus.fr*
Organised bike rides around the bay of Mont St Michel and the
countryside around St Malo. Rides take place from March to
October and on request the rest of the year.

Espace Nicole Deux Roues, 11 rue   ☎ 02 99 56 11 06
Robert Schumann, Paramé
(just inland from the Rochebonne beach)
Bike hire. Open from Tuesdays to Saturdays.

Fishing

Maps are available from fishing shops and tourist offices showing local
fishing waters. If there's a lake locally, permits will be on sale in nearby
tabacs and fishing shops and at the *mairie*.

Bain-de-
Bretagne
    River fishing in the area at Moulin de la Plesse, Ercé-en-
Lamée, Moulin de l'Ardouais and Pléchâtel.
Day permit €7.50. Fishing in the lake: €3 for a day permit.

Etang de la Huais   ☎ 02 99 43 71 15
Trout fishing lake open every day. Full or half-day permits.

Fishing permits for sale at the bar Le Cyrano on Grande
Rue and Café Messu on rue de l'Hôtel de Ville.

Combourg   Les Pêcheurs de la Dore   ☎ 02 99 73 04 84
Local fishing group. Contact M. Bidel.

Ecole de Pêche et Courant Mitchell   ☎ 02 99 73 04 84
Fishing school. Contact Mme Bidel.

Fougères   AAPPMA Gaule Fougeraise, Mairie de ☎ 02 99 99 68 08
Fougères, 2 rue Porte Léonard
There are 400km (248mi) of fishing on the rivers and lakes in
the area. Fishing school and courses on fly fishing. Contact
M. Leduc.

Redon   There are many lakes and waterways around Redon
                   suitable for fishing, including L'Ile-aux-Pies and La
                   Potinais at Bains-sur-Oust, and L'Ecluse de Limur at
                   Peillac; on the river Vilaine, La Goule d'Eau at Redon and
                   Les Bellions at Fégréac.

Rennes   Ecole de Pêche de la Fédération, Etang   ☎ 02 99 22 81 80
                   des Gayeulles
                   Fishing school on Wednesdays from 2 to 5pm.

Football

Bain-de-   USB Section Football, avenue Guillotin   ☎ 02 99 43 88 10
Bretagne   de Corson
                   Teams for all age groups from six-year-olds upwards. Training
                   for children on Wednesday afternoons, adults on Tuesday and
                   Friday evenings. Contact M. Habelin.

Fougères   AG, Stade AGL de Paron Sud, route de   ☎ 02 99 95 40 88
                   la Chapelle Janson
                   Teams for all ages from four-year-olds upwards, plus a
                   women's team. Contact M. Meigne.

Redon   Football Club Atlantique Vilaine, Stade   ☎ 02 99 71 13 34
                   Municipal, avenue Joseph Ricordel
                   The office is open Mondays to Saturdays from 11am to noon.

Rennes   ASPTT, Stade Robert Launay, 1 rue   ☎ 02 23 21 13 13
                   Pierre Nougaro
                   ✉ asptt-rennes@wanadoo.fr

St Malo   AS Château-Malo, Stade Château-   ☎ 02 99 82 26 08
                   Malo

Golf

Cesson-Sévigné Golf de Cesson-Sévigné, 43 boulevard   ☎ 02 99 83 19 69
                   de Dézerseul
                   ⌨ www.cesson-sevigne.fr
                   9 holes, par 35, 2,703m. Green fees €10.50 to €12.25.

Dol-de-   Golf Club du Château des Ormes,   ☎ 02 99 73 53 00
Bretagne   Epiniac
                   ⌨ www.lesormes.com
                   (south-east of St Malo)
                   18 holes, par 72, 6,013m. Driving range, lessons, putting green
                   and golf buggies for hire. Open from February to November.
                   Green fees €34 to €46.

| Rennes | Golf Public de Rennes, Le Temple du Cerisier, St Jacques de la Lande | ☎ 02 99 30 18 18 |

(south-west of the city)
18 holes, par 72, 6,106m. Restaurant and bar. Green fees November to February €27, March to October €34.

| Le Rheu | Golf de la Freslonnière | ☎ 02 99 14 84 09 |

18 holes, par 72, 5,645m. Green fees €32 to €44.

| Vitré | Golf Club des Rochers, route d'Argentré du Plessis | ☎ 02 99 96 79 34 |

🖳 *www.vitre-golf.com*
(directly east of Rennes)
18 holes, par 71, 5,687m. Golf school for 7 to 18 year-olds. Driving range, golf carts, buggy and club hire. Restaurant open March to October. Green fees €32 to €40.

Hockey

| Combourg | Hockey Subaquatique, Piscine de Combourg, allée des Primevères | ☎ 02 99 73 39 98 |

Underwater hockey. Training on Wednesday nights. This form of hockey started in England in the '50s, came to France in the '80s and is now played in over 30 countries.

| Rennes | Centres d'Initiation Sportive, 2 rue Gambetta | ☎ 02 99 78 09 40 |

✉ *ds@ville-rennes.fr*
Field hockey.

| | Skating de Rennes, le Blizz, 8 avenue des Gayeulles | ☎ 02 99 36 28 10 |

🖳 *www.leblizz.com*
Ice hockey.

| | REC Roller, 5 square René Coty | ☎ 02 99 59 69 29 |

🖳 *www.rec-roller.chez.tiscali.fr*
Roller hockey.

| St Malo | AS Jeanne d'Arc, Stade de Marville, 22 avenue de Marville | ☎ 02 99 19 82 19 |

Field hockey.

Horse Riding

| Bain-de-Bretagne | Centre Equestre du Fresne, Le Frêne, Bourg-des-Comptes | ☎ 02 99 57 42 05 |

Indoor and outdoor riding schools.

Bains-sur-Oust	Centre Equestre Poney Club du Ménaret, Ménaret (just north of Redon) Riding for all ages and levels. Hacks, summer camps and week long courses during the school holidays.	☎ 02 99 91 61 98

Combourg   Centre Equestre du Parc, Le Parc,   ☎ 02 99 81 71 34
Meillac
✉ *leparc-fd@wanadoo.fr*
(just west of the town)

Fougères   Centre Hippique de Montaubert,   ☎ 02 99 99 03 52
Montaubert
(on the north side of the town)
Beginners, experienced riders, competitions and polo. Hacks through the forest and across the bay of Mont St Michel. Open all year.

    Centre Initiation aux Activités de Plein   ☎ 02 99 97 35 46
Air, La Ferme de Chênedet, Landéan
(just north of the town)
This group organises hacks across the bay of Mont St Michel.

Rennes   Centre Equestre Poney Club de Cesson-   ☎ 02 99 83 48 53
Sévigné, Les Conillaux
(east of Rennes)

St Malo   Poney Club de St Malo, Le Petit Vau   ☎ 02 99 19 08 61
Garni, La Briantais
(west of the town centre in the direction of the estuary/airport)
Horses and ponies, hacks on the beach, lessons and courses. Closed Mondays out of season, Sundays in the summer.

Land Yachting

St Malo   Surf School, 2 avenue de la Hoguette   ☎ 02 99 40 07 47
💻 *www.surfschool.ass.fr*

Motorsports

Cars

See general information on page 112.

Karts

Rennes   Karting, La Haie Gautrais, Bruz   ☎ 02 99 05 96 05

St Malo   Karting des Nielles, Les Nielles, St   ☎ 02 99 89 16 88
Méloir-des-Ondes

🖥 *www.karting-saint-malo.com*
(south of the town)
900m karting track and quad bikes. Open all year (closed
Tuesdays out of season).

Motorbikes

Combourg Bol l'Air   ☎ 02 99 73 19 97
          Contact M. Dardeval.

Rennes   Moto Club Randonneurs de l'Ouest,   ☎ 02 99 58 65 18
          31 Grande Rue, Vildé-la-Marine, Hirel
          ✉ *p.gorgiard.mcro.vilde@wanadoo.fr*

Quad Bikes

St Malo   Karting des Nielles, Les Nielles, St   ☎ 02 99 89 16 88
          Méloir-des-Ondes
          🖥 *www.karting-saint-malo.com*
          (south of the town)
          Quad bike rides out into the countryside around St Malo. Open
          all year (closed Tuesdays out of season).

Paint Ball

Dol-de-   Air Game Paintball   ☎ 06 63 29 17 65
Bretagne 🖥 *www.rgame-paintball-bretagne.com*
          (directly north of Combourg)
          Prices from €20 depending on how many pellets are bought
          and how many players. Booking required.

Rollerskating

Bain-de- USB Section Roller Skating   ☎ 02 99 44 87 19
Bretagne Held at Salle Omnisport, rue du Semnon or at the skate park
          on avenue Patton, opposite Collège du Chêne Vert.

Fougères Roulette Club Fougerais, 10 rue Père Le ☎ 02 99 99 05 28
          Taillander
          Various groups according to age and ability. Roller
          hockey, dance and competitions. Most activities are held
          in the gymnasium of the Collège Jeanne d'Arc, rue
          Jeanne d'Arc.

Redon   Le Roller, l'Amical Laïque, Gymnase   ☎ 02 99 72 73 35
          de Beaumont, avenue de Beaumont
          This club has various sessions throughout the week for adults
          and children, including roller hockey, roller basketball, speed
          skating and relay races. Contact Mme Rouxel for relevant
          groups and venues.

Rennes	Get High Skate Park, 10 rue de la Retardais	☎ 02 99 54 13 26

Cercle Paul Bert, 4bis square du Berry ☎ 02 99 54 10 40
💻 *www.cerclepaulbert.asso.fr*
Rollerskating club.

St Malo ASPTT, Salle Surcouf, rue de la ☎ 02 99 56 78 84
Chaussée
✉ *asptt.stmalo@wanadoo.fr*
Rollerskating club with training on Wednesdays and Fridays
from 6 to 8pm.

Shooting

Fougères Société de Tir la Fougeraise, 54 ☎ 02 99 99 65 99
boulevard Edmond Roussin
Groups held throughout the week for juniors, adults, 'seniors'
and women. Open September to June.

Redon Tir Olympic Redonnais, Chemin du ☎ 02 99 72 16 56
Bois des Chapelets, route de la Gacilly
Contact M. Gautier.

St Malo Société Tir Emeraude, Stand Municipal ☎ 02 99 81 68 88
de la Gilbardais

Squash

Fougères Tennis Club de Fougères, La Rivière, ☎ 02 99 94 09 74
route de Vitré
Squash court and outdoor tennis courts.

Rennes Le Garden Rennes, Base de Loisirs des ☎ 02 99 36 34 87
Gayeulles, rue Pierre Nougaro
Squash, badminton and tennis courts.

St Malo AS Jeanne d'Arc, 17 boulevard Gouazon ☎ 02 99 19 82 19
Leisure and competitive squash.

Swimming

Bain-de- Piscine, avenue Guillotin de Corson ☎ 02 99 43 71 19
Bretagne Indoor heated pool. Open from the end of June to the end
of August.

Combourg Piscine, allée des Primevères ☎ 02 99 73 06 74
(east of the town centre, off avenue de la Libération)

Fougères	Piscine, 49 avenue Georges Pompidou ☎ 02 99 94 37 93
	Two pools, toboggan, diving pool and sauna. Swimming club, water polo, swimming lessons for all ages and aqua-gym.
Redon	Sport Loisirs du Pays de Redon, rue ☎ 02 99 71 08 49 Lucien Poulard
	This centre has a flume and variety of pools.
Rennes	There are four indoor swimming pools in the city:
	Piscine Bréquigny, 12 boulevard Albert ☎ 02 99 35 21 30 1er
	(on the south-west side of the city, in the Complexe Sportif Bréguigny)
	Piscine Gayeulles, avenue des Gaveulles ☎ 02 23 21 11 50
	(north-east of the city, part of a large sports and leisure area)
	Piscine St Georges, 2 rue Gambetta ☎ 02 99 28 55 94
	(in the city centre, by the fire station)
	Piscine Villejean, Square d'Alsace ☎ 02 99 59 44 83
	(north-east of the city centre, near the university)
St Malo	Piscine, Terre Plein du Naye ☎ 02 99 81 61 98

Tennis

Bain-de-Bretagne	Tennis Club, rue du Semon ☎ 02 99 43 87 79
	(off rue de Chêne Verte, west of the town centre)
	Two indoor and two outdoor courts. Open to all levels and ages. Tennis school every evening from 5pm, September to June. Contact Mme Oger. Bookings for the tennis courts are made at the Café Barbotin, 10 place de la République; €8 per hour.
Combourg	Tennis club, avenue de Waldmünchen ☎ 02 99 73 23 16
	(by the campsite on the south side of the lake)
Fougères	Tennis Club de Fougères, La Rivière, ☎ 02 99 94 09 74 route de Vitré
	Outdoor tennis courts, a squash court and tennis school for all ages and abilities.
Redon	Tennis Club de Redon, Stade ☎ 02 99 72 19 46 Municipal, route de la Gacilly
Rennes	Centres d'Initiation Sportive, Palais St ☎ 02 99 78 09 40

Georges, 2 rue Gambetta
✉ *ds@ville-rennes.fr*

St Malo   AS Jacques Cartier, 5 avenue de la   ☎ 02 99 56 54 86
Borderie
Competitions, leisure and lessons.

Tree Climbing

See general information on page 113.

Walking & Rambling

The river Vilaine, from which the department takes its name, is the largest
river in Brittany and has a 37km (23mi) towpath from Guipry to Redon.

General   Comité Départemental de la Fédération   ☎ 02 99 54 67 61
Française de Randonnée Pédestre, 13b avenue
de Cucillé, Rennes
💻 *www.rando35.com*
This is the main office for all walking information in the
department.

Bain-de-   There are three walks around the town and surrounding
Bretagne   area departing from the lake. Details are available from
the *syndicat d'initiative* or the *mairie*.

Throughout July and August there are organised walks
every other Tuesday at 3pm. Departing from in front of
the *syndicat d'initiative*.

Combourg   There are two leaflets available free from the tourist office
giving details of two walks in the area around Combourg.

Fougères   Club Fougerais de Randonnées   ☎ 02 99 99 56 28
Pédestres
This local walking group goes on walks of around 20 to 25km
(12 to 16mi) the first Tuesday and third Sunday of the month.

Redon   Various booklets (*Topoguides*) are available from the
tourist office giving details of walks in the area, from 6 to
154km (4 to 95mi) and costing €2 to €13.50 depending on
how many routes are included.

Randonnées Pédestres   ☎ 02 99 71 28 71
This group organises two walks a month, both setting off from
the tourist office: the second Sunday of each month at 9am, the
fourth Sunday of each month at 2pm. Contact Mme Année.

Rennes	There are 50 marked walks in and around Rennes. Details are available from the tourist office; ask for the leaflet *Le Pays de Rennes à Pied*.

La Bellangerais, Maison de Quartier, 5   ☎ 02 99 27 21 1
rue du Morbihan0
🖥 *www.labellangerais.org*
Local walking group.

St Malo	Association Balades Entre Rance et ☎ 02 99 23 88 12
Couesnon, Maison des Associations, rue
Ernest Renan
Three walks organised each month. Contact Mme Hemon.

Watersports

Canoeing & Kayaking

Bain-de-   Club Nautique, avenue Guillotin de   ☎ 02 99 43 72 03
Bretagne   Corson
✉ *mail.cnbv@laposte.fr*
Open from Tuesdays to Saturdays all year.

Redon   Canoë Kayak Redonnais, La Digue, St   ☎ 06 32 15 30 03
Nicolas-de-Redon
✉ *ckredonnais@hotmail.com*
Open for group instruction all year round, adults and children.
Competitions and leisure activities, including evening trips
around the small Ile aux Pies. Contact M. Ripoche.

Rennes   Base Nautique de la Prévalaye,   ☎ 02 99 79 37 37
chemin rural 72 du Moulin d'Apigné
(south-west of the city)

St Malo   Plage de Bon Secours   ☎ 02 99 40 11 45
🖥 *www.snbsm.com*
Open all year for canoeing, sailing, windsurfing and rowing.

Rowing

Redon   Société d'Aviron de Redon et Vilaine,   ☎ 02 99 72 75 44
rue de la Vilaine, St Nicolas-de-Redon
✉ *aviron.redon@wanadoo.fr*
Contact M. Jaffray or M. Bidaud.

Rennes   Société des Régates Rennaises, Base   ☎ 02 99 36 65 75
Nautique de la Plaine de Baud, 35 rue
Jean Marie Huchet
🖥 *www.regates.rennaises.free.fr*

St Malo	Société Nautique de la Baie de St Malo, ☎ 02 99 56 39 41

St Malo   Société Nautique de la Baie de St Malo,   ☎ 02 99 56 39 41
           quai Bajoyer
           🖳 *www.snbsm.com*
           (based at Cale de Bon Secours west of the fort on the northern
           tip of St Malo and Plage du Havre to the east of the town)

Sailing

Bain-de-   Club Nautique, avenue Guillotin de   ☎ 02 99 43 72 03
Bretagne   Corson
              ✉ *mail.cnbv@laposte.fr*
              Open from Tuesdays to Saturdays all year.

Redon   L'Etang Aumée, St Nicolas de Redon   ☎ 02 99 72 12 67
              ✉ *nvcr@wanadoo.fr*
              Open every day from mid-June to mid-September and
              weekends from April to October. Catamarans available to hire
              by the hour or the day. Individual or group courses available
              July and August.

Rennes   Centre Nautique de Rennes, Le Moulin   ☎ 02 99 58 48 80
              d'Apigné
              🖳 *www.centrenautique.org*

St Malo   Société Nautique de la Baie de St Malo, ☎ 02 99 56 39 41
              quai Bajoyer
              🖳 *www.snbsm.com*
              (based at Cale de Bon Secours west of the fort on the northern
              tip of St Malo and Plage du Havre to the east of the town)
              Sailing school with courses, individual lessons and yacht hire.

Scuba Diving

Bain-de-   Club de Plongée, avenue Guillotin de   ☎ 02 23 40 26 98
Bretagne   Corson
              🖳 *www.zomards.free.fr*
              Introduction and training; sea and quarry dives. Open from mid-
              September to June. Contact M. Marchand.

Combourg   Combourg Suba, Piscine Municipale,   ☎ 02 99 73 06 74
              allée des Primevères
              ✉ *alaindubos@free.fr*

Fougères   Subaquatique Club Fougères, 47 rue   ☎ 02 99 94 86 20
              Georges Pompidou
              The group meets at 47 rue de Laval on Wednesday evenings,
              training and courses held on Wednesday evenings from 7.30 to
              10pm at the pool on rue Georges Pompidou. Minimum age 16.

Redon	Groupe d'Activitiés Subaquatiques du Pays de Redon, La Digue, St Nicolas-de-Redon ✉ *roger.ch@libertysurf.fr*	☎ 06 03 88 00 04

Rennes	Rennes Sports Sous-marins, 14 allée des Asturies 💻 *www.rssm.asso.fr* Groups for ten-year-olds upwards.	☎ 02 23 36 09 26

St Malo	Comarin, Port de Plaisance des Bas Sablons, St Servan 💻 *www.comarin.fr* (on the marina, opposite Ponton C) Hire of equipment and group courses.	☎ 02 99 21 38 38

Windsurfing

Bain-de-Bretagne	Club Nautique, avenue Guillotin de Corson ✉ *mail.cnbv@laposte.fr* Open from Tuesdays to Saturdays all year.	☎ 02 99 43 72 03

Cherrueix	Noroît Club, 1 rue de la Plage 💻 *www.noroitclub.fr.fm* (on the coast east of St Malo)	☎ 02 99 48 83 01

Redon	L'Étang Aumée, St Nicolas de Redon ✉ *nvcr@wanadoo.fr* Open every day from mid-June to mid-September and weekends from April to October. Hire by the hour or by the day. Individual or group courses available in July and August.	☎ 02 99 72 12 67

Rennes	Club Nautique de Rennes, Le Moulin d'Apigné 💻 *www.centrenautique.org*	☎ 02 99 58 48 80

St Malo	Surf School, 2 avenue de la Hoguette 💻 *www.surfschool.asso.fr* Surf school with lessons, courses and board hire.	☎ 02 99 40 07 47

Tourist Offices

General	Comité Départemental du Tourisme Haute-Bretagne, 4 rue Jean Jaurès, Rennes 💻 *www.pays-des-portes-de-bretagne.com* 💻 *www.bretagne35.com*	☎ 02 99 78 47 47

Bain-de-Bretagne	Syndicat d'Initiative, 6 rue Bertrand	☎ 02 99 43 98 69

✉ si-baindebretagne@wanadoo.fr
Open September to mid-June Mondays and Saturdays from 10am to noon; mid-June to the end of August (at 17 rue de l'Hôtel de Ville) Mondays to Saturdays 10am to 1pm and 2.30 to 6.30pm, Sundays 10am to noon.

Combourg Maison de la Lanterne, 21 place Albert ☎ 02 99 73 13 93
Parent
💻 www.combourg.org
💻 www.asteria.fr
Open September to June Tuesdays to Saturdays from 10am to 12.30pm and 2.30 to 6pm; July and August, Mondays 10am to 1pm, Tuesdays to Saturdays 10am to 1pm and 2 to 6.30pm, Sundays 10am to 12.30pm.

Fougères 2 rue Nationale ☎ 02 99 94 12 20
💻 www.ot-fougeres.fr
💻 www.fougeres-web.com
💻 www.bretagne-fougeres.com
Open Easter to June, September and October, Mondays to Saturdays 9.30am to 12.30pm and 2 to 6pm, Sundays and bank holidays 1.30 to 5.30pm; July and August, Mondays to Saturdays 9am to 7pm, Sundays and bank holidays 10am to noon and 2 to 4pm; November to Easter, Mondays 2 to 6pm, Tuesdays to Saturdays 10am to 12.30pm and 2 to 6pm.

Redon place de la République ☎ 02 99 71 06 04
💻 www.tourisme-pays-redon.com
💻 www.redon.fr
Open September to June Mondays to Fridays from 9.30am to noon and 2 to 6pm, Saturdays 10am to 12.30pm and 3 to 5pm (closed Tuesday mornings); July and August Mondays to Saturdays 9.30am to 12.30pm and 1.30 to 6.30pm, Sundays and bank holidays 10am to 12.30pm and 3 to 5.30pm.

Rennes 11 rue St Yves ☎ 02 99 67 11 11
💻 www.rennes.fr
💻 www.tourisme-rennes.com
Open April to September Mondays to Saturdays from 9am to 7pm, Sundays and bank holidays 11am to 6pm; October to March Mondays to Saturdays 9am to 6pm, Sundays and bank holidays 11am to 6pm.

St Malo Esplanade St Vincent ☎ 08 25 16 02 00
💻 www.saint-malo-tourisme.com
💻 www.saint-malo.fr
Open April to June and September Mondays to Saturdays from 9am to 12.30pm and 1.30 to 6.30pm, Sundays and bank

holidays 10am to 12.30pm and 2.30 to 6pm; July and August
Mondays to Saturdays 9am to 7.30pm, Sundays and bank
holidays 10am to 6pm; October to March Mondays to
Saturdays 9am to 12.30pm and 1.30 to 6pm (closed Sundays
and bank holidays).

Tradesmen

Architects & Project Managers

General   Burrows-Hutchinson, Ploerdut   ☎ 02 97 39 45 53
     ✉ *burrowhutch@aol.com*
English-speaking architectural practice offering interior design,
project management, building surveys and reports.

Max Lenglet, Plérin   ☎ 02 96 74 49 22
English-speaking project manager for building and renovation
work, specialising in 'green' and eco-friendly buildings and
materials.

Mike McCoy, Pen-ar-Vern, Bourbriac   ☎ 02 96 43 44 23
✉ *therealmccoy999@aol.com*
Bi-lingual draughtsman for architectural design and planning,
renovations and septic tank applications.

View Brittany, Le Kanveze, Remungol   ☎ 02 97 60 94 57
✉ *vb.caro@wanadoo.fr*
New builds, renovation, surveys and project management.
English-speaking.

Combourg   JFH, Maitre d'Oeuvre, rue de la Mairie   ☎ 02 99 73 06 92
Architect and project management for new builds and
renovations. English speaking.

Builders

General   View Brittany, Le Kanveze, Remungol   ☎ 02 97 60 94 57
     ✉ *vb.caro@wanadoo.fr*
New builds, renovation, surveys and project management.
English-speaking.

Carpenters

See general information on page 115.

Chimney Sweeps

See general information on page 115.

Electricians & Plumbers

See general information on page 116.

Planning Permission

See general information on page 116.

Translators & Teachers

French Teachers & Courses

Combourg	Mme Porée ✉ *fab.poree@wanadoo.fr*	☎ 06 77 57 43 76
Fougères	La CCI, 50 rue Nationale	☎ 02 99 94 75 75
Redon	French Lessons for English Speakers, 7 rue St Conwoïon	☎ 02 99 72 22 40
Rennes	Langue et Communication, 55 rue Jean Guéhenno 🖳 *www.fle.fr/lc*	☎ 02 99 38 12 55
St Malo	Caplangue, Créhen, Pleurtuit ✉ *caplangue@aol.com*	☎ 02 99 88 54 79

Translations

See general information on page 116.

Translators

See general information on page 117.

Utilities

See general information on page 117.

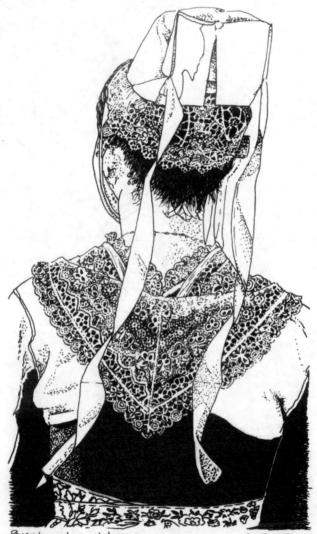

Breton headdress   JoTaylor

6

Morbihan

This chapter provides details of facilities and services in the department of Morbihan (56). General information about each subject can be found in **Chapter 2**. All entries are arranged alphabetically by town, except where a service applies over a wide area, in which case it's listed at the beginning of the relevant section under 'General'. A map of Morbihan is shown below.

Accommodation

Various tourist office websites have details of camping, B&B, *gîte* and hotel accommodation, including the following:

    🖥 *www.brittanytourisme.com*
    🖥 *www.lorient-tourisme.com*
    🖥 *www.morbihan.com*
    🖥 *www.paysroimorvan.com*
    🖥 *www.tourisme-vannes.com*

Camping

Arradon   Camping de Penboch   ☎ 02 97 44 71 29
Four-star campsite with swimming pool, 200m from the sea. Mobile homes and chalets for rent.

Erdeven   Camping les Sept Saints   ☎ 02 97 55 52 65
🖥 *www.septsaints.com*

Four-star campsite with swimming pool and evening events in the summer. Chalets and mobile homes for hire.

Le Faouët	Beg-er-Roch, route de Lorient	☎ 02 97 23 15 11

Three-star campsite open from March to September.

Gourin	Camping Municipal de Pont-Min, route de Quimper	☎ 02 97 23 42 74

Open in July and August.

Guémene	Le Palevart	☎ 02 97 51 20 23

A basic campsite close to the river Scorff. Open from June to mid-September.

Plœmeur	Camping Kerpape, route de Lomener	☎ 02 97 82 94 55

🖳 *www.vacanciel.com*

Three-star campsite with direct access to the sea. Mobile homes for rent.

Priziac	Le Bel Air, Lac du Bel Air	☎ 02 97 34 63 55

Three-star campsite on the edge of a large lake. Open from March to September.

Taupont	La Vallée du Ninian, Le Rocher	☎ 02 97 93 53 01

🖳 *www.camping-ninian.com*
(on the north-west outskirts of Ploërmel)
Three-star campsite with swimming pool, paddling pool, launderette and groceries. Open from May to September.

Vannes	Camping Municipal de Conleau, 188 avenue du Maréchal Juin	☎ 02 97 63 13 88

(on the south side of the town on the water front)

Chateaux

Rochefort-en-Terre	Château de Talhouët	☎ 02 97 43 34 72

🖳 www.chateaudetalhouet.com
A traditional Breton manor house built in the 16th century and surrounded by 20ha (49 acres) of parkland. Rooms from €120 to €200 per night. Evening meal available, English spoken.

Gîtes and Bed & Breakfast

General	Gîtes de France Morbihan, 42 avenue Wilson, Auray	☎ 02 97 56 48 12

🖳 *www.gites-de-france-morbihan.com*

	Clévacances, Pibs Kérino, allée Nicolas Le Blanc	☎ 02 97 54 14 56

🖳 *www.clevacances.com*

Hotels

Three hotel suggestions are listed in price order for each town, where possible covering all budgets. Many towns have the national chains such as those given on page 51.

Le Faouët   There's only one hotel in Le Faouët, listed below.

La Croix d'Or, 9 place Bellanger   ☎ 02 97 23 07 33
💻 *www.lacroixdor.fr*
Double rooms from €46 per night. Closed mid-December to mid-January.

Lorient   Le Square, 5 place Jules Ferry   ☎ 02 97 21 06 36
Double rooms from €25 to €30 per night.

Central Hotel, place Jules Ferry   ☎ 02 97 21 16 52
💻 *www.centralhotellorient.com*
Double rooms from €48 to €80 per night.

Hôtel Mascotte du Centre, 30 rue   ☎ 02 97 64 13 27
Ducouédic
💻 *www.hotelmascotte-lorient.com*
Double rooms from €52 to €56 per night.

Ploërmel   Retour de Pêche, 70 rue de la Gare   ☎ 02 97 74 05 32
💻 *www.retourdepeche.com*
Double rooms from €36 to €38 per night.

Le Cobh, 10 rue des Forges   ☎ 02 97 74 00 49
Three-star hotel with double rooms from €55 to €100 per night.

Le Roi Arthur, Lac au Duc   ☎ 02 97 73 64 64
💻 *www.hotelroiarthur.com*
Three-star hotel overlooking a lake and golf course. Various gourmet and relaxation weekends. Double rooms from €87 to €127 per night.

Vannes   Le Richemont, 26 place de la Gare   ☎ 02 97 47 17 24
💻 *www.hotel-richemont-vannes.com*
Double rooms from €50 per night.

Hôtel Marina, 4 place Gambetta, Port   ☎ 02 97 47 22 81
de Vannes
Double rooms from €57 per night. Dogs accepted.

La Marébaudière, 4 rue Aristide Briand   ☎ 02 97 47 34 29
💻 *www.marebaudiere.com*

Three-star hotel with private parking, dogs accepted. Double
rooms from €78 per night.

Long-term Rentals

See general information on page 52.

Administration

See general information on page 52.

Banks

See general information on page 55.

Business Services

Computer Services

General	M2 Services Informatique, 17 rue St Jean, Moncontour	☎ 02 96 73 46 31

Computer repairs, call-out service and custom-built systems.
English-speaking company, covering the north side of the
department. There's also a recording studio for rent.

Le Faouët	Trucs et Astuces, Le Léannec, Berne (just to the south-east of the town)	☎ 02 97 34 24 54

Lorient	Cap Informatique, 109 rue Paul Guieysse	☎ 02 97 21 49 56

✉ *cap.informatique56@wanadoo.fr*
Sale, repair, software and accessories.

Ploërmel	Giga Hertz, 13 place de l'Union	☎ 02 97 73 31 71

Computers made to order, sales, repairs and consumables.

Vannes	Alias Informatique, 3 rue Madame Lagarde	☎ 02 97 47 00 20

Sales and repairs. Repair work carried out at your home or in
the workshop.

Computer Training

Le Faouët	Médiathèque, 54 rue de St Fiacre	☎ 02 97 23 15 39

Introductory sessions given to individuals or couples, free to
residents of Le Faouët.

| Lorient | Mediathèque – Logithèque ☎ 02 97 84 33 60 |
| | Group sessions throughout the week. Contact M. Brunel. |

Ploërmel   Club Informatique de Taupont, Annexe ☎ 02 97 74 11 10
de la Mairie, avenue Porhoët, Taupont
Contact M. Dauvergne.

Vannes   Mediacap, rue Henri Becquerel   ☎ 02 97 01 55 55
🖳 *www.mairie-vannes.fr/cybercentres*
Various workshops to introduce you to the internet, software
packages and basic computer skills.

Employment Agencies

See general information on page 58.

Communications

Telephone

See also general information on page 59.

Fixed Line Telephone Services

General   France Télécom   ☎ 1014
🖳 *www.francetelecom.fr*
Local France Télécom shops are listed below.

Lorient   Géant Complex, Parc des Expos, Lanester
(north of the town; from the N165 take the turning to Lanester)
Open Mondays to Fridays from 9am to 8.30pm, Saturdays 9am
to 8pm.

Vannes   15 place de la République

Internet

Broadband

See general information on page 62.

Public Internet Access

Le Faouët   Médiathèque, 54 rue de St Fiacre   ☎ 02 97 23 15 39
Open Tuesdays from 2 to 6pm, Wednesdays 9am to noon and
2 to 5pm, Thursdays 9am to noon, Saturdays 9am to noon and
2 to 5pm.

Lorient	Webbow Cybercafé, 13 place Jules Ferry	☎ 02 97 21 46 51

www.webbow.net
Open Mondays to Saturdays from 1pm to 1am, Sundays 4 to 11pm.

Ploërmel	K-Var Espace Informatique, 3 rue de la Gare	☎ 02 97 73 30 13

Open Mondays to Fridays from 9am to 12.30pm and 2 to 6.30pm, Saturdays 9am to noon.

Vannes	Cybercentre, Bureau Information Jeunesse, 22 avenue Victor Hugo	☎ 02 97 01 61 00

✉ *bij@mairie-vannes.fr*
Open Mondays from 1.30 to 6pm, Tuesdays to Fridays 10am to noon and 1.30 to 6pm.

Useful Web Addresses

See general information on page 63.

Television & Radio

See general information on page 63.

Domestic Services

Bouncy Castle Hire

See general information on page 65.

Clothes Alterations

Lorient	Rapid' Couture, 37 rue Paul Guieysse	☎ 02 97 21 87 61
Ploërmel	Marie-Line Couture, rue Fossés	☎ 02 97 73 34 99
Vannes	L'Atelier d'Ces Dames, 4 place Cabello	☎ 02 97 54 38 96

Clothes made to measure and altered, and theatrical costumes supplied.

Crèches & Nurseries

Lorient	Halte-garderie du Pôle Enfance, 2 rue François Le Brise	☎ 02 97 64 23 37

Babies and children from three months to six-year-olds. Closed for one week in April and all of August.

| Vannes | Halte-garderie de Richemont, 24 rue Richemont | ☎ 02 97 63 25 85 |

Children from three months to six years old. Open Tuesdays and Thursdays from 9am to 5pm, Wednesdays and Fridays 8.45am to 12.15pm and 1.45 to 5.45pm, Saturdays 9am to 12.15pm.

| | BIJ Service Baby Sitting, 22 avenue Victor Hugo | ☎ 02 97 01 61 00 |

Equipment & Tool Hire

| Lorient | Bretagne Nacelle, 8 avenue Kergroise | ☎ 02 97 83 50 60 |

| Ploërmel | Locarmor, ZI Bois Vert | ☎ 02 97 74 10 20 |

| Vannes | Loxam, ZI Prat, 29 avenue Gontran Bienvenu | ☎ 02 97 54 27 58 |
💻 *www.loxam.fr*

Fancy Dress Hire

See general information on page 66.

Garden Services

| General | Central Brittany Gardening, Kroas-ar-Pichon, Paule | ☎ 02 96 29 68 47 |

English-speaking garden maintenance, hedge cutting and tree felling. Covers the north-west of the department.

| | Squire Services, Kerguédalen, St Caradec Tregomel | ☎ 06 30 59 34 34 |
✉ *john@squirearbo.com*

Internationally qualified, English-speaking arborist for all tree, hedge and woodland work. Tree felling and crowns lifted.

| Campénéac | Bruno Bargain, Mauny | ☎ 02 97 93 45 07 |
💻 *www.atoutvert.fr*

Gardens designed and maintained.

| Larmor-Plage | Kerhoas Services, ZA Armor Océan | ☎ 02 97 83 52 52 |

General garden maintenance.

| Lorient | Didier Lailic, 38 rue Kerguillette | ☎ 02 97 83 33 25 |

| Vannes | Propreté Morbihannaise, ZA de la Trehuinec, Plescop | ☎ 02 97 46 92 92 |

Garden design and maintenance.

Launderettes

Lorient   Laverie Multiservices, 2 rue Georges   ☎ 02 97 64 65 98
                 Gaigneux

Vannes   Le Priol Gilles, 8 rue 116ème RI   ☎ 02 97 47 01 56

Marquee Hire

Pleucadeuc   Location Chapiteaux Ayoul O, Les   ☎ 02 97 26 94 67
                 Fontenelles
                 💻 *www.cortix.fr/ayoul-chapiteaux.com*
                 (south of Ploërmel)
                 Marquees, tents and rigid structures and all equipment needed
                 for a party.

Vannes   Rault Location, ZAC Kerniol, 15 rue   ☎ 02 97 40 61 14
                 Frères Lumière
                 💻 *www.rault.fr*
                 Sale and hire of marquees.

Party Services

See general information on page 66.

Septic Tank Services

Carnac   ADS-AAE, Kergroix   ☎ 02 97 56 85 48
                 (on the coast south-east of Lorient)
                 Pumping out, unblocking, installation and repair of septic tanks.

Quiberon   Claude Le Pennec, 2 rue Surcouf   ☎ 02 97 50 05 65
                 ✉ *clepennec@wanadoo.fr*
                 (on the peninsula out towards Belle Ile, south-west of Vannes)
                 Empting and cleaning of septic tanks.

Vannes   Sita Ouest, 27 avenue Edouard Michelin ☎ 02 97 26 70 90

Entertainment

Cinemas

Le Faouët   Cinéma Ellé, place Corderie   ☎ 02 97 23 20 94

Lorient   Ciné Stars, Parc des Expos, Lanester   ☎ 08 92 68 20 15
                 💻 *www.cinefil.com*
                 (north of Lorient; from the N165 take the turning for the Géant
                 hypermarket)
                 11-screen cinema complex.

Cineville, 4 boulevard Maréchal Joffre   ☎ 02 97 64 78 00
Art cinema frequently showing films in English.

Ploërmel   Cinéma Syrius, place Mairie   ☎ 02 97 73 35 24
                    💻 *www.cinefil.com*

Vannes   La Garenne, 12 bis rue Alexandre Le   ☎ 08 92 68 06 66
                    Pontois
                    Five-screen cinema.

English Books

General   Le Chat qui Lit, Pempoulrot, Kergrist-   ☎ 02 96 36 59 00
                    Moëlou
                    💻 *www.chatquilit.com*
                    (north-east of Le Faouët , just over the border into Côtes-
                    d'Armor))
                    Second-hand English books. Open Tuesdays to Thursday from
                    2 to 6pm, Fridays and Saturdays 10am to 6pm.

Festivals

There are many festivals in this department, and just a small selection is
detailed here. Further details are available from tourist offices. All events
are annual unless otherwise stated.

February   Lorient
                    Deiziou Pays de Lorient   ☎ 02 97 21 37 05
                    A traditional Breton festival with exhibitions, concerts, theatre
                    and dancing.

March   Lorient
                    Mars m'Enchante   ☎ 02 97 76 01 47
                    A festival of French singers held annually at Lanester, north-
                    east of the town.

April   Lorient
                    BD de Lorient   ☎ 02 97 21 07 84
                    💻 *www.bullesanoriant.com*
                    Cartoon festival, generally the first weekend of April. Multimedia
                    exhibitions, workshops and films.

May   Lorient
                    Fête Nationale du Nautisme, Larmor-   ☎ 02 97 33 77 78
                    Plage
                    Two-day nautical festival around the middle of the month.

                    Vannes
                    Semaine du Golfe   ☎ 02 97 47 24 34

All the communities around the Gulf of Morbihan take part in this week-long maritime festival every other year (the next is in 2007) around the Ascension bank holiday (sixth Thursday after Easter).

July	**Guidel** Polignac des "7 Chapelles"	☎ 02 97 65 06 13

🖥 *www.festival7chapelles.com*
A music festival with some of the greatest classical artists from around the world.

Hennebont
Les Fêtes Médiévales d'Hennebont   ☎ 02 97 36 24 52
Medieval festival with a carnival procession, street entertainment, shows and a market late into the night.

Lorient
Le Festival 'Saumon', Pont-Scorff   ☎ 02 97 32 50 27
A three-day salmon festival, unique in France.

Vannes
Jazz à Vannes   ☎ 02 97 47 24 34
Jazz festival.

August   **l'Ile-aux-Moines**
Festival de la Voile   ☎ 02 97 26 32 4
Sailing festival on an island just south of Vannes.

Surzur
Fête de l'Huître   ☎ 02 97 42 12 52
Oyster festival.

October   **Sulniac**
Fête de la Pomme   ☎ 02 97 53 23 02
Apple festival.

Libraries

Le Faouët   Médiathèque, 54 rue de St Fiacre   ☎ 02 97 23 15 39
Open Tuesdays from 2 to 6pm, Wednesdays 9am to noon and 2 to 5pm, Thursdays 9am to noon, Saturdays 9am to noon and 2 to 5pm. This library doesn't currently have any books in English.

Lorient   Bibliothèque de Kéryado 24 rue   ☎ 02 97 35 33 12
Kersabiec
Open Tuesdays, Thursdays and Fridays from 2.30 to 6.30pm, Wednesdays 10am to noon and 2 to 6.30pm, Saturdays 10am to noon and 1.30 to 5.30pm. This library has a small selection of English books.

Ploërmel	Bibliothèque/Médiathèque de	☎ 02 97 74 28 25

Ploërmel, Centre Culturel, avenue de Guibourg
Open Mondays from 10am to noon and 3.30 to 6.15pm,
Tuesdays 3.30 to 6.15pm, Wednesdays 10am to noon and
2.30 to 6pm, Thursdays 12.30 to 1.30pm and 3.30 to 6.15pm,
Fridays 3.30 to 6pm, Saturdays 9.30am to 12.30pm. This
library has a selection of English books.

Vannes	Médiathèque du Palais des Arts, place	☎ 02 97 01 62 62

de Bretagne
Open Tuesdays and Thursdays from 1.30 to 6pm, Wednesdays
9am to 12.30pm and 1.30 to 6pm, Fridays noon to 6pm,
Saturdays 9am to 12.30pm and 1.30 to 5.30pm. This library
has a selection of English books.

Theatres

Lorient	Théâtre de Lorient, 11 rue Claire Droneau	☎ 02 97 83 51 51
Pont-Scorff	Théâtre de l'Echange, St Urchaut ✉ *theatredelechange@wanadoo.fr*	☎ 02 97 32 68 69
	Théâtre Le Strapontin, rue Docteur Rialland	☎ 02 97 32 63 91

Video & DVD Hire

See general information on page 68.

Leisure

This section isn't intended to be a definitive guide but gives a wide range
of ideas for the department. Prices and opening hours were correct at the
time of writing, but it's best to check before travelling long distances.

Arts & Crafts

Le Faouët	Ateliers de la Vieille Ecole	☎ 02 97 34 40 79

Sculpture and painting workshops. Contact Rémy Mounier.

Lorient	Les Ateliers de l'Arc, 26 rue de	☎ 02 97 83 57 57

Kersabiec
🖳 *www.lesateliersdelarc.om*
Sculpture and drawing workshops.

	Artoiles	☎ 06 07 27 75 47

Oil painting and watercolour. Contact M. Dumont.

| Ploërmel | Office Culture Mystringue, 3 avenue de Guibourg | ☎ 02 97 74 08 21 |

Various workshops for all ages including painting, sculpture, modelling and drawing.

| Vannes | Ateliers Artistiques Municipaux, Manoir de Trussac, 60 rue Albert 1er | ☎ 02 97 40 84 01 |

Drawing, watercolour and oil painting, modelling and engraving.

Bowling

| Lorient | Bowling de Larmor-Plage, 12 rue Minio, Larmor-Plage | ☎ 02 97 33 70 60 |

(on the coast, south of the town)

| Vannes | Le Master, rue Gilles Gahinet | ☎ 02 97 46 09 00 |

Bowling, pool tables and a disco.

| | Superbowl, 1 rue marcel Dassault, St Avé | ☎ 02 97 60 62 89 |

(north of the town)
14 bowling alleys, pool tables, crazy golf, bar, video games and a giant TV screen.

Bridge

| Lorient | AVF, Maison des Associations, Cité Allende, 12 rue Colbert | ☎ 02 97 84 85 39 |

Contact M. Le Verger or Mme Pèlerin.

| Ploërmel | Club de Bridge, Office Culturel Mystringue, 3 avenue de Guibourg | ☎ 02 97 93 24 97 |

Mondays from 8.15pm, Wednesdays from 2.30pm, Thursdays from 8.15pm and one Sunday each month. Contact Mme Séguineau.

| Vannes | Bridge Club Vannetais, 23 rue Emile Jourdan | ☎ 02 97 63 41 76 |

Courses from Tuesdays to Fridays at 9.30am, Wednesdays 8.30pm and Thursdays 2pm. Matches Mondays to Fridays, beginners' matches Wednesdays 8pm and Thursdays 2pm.

Children's Activity Clubs

| Le Faouët | Point Information Jeunesse, rue Victor Robic | |

(down the driveway to the right of the *mairie*)
Open Saturdays from 10am to noon, this is part of a larger organisation that works with youngsters.

| Lorient | Maison pour Tous de Kervénanec, | ☎ 02 97 37 29 86 |

2 rue Maurice Thorez
Open Wednesdays and Saturday afternoons. Courses and
activities during the school holidays.

Vannes   Espace Henri Matisse, rue Emile Jourdan ☎ 02 97 62 68 10
Leisure activities for 4 to 11-year-olds. Open Wednesdays and
school holidays.

Choral Singing

Lorient   Accord Parfait Lorientais, Maison des   ☎ 02 97 33 35 15
Associations, Cité Allende, 12 rue Colbert
Contact Mme Carado.

Ploërmel   Office Culture Mystringue, 3 avenue de ☎ 02 97 74 08 21
Guibourg
Mixed, women's and junior choirs.

Vannes   Ecole Nationale de Musique, 16 place   ☎ 02 97 01 67 00
Théodore Decker
✉ enm@mairie-vannes.fr

Circus Skills & Magic

Vannes   Gymmome-Les Acrofils, Gymnase du   ☎ 02 97 46 04 14
Lycée St Paul
🖥 www.multimania.com/gymmome
Circus skills including acrobatics, trapeze, tight rope walking
and trampoline. Contact Mme Menanteau.

Dancing

Le Faouët   Danserien an Ellé   ☎ 02 97 23 02 31
Breton dancing.

Lorient   Ecole de Danse Nicole Mouton, Cité   ☎ 02 97 84 87 24
Allende, 12 rue Colbert
Ballet, jazz and tap classes.

Ecole de Danse Colette Gauthier   ☎ 02 97 64 55 71
Rock, salsa, tango and other Latin American dances.

Ploërmel   Attitude Pointes, Office Culturel   ☎ 02 97 22 30 54
Mystringue, 3 avenue de Guibourg
Ballet classes.

Ecole de Danse F. Chardevel, Office   ☎ 06 88 08 86 78
Culturel Mystringue, 3 avenue de Guibourg
Jazz classes.

| Vannes | LA Danse Association, 18 rue Fravel et Lincy | ☎ 02 97 42 61 72 |

Ballet, jazz, keep fit, and African dance. Groups for all ages
from 4-year-olds.

| | CA Danse, avenue Borgnis Desbordes | ☎ 02 97 40 51 69 |

Ballroom and Latin American.

Drama

| Lorient | Centre Dramatique de Bretagne, Théâtre de Lorient, 11 rue Claire Droneau | ☎ 02 97 83 51 51 |

| | Plateau en Toute Liberté | ☎ 02 97 83 65 76 |

Children's and adult groups. Contact Mme Paugam.

| Ploërmel | Cailloux et Allumettes | ☎ 06 65 37 25 15 |

Various groups held on Wednesdays. Contact Luisa Tonini.

| Vannes | Ateliers Théâtre de la Ville de Vannes, Manoir de Trussac, 60 rue Albert 1er | ☎ 02 97 40 84 01 |

Dress Making

| Ploërmel | Office Culture Mystringue, 3 avenue de Guibourg | ☎ 02 97 74 08 21 |

| Vannes | Centre Communal d'Action Sociale, 22 avenue Victor Hugo | ☎ 02 97 54 64 60 |

Courses for beginners and intermediates, adults and
youngsters, Mondays to Fridays.

Flower Arranging

| Lorient | Fleur-en-Art, Cité Allende, 12 rue Colbert | ☎ 06 22 08 62 40 |

Contact Gwenola Collin.

| Ploërmel | Art Floral | ☎ 02 97 73 37 74 |

Courses held Tuesday afternoons and Thursday evenings.
Contact Mado Cottenceau.

| Vannes | Société d'Horticulture du Pays de Vannes | ☎ 02 97 60 73 90 |

🖥 *www.vannes-horticulture.asso.fr*
Contact Mme Lorec.

Gardening

See general information on page 70.

Gym

Lorient	Les Ateliers de l'Arc, 7 rue Jules Legrand ☎ *www.lesateliersdelarc.com* Classes for teenagers and adults.	☎ 02 97 64 64 21
Ploërmel	Club de Gym EPMM de Ploërmel Various classes for adults and seniors.	☎ 02 97 74 25 81
Vannes	Club Gym, 19 rue Tannerie A wide range of classes from cardio to stretching.	☎ 02 97 54 28 88

Gyms & Health Clubs

Lorient	Fitness Club, 87 boulevard Cosmao Dumanoir	☎ 02 97 83 39 05
Vannes	Atlantic Fitness, 18 rue Alsace, Séné (south of the town, on the coast) Group classes and personal training. Sauna. Open daily all year.	☎ 02 97 42 77 49
	Somao Fitness, 53 rue Ste Anne ☎ *www.somao-fitness.com* Swimming pool, sauna and various fitness classes. Open daily.	☎ 02 97 46 35 34

Ice Skating

Lorient	La Patinoire du Scorff, Parc des Expositions, rue JM Djibaou, Lanester (north-east of the town)	☎ 02 97 81 07 83
Vannes	Patinium, route de Ste Anne ☎ *www.patinium.com* Ice rink open all year.	☎ 02 97 40 91 23

Music

Lorient	Ecole Nationale de Musique et de Danse, 7 rue Armand Guillemot ✉ *enmdlor@mairie-lorient.fr* Wide range of instruments taught, including guitar, clarinet, flute, piano and drums.	☎ 02 97 02 23 00
Ploërmel	Ecole Municipale de Musique, Office Culture Mystringue, 3 avenue de Guibourg Choir, chamber music, rock and jazz workshops, computer-assisted music and drums.	☎ 02 97 74 08 21

| Vannes | Ecole Nationale de Musique, 16 place T. Decker | ☎ 02 97 01 67 00 |

Vocal and instrumental activities, orchestra, choir and lessons on 19 different instruments.

Photography

| Lorient | Club Culturel et Artistique de la Défense | ☎ 02 97 12 21 63 |

Contact M. Lunelli.

| Ploërmel | Office Culture Mystringue, 4 rue Sénéchal Thuault | ☎ 02 97 74 08 21 |

Contact M. Sasso.

| Vannes | Espace Henri Matisse, 13 rue Emile Jourdan | ☎ 02 97 62 68 10 |

Introductory courses on Monday evenings and a photographic club on Fridays at 6pm.

Scouts & Guides

| Lorient | Guides de France | ☎ 02 97 82 74 86 |

Weekly meetings plus several weekends each year and a summer camp. Contact Mme Loriot.

| | Scouts de France | ☎ 02 97 43 92 97 |

Contact M. Roszo.

| Vannes | Guides de France | ☎ 02 97 60 77 98 |

Saturday afternoon meetings, weekend trips and summer camps. Contact Mme Le Neillon.

| | Scouts de France Groupe Beaumanoir, 10 rue de Nomeny | ☎ 02 97 44 45 56 |

This group meets every Saturday (except school holidays) from 2 to 5pm. Contact M. Le Corre.

Social Groups

Town Twinning

| Le Faouët | Comité de Jumelage | ☎ 02 97 23 10 45 |

Twinned with Headford in Ireland. Contact Mme Le Ny.

| Ploërmel | Comité de Jumelage Ploërmel/Cobh | ☎ 02 97 74 21 01 |

Twinned with Cobh in Ireland.

| | Les Amis de Gorseinon | ☎ 02 97 74 64 96 |

An exchange group with Gorseinon in Wales.

| Vannes | Comité Vannes-Fareham
Twinned with Fareham in England. | ☎ 02 97 63 16 73 |

Welcome Groups

| Lorient | AVF, Maison des Associations, Cité
Allende, 12 rue Colbert
✉ *avf-lorient@wanadoo.fr* | ☎ 02 97 84 85 39 |

| Vannes | AVF Vannes, 14 rue Francis Decker | ☎ 02 97 42 72 23 |

Spas

See general information on page 71.

Stamp Collecting

| Lorient | Association Philatélique Armoricaine,
Maison des Associations, Cité Allende, 12 rue Colbert
Separate groups for adults and children. | ☎ 02 97 83 82 54 |

| Vannes | La Philatélie Vannetaise, Maison des
Associations, 6 rue de la Tannerie
Monthly meetings for adults and youngsters. Contact
M. Pennes. | ☎ 02 97 60 65 97 |

Yoga

| Lorient | Cercle de Yoga, Le Polygone, 80
avenue du Général de Gaulle
Contact Mme Stéphan. | ☎ 02 97 83 31 01 |

| Ploërmel | Ecole St Louis, 18 avenue Rioust des
Villes Audrains
Classes on Mondays and Wednesdays. Contact Mme
Chauvensy. | ☎ 02 97 93 89 01 |

| Vannes | Shivaree Om Relaxation, 5 rue
Maréchal Foch, Sarzeau | ☎ 06 16 02 94 67 |

Medical Facilities & Emergency Services

Ambulances

See general information on page 72.

Doctors

English-speakers may like to contact the following doctors:

Le Faouët	Cabinet Médical, 18 rue Quimper	☎ 02 97 23 12 79
Lorient	Cabinet Médical, 55 rue Claire Droneau	☎ 02 97 21 04 34
	Emergency doctor ☎ 08 25 85 03 08
Ploërmel	Dr Lechesne, 52 rue Général Dubreton	☎ 02 97 93 69 12
Vannes	Dr Legrand, 22 place Fareham	☎ 02 97 46 00 66

Emergencies

See general information on page 73.

Fire Brigade

See general information on page 76.

Health Authority

| Le Faouët | 9 rue Victor Robic |
| | There's a representative from the CPAM here every Wednesday from 1.30 to 4.30pm. The office is in the building to the right of the courtyard of the *mairie*. |

| Lorient | 3 avenue Anatole France | ☎ 02 97 84 18 28 |

| Ploërmel | Les Carmes, 9 rue du Val   ☎ 02 97 72 02 66 |
| | There's a CPAM representative here the first and third Tuesday of each month from 9am to noon and 1.30 to 4.30pm. |

Vannes	CPAM du Morbihan, 73 rue du Général ☎ 08 20 90 41 49 Weygand
	🖥 *www.cpam56.fr*
	This is the main office for the department. Open Mondays to Fridays from 8am to 5pm.

Hospitals

All the following hospitals have an emergency department.

Caudan	Centre Hospitalier Charcot, route Pont- ☎ 02 97 02 39 39 Scorff
	🖥 *www.ch-charcot56.fr*
	(just outside Lorient, off the D769, directly north of Lanester)

| Lorient | Centre Hospitalier de Bretagne Sud, 27 ☎ 02 97 64 90 00 rue Docteur Lettry |

Pontivy	Centre Hospitalier de Pontivy, place Ernest Jan 🖳 *www.ch-pontivy.fr*	☎ 02 97 28 40 40
Vannes	Centre Hospitalier Bretagne Atlantique, 20 boulevard du Général Maurice Guillaudot	☎ 02 97 01 41 41

Police

See general information on page 77.

Motoring

See general information on page 79.

Nightlife

This section isn't intended to be a definitive guide but gives a wide range of ideas for the department. Prices and opening hours were correct at the time of writing, but it's best to check before travelling long distances.

Arzon	Casino Port Crouesty Le Grand Jeu, Rond-point du Crouesty (at the end of the peninsula that curves around the south of Vannes) Games machines, gambling tables, restaurant and bar.	☎ 02 97 53 99 44
Le Faouët	Au Bon Abri, 1 îlot Congrégation Restaurant/bar in the centre of town. Draught cider, pool tables and Celtic entertainment in the evenings.	☎ 02 97 23 09 98
Lorient	The Galway Inn, 18 rue de Belgique Irish bar open late.	☎ 02 97 64 50 77
	Le Pacific, 4 place Jules Ferry Disco.	☎ 02 97 21 30 90
	Tavarn ar Roue Morvan, 17 rue Poissonnière Late bar.	☎ 02 97 21 61 57
Séné	Le Yanis Club, route de Nantes, Rond-point du Poulfanc Disco.	☎ 02 97 42 51 10

Sérent	Le Conc'ker, Trégaro	☎ 06 77 81 54 27

(south-west of Ploërmel)
Disco, concerts and pizza/snack bar. Open from 11.30pm
to 5am.

Vannes	Le Bar Bi, Parc du Golfe	☎ 02 97 46 05 55

Late bar/club.

D'Ici et d'Ailleurs, 24 rue du Maréchal   ☎ 02 97 63 04 52
Juin
Concert/cafe.

John O'Flaherty's, 22 rue Hoche   ☎ 02 97 42 40 11
Late bar.

Le Master, Parc du Golfe   ☎ 02 97 46 09 00
A large complex with bowling, pool tables and disco.

Le River Side, 2 rue Campen   ☎ 02 97 40 43 32
An Irish pub with snack food and a wide range of beers.

Superbowl, 1 rue marcel Dassault, St Avé ☎ 02 97 60 62 89
(north of the town)
14 bowling alleys, pool tables, crazy golf, bar, video games and
giant TV screen.

Le Swansea, 3 rue du Four   ☎ 02 97 42 74 92
Late bar.

Villa Kirov, Parc du Golfe   ☎ 02 97 62 08 29
Disco within the Hôtel Mercure.

Pets

Dog Hygiene

See general information on page 84.

Dog Training

See general information on page 84.

Farriers

General	Sylvain Guyonvarho, Kerjustic,	☎ 02 97 65 29 46

Languidic
(north-east of Lorient)

M. Penneroux, Rhe, Questembert   ☎ 02 97 26 13 44
(directly east of Vannes)

Horse Dentists

See general information on page 84.

Horse Feed

General   Joe Denham, La Garenne, Langonnet   ☎ 02 97 23 91 65
✉ *lagarenne2004@yahoo.co.uk*
Quality hay and haylage (preserved hay with a slightly higher
protein/energy content). English-speaking.

Horse Vets

Guidel   Dr Ridoux, 24 rue St Maurice   ☎ 02 97 65 03 17

Identification

See general information on page 85.

Kennels & Catteries

See general information on page 85.

Pet Parlours

See general information on page 86.

Pet Travel

See general information on page 86.

Riding Equipment

Sarzeau   Equilance, 13 rue Père JM Coudrin   ☎ 02 97 41 76 36
(on the larger peninsula curving east below Vannes)
Equipment for horse and rider. Spillers distributor.

Vannes   Sellerie du Golfe, ZC du Parc Lann, rue ☎ 02 97 63 25 49
Marcellin Berthelot
✉ *selleriedugolfe@wanadoo.fr*
Saddlery, equipment supplier and Spillers distributor.

SPA

Lorient   SPA, 80 Kercaves, Larmor-Plage   ☎ 02 97 33 70 90

Vannes   ZI Le Prat, avenue Edouard Michelin   ☎ 02 97 42 43 74
Open every day from 10am to noon and 2 to 5pm.

Veterinary Clinics

See general information on page 87.

Places to Visit

This section isn't intended to be a definitive guide but gives a wide range of ideas for the department. Prices and opening hours were correct at the time of writing, but it's best to check before travelling long distances.

Animal Parks & Aquariums

Le Faouët — L'Abeille Vivante/La Cité des Fourmis, ☎ 02 97 23 08 05
Kercadoret
🖥 *www.abeilles-et-fourmis.com*
There are two centres on this site: the bee centre has a collection of bee hives and an exhibition of honey production, queen bees and equipment used; the ant exhibition has a variety of ant colonies that show you the different ways in which they work, their strength and a detailed insight into their lives. Commentaries available in English. Open every day April to June and September from 10am to 12.30pm and 1.30 to 6pm; July and August 10am to 7pm. Under 16s €4, others €6.

Le Guerno — Parc Zoologique de Branféré, Branféré   ☎ 02 97 42 94 66
🖥 *www.branfere.com*
Botanical gardens and animal park; animals include zebras and kangaroos. Restaurants, shop and picnic area. Open daily February, March, October and November from 1 to 5.30pm; April to June and September Mondays to Fridays 10am to 6.30pm, weekends and bank holidays 10am to 7.30pm; July and August daily 10am to 7.30pm. Over 12s €10, 4 to 12-year-olds €7, under fours free.

Languidic — La Ferme du Cheval de Trait, Château   ☎ 02 97 65 83 96
de la Vigne
A farm dedicated to working horses. There's a forge and saddlery, and an exhibition of modern and ancient equipment used by horses. Wagon rides in the Blavet valley. Open May to September Tuesdays to Sundays from 10am to 5pm. Adults €3, children €1.50; wagon rides €10 adults, €5.50 children.

Larmor-Baden — Réserve Naturelle des Marais de Séné   ☎ 02 97 66 92 76
🖥 *www.reservedesene.com*
(on the coast, west of Vannes)
This bird reserve is an important refuge for sea birds, particularly ducks, terns and waders. Open from February to mid-September.

Meslan   Chez Dame Nature, Pencleux   ☎ 02 97 34 26 72
Animal park, picnic area, playground and in the summer a corn maze. Open Easter to September from 11am to 7pm. 4 to 12-year-olds €3.50, over 12s €5.50.

Pont-Scorff   Odyssaum, Moulin des Princes   ☎ 02 97 32 42 00
✉ *decouverte@sellor.com*
Discover everything to do with the life cycle of wild salmon. Open September to June, Tuesdays to Fridays from 9am to 12.30pm and 2 to 6pm, Saturdays to Mondays 2 to 6pm (open Monday mornings in school holidays); July and August every day 9am to 7pm. Adults €5.20, children €3.90.

Zoo de Pont-Scorff, Keruisseau   ☎ 02 97 32 60 86
🖥 *www.zoodepontscorff.com*
(north-west of Lorient)
There are 600 animals, including black rhinos, giraffes, hippopotamuses and zebras, an elephant breeding centre and a monkey island. Open every day all year: September to June 9.30am to 5pm; July and August 9.30am to 7pm. Three shows daily from Easter to the end of September. Restaurant open from March to October and a picnic area. 3 to 11-year-olds €7.40, over 11s €12.40.

Vannes   Aquarium de Vannes, Parc du Golfe, ☎ 02 97 40 67 40
rue Daniel Gilard
🖥 *www.aquarium-du-golfe.com*
(near the sea front, south of the town)
Large aquarium with a wide variety of fish including piranha and fish with four eyes! Open every day: February, March, September, October and winter school holidays 10am to 12.30pm and 2 to 6.30pm; April to June 10am to 12.30pm and 2 to 7pm; July and August 9am to 7.30pm; November to January 2 to 6pm. 4 to 11-year-olds €5.50, over 11s €8.50.

Jardin des Papillons, rue Daniel Gilard ☎ 02 97 46 01 02
🖥 *www.jardinauxpapillons.com*
Hundreds of varieties of butterfly in their various stages of growth. Open every day: April to June and September 10am to 12.30pm and 2 to 6.30pm; July and August 10am to 7.30pm. 4 to 11-year-olds €5, over 11s €7.

Beaches & Leisure Parks

There are several beaches along the coast of Morbihan; the largest are Carnac Plage between Lorient and Vannes and Larmor-Plage south of Lorient.

Brandivy   Base de Loisirs de l'Etang de la Forêt, ☎ 02 97 56 02 75
Lann-Kerhoarno
Various activities based around a lake.

Ploërmel   Le Lac au Duc
                   Beach and water slides, bike hire, pedalos, tennis, horse riding,
                   volley ball, fishing and a restaurant.

Boat, Train & Wagon Rides

Boat Trips

Baden   Izenah Croisières, Le Port, Ile-aux-   ☎ 02 97 26 31 45
                   Moines
                   🖥 *izenah-croisieres.com*
                   Regular crossings all year between Port Blanc and Ile-aux-
                   Moines. Cruises on the Gulf of Morbihan from April to
                   September.

Larmor-Baden   Les Vedettes Blanches, Quai de Pen-   ☎ 02 97 57 15 27
                   Lannic
                   🖥 *www.croisieres-golfe-du-morbihan.com*
                   Cruises across the Gulf of Morbihan to the Ile-aux-Moines.

Lorient   Analogie, 21 rue du Fort Bloqué,   ☎ 02 97 86 79 24
                   Plœmeur
                   🖥 *www.analogie-ncm.com*
                   This is a large sailing yacht that departs from Lorient for half-
                   day and weekend trips out to sea. You're invited to help with
                   the sails and winches and take the wheel, or you can just relax
                   and sunbathe. Half-day trip from €35, sunset trip €25.

                   SMN Navigation, Gare Maritime, rue   ☎ 08 20 05 60 00
                   Gilles Gahinet
                   🖥 *www.smn-navigation.fr*
                   Boat trips to the islands of Ile-de-Groix; foot passengers and
                   cars (you're advised to book if taking a car). 45-minute
                   crossing. Adults €23 return, children €14 (prices may vary
                   slightly according to the time of year). Trips to Belle-Ile; foot
                   passengers only, no bicycles or surf boards. One hour
                   crossing. Adults €27 return, 12 to 18-year-olds €19, under
                   12s €13.50.

                   SPI, Pont de Kenével, Larmor-Plage   ☎ 02 97 84 60 80
                   🖥 *www.spi-location.com*
                   Sailing yachts from 6 to 13m and two motor yachts for hire.

Vannes   Navix, Gare Maritime, Parc du Golfe   ☎ 08 25 16 21 00
                   🖥 *www.navix.fr*
                   Cruises in the Gulf of Morbihan and between the islands. €25
                   for adults, €14 children; dinner cruises from €20 to €28.

                   Compagnie des Iles, Gare Maritime,   ☎ 08 25 16 41 00
                   Parc du Golfe

🖳 *www.compagniedesiles.com*
Cruises across and around the Gulf of Morbihan.

Train Rides

Vannes   Petit Train Touristique   ☎ 02 97 24 06 29
                 This 'train' offers half-hour tours of the town from Easter to mid-
                 October 10am to 7pm (July and August 10am to 10.30pm).
                 Departs from the Port de Plaisance (marina). Adults €5,
                 children €2.50.

Wagon Rides

See general information on page 88.

Chateaux

Josselin   Château Josselin   ☎ 02 97 22 36 45
                 An imposing chateau on the banks of the river Oust with turrets
                 and gabled roof. The chateau was fortified during the Hundred
                 Years War and remains of the fortifications can still be seen. In
                 the 16th century it was converted into a more comfortable
                 residence and is still a private residence today. The chateau is
                 open April, May and October on Wednesdays, Saturdays,
                 Sundays and bank holidays from 2 to 6pm; June and
                 September every day 2 to 6pm; July and August every day
                 10am to 6pm. Adults €6.80, children €4.70.

Sarzeau   Château de Suscinio   ☎ 02 97 41 91 91
                 ✉ *suscinio@sagemor.fr*
                 A medieval fortress between the forest and the sea. There are
                 four magnificent towers and thousands of medieval paving
                 stones, making it a unique example of art from the Middle
                 Ages. Open January, November and December daily from
                 10am to noon and 2 to 5pm; February, March and October
                 10am to noon and 2 to 6pm; April to September every day
                 10am to 7pm. Closed Wednesdays in term time October to
                 March. Adults €5, 8 to 18-year-olds €2, under eights free.

Churches & Abbeys

See general information on page 88.

Miscellaneous

Brandérion   La Tisserie, rue Vincent Renaud   ☎ 02 97 32 90 27
                 (east of Lorient)
                 Exhibition and workshop of traditional and contemporary
                 methods of weaving. Open May, June and September
                 Saturdays and Sundays from 2 to 6pm (May school holidays
                 Sundays to Fridays 2 to 6pm); July and August every day 10am
                 to 12.30pm and 2 to 6pm. Adults €3.50, children €2.60.

Elven	Tours de l'Argoët ☎ 02 97 53 35 96

✉ *forteresselargoet@free.fr*
(north-east of Vannes, by the N166)
The tallest octagonal keep in France. Open June and
September Mondays and Wednesdays to Sundays from
10.30am to noon and 2.20 to 6.30pm; July and August every
day 10.30am to noon and 2.20 to 6.30pm. Entry €4, under
tens free.

Guidel-Plages	Labyrinthe du Corsaire ☎ 02 99 81 17 23

🖥 *www.labyrintheducorsaire.com*
(just to the west of Lorient)
Four routes and more than 10km (6mi) of pathways in one of
the largest mazes in Europe. Playground, bouncy castles,
snack bar and picnic area. Open from the end of June to the
first week in September. Entry €7.

Hennebont	Haras National, rue Victor Hugo ☎ 02 97 89 40 30

(just north-east of Lorient)
Opened in 1857 this stud farm has 70 stallions. Guided tours
available and carriage rides on Sunday afternoons. Open
September to June Saturdays to Mondays from 2 to 6pm,
Tuesdays to Fridays 9am to 12.30pm and 2 to 6pm (open
Monday mornings in school holidays); July and August, every
day 9am to 7pm.

L'Ile-d'Arz	Moulin du Berno ☎ 02 97 40 45 38

(west of Vannes)
This is a working flour mill that was restored in 1995. Open July
and August 10am to 5pm; rest of the year by appointment.

Ile-aux-Moines	An island full of charm with fishermen's cottages, manor houses and plentiful flowers. Ideal for walking and cycling. Accessed by regular boat crossings from Vannes.

Yakapark, Le Paradis des Enfants, Zone ☎ 02 97 76 68 50
de Manébos, rue JM Djibaou, Lanester
(north-east of the town)
An indoor playground for children up to 12. Monkey bridges,
ball pools and inflatables. Open every day in the school
holidays 10am to 7pm; term time Wednesdays, Saturdays,
Sundays and bank holidays 10am to 7pm, Tuesdays and
Fridays 3.30 to 7pm. Entry €7, Tuesday and Friday afternoons
term time €5.50.

Lanvenegen	Parc du Roi Morvan, Les Kaolins ☎ 02 97 34 00 00

🖥 *www.parcduroimorvan.com*
(south-west of Le Faouët)
Leisure park for all ages. Karting, quad bikes, mini-port, water
park, tree climbing, indoor playground, pedal boats, picnic area,

mini-farm, clay pigeon shooting and crazy golf. Open May, June, September to mid-October Saturdays, Sundays and bank holidays 11am to 6pm; July and August every day 11am to 7pm. Entry out of season €10, July and August €12.

Lorient	L'Abri Anti-Bombes, place Alsace Lorraine	☎ 02 97 21 07 84

A restored Second World War bomb shelter designed to take 400 people and a memorial to the people affected by the war. Open July and August every day for guided tours only at 4pm and 5pm. Adults €3.50, children €2.50.

La Thalassa, quai de Rohan   ☎ 02 97 35 13 00
An ancient ship moored at Lorient. Explore the bridge, laboratories, dining rooms and cabins and get the feeling of life on board. Open July and August every day 9am to 7pm; September to June Tuesdays to Fridays 9am to 12.30pm and 2 to 6pm, Saturday and Sundays 2 to 6pm (during school holidays open Monday mornings).

Melrand   Le Village de l'An Mil, Lann-Gough   ☎ 02 97 39 59 50
(south-east of Le Faouët, north-east of Lorient)
This is a reconstruction of a Breton village of 1,000 years ago. There are huts, gardens and rare animals. Open every day May to August from 10am to 7pm; September to April Mondays to Fridays 11am to 5pm, Saturdays and Sundays 11am to 6pm. Adults €3.50, children €2.50.

Pontivy   Hippodrome de Kernivinen   ☎ 02 97 60 05 65
Trotting, flat racing and steeplechase.

Quistinic   Village de Poul-Fetan   ☎ 02 97 39 51 74
💻 www.patrimoine.morbihan.com
(north-east of Lorient)
A recreation of life in Brittany in the 16th century. There's a selection of trades from the period including wool spinning, butter making, lavender drying and the use of working animals. Guided tours in the mornings, shows every afternoon. Open April to October from 1 to 7pm. 6 to 12-year-olds €3, over 12s €6.

Vannes   Hippodrome de Cano   ☎ 02 97 40 96 70
Trotting and flat racing.

Museums, Memorials & Galleries

Le Faouët   Musée du Faouët, 1 rue de Quimper   ☎ 02 97 23 15 27
✉ musee.du.faouet@wanadoo.fr
Housed in an ancient convent, this museum holds a collection of paintings donated by artists who stayed in Le Faouët

between 1850 and the Second World War. Open every day from 10am to noon and 2 to 6pm. Adults €4, children €1.55.

Lorient

Galerie Compagnie d'Artistes, 55 rue de Liège   ☎ 02 97 35 21 82

💻 *www.cnap.culture.gouv.fr*
This gallery displays creative contemporary art in the form of paintings, engravings, sculptures and ceramics. Open Tuesdays to Saturdays from 10am to noon and 2.30 to 7pm.

Galerie Le Lieu, Maison de la Mer, quai de Rohan   ☎ 02 97 21 18 02

💻 *www.galerielelieu.com*
Photograph gallery with six to seven exhibitions a year. Open Tuesdays to Fridays from 11am to 6pm, Saturdays and Sundays 3 to 6pm. Free entry.

Musée de la Compagnie des Indes & Musée d'Art et d'Histoire de Lorient, Citadelle de Port Louis   ☎ 02 97 82 19 13

This museum has a collection of documents, model boats, engravings and porcelain with maritime and exotic origins relating to Breton trading with Africa and Asia in the 17th and 18th centuries. Open every day April to mid-September 10am to 6.30pm; mid-September to mid-December, February and March Mondays and Wednesdays to Sundays 2 to 6pm. Adults €4.60, children free.

La Tour Davis, Base des Sous-Marins de Keroman   ☎ 06 07 10 69 41

💻 *www.tour-davis.com*
The guides at this sub-mariners' museum are specialists in diving. There's a simulator built in 1942 that was used to train the divers. Open Sundays September to June from 2 to 6pm; July and August every day 1.30 to 6.30pm. Adults €4, children €2.50.

St Marcel

Musée de la Résistance Bretonne   ☎ 02 97 75 16 90

💻 *www.resistance-bretonne.com*
(south of Ploërmel)
Six exhibition areas showing the work of the Resistance in Brittany during the Second World War. Open mid-September to mid-June Mondays and Wednesdays to Sundays from 10am to noon and 2 to 6pm; mid-June to mid-September every day 10am to 7pm.

Treffléan Musée des Châteaux en Allumettes, 12 rue du Clavaire, Bizole   ☎ 02 97 43 03 20

(east of Vannes)

An exhibition of chateaux and other monuments, all made from matchsticks. Open May to October Mondays to Tuesdays from 1 to 7pm, Wednesdays to Saturdays 9am to noon and 2 to 7pm.

Vannes   Musée Aéronautique de Vannes,   ☎ 02 97 44 66 60
                Monterblanc
                Aviation museum with a variety of engines, ejector seats and
                flying memorabilia. Open from March to October.

                Musée des Beaux Arts de Vannes, place   ☎ 02 97 01 63 00
                St Pierre
                ✉ *musees@mairie-vannes.fr*
                Situated in a medieval hall, the museum includes paintings,
                sculptures, engravings and furniture. Open mid-June to
                September every day 10am to 6pm (including bank holidays);
                October to mid-June 1.30 to 6pm (closed bank holidays).

                Musée d'Histoire et d'Archéologie de   ☎ 02 97 01 63 00
                Vannes, Château Gaillard, 2 rue Noé
                An archaeological collection from megalithic sites across the
                department. Open mid-June to September, every day 10am to
                6pm. Adults €3, children €1.50.

                Musée Maritime Capitaine d'un Jour,   ☎ 02 97 40 40 39
                Parc du Golfe
                ✉ *capitaine-dun-jour@wanadoo.fr*
                A maritime museum. Open February to December. Adults €6,
                children €4.50.

Parks, Gardens & Forests

Hennebont   Le Parc de Kerbihan
                (just north-east of Lorient)
                A large botanical garden, orchard, bamboo forest and
                playground. Open access.

Ile-de-Groix   Réserve Naturelle François-Le-Bail,   ☎ 02 97 86 55 97
                Maison de la Réserve, Le Bourg-de-Groix
                (an island just south of Lorient)
                This nature reserve is a protected site. Open all year with free
                access. Various shows are put on throughout the year for which
                there's a charge: €5 adults, €2.50 children, free for under 12s.
                No charge to enter the reserve.

St Avé   Le Jardin de Maire Cécile   ☎ 02 97 60 71 81
                This garden has various features including rockeries and
                English gardens. Open mid-May to mid-July and from the end
                of August to the end of September.

Trédion   Parc du Château de Trédion   ☎ 02 97 67 15 67
                🖳 *www.chateauxcountry.com/chateaux/tredion*
                A large park and lake surrounding the 16th century chateau.
                The park is open from June to September. €3 entry.

Vannes   Le Jardin aux Papillons, Parc du Golfe ☎ 02 97 46 01 02
                (south of the town)
                Hundreds of exotic butterflies in a tropical climate and an
                exhibition of orchids from all over the world. Open every day
                from 10am to 12.30pm and 2 to 6.30pm; July and August 10am
                to 7pm. Adults €7, children €5, under fours free.

Regional Produce

Guidel   Autruches de la Saudraye   ☎ 02 97 65 04 54
                (west of Lorient)
                Open all year for ostrich products including meat, leather goods
                and decorative eggs.

                Cidrerie des Vergers de Kermabo,   ☎ 02 97 65 94 38
                Kermabo
                ✉ *leguerroue@wanadoo.fr*
                Tastings and sale of cider, *Pommeau* and apple juice.

Hézo   Musée du Cidre du Pays Vannetais   ☎ 02 97 26 47 40
                🖳 *www.museeducidre.com*
                (south-east of Vannes)
                A museum of cider and its production. Open April to June,
                September and October Tuesdays to Saturdays from 10am to
                noon and 2.30 to 6.30pm, Sundays 2.30 to 6.30pm; July and
                August every day 10am to 7pm. Over 15s €4, 8 to 15-year-olds
                €2, under eights free.

Ile-de-Groix   l'Escargoterie, Kerbus   ☎ 02 97 86 58 94
                Sale of farm produce including snails, sea food, cider and
                ostrich meat.

Theix   Morbraz, Zone St Léonard Nord   ☎ 02 97 42 53 53
                🖳 *www.morbraz.com*
                (just south-east of Vannes, off the N165)
                Large brewery. Open all year.

Standing Stones & Megaliths

La Chapelle   There are various standing stones around this town,
Caro   including the Dolmen de la Maison Trouée.
                (in the village of Ville-au-Voyer on the way to Monterrein)

Ile de Gavrinis Site de Gavrinis   ☎ 02 97 57 19 38
                (south of Larmor-Baden)

A dolmen with a 14m long gallery leading to the burial chamber. The corridor and chamber are constructed from 29 stone pillars. Open April to October.

On the neighbouring island of Ilot-er-Lannic is a stone circle that stretches into the sea.

Ménéac

Menhir de Bellouan
(on the Illifaut road, in the village of Bellouan, turn towards Tréaulé)
Nine-metre tall, 25 tonne stone.

Menhir of Camblot
(on the Coëtlogon road, on the left on leaving the town)
Standing stone.

Vannes

By the roads around the town are innumerable standing stones and small dolmens.

Professional Services

The following offices have an English-speaking professional.

Accountants

Vannes   Cabinet Chevallier-Giard, 80 allée du   ☎ 02 97 63 32 63
                  Bois du Vincin

Architects & Project Managers

See page 367.

Solicitors & Notaires

Vannes   Maître Bernard, rue Richemont   ☎ 02 97 47 38 88

Property

See general information on page 90.

Public Holidays

See general information on page 95.

Religion

Anglican Services in English

Guénin   St Andrews Church, Foyer Communal ☎ 02 97 38 14 10
                (on the D197, north-east of Lorient)
                English-language church services, usually followed by Holy
                Communion, held twice a month. All denominations welcome.
                Contact John Fox for further information.

Ploërmel   Christ Church, Maison Mère des Frères ☎ 02 97 74 97 73
                ✉ fraylesnot@aol.com
                English-language church services are held every Sunday.
                The first three Sundays of the month, communion with
                children's activities at 11am; the fourth Sunday, an informal,
                non-communion service for all ages at 11am; fifth Sunday,
                family communion. Contact Revd. Roger Fray for further
                information.

Catholic Churches

See **Religion** on page 96.

Restaurants

Arzon   Le Jules Verne, Rond-point du Crouesty ☎ 02 97 53 99 44
                Within the casino, this restaurant is open every evening from
                7.30 to 11.30pm and at lunchtime on Saturdays and Sundays.

Auray   Manoir de Kerdréan, Le Bono   ☎ 02 97 57 84 00
                🖥 www.abbatiales.com
                This restaurant is part of an 14th century abbey. Open every
                day. Set menus from €22 to €45.

Lorient   Buffalo Grill, ZI de Kerpont   ☎ 02 9781 43 00
                (just off the N165 at Lanester, north-east of the town)
                Steak house-style restaurant with continuous service from noon
                to 11pm.

                Chicanos Restaurant, 26 rue Maréchal   ☎ 02 97 84 90 90
                Foch
                Texan and Mexican food.

                La Pause Bio, 4 rue Clairambault   ☎ 02 97 64 21 92
                An organic restaurant with an à la carte menu. Open for lunch
                Mondays to Saturdays and in the evenings Fridays and
                Saturdays.

La Taverne de Maître Kanter, 23 place   ☎ 02 97 21 32 20
Aristide Briand
Restaurant open daily from noon through to midnight. Seafood
a speciality.

Ploërmel   Le Roi Arthur, Golf du Lac au Duc   ☎ 02 97 73 64 64
💻 *www.hotelroiarthur.com*
(by the golf course, north-west of the town)
Traditional and gastronomic cuisine, set menus from €28 to
€45 plus *à la carte*. The restaurant has a veranda overlooking
the lake, golf course and flower gardens.

Le Saïgon, 4 rue Alphonse Guérin   ☎ 02 97 74 28 82
Chinese and Vietnamese cuisine.

Vannes   L'Andaluz, 18 rue des Vierges   ☎ 02 97 54 26 09
Spanish restaurant open Monday evenings to Sunday
evenings. Lunch time menus €8.

L'Atlantique, Port de Vannes   ☎ 02 97 54 01 58
Brasserie and seafood restaurant overlooking the marina.
Service all day from noon to midnight. Set menus and *à
la carte*.

La Brasserie des Halles, 9 rue des Halles ☎ 02 97 54 08 34
💻 *www.brasserie-des-halles.com*
This restaurant has an *art déco* interior with windows
overlooking an exhibition of 1930s porcelain. Classic brasserie
food and a variety of seafood. Service continuously from noon
to midnight in July and August.

Navix, Gare Maritime, Parc du Golfe   ☎ 08 25 16 21 00
💻 *www.navix.fr*
Dinner cruises in the Gulf of Morbihan. Panoramic views,
candle-lit dinners and a dance floor. Three-and-a-half hour
cruises lunchtimes and evenings. Cruises €25 for adults, €14
for children; menus from €20 to €28.

Rubbish & Recycling

See general information on page 97.

Schools

See general information on page 100.

Shopping

When available, the opening hours of various shops have been included, but these are liable to change and so it's advisable to check before travelling long distances to a specific shop.

Architectural Antiques

Baud   Poulain, 7 rue de Kérentrée, Ancienne   ☎ 02 97 51 01 33
                route de Locminé
                Reclaimed stone.

St Congard   Loic Bougo, Le Bourg   ☎ 02 97 43 50 08
                💻 *www.antiquites-bretagne.com*
                (by the river, south of Ploërmel)
                Specialising in reclaimed fireplaces, staircases, windows
                and doors.

Bakeries

See general information on page 103.

British Groceries

Séglien   La Crème Anglaise, place de l'Eglise   ☎ 02 97 28 02 03
                ✉ *lacremeanglaise@aol.com*
                (north-east of La Faouët)
                British groceries including gluten-free, diabetic and vegetarian
                products. Open Tuesdays to Saturdays from 8am to noon and
                2 to 6pm, Sundays 8.30am to 12.30pm.

Building Materials

See general information on page 103.

Chemists'

See general information on page 103.

Department Stores

Lorient   Les Nouvelles Galeries, place Alsace   ☎ 02 97 64 14 58
                Lorraine
                Open Mondays to Saturdays from 9.30am to 7.30pm.

DIY

See general information on page 104.

Dress Making & Crafts

Lorient   Duret Tissus, 15 rue Fontaines   ☎ 02 97 64 28 48
                   Clothes and furnishing fabric and haberdashery.

Ploërmel   L'Etoffe, 20 rue St Armel   ☎ 02 97 63 68 01

Vannes   Self Tissus, ZAC Poulfanc, rue Vosges,   ☎ 02 97 47 46 04
                   Séné
                   🖳 www.self-tissus.fr
                   Clothes and furnishing fabrics, haberdashery and craft
                   supplies.

Fireplaces & Log Burners

See general information on page 104.

Fishmongers'

See general information on page 104.

Frozen Food

Kervignac   Argel Ouest, Kermaria   ☎ 02 97 65 64 22
                   (east of Lorient)
                   Home deliveries only, telephone for a catalogue.

Lorient   Picard, 8 rue Georges Brassens   ☎ 02 97 35 30 05
                   🖳 www.picard.fr

Vannes   Picard, route Nantes, Séné   ☎ 02 97 68 82 01

Garden Centres

See general information on page 105.

Hypermarkets

See **Retail Parks** on page 354 and general information on pages 105 and 108.

Key Cutting & Heel Bars

See general information on page 106.

Kitchens & Bathrooms

See general information on page 106.

Markets

Arradon	Tuesday and Friday mornings
Le Faouët	First and third Wednesdays of the month
Gâvres	Tuesday and Saturday mornings
Gourin	Monday mornings
Guidel	Wednesday and Saturday mornings
Hennebont	Thursday mornings
Ile-aux-Moines	Wednesday mornings
Ile-de-Groix	Tuesday and Saturday market; fresh fish sold every day
Lorient	There are markets Tuesday to Saturday mornings (except bank holidays) at Halles de Merville and Halles St Louis
	Tuesday mornings at Lanester
	Wednesday and Saturday morning markets at cours de Chazelles, Merville and St Louis
Le Palais	Tuesday and Friday mornings
	Organic market Thursday mornings at place de l'Eglise, Quéven from 4 to 8pm
	Sunday mornings and Tuesday evenings in the summer at Larmor-Plage
Ploëmeur	Wednesday and Sunday mornings
Ploërmel	Monday and Friday mornings
Plougoumelen	Friday mornings
St Avé	Organic market Tuesday mornings, traditional market Sundays
Séné	Traditional market Friday mornings, organic market Friday evenings

Vannes   Outdoor market Wednesday and Saturday mornings

                      Tuesday to Friday mornings at La Halle des Lices
                      November to April, every morning May to October

                      Tuesdays to Saturdays at La Halle aux Poissons

Mobile Shops

See general information on page 106.

Music

See general information on page 107.

Newsagents'

See general information on page 107.

Organic Produce

Lorient   Ti Bio, 125 rue de Belgique   ☎ 02 97 37 33 92
               Open Mondays from 3 to 7pm, Tuesdays to Saturdays 8.15am
               to 12.30pm and 3 to 7pm (closed Thursday afternoons).

Ploërmel   Dietetic-Natur, 6 rue des Herses   ☎ 02 97 93 66 01
               Open Monday afternoons and Tuesdays to Saturdays.

Vannes   Vannes Nature, 25 rue des Halles   ☎ 02 97 54 11 22
               Open Mondays from 2 to 7pm, Tuesdays to Saturdays 8.45am
               to 12.30pm and 2 to 7pm.

Passport Photos

See general information on page 108.

Post Offices

See general information on page 108.

Retail Parks

Lorient   Parc des Expositions, Lanester
               (north of the town; from the N165 take the turning to Lanester)
               Like many retail parks, this one is centred around a major road
               junction – in this the case the N165 junction. Unfortunately it's a
               maze of slip roads and roundabouts. Shops include:
               ● Aubert – baby goods;
               ● Buffalo Grill – steak house restaurant;
               ● BUT – furniture and household accessories;
               ● Casa – gifts and furnishings;

- Cuisines Plus – kitchens;
- Feu Vert – tyre and exhaust centre;
- Fly – furniture and household accessories;
- Géant – hypermarket   ☎ 02 97 89 24 00
  Open Mondays to Fridays from 9am to 9pm, Saturdays
  9am to 8.30pm. Shops in the surrounding complex
  including a florist's, post office, heel and key bar, dry
  cleaner's, jeweller's, chemist's, France Télécom, optician's
  and several restaurants;
- Go Sport – sports goods;
- La Halle – clothes;
- Halle aux Chaussures – shoes;
- Mobalpa – kitchens;
- Philanima – pet products;
- Saint Maclou – paint and decorating materials.

Vannes   Le Fourchêne
            (on the north-west side of the town, take the Vannes
            Ouest/Arradon exit from the N165)
            Shops include:
            - Carrefour – hypermarket   ☎ 02 97 63 07 63
              💻 www.carrefour.fr
              The complex has many shops including an optician's,
              chemist's, clothes shop, post office, heel bar, dry cleaner's
              and jeweller's, computer games and photograph
              developing, and a cafe and bars. Carrefour is open
              Mondays to Thursdays 8.30am to 9pm, Friday 8.30am to
              10pm, Saturdays 8.30am to 8pm;
            - Sports Village – sports goods.

Second-hand Shops

See general information on page 108.

Sports Goods

See general information on page 108.

Supermarkets

See general information on page 108.

Wine & Spirits

See general information on page 109.

Sports & Outdoor Activities

The following is just a selection of the activities available, the large towns
having a wide range of sports facilities. Details are available from the
tourist office or the *mairie*.

Aerial Sports

Ballooning

Arradon   La Montgolfière Morbihan, 9bis rue de   ☎ 06 07 64 91 91
             la Chapelle

Vannes   Bretagne Sud Montgolfières, 30bis rue   ☎ 02 97 46 40 58
             Pierre de Coubertin
             ✉ *bsmontgolfieres@voila.fr*
             A club that organises training, basket construction and
             participation in ballooning events.

Flying

Guiscriff   Aérodrome Bretagne Atlantique, Pont   ☎ 02 97 34 08 55
             Person
             🖥 *www.aerodrome-bretagne.com*
             (west of Le Faouët)
             Sight-seeing flights. Helicopters and charter planes available.

Ploermel   Aéro Club de Brocéliande, Aérodrome   ☎ 02 97 93 00 80
             de Ploërmel, Loyat
             Flying school.

Vannes   Aéro Club de Vannes, Aérodrome de   ☎ 02 97 60 73 08
             Vannes-Meucon, Monterblanc

Parachuting

Lorient   Para Club de Lorient, Maison des   ☎ 02 97 60 78 69
             Associations, Cité Allende, 12 rue Colbert
             ✉ *paraclublorient@voila.fr*
             This club meets at the Centre Ecole de Parachutisme at
             Meucon, Vannes.

Vannes   Le Para Club de Vannes, l'Aérodrome   ☎ 02 97 60 78 69
             Vannes-Meucon

Archery

Lorient   Patronage Laique de Lorient, Gymnase   ☎ 02 97 83 69 64
             de Kerjulaude
             ✉ *plloirient@wanadoo.fr*

Ploërmel   Archers de la Table Ronde, rue   ☎ 02 97 74 12 46
             Sénéchal Thuault

Vannes   Les Archers de Richemont, Centre   ☎ 02 97 53 20 87
             Sportif de Kercado

Badminton

Lorient   Patronage Laïque de Lorient, Salle   ☎ 02 97 83 69 64
                 Svob, rue Madeleine Desroseaux
                 Competitive and leisure badminton.

Ploërmel   Ploërmel Badminton Club, Gymnase de ☎ 06 03 79 74 20
                 Ploërmel
                 💻 www.ploermel-badminton.com

Vannes   ASPTT Badminton, 2 place de la   ☎ 02 97 54 08 09
                 République
                 💻 www.asso.wanadoo.fr/asptt.vannes
                 Contact M. Musset.

Boules/Pétanque

Lorient   Boule Lorientaise, Boulodrome   ☎ 02 97 64 37 93
                 Municipal, rue Beauvais
                 Contact M. Collobert.

Ploërmel   Amicale Pétanque Ploërmelaise, place   ☎ 02 97 74 27 39
                 de l'Ancienne Gare
                 This group meets on Friday evenings from 6.30pm. Contact
                 M. Davoine.

Vannes   There's a boulodrome at the Complexe Sportif de Bécel.
                 (west of the town centre)

                 Vannes Pétanque Club, bar 'Le Club',   ☎ 02 97 63 57 44
                 4 place de la Madeleine

Climbing

Lorient   Club Omnisports de Kerentech,   ☎ 02 97 21 67 56
                 Gymnase de Kerentrech

Vannes   Escalade 5+, 33 avenue du 4 août 1944 ☎ 06 80 07 13 81
                 Indoor climbing wall and outdoor sites.

Cycling & Bike Hire

Le Faouët   Club de Cyclorandonneurs   ☎ 02 97 23 22 20
                 Contact M. Biscaro.

Ile -de-Groix   There are two cycle routes (8km/5mi and 15km/10mi)
                 around this island just off the coast south of Lorient.
                 Regular boats cross to the island from the port at Lorient.
                 See **Boat, Train & Wagon Rides** on page 341.

Coconut's Location, Port Tudy ☎ 02 97 86 81 57
🖳 *www.coconutslocation.com*
(opposite the landing stage on the island)
Adults' and children's bikes and adults' mountain bikes.

Lorient   Vélo Loca Service, 1 place Yann Sohier ☎ 06 70 97 88 73
Bike hire

Cyclotourisme, Foyer Laïque de ☎ 02 97 83 81 64
Keryado
Road cycling. Contact M. Amalir.

Club Alpin Français du Pays de Lorient ☎ 02 97 65 60 43
✉ *cafpaysdelorient@multimania*
Mountain biking. Contact M. Simon.

Ploërmel   Club VTT de Ploërmel, Lycée La Touche ☎ 02 97 93 64 26
Mountain bike club.

Avenir Cyclisme Guer-Ploërmel, Stade ☎ 02 97 74 19 53
de St Jean de Villenard
Cycle club including groups for children. Contact M. Guilloux.

Vannes   Abbis Location, 11 quai des Voiliers, ☎ 02 97 53 64 64
Arzon-Le-Crouesty
Bike hire.

Vannes Cyclo Randonneurs + VTT, 14 ☎ 02 97 40 52 13
rue Nicolazic

Vannes Racing Team ☎ 02 97 57 83 93
Road racing and mountain biking. Contact M. Gicquel.

Fishing

Maps are available from fishing shops and tourist offices showing local
fishing waters. If there's a lake locally, permits will be on sale in nearby
tabacs and fishing shops and at the *mairie*.

Le Faouët   The rivers Ellé and Scorff are near Le Faouët. Fishing
guides are available from the tourist office and fishing
permits for sale at the Maison de la Presse (☎ 02 97 23
09 01).

Entente Haut Ellé/Pêche ☎ 02 97 51 68 80
Fishing club. Contact M. Le Chat.

Lorient	There's a variety of fishing opportunities. including the Etang de Kergoff at Caudan, just north of the town.	

Pêche à Soutenir   ☎ 02 97 21 07 84
Sea fishing trips during July and August. Departing from quai de la Pointe at Port-Louis and Kernével at Larmor-Plage. Bookings made at the tourist office. Adults €37, children €23.

Ste Hélène-sur-Mer	Le Loup Bar, Centre de Pêche de la Ria d'Etel	☎ 02 97 36 63 01

🖳 www.leloupbar.free.fr
Professional fishing instructor and guide.

Vannes	La Gaule Vannetaise, 6 rue de la Tannerie	☎ 06 30 57 29 96

Fishing school and club.

Football

Le Faouët	Union Sportive Faouëtaise	☎ 02 97 23 17 77

Contact M. Le Guennic.

Lorient	Football Club 56 Lorient, Stade du Moustoir, 20 rue Jean Le Coutaller	☎ 02 97 84 12 20

Training Wednesday afternoons and Tuesday to Friday evenings. Matches at weekends for all ages. Contact M. Le Herdy.

Ploërmel	Ploërmel Football Club, Complexe Sportif, route de Redon	☎ 02 97 74 14 04

Contact M. Guillerm.

Vannes	ASPTT Section Football, 2 place de la République	☎ 02 97 54 08 09

✉ www.asptt.vannes@wanadoo.fr
Junior, men's, women's and veterans' teams.

Golf

Bieuzy-les-Eaux	Golf de Rimaison	☎ 02 97 27 74 03

✉ golfderimaison@europe.com
9 holes, par 35, 2,582m. Green fees €23 to €26. Equipment hire and bar.

Lorient	Plœmeur Océan, St Jude Kerham, Plœmeur	☎ 02 97 32 81 82

🖳 www.formule-golf.com

(south-west of the town)
18 holes, par 72, 5,819m. Links course. Putting green, covered driving range, club and trolley hire, pro-shop, bar and restaurant. Green fees €33 to €47.

Golf de Val Quéven, Quéven ☎ 02 97 05 17 96
💻 *www.formule-golf.com*
(north-west of the town)
18 holes, par 72, 6,140m. Driving range and putting green. Green fees €33 to €47.

Ploërmel   Golf du Lac au Duc, Clos Hazel ☎ 02 97 74 19 55
(north-west of the town, off the ring road, rue du Pardon)
9 holes, par 36, 2,901m. Restaurant, clubhouse, buggy and trolley hire, driving range, hotel and swimming pool. Green fees €22. Open every day unless there's a competition.

Hockey

Lorient   Foyer Laïque de Lanester, 4 rue Gérard ☎ 02 97 76 11 50
Philippe
Ice hockey.

Vannes   Patinium Sports de Glace, 6 rue ☎ 02 97 40 91 23
Georges Caldray
💻 *www.patinium.com*
Ice hockey.

Avril Association, 59 rue Amiral ☎ 06 87 39 58 10
Desforges
Roller hockey.

Horse Riding

Le Faouët   Les Ecuries du Triskel, Guervienne ☎ 02 97 23 22 91
Hacks by the hour, day or up to five days.

Lorient   Kerguélen Equitation, Village de ☎ 02 97 33 60 56
Kerguélen, Larmor-Plage
✉ *kerguelen.equitation@wanadoo.fr*
Open all year for individual and group lessons, hacks, competitions, dressage and jumping.

Ploërmel   Centre Equestre La Touche, La Touche ☎ 02 97 73 39 24
💻 *www.lycee-latouche.com*
Riding lessons and stabling.

Vannes   Centre Equestre de Bilaire, 8 chemin de ☎ 02 97 47 47 27
Bilaire

Land Yachting

Lorient   Char à Voile, Les Passagers du Vent,   ☎ 02 97 52 40 60
                 avenue de l'Océan, Plouharnel
                 Introductory sessions, courses and competitions.

Motorsports

Cars

Lorient   Automobile Club de l'Ouest, 61 rue   ☎ 02 97 21 03 07
                 Maréchal Foch

Karts

Guillac   Circuit de la Pyramide   ☎ 02 97 74 13 48
                 💻 *www.3gkarting.com*
                 Leisure and competitive karting for seven-year-olds upwards.

Lanester   Un Tour de Karting, Parc des   ☎ 02 97 76 09 51
                 Expositions du Pays de Lorient
                 Competitions, leisure days and parties. Adult and junior karts.
                 Open Wednesdays to Fridays from 4 to 10pm, Saturdays 2.30
                 to 10pm, Sundays 2.30 to 7.30pm (open every day during
                 school holidays). 7 to 14-year-olds €8 for eight minutes, over
                 14s €11 for ten minutes.

Ploemel   Karting de Ploemel, RD22, ZA la   ☎ 02 97 56 71 71
                 Madeleine
                 💻 *www.ajf-karting.com*
                 (mid-way between Lorient and Vannes)
                 800m floodlit track. Karts for adults and children. Open term
                 time Mondays, Thursdays and Fridays from 1 to 7pm,
                 weekends 10.30am to 8pm; during the school holidays every
                 day 10am to 8pm.

Saint Avé   Karting Indoor, ZI de Kermelin   ☎ 02 97 44 57 03
                 Indoor karting.

Motorbikes

Ploërmel   Moto Verte Ploërmel   ☎ 02 97 93 50 27
                 Contact M. Mahias.

Quad Bikes

Locmalo   Quad Tri Mil, Rozulair Bras   ☎ 06 30 88 76 17
                 Quad rides around a 70ha (173-acre) site.

Quelneuc   Adventure Quad, Le Bois Pierre   ☎ 06 63 29 17 65
                 ✉ *rgame@wanadoo.fr*

Open Wednesdays to Sundays from 9.30am to 12.30pm and 2 to 7pm (every day in the summer holidays).

Paint Ball

Quelneuc   Air Game Paintball, le Bois Pierre   ☎ 06 63 29 17 65
✉ *rgame@wanadoo.fr*
(north-east of Vannes)

Rollerskating

Ile-de-Groix   There's a skate park in the centre of the town on impasse de la Mairie.

Lorient   Club de Patinage a Roulettes   ☎ 06 07 51 96 05
Leisure and competitive skating at Salle Carnot and Gymnase Kerolay. Contact M. Ghersin.

There's a skate park at the Complexe Sportif du Moustoir, rue Jean Le Coutaller

Vannes   Skate Parc, Centre Sportif de Kercado, rue Montaigne.
(on the south-west side of the town centre)

Avril Association, 59 rue Amiral   ☎ 06 87 39 58 10
Desforges
In-line skating including roller hockey. Skating school and excursions.

Postakitsch, 3 allée de la Corderie   ☎ 02 97 40 82 00
Skateboarding club.

Shooting

Lorient   Tir au Pistolet, Association Sportive   ☎ 02 97 12 16 89
Arsenal de Lorient, Stand de Tir de l'ASAL

Vannes   Société d Tir l'Impact   ☎ 02 97 48 11 61
Contact Mme Guillaume.

Squash

Lorient   Top Squash, ZA de Kerhoas, Larmor-   ☎ 02 97 83 62 44
Plage
🖥 *www.chez.com/topsquash*
Open Mondays to Fridays from 10am to 10.30pm, Saturdays 10am to 8pm, Sundays 10am to 1pm and 4 to 7pm (Sunday afternoon sessions must be booked).

| Vannes | Squash des Iles, Parc du Golfe
Squash courts, gym and weights. | ☎ 02 97 40 79 80 |

Swimming

| Le Faouët | Piscine Municipale du Faouët, cours Carré
Swimming pool. Swimming hats must be worn. | ☎ 02 97 23 12 34 |

Lorient	Aqualanes, rue René Cassin, Lanester (north-east of the town) Indoor water complex.	☎ 02 97 81 42 42
	Piscine du Bois du Château, rue Bois du Château	☎ 02 97 83 84 89
	Piscine du Moustoir, rue Jean Le Coutaller	☎ 02 97 02 22 65
	Océanis, boulevard François Mitterrand, Plœmeur 💻 *www.Plœmeur.com* (south-west of the town) Indoor water complex.	☎ 02 97 86 41 00

| Ploërmel | Piscine Municipale, route de Redon | ☎ 02 97 93 67 74 |

| Vannes | Piscine de Kercado, rue Winston Churchill | ☎ 02 97 62 69 00 |
| | Piscine VanOcéa, boulevard de Pontivy
Water complex with a variety of pools, water slide, gym and fitness classes. | ☎ 02 97 62 68 00 |

Tennis

| Lorient | Tennis Club de Lorient, Stade du Moustoir, rue Jean Le Coutaller
Contact M. Girot. | ☎ 02 97 83 53 98 |

| Ploërmel | Tennis Club Ploërmelais, Complexe Sportif, rue de Ronsouze
Contact M. Périer. | ☎ 02 97 73 32 11 |

| Vannes | Tennis Club Vannetais, allée du Clos Vert
Competitions, recreational tennis and courses. | ☎ 02 97 63 14 66 |

Tennis Club Vannes-Ménimur, rue H.   ☎ 02 97 63 70 03
Matisse
Courts for hire.

Tree Climbing

Camors
Camors Aventure Forest, Site du Petit   ☎ 02 97 39 28 69
Bois
Various tree-top adventure courses including aerial runways
and monkey bridges. Full safety equipment provided. Open
April to mid-November: school holidays every day from 9am to
noon and 1.30 to 6pm; term time Wednesdays to Sundays 9am
to noon and 1.30 to 6pm. Over 16s €20, under 16s over 1m 45
€15, under 16s between 1m 20 and 1m 45 €8.

Carnac
Forêt Adrénaline, Fontainebleau, route   ☎ 06 72 07 35 90
du Hahon
🖳 www.foretadrenaline.com
Large adventure forest with eight tree-top courses. Open to all
ages from five-year-olds upwards. Booking recommended, by
phone or internet. Open March to November Wednesdays,
weekends and school holidays with departures from 2.30pm
(high season from 9am). Over 15s €10, 10 to 15-year-olds €16,
five to nine-year-olds €10.

Nivillac
Coëtarlann Aventures, Trévineuc   ☎ 02 99 90 97 03
🖳 www.parc-aventure-bretagne.com
(south-west of Vannes, off the N165 at junction 16)
An adventure forest with aerial runways, rope ladders (safety
equipment supplied), pony rides, animals and paths in the
forest. Minimum age seven and minimum height 1m 20 for the
tree-climbing activities; minimum age ten and minimum height
of 1m 50 for high climbs. Suitable footwear to be worn. Tree-
climbing: adults €13 to €18, children €11 to €16 dependent on
climb height. Aerial runways €5. Access to park €2. Canoeing
€12. Orienteering €3. Open Tuesdays to Sundays from 9am to
6pm.

Quelneuc
Aventure Park, le Bois Pierre   ☎ 02 99 93 78 78
🖳 www.aventure-parc.fr
Aerial runways, monkey bridges, Tarzan swings, all up in the
tree-tops. Three routes for adults and another for children.
Open all year, weekends and school holidays 10am to 5pm.
Full safety equipment provided, but wear sensible sports
shoes. Adults €19.50, children €15.50. To participate in the
adult courses you must be at least 1m 80 with your arms raised
above your head.

Walking & Rambling

General
La Voie Verte

This is the route of an old railway line that is now dedicated to walkers, cyclists and roller skaters. 53km (33mi) long, it stretches from Questembert to Mauton and can be joined at various points including by the lake at Ploërmel.

Le Faouët	The tourist office has full details of local walks and a calendar of organised walks.	
	Randonnées Pédestres Contact M. Lefèvre.	☎ 02 97 23 08 52
Lorient	AVF, Maison des Associations, Cité Allende, 12 rue Colbert Regular walks arranged. Contact Mme Cosson.	☎ 02 97 84 85 39
Ploërmel	There are two walking routes near the lake that take you around the flower gardens.	
	Chemins Faisant Organised walks the third Sunday of the month. Departing from place de la Mairie. Contact M. Gavaud.	☎ 02 97 93 56 33
Vannes	There are four walks around the town and surrounding areas, all around 6km (4mi), details available from the tourist office.	
	Randonneurs du Pays de Vannes, Maison des Associations, 6 rue de la Tannerie Organised walks the third Sunday of each month.	☎ 02 97 40 96 97

Watersports

Canoeing & Kayaking

Le Faouët	Base Nautique Itinérante du Pays du Roi Morvan Open April to mid-October.	☎ 02 97 34 65 86
Lorient	Centre Nautique de Kerguélen, Larmor-Plage Hire of kayaks.	☎ 02 97 33 77 78
Ploërmel	Club Nautique Ploërmel-Taupont, Lac au Duc	☎ 02 97 74 14 51
Vannes	Canoe-Kayak Club de Vannes, 40 rue du Commerce	☎ 02 97 01 35 35

Rowing

Lorient   Aviron du Scorff, rue Amiral Favereau   ☎ 02 97 84 04 96
                Introductory sessions, courses and trips on the river.

Vannes   Cercle d'Aviron de Vannes, 42 rue du   ☎ 02 97 47 55 03
                Commerce

Sailing

Le Faouët   Base Nautique Itinérante du Pays du   ☎ 02 97 34 65 86
                Roi Morvan
                Open April to mid-October.

Lorient   Base Nautique du Ter, boulevard du   ☎ 02 97 37 45 25
                Ter
                See also **Boat, Train & Wagon Rides** on page 341.

                Centre Nautique de Kerguélen, Larmor-   ☎ 02 97 33 77 78
                Plage
                Hire of sailing dinghies.

Ploërmel   Club Nautique Ploërmel-Taupont, Lac   ☎ 02 97 74 14 51
                au Duc

Vannes   Cata School, Pen-Lannic, Larmor-Baden   ☎ 02 97 57 20 80

Scuba Diving

Lorient   Centre Nautique de Kerguélen, Larmor-   ☎ 02 97 33 77 78
                Plage
                Trial dives and training from beginners to instructor level.

Ploërmel   Atlantis Club Ploërmel, Piscine   ☎ 02 97 74 00 85
                Municipale, route de Redon
                Training sessions on Mondas from 8.30 to 11pm. Contact
                M. Cocaud.

Vannes   Les Vénètes, 5 avenue Wilson   ☎ 02 97 42 47 00

Windsurfing

Lorient   Centre Nautique de Kerguélen, Larmor-   ☎ 02 97 33 77 78
                Plage
                Lessons and hire of windsurf boards.

Ploërmel   Club Nautique Ploërmel-Taupont, Lac   ☎ 02 97 74 14 51
                au Duc

Vannes | Centre Nautique d'Arradon, La Pointe, | ☎ 02 97 44 72 92
Arradon
(west of the town)

Tourist Offices

General | Comité Départemental du Tourisme, | ☎ 02 97 54 06 56
allée Nicolas Le Blanc, Vannes
🖳 *www.morbihan.com*

Le Faouët | Office de Tourisme du Pays du Roi | ☎ 02 97 23 23 23
Morvan, rue des Cendres
🖳 *www.paysroimorvan.com*
Open Tuesdays to Saturdays from 10am to 12.30pm and 2
to 5.30pm.

Lorient | Maison de la Mer, quai de Rohan | ☎ 02 97 21 07 84
🖳 *www.lorient-tourisme.com*
🖳 *www.lorient.com*
Open all year Mondays to Fridays from 9am to 12.30pm and
1.30 to 6pm, Saturdays 9am to noon and 2 to 5pm (July and
August open later in the evening).

Ploërmel | 5 rue du Val | ☎ 02 97 74 02 70
🖳 *www.ploermel.com*
Open September to June Mondays to Saturdays from 10am to
12.30pm and 2 to 6.30pm; July and August Mondays to
Saturdays 9.30am to 7pm, Sundays and bank holidays 9.30am
to 12.30pm.

Vannes | 1 rue Thiers | ☎ 02 97 47 24 34
🖳 *www.tourisme-vannes.com*
🖳 *www.mairie-vannes.fr*
🖳 *www.agglo-vannes.com*
Open September to June Mondays to Saturdaysfrom 9.30am
to 12.30pm and 2 to 6pm; July and August Mondays to
Saturdays 9am to 7pm, Sundays 10am to 6pm.

Tradesmen

Architects & Project Managers

General | Burrows-Hutchinson, Ploerdut | ☎ 02 97 39 45 53
✉ *burrowhutch@aol.com*
English-speaking architectural practice offering interior design,
project management, building surveys and reports.

Max Lenglet, Plérin   ☎ 02 96 74 49 22
English-speaking project manager for building and
renovation work, specialising in 'green' and eco-friendly
buildings and materials.

Mike McCoy, Pen-ar-Vern, Bourbriac   ☎ 02 96 43 44 23
✉ therealmccoy999@aol.com
Bi-lingual draughtsman for architectural design and planning,
renovations and septic tank applications.

View Brittany, Le Kanveze, Remungol   ☎ 02 97 60 94 57
✉ vb.caro@wanadoo.fr
New builds, renovation, surveys and project management.
English-speaking.

Builders

General   View Brittany, Le Kanveze, Remungol   ☎ 02 97 60 94 57
✉ vb.caro@wanadoo.fr
New builds, renovation, surveys and project management.
English-speaking.

Carpenters

See general information on page 115.

Chimney Sweeps

See general information on page 115.

Electricians & Plumbers

General   T Electrics, 5 Kerroc'h, Plougonver   ☎ 02 96 21 67 11
✉ electrics@tiscali.fr
Large and small jobs and 24-hour emergency call-out.

Will Morgan, Melrand   ☎ 02 97 39 50 38
✉ will.morgan@wanadoo.fr
Electrical work, rewiring and equipment installation. Covering
the west of Morbihan. English-speaking.

Yves Borrely, St Adrien, St Barthelemy   ☎ 02 97 27 14 29
English-speaking plumber for general plumbing and heating
appliances.

Planning Permission

See general information on page 116.

Translators & Teachers

French Teachers & Courses

Lorient	Greta Lorient Quimperlé, 117 boulevard Léon Blum 💻 *www.greta-bretagne-ac-rennes.fr*	☎ 02 97 87 15 60
Ploërmel	AREP, Lycée La Touche French courses. Contact Mme Delarbre.	☎ 02 97 73 32 90
Vannes	Greta du Golfe, 6 avenue de Lattre de Tassigny	☎ 02 97 46 66 66

Translations

See general information on page 116.

Translators

See general information on page 117.

Utilities

See general information on page 117.

INDEX

N

O

P

T

U

BUYING A HOME SERIES

Buying a Home books, including **Buying, Selling & Letting Property**, are essential reading for anyone planning to purchase property abroad. They're packed with vital information to guide you through the property purchase jungle and help you **avoid the sort of disasters that can turn your dream home into a nightmare!** Topics covered include:

- Avoiding problems
- Choosing the region
- Finding the right home and location
- Estate agents
- Finance, mortgages and taxes
- Home security
- Utilities, heating and air-conditioning
- Moving house and settling in
- Renting and letting
- Permits and visas
- Travelling and communications
- Health and insurance
- Renting a car and driving
- Retirement and starting a business
- And much, much more!

Buying a Home books are the most comprehensive and up-to-date source of information available about buying property abroad. Whether you want a detached house, townhouse or apartment, a holiday or a permanent home, these books will help make your dreams come true.

Save yourself time, trouble and money!

Order your copies today by phone, fax, post or email from: Survival Books, PO Box 3780, YEOVIL, BA21 5WX, United Kingdom (☎/▤ +44 (0)1935-700060, ✉ sales@survivalbooks.net, 💻 www.survivalbooks.net).

LIVING AND WORKING SERIES

Living and Working books are essential reading for anyone planning to spend time abroad, including holiday-home owners, retirees, visitors, business people, migrants, students and even extra-terrestrials! They're packed with important and useful information designed to help you **avoid costly mistakes and save both time and money.** Topics covered include how to:

- Find a job with a good salary & conditions
- Obtain a residence permit
- Avoid and overcome problems
- Find your dream home
- Get the best education for your family
- Make the best use of public transport
- Endure local motoring habits
- Obtain the best health treatment
- Stretch your money further
- Make the most of your leisure time
- Enjoy the local sporting life
- Find the best shopping bargains
- Insure yourself against most eventualities
- Use post office and telephone services
- Do numerous other things not listed above

Living and Working books are the most comprehensive and up-to-date source of practical information available about everyday life abroad. They aren't, however, boring text books, but interesting and entertaining guides written in a highly readable style.

Discover what it's *really* like to live and work abroad!

Order your copies today by phone, fax, post or email from: Survival Books, PO Box 3780, YEOVIL, BA21 5WX, United Kingdom (☎/🖨 +44 (0)1935-700060, ✉ sales@survivalbooks.net, 💻 www.survivalbooks.net).

OTHER SURVIVAL BOOKS

The Alien's Guides: *The Alien's Guides to Britain and France* provide an 'alternative' look at life in these popular countries and will help you to appreciate the peculiarities (in both senses) of the British and French.

The Best Places to Buy a Home in France/Spain: The most comprehensive homebuying guides to France or Spain, containing detailed profiles of the most popular regions, with guides to property prices, amenities and services, employment and planned developments.

Buying, Selling and Letting Property: The most comprehensive and up-to-date source of information available for those intending to buy, sell or let a property in the UK.

Foreigners in France/Spain: Triumphs & Disasters: Real-life experiences of people who have emigrated to France and Spain, recounted in their own words – warts and all!

Lifelines: Essential guides to specific regions of France and Spain, containing everything you need to know about local life. Titles in the series currently include the Costa Blanca, Costa del Sol, Dordogne/Lot, Normandy and Poitou-Charentes; Brittany Lifeline is to be published in summer 2005.

Making a Living: Essential guides to self-employment and starting a business in France and Spain.

Renovating & Maintaining Your French Home: The ultimate guide to renovating and maintaining your dream home in France: what to do and what not to do, how to do it and, most importantly, how much it will cost.

Retiring Abroad: The most comprehensive and up-to-date source of practical information available about retiring to a foreign country, containing profiles of the 20 most popular retirement destinations.

Broaden your horizons with Survival Books!

Order your copies today by phone, fax, post or email from: Survival Books, PO Box 3780, YEOVIL, BA21 5WX, United Kingdom (☎/🖷 +44 (0)1935-700060, ✉ sales@survivalbooks.net, 🖳 www.survivalbooks.net).

Qty.	Title	Price (incl. p&p)			Total
		UK	Europe	World	
	The Alien's Guide to Britain	£6.95	£8.95	£12.45	
	The Alien's Guide to France	£6.95	£8.95	£12.45	
	The Best Places to Buy a Home in France	£13.95	£15.95	£19.45	
	The Best Places to Buy a Home in Spain	£13.95	£15.95	£19.45	
	Buying a Home Abroad	£13.95	£15.95	£19.45	
	Buying a Home in Cyprus	£13.95	£15.95	£19.45	
	Buying a Home in Florida	£13.95	£15.95	£19.45	
	Buying a Home in France	£13.95	£15.95	£19.45	
	Buying a Home in Greece	£13.95	£15.95	£19.45	
	Buying a Home in Ireland	£11.95	£13.95	£17.45	
	Buying a Home in Italy	£13.95	£15.95	£19.45	
	Buying a Home in Portugal	£13.95	£15.95	£19.45	
	Buying a Home in South Africa	£13.95	£15.95	£19.45	
	Buying a Home in Spain	£13.95	£15.95	£19.45	
	Buying, Letting & Selling Property	£11.95	£13.95	£17.45	
	Foreigners in France: Triumphs & Disasters	£11.95	£13.95	£17.45	
	Foreigners in Spain: Triumphs & Disasters	£11.95	£13.95	£17.45	
	Costa Blanca Lifeline	£11.95	£13.95	£17.45	
	Costa del Sol Lifeline	£11.95	£13.95	£17.45	
	Dordogne/Lot Lifeline	£11.95	£13.95	£17.45	
	Normandy Lifeline	£11.95	£13.95	£17.45	
	Poitou-Charentes Lifeline	£11.95	£13.95	£17.45	
	Living & Working Abroad	£14.95	£16.95	£20.45	
	Living & Working in America	£14.95	£16.95	£20.45	
	Living & Working in Australia	£14.95	£16.95	£20.45	
	Living & Working in Britain	£14.95	£16.95	£20.45	
	Living & Working in Canada	£16.95	£18.95	£22.45	
	Living & Working in the European Union	£16.95	£18.95	£22.45	
	Living & Working in the Far East	£16.95	£18.95	£22.45	
Total carried forward (see over)					

ORDER FORM

Qty.	Title	UK	Europe	World	Total
				Total brought forward	
		Price (incl. p&p)			
	Living & Working in France	£14.95	£16.95	£20.45	
	Living & Working in Germany	£16.95	£18.95	£22.45	
	L&W in the Gulf States & Saudi Arabia	£16.95	£18.95	£22.45	
	L&W in Holland, Belgium & Luxembourg	£14.95	£16.95	£20.45	
	Living & Working in Ireland	£14.95	£16.95	£20.45	
	Living & Working in Italy	£16.95	£18.95	£22.45	
	Living & Working in London	£13.95	£15.95	£19.45	
	Living & Working in New Zealand	£14.95	£16.95	£20.45	
	Living & Working in Spain	£14.95	£16.95	£20.45	
	Living & Working in Switzerland	£16.95	£18.95	£22.45	
	Making a Living in France	£13.95	£15.95	£19.45	
	Making a Living in Spain	£13.95	£15.95	£19.45	
	Renovating & Maintaining Your French Home	£16.95	£18.95	£22.45	
	Retiring Abroad	£14.95	£16.95	£20.45	
				Grand Total	

Order your copies today by phone, fax, post or email from: Survival Books, PO Box 3780, YEOVIL, BA21 5WX, United Kingdom (☎/▤ +44 (0)1935-700060, ✉ sales@ survivalbooks.net, ▣ www.survivalbooks.net). If you aren't entirely satisfied, simply return them to us within 14 days for a full and unconditional refund.

I enclose a cheque for the grand total/Please charge my Amex/Delta/Maestro (Switch)/MasterCard/Visa card as follows. (delete as applicable)

Card No. _ _ _ _   _ _ _ _   _ _ _ _   _ _ _ _   Security Code* _ _ _

Expiry date _____ Issue number (Maestro/Switch only) _____

Signature _____ Tel. No. _____

NAME _____

ADDRESS _____

_____

_____

* The security code is the last three digits on the signature strip.

NOTES

NOTES